SANCTUARY
—OF THE—
SHADOW

SANCTUARY
—OF THE—
SHADOW

THE ELEMENTAL EMERGENCE SERIES

AURORA ASCHER

Preview of *Star Bringer* copyright © 2023 by
Tracy Deebs-Elkenaney and Nina Croft

Entangled Publishing, LLC
644 Shrewsbury Commons Ave., STE 181
Shrewsbury, PA 17361
rights@entangledpublishing.com

Red Tower Books is an imprint of Entangled Publishing, LLC.

Visit our website at www.entangledpublishing.com.

Edited by Molly Majumder
Cover art and design by Bree Archer
Stock art by macniak/Depositphotos, maykal/Depositphotos
Interior map design by Heidi Pettie
Interior design by Toni Kerr

HC ISBN 978-1-64937-411-0
Ebook ISBN 978-1-64937-311-3

Printed in China
First Edition January 2024

10 9 8 7 6 5 4 3 2 1

RED TOWER BOOKS™

For you.
Because you believed in yourself.

THE FIVE TERRITORIES

NORTHERN TERRITORY
QUEEN TIERRA

GLIMRA RIVER

BEIRSTAD

EASTERN TERRITORY
QUEEN AUDRA

CENTRAL TERRITORY
QUEEN NASHIRA

RYLKA

AIRDRIE

STELIÓRN RIVER

ETHEREAL FOREST

KEREZA

FORT MERSON

KAMBU VALLEY

SOUTHERN TERRITORY
QUEEN FURIE

N
W   E
S

CHAPTER ONE

H arrow hurried down the narrow path between colorful caravans. Lifting a hand to her chest, she curled her fingers into the fabric of her warm cloak, feeling her heart race beneath her grip. She forced herself to maintain a walking pace when what she really wanted to do was run.

Across the fairgrounds, friendly chatter brightened the morning. The laborers were already busy setting up the big top, pounding pegs into the earth with heavy mallets. Encircling the bustling grounds and the surrounding town of Beirstad, snow-capped mountains framed the clear sky. Though the air was cool, the sun's rays brought a welcome warmth.

Harrow stayed huddled in her cloak, however. Inside, her blood ran cold.

In just a few days, the setup would be complete, and the extravagance of Salizar's Incredible Elemental Circus would come fully alive. The enchanted lights would glow in the big top and down the rows of caravans and tents where mysterious, hidden side attractions awaited—Harrow's fortune-telling booth included. The humans would come in droves to gape and indulge, and Salizar would ensure he wrung them dry of every coin they could spare.

As soon as Harrow saw her destination ahead, she quickened her pace.

Outside a red and blue caravan, a woman with midnight skin and long braids reclined in a chair in the sun, a peaceful smile on her face. She heard Harrow's approach before she had a chance to announce herself, and her amber eyes popped open.

"Morning, Harrow!" she called, stretching her arms wide. They were toned with muscle from years of training. "The Amazing Malaikah" had worked harder than anyone to earn her place as the star acrobat of their show. "How nice is this sunshine? I was beginning to think it was always cold in the North, but—" She broke off and her smile faded. "What's wrong?"

Harrow and Malaikah had been close friends for decades, and she wasn't surprised Malaikah had sensed something was amiss with a single glance.

"I woke up with this terrible feeling, Mal," Harrow said without preamble, "and I think there might be trouble coming. But when I did my scrying ritual, I didn't see any—"

Malaikah stood suddenly, glancing around to check they were alone. "Why don't we go inside to talk?"

If Harrow had been thinking clearer, she would have done the same before speaking. She knew she shouldn't talk openly about her gifts where there was a risk of being overheard. She couldn't afford to let anything slip about her true nature.

With a gentle hand, Mal led her toward the narrow door

of her caravan. Inside, there was a bed at the far end with curtains, a tiny wood stove and counter, and a wardrobe stuffed full of sparkling costumes. They took a seat at the small table opposite the stove.

"Tell me what's going on," Mal said when they were settled, her tail flicking with subtle tension. Malaikah was a black panther Hybrid, one of the species variants of the Earth Queen's Elementals. Like all Hybrids, she displayed certain features of her animal in appearance and ability—for Mal, a sinewy tail, catlike ears, and sharp canines.

Harrow twisted her hands on the table in front of her. "Since waking this morning, I've had this feeling that something is coming, but I can't decipher it beyond a general sense of dread. I feel like there's someone who needs my help, and if they don't get it, something terrible will happen. But I don't know who it is or how to find them."

Malaikah frowned. "Is it the Water telling you this?"

"It's always the Water." The Water was the elemental source of all her visions and premonitions. She was the conduit through which the powerful force spoke its wisdom.

"I did my morning scrying ritual," Harrow continued, "but it didn't give me any answers. All I saw when I looked into the bowl of water was an image of flames, and then perhaps some kind of shadow streaking across a full moon? Which makes no sense to me."

"Hm." Mal slumped in her seat. "The moon thing doesn't mean anything to me either, but thanks to Queen Furie, I think we all have a healthy fear of anything fire related."

"I just can't shake the feeling that there's something I'm supposed to be doing. Maybe I need to go search for someone. But where?" Harrow dragged her hands over her mane of curly hair in frustration. "Or maybe I'm misinterpreting it, and this is a warning that the circus is in danger. I just don't know."

"If you think there's potential danger, we should take it seriously. Maybe you could tell Salizar?"

"Why would he believe me?" She traced the edge of the folded headband she wore every day to hide her pointed ears. "He thinks I'm human. He'll want to know why I think there's a threat, and he has no cause to trust my instincts. If I try to convince him, it'll only give him more reason to suspect what I am."

"I keep telling you, I think Salizar already knows. Why else would he have taken you in?"

"Because I was a ten-year-old orphan who'd witnessed a massacre. Human or Elemental, I was still a child. He helped Loren, too, didn't he?"

Harrow didn't want Salizar to know who she was. There wasn't much that got past him, but being in control of her secret was important to her. And she certainly didn't want people prying into what she remembered of that night, especially since it was nothing at all.

Well, mostly nothing. *Blood on her hands. A warm body growing cold beside her.* But this wasn't the time to dredge up that old pain.

"It doesn't matter right now anyway," she said, waving a hand. "Something bad is coming, and I don't know what to do about it."

Malaikah stood decisively, her posture tense. Among her other tumultuous emotions, Harrow felt a twinge of regret for getting her friend worked up only a few days before opening night. "If there's really danger, we have to warn people," Mal said. "Why don't I go talk to Salizar for you? I'll just tell him I have reason to believe there's—"

She broke off suddenly and stiffened. Twisting toward the open window over the bed, she tilted her head, her ears twitching.

"What is it?" Harrow whispered. As a Hybrid, Malaikah's hearing was far better than hers, but Harrow had a terrible suspicion she already knew what Mal was going to say.

"I think it might be too late for warnings. There's some kind of commotion at the front gate. I hear shouting."

Harrow jumped up, dread coursing through her. "Let's go!"

Both women hurried outside. In the open air, Harrow could hear distant, angry voices, and they ran toward the source of the noise. She hiked up her skirts and tried to match Malaikah's rapid pace, but there was no keeping up with a panther Hybrid running at full speed.

Closer to the entrance, there were storage wagons, rolled up tents, and building supplies laid out to be set up. Beside the tall gates, the ticket booth was half built, its colorfully painted walls erected but the roof still missing. As Harrow passed the last wagon and finally caught up with Mal, she skidded to a halt. They faced the tall arch over the wrought-iron gates to the fairgrounds.

And the mob of angry humans that had gathered outside them.

About fifty people strong, the crowd seemed to be made up of average citizens of the town, not dressed in wealthy finery nor clad in the rags of the destitute. The men and women carried torches and weapons, and metallic clanging rang out as they struck them against the bars.

The padlock and chain wrapped between the gates suddenly seemed a pitiful defense. Especially because a large man in the front hacked at the length with a heavy axe.

"Elemental filth!" someone hollered as they noticed Harrow and Malaikah. In the bright morning sunshine, the enraged display felt decidedly incongruous. "Servants of the bitch Queens! Your kind aren't welcome here!"

Harrow had no doubt they would break through if left to their own devices. The fury on their faces made clear their determination to inflict violence upon the Queen's forsaken chosen ones.

Their hatred was as misguided as it was ignorant. Humans and Elementals alike had paid the price for the Queens' endless feuding. Harrow knew better than anyone how high the cost of war could be.

"Go back where you came from!" another cried, and the clanging against the bars amplified in emphasis.

"Where do you want us to go?" Malaikah shouted back, ever the fearless one. She bared her sharp white canines. "We came from here the same as you did!"

To Harrow, she added, "I mean, really. Servants of the Queens? What kind of logic is that? In case these fools hadn't noticed, the Queens don't give a fuck about us anymore."

Following an intuition, Harrow grabbed Mal's hand and pulled her back behind the wagon for cover. "These people have no logic, Mal. Don't try to reason with them. It'll only enrage them."

"Oh, I think they're enraged enough already."

As if to punctuate her point, a volley of stones launched over the gates, accompanied by more verbal abuse. All the while, the clanging of the axe striking the chain continued.

"Damn it." Malaikah looked around the wagon and pointed. "Look. Oli is stuck in the ticket booth."

Harrow leaned over and followed her finger. It took her a moment to see the fox Hybrid hiding in the corner inside the half-finished structure, but a glimmer of his bright red hair was just visible through the window.

"What in the Goddess's name is he doing there?" Mal hissed. "Why doesn't he run?"

The booth was against the fence and within striking distance of the humans if they reached through the bars. But it was inside the grounds, and the open doorway faced away from the mob, which meant Oli could escape if he moved quickly.

"They're throwing stones." Harrow ducked as one came flying over the wagon. She certainly wouldn't be keen to run out of a safe hiding spot directly into the firing line of an enraged mob.

"He's a fox," Mal said. "He's faster than all of them combined."

"Maybe he's too scared to run." Hybrids were the physically strongest of all Elementals, but Oli wasn't a fighter, and it seemed likely he'd simply frozen in fear.

"Oli's in there!" someone called out, and Harrow glanced back. Behind another wagon, several of the circus laborers had gathered to watch the spectacle.

"Oli, run!" another called out.

"Shut up!" Mal hissed at them, but unfortunately, her warning came too late. Some of the humans heard and caught on to the location of their trapped comrade. Weapons were thrust through the bars, battering the sides of the booth. Others threw more stones. Oli paled and flattened himself against the wall as if trying to disappear.

As Harrow watched, the Water suddenly rose inside her, turbulent and insistent.

"Mal," she bit out, fighting the sudden onslaught of her magic as it surged in response to the threat. "We have to get Oli out of there now." She closed her eyes and took a breath, willing the Water to subside. Oli needed help, but she couldn't afford to unleash her defenses, not here in the middle of the circus in front of a horde of humans.

Gaining a sliver of control, she opened her eyes again, preparing to run into the melee. She may not have been able to use her abilities, but that didn't mean she wasn't going to help.

Then she noticed the empty space beside her where Mal had been.

She looked up just in time to see a shadow streaking toward the gate. A second later, Malaikah appeared inside the booth.

Harrow leaned around the wagon to get a better view, fingers clenching on the wooden side. She watched with bated breath as Mal spoke to Oli, reassuring him, while simultaneously slashing her claws at any weapons that strayed near.

The Water surged again, and this time Harrow obeyed it. "Run, Mal!" she shouted.

Malaikah glanced back through the window.

"Run, now!"

Malaikah seized Oli's hand and finally, they started moving. At the same moment, someone threw a torch.

It sailed through the air and went through the open roof of the structure. They'd barely made it through the door when it hit, spilling fuel and fire across the floor. Immediately, the old, dry wood went up in flames. By the time Oli and Malaikah reached Harrow's hiding spot, the entire booth was engulfed.

They dropped to the ground, their backs against the wagon wheels. "That was way too close," Malaikah breathed, but she looked exhilarated, her amber eyes alight with the thrill of battle. Poor Oli looked shell-shocked.

And then Salizar arrived.

"Thank the sweet mother Goddess," Oli whispered, pressing his palms to his cheeks.

Their intimidating ringmaster cut an impressive silhouette as he strode toward the gates. Tall and foreboding, he held his enchanted staff aloft, his long coat billowing behind him. As his rapid strides carried him toward the mob, the irate humans appeared to lose some of their bluster.

It seemed Salizar's reputation preceded him, but that wasn't a surprise. He was nearly as infamous as his circus was.

When he reached the gates, he didn't bother combatting anyone directly. Instead, he raised the staff and pointed it toward the iron bars.

Bolts of silver lightning traveled from the tip of the weapon across the metal, down the crossbeams connecting the bars and shooting all the way to the top. The current struck anyone touching them, and cries rang out as the crowd lurched back.

As a final warning, Salizar struck again, but this time he targeted the man with the axe who'd been trying to break the chain. Lightning coursed over his body, and the human dropped like a stone. He didn't even have time to scream.

Message received, the crowd began to retreat. Their weapons lowered, and their raucous slurs faded until the only sound was the crackle of burning wood. Salizar stepped back, and there was a tense pause, the ringmaster challenging anyone to come closer, and the humans debating whether to attack again.

In the end, of course, they relented, backing down the road, once again hollering threats and insults to appease their wounded pride. The unconscious man with the axe had to be carried away with the group, his arms and legs suspended while his torso hung like a sack of grain.

Salizar turned his back on the humans and approached the gathered members of his circus.

"That was awesome, sir," Oli whispered, still slumped against the wagon wheel and looking utterly exhausted.

The ringmaster glanced over at him and Malaikah. "Are you all right?"

"We're fine," Mal said, grinning. She was back on her feet, looking as though she was half considering chasing after their fleeing aggressors. "Especially after watching those humans scatter like frightened chickens."

Salizar addressed the others. "Go start packing up. We're leaving. Spread the word to everyone else."

There was a moment of stunned silence, and their victorious smiles faded.

"But, sir," Oli said, "we just got here."

"And now we're leaving," Salizar replied. "I refuse to perform in a town that couldn't bother to ensure we had a safe reception after they invited us, and I won't risk any of those humans getting past the gates and posing a threat during a show. So go pack up. We leave for Allegra first thing tomorrow."

With that pronouncement, he departed down the center lane, the ticket booth still flaming behind him. Groans and murmurs of disbelief followed in his wake, but no one protested his decision.

Harrow almost couldn't believe they were about to turn around and go after traveling weeks to get here, but she also knew that Salizar took the protection of the circus seriously. She hated the thought of Malaikah being in danger from the audience while she was performing. What if someone threw something at her while she balanced on the trapeze? A fall from that height could mean serious injury or even death.

Soon the others dispersed to fulfill their orders, undoing the work they'd just begun, while a couple people stayed to put out the ticket booth's fire. Malaikah offered to walk Harrow back to her caravan, and she was glad for the company, still feeling unsettled.

"It's uncanny how you do that," Mal said as they walked, careful to keep her voice low. "I don't think I'll ever get used to it. You said you saw fire in your vision, and you told me you felt there was someone who needed your help. Well, that was obviously Oli. If we hadn't showed up when we did, I shudder to think what could've happened."

They stopped outside Harrow's caravan. She forced a smile. "It was lucky, that's for sure."

"It wasn't luck, and you know it," Mal said, nudging her gently.

Harrow knew. But for some reason, she didn't share Malaikah's sense of relief.

They bid each other farewell, promising to meet for the next meal, and then Harrow ducked through the fabric entrance to her fortune-telling booth. An awning extended out from the back end of her caravan over the narrow door, and she hung brightly patterned fabrics from the edges to serve as walls.

The rest of the booth had yet to be set up, however. At least she wouldn't have to put anything else away. She crossed the empty space and went straight into the caravan, closing the door and leaning against it.

Closing her eyes, she took a breath and then finally released the power she'd been holding back.

An invisible forcefield pulsed outward, rattling the objects in her tiny home, condensation forming on the walls and windows. Here, in secret, she could give in to the Water. Not out there. Not in front of everyone.

When the wave passed, she opened her eyes and looked around. Last night's lantern sat atop the table. The sight of the blackened, dead wick sent another strange chill through her.

Malaikah was right, she told herself. The fire in the ticket booth coincided with the fire she'd seen while scrying. And the strange shadow... Well, Mal moving with panther quickness was undeniably shadow-like.

But the shadow was fluid in your vision, her mind whispered. *It wasn't a solid shape.*

She shook her head, refusing to listen to doubt. Oli *had* needed their help. If they hadn't been there, he could have been seriously hurt. The connection was obvious.

It was broad daylight, but only slivers of light snuck through the cracks between the window curtains. Suddenly, the darkness bothered her. Darkness was where the unknown lurked. Darkness was the birth of unwelcome change.

She crouched, searching around the floor for where she'd dropped the matchbox last night. Spying it beneath the table, she grabbed it, struck a match, and relit the lantern.

She stood beside the table and peered at the tiny flickering flame. It put out a comforting orange glow, bringing a measure of relief. A light amid the darkness.

The danger had been circumvented. They'd rescued someone in need, Salizar had chased away the mob, and now they were leaving Beirstad completely. So why did she feel the same sense of dread? Why did her heart still ache and her blood run cold?

Why did she feel a shadow hanging over her?

CHAPTER TWO

The sun crept under his eyelids as he gradually pulled himself from unconsciousness. Instinct told him to sharpen his awareness, survey his surroundings, scan for threats. He only managed to shift his eyes beneath their too-heavy lids.

Pain assailed him as he slowly became aware of his body. Everything hurt.

He finally peeled his eyes open, only to close them immediately as the glaring sun scalded him. He tried again, squinting into the intense light, and saw blue. Clear sky, not a cloud in sight.

Battling intense weakness, he turned his head to one side. Beside him, the ground was cracked and dusty, an impenetrable, hardened crust. In the distance, a lone shrub struggled for life.

A bird's faraway scream had his gaze shifting back to the sky. Vultures were circling above, waiting for their prey to be weak enough to swoop down and consume while its meat was still fresh. He wondered what wretched creature was stranded out here waiting to die.

Then he realized that wretched creature was him.

He had no intention of becoming vulture food, but when he tried to move, he found the task excruciatingly difficult. But he had to try. After everything he'd endured, there was no way he was going to lie here helpless and surrender to death—

After everything he'd endured...?

What had he endured?

A wave of cold realization washed over him. Fighting to open his eyes under the blazing sun, his body too weak to move, was the only memory he had of anything. Ever.

He didn't even know his own name.

The burden of flesh was an entirely foreign concept, of that he was certain. The blue sky, the cracked earth, the birds above him—these things were familiar. But this debilitating weakness, this feeling of being tethered to a withering sack of skin and bones...

This was something else entirely.

Evidently, whoever he'd been was someone who didn't give up easily, because, despite the hopelessness of his situation, he forced himself to roll over. Shoving onto his hands with all his feeble strength, he pushed his torso up.

To his left, there was nothing but barren desert as far as the eye could see. To his right, a towering cliff face rose proudly toward the sky. At its base, a few measly shrubs and scraggly grasses grew.

At its base...was shade.

Focusing on his new objective, he began to drag his heavy body across the burning dust toward that little strip of shelter. He was naked, he realized. Of course he was. Awareness of his nakedness, the desire to clothe his bare skin... These were other sensations that felt foreign.

Humiliating.

A cold wrath rose within, the urge to annihilate whatever unseen foe had landed him in this predicament.

For now, he quelled it and focused on the immediate objective: survival. He reached forward and dug his claws into the cracked earth, dragging himself inch by inch until he finally reached his destination.

Sheltered from the sun at last, he collapsed in exhaustion.

He cursed his foreign flesh prison and its debilitating weakness. He'd once been powerful. Invincible. Now, he was nothing. Now, he could only lie there and hope he wouldn't feel it when the vultures started to eat him.

With that final morbid wish, he slipped away into oblivion.

Deep in the Southern Territory, the land of the Fire Queen, a human named Cragar led a small procession across the baking desert.

Three riders atop weary horses rode in formation around a four-wheeled cart, pulled by a camel. Their two-day journey to the nearest village had been fruitful, and they were laden with supplies for upcoming travels. The skin on their faces had tanned to shades of deep brown after days exposed to the sun—except for Anzo, who was just red and peeling no matter how much he covered.

Everyone was thirsty, even the camel, but Cragar pushed his men onward regardless. He knew they were close to their camp, and there was no water to be found nearby anyway.

The sun was sinking low on the horizon, that vivid orange

ball close to disappearing. Once it did, the temperature would drop to near freezing, and lack of water wouldn't be the only survival concern. High above, vultures circled the darkening sky, their lonely cries the only sound in the desolate silence.

Ahead, a dark cliff towered above the flat earth. There was only one path to reach the top—a narrow traverse diagonally across the face. It was this path that Cragar would lead his men up on the final push toward their camp. If all went well, he hoped to reach it by nightfall.

As they neared the cliff base, however, his eyes caught upon a dark object in the distance that seemed incongruous with the landscape. He watched as a vulture swooped toward it before angling sharply back to the sky. Another followed.

Pointing it out to his men, they veered off course and headed toward it to investigate. As they approached, his confusion morphed into bewilderment and even trepidation.

The shape was vaguely humanlike. Long legs, arms splayed out. Except its appearance was…wrong. It was like a shadow, but empty of all shade and tone. It was darkness without depth, a void that absorbed light like a sponge. The harder he tried to focus upon it, the more his eyes seemed to blur.

"Is it dead?" one of his men asked as they stopped their horses a safe distance away.

"If it isn't, it will be soon," the other replied, "else the vultures wouldn't be circling."

Cragar dismounted and cautiously approached the strange figure. As he neared, he saw it was indeed a humanoid male. There was no mistaking it, seeing as it was quite naked.

It—*he*—lay on his side, one arm under him, the other stretched forward, long legs sprawled on the dirt. Sleek black hair fanned out around his head, hiding his face. His body was built with the strength of a warrior, though it was impossible to discern any details on his skin because of its eerie lightlessness. To gaze upon him was like peering into an abyss.

Cragar approached the figure, lifted a sandaled foot, and prodded him lightly on the shoulder. The shadow man didn't move. Cragar prodded him again, this time hard enough to nudge him over onto his back.

The creature groaned softly.

He leaped back. "By the Goddess, it's alive!"

"What sort of man is this? He looks like a demon from the dark Shades."

"I've no idea," Cragar replied, "but I don't know that I'd call it a *man* of any sort."

Only an Elemental could have such unnatural characteristics, though he'd never heard of any of their kind with such otherworldly skin. But he'd never particularly cared to learn more about the Queens' magic-infused abominations either.

As far as he was concerned, the world would be a better place if Elementals and their vile Queens were wiped off it. The only thing Elementals were good for was procuring gold when he sold them as chattel at the market.

"A Hybrid, perhaps?" one of the other men ventured, still staring at the monstrous creature sprawled in the sand.

"He has no animal characteristics to speak of," the second said.

"He has claws. Look."

There was a silence as they studied their strange discovery.

And then Cragar said, "Whatever he is, he'll fetch us a handsome sum."

The gazes upon the naked figure flared with sudden avarice. "Let's take him."

Cautiously, the three men approached the male. They seized him by his arms and legs and hefted his considerable bulk off the desert floor, shuffling awkwardly toward the cart.

Halfway there, he awoke.

Delirious and weakened by whatever ordeal had left him stranded in the desert, the creature could not attack anywhere near as effectively as he might have been able to. He simply jerked in the men's holds and lashed out with his claws, an ominous growl rumbling in his chest. Reflexively, they dropped him and jumped back, and the male hit the ground.

His eyes snapped open.

They gasped.

"By the Goddess, what is this beast?"

The creature snarled and, though he seemed to be hovering on the brink of unconsciousness, slowly began to climb upright. He painstakingly stood before them, stretching to his full height and swaying on his feet. He blinked heavily, revealing unnatural eyes—twin pits of darkness with wreaths of flame at their centers. Flexing his claws, he sank into an unsteady attack position.

And then two enormous, leathery wings burst from his back.

The men stumbled back, one falling to the ground. Seemingly from nowhere, those wings had appeared. There'd been no sign of them moments ago.

The male snarled, the curling of his lip revealing gleaming white fangs. He was fear personified. A living shadow of death.

"Get the chains," Cragar commanded, facing off with the

creature. He didn't care what it was. He was looking at that shadow of death and seeing gold raining down.

One did not flourish in his line of work without getting an acute sense of what was sought after. In fact, he was already thinking of one buyer in particular who would be interested in this specimen.

There was a male of indeterminate species—some said human; others, Enchanter—who traveled the Territories with his troupe of Elementals, charging a sizable fee to showcase them to curious patrons.

What might this creature of shadows be worth to such a man? Surely nothing short of a fortune.

"Get the chains," Cragar repeated, "and secure him tightly. We'll take him to Allegra and sell him to the Fiend Collector."

The creature resisted capture with everything he had, as feral things were wont to do. Cragar's men sustained several lacerations that would require the use of precious medical supplies.

But in the end, the creature's debilitating weakness was no match for three humans motivated by the prospect of wealth. A strike to the temple finally took him down, and his wrists and ankles were securely bound.

He was loaded onto the back of the cart and hauled back to camp. The following morning, they packed up again and hit the dusty road for Allegra, Central Territory.

There was business to be done.

The human woman cast a nervous glance over her shoulder as she slipped into Harrow's tent. It was always this way— no one wanted to be recognized visiting a phony psychic, but the lure of knowing the unknown was too great for them to stay away.

Sitting neatly in the empty chair, the woman smoothed her skirts, eyes widening as she took in the appearance of her "fortune teller." Harrow was used to such reactions.

Today, she wore a red shift with a patterned silk robe on top, the loose sleeves and bottom decorated with tassels. Heavy teardrop earrings and a silken headband to hide her pointed ears contrasted with her thick black hair. A locket nestled between her breasts inside her dress, hanging from a delicate chain.

Her clothing helped her look the part, but that was mostly because it was how the Seers of old traditionally dressed. And her locket was her most precious possession—it was her mother's, the only thing Harrow had of hers. Inside was a tiny shard of crystal, the last remaining piece of her mother's casting stones.

As for Harrow's customer, she was nearly the opposite of Harrow in every way. Pale-skinned, human, wealthy—likely the wife of a successful merchant. Allegra was smack dab in the middle of the Central Territory, the Ether Queen's domain, making it an ideal trading hub for all five Territories.

"How much for a reading?"

"Ten pieces." It was the highest price Harrow ever asked for, but the woman's clothing told her she could afford it.

The customer balked at the price momentarily but soon reached into the pocket of her dress and deposited ten gold coins on the table.

"Let me see your hands, please."

The woman held out her hands, and Harrow clasped them, turning them over so her palms faced up. She studied them—soft, unlined—allowing the Water to rise with every breath. "What's your name?"

"Rosemary."

Harrow closed her eyes, repeating the woman's name in her mind as her power rose steadily higher, its current rushing through her blood.

Out of nowhere, an unexpected wave of darkness overtook her like a flood, and her awareness was swept away. Images and sounds flashed across her mind. She saw a circle of caravans in a forest clearing. A group of women gathered around a fire. A shadow streaking across the full moon.

And then she saw fire, and she heard screams. *Familiar* screams.

Harrow jerked her hands back from Rosemary's and opened her eyes. The vision faded as she looked into the concerned face of her customer. Her heart pounded and her palms shook, but she tried not to betray how rattled she was.

"Is everything all right?" Rosemary asked.

She had just seen memories, ones she'd never been able to access before. Of all the times for her mind to open to her, why now? *That shadow on the moon...* She'd seen the same thing in her scrying bowl a month ago, not realizing it was a memory. But what was it?

Of course she'd heard the stories of the Fire Queen's fabled incorporeal assassins, but she'd always thought them to be rumors. Everyone did. It helped that no one could agree on what they were. Formless, ghostly warriors? Beings capable of killing with a single touch? It was too fantastical to be real. The genocide of her people was terrible enough without needing to invent invisible, invincible foes to be responsible for it.

But then, what had really happened that night?

Rosemary had begun eyeing the exit as if debating

whether to flee. She likely believed Harrow's sudden tension was in relation to her reading.

"Everything's fine." Harrow shook her head roughly. "My apologies. Let's continue."

With some hesitation, Rosemary nodded.

Harrow closed her eyes once more. She was almost wary of sinking fully into her power again, but thankfully, this time nothing unusual reached out to her from the darkness.

When she was ready, she reached for her Seer cards and shuffled them. The methods human fortune tellers used were usually in imitation of the Seers, so Harrow was free to use these methods without fear of revealing herself.

For a reading, six cards were dealt from the deck of twenty-four. Each was a different type of water with a variable meaning, depending on how it was drawn.

"Rain, Waterfall, Snow, Spring, Wave, and River," Harrow read as she placed each card, taking time to listen to what the Water told her. "Wave and River are powerful cards, and their placement as the final two is telling."

"Telling how?"

Harrow studied her customer, deciding how much to reveal. She tried to limit the number of true readings she gave out, withholding specific details to lessen the chance of her identity being discovered. She couldn't lie outright, however. It went against everything she was to be dishonest about what the Water told her. But the risk of exposure always lingered, and she had a duty to herself to survive, too.

Rosemary was different from her usual customers, however. The Water had told Harrow a great deal, and she sympathized with the woman's plight. She decided to throw caution to the wind and tell her everything.

"You're pregnant."

Rosemary leaped out of her chair, eyes round as saucers. "I'm what?"

"Pregnant, dear."

"Are—are you sure?"

"Very."

Those saucer-like eyes filled with tears.

"This is good news." It wasn't a question. It was all in the cards. "You've been trying for a long time. Long enough that you feared you were unable."

With shaking hands, Rosemary straightened her chair and sat heavily upon it once more. "Y-yes."

"You will have a son."

"By the Goddess." The tears started to fall.

"But you must be careful. There are several potential futures where you could lose the child."

The woman seized the edge of the table with a white-knuckled grip. "What should I do? How do I prevent this?"

Harrow hesitated. This was where her job got difficult. Being the bearer of good tidings was always pleasant, but the reverse…not so much. "You've been trying for a child long enough that unrest has stirred in your marriage. You feared your husband might cast you aside if you couldn't provide him with children."

Such a human problem, Harrow mused distantly. Elementals would never base a mating off the desire for an heir—a couple could be together their entire thousand-year lifespan without ever conceiving.

Long ago, Harrow's mother had told her that because Elementals lived so much longer than humans, the Goddess hadn't blessed them with the same rate of fertility to maintain balance. Harrow had been the first Water Elemental born in a century, and her clan had always told her she was a gift.

Now she was the only one of them left. And she didn't feel like a gift anymore.

"Yes, that's t-true," Rosemary said.

"You will discover something about your husband that will upset you greatly. Though you have every right to be angry, you must not fall prey to dark emotions. Remember your joy for your unborn child. Hold onto your peace for his sake."

"My son…" Rosemary's eyes were still spilling tears, but there was also a hard look in them that told Harrow she might already have suspicions about what her husband was up to.

"Thank you." The woman rose shakily from her chair. Leaning over the table, she grasped Harrow's hands tightly and held them to her bosom. "Thank you so much. I can never thank you enough."

After leaving another three gold pieces on the table, Rosemary left. Harrow reorganized her cards into a neat pile and tidied the rest of her workspace, trying to recall more details from the memory flashes she'd seen. Nothing more came to her, however, and she knew better than to force it. The Water would reveal more when it was ready.

Besides, she wasn't entirely sure she wanted these memories. Whatever they uncovered would bring her nothing but more grief and pain.

Her fortune-telling booth was set up as it always was. Beneath her awning tent, the writing desk from her caravan became the table she laid readings on, and her clients sat on the desk's chair. Harrow sat upon a small chaise with clawed feet. When traveling, it fit beside the wardrobe inside. Like Malaikah's, her portable home also had a mini wood stove with two burners for cooking.

The circus had set up camp for the next month at Allegra's fairgrounds. Dinner was served in the meal tent at sunset—which was already well underway—and the main performance in the big top started at nightfall. Harrow tried to catch Malaikah's show every night. She never tired of watching Mal backflip through space as the crowds gasped in awe.

Ducking outside, she flipped over the READING IN SESSION sign on her tent and headed down the rows of colorful caravans. Ahead, the big top loomed in the fading light, the enchanted lights within already illuminated, giving the canvas a soft glow.

Salizar's Incredible Elemental Circus was an elaborate setup. It never ceased to amaze her how much stuff they managed to pack into their tiny wagons and how quickly they were able to reconstruct their playground of weird and impossible things.

Maybe this wasn't the life she would have chosen for herself, but over the years, she'd learned to love the mayhem of the circus and felt grateful to be part of it. And what else could one do in life besides be grateful?

At the meal tent, she piled a plate full of food and then took a seat across from "Lenny the Lizard Contortionist" and "Claudia Sky Tamer," an eagle Hybrid with an impressive aerial show. Everyone was artfully dressed for tonight's main performance, and the familiar preshow buzz filled the air.

Claudia and Lenny were already mid-conversation. "You must have heard about the human at Lady Absynthe's show last night?"

Lenny's reptilian eyes lit with the thrill of gossip. "What happened?"

"He managed to hide under the stage until after closing,

and then he followed her back to her caravan to proclaim his undying love."

Lenny cackled. "She told me her nipple tassels fell off during her final reveal."

"Well, that explains it! If she flashed those puppies at me, I'd fall in love too."

They dissolved into laughter together while Harrow rolled her eyes and took a bite of food to hide her grin.

Loren the Human sat down beside her and smiled shyly. "Hi, Harrow."

"Hi, Loren." She smiled in return, but inside, she tensed. "How are you today?" The only human employed at the circus (besides Harrow, or so everyone assumed), Loren was often referred to as such. Harrow, grateful she hadn't earned a similar nickname, took pity on him. But every time he spoke to her, she felt as though her life of stability flashed before her eyes.

She'd been ten years old when she joined the circus. That was five decades ago now. For an Elemental, sixty was young, but for a human, she should have been showing her age. Loren had joined years after her and was around twenty years younger, but lately, he'd begun to look older.

Most of the Elementals in the circus were pretty ignorant of the human aging process, but Harrow knew it was only a matter of time before Loren or someone else noticed her appearance, and she'd have to choose whether to reveal her secret or leave her home forever.

In the meantime, she avoided Loren as much as she could, which wasn't always easy. She got the impression he sought out her company, likely believing they had a connection as the only two humans in an Elemental circus.

"Oh, I'm fine," he replied around a mouthful of food.

"Been busy all day helping the boss work on security at the front gate. After what happened at—"

"Loren."

He stiffened and twisted around.

Everyone's heads turned as the boss himself strode through the tent. Along with his imposing height, Salizar had olive skin, dark hair, and the same pointed ears as all Elementals. In his case, they were proof of his Enchanter blood and the Air magic he possessed, but he always kept them hidden beneath a short top hat.

The common theory was that he pretended to be human to put his customers at ease. Though the illusion only went so far. After the display at Beirstad, there was likely no one in that particular region who didn't know what he was.

He never went anywhere without his formidable enchanted staff. Malaikah called it the "witch stick," and the circus had been abuzz ever since a few of them had seen the weapon in action last month. Oli had retold the story a dozen times, each telling more grandiose than the last.

For the most part, however, Salizar had never given anyone he employed reason to fear him. He kept safe those he considered under his protection, but Harrow wished the Goddess's blessing on anyone who crossed him or got on his bad side.

Loren stood immediately and came to stiff attention as Salizar approached their table. For years, he had served as Salizar's personal assistant. "Sir."

Everyone stared and conversation hushed. It was rare indeed to see their aloof leader in the common areas. He tended to keep to his caravan or private tent, always pitched beside the big top. He would show up for performances and in times of need and then disappear again, and there was no one who dared disturb him.

"I'm going to the market tonight," he said, "immediately after the performance. Assign another to cover your duties—I want you with me."

Loren tensed visibly at this pronouncement. "Just us two, sir? Shouldn't we bring a few more?"

"No. Be at my tent after the show." Without waiting for a response, Salizar spun on a heel and strode away, long coat swooshing behind him.

Loren looked pale.

"What's happening?" Harrow asked him, her senses immediately on alert. "Why are you going to the market?"

"I don't know." It was easy to see he was lying. "Excuse me, Harrow." Before she could say another word, he hurried off in the direction Salizar had gone, leaving his plate of food behind.

Lenny rolled his eyes and grabbed it, shamelessly adding the contents to his own plate. "Bloody Salizar. Always so mysterious." Harrow noticed he checked that their boss was out of earshot before speaking. "If I could make lightning like that, you bet I'd be shocking people left and right."

Claudia snatched Loren's bread roll and took a bite. "If you did, you'd bring another mob down on your head in days. I still don't think it was wise to stir things up that much. We'll never be able to go back to Beirstad now."

Lenny scoffed. "Like we'd want to anyway. I'll stay far away from anywhere that greets us with torches and spears, thank you very much."

The conversation continued as they divvied up portions of the abandoned meal, but Harrow barely heard them. She was still staring after Loren, suddenly feeling that sense of dread and impending upheaval all over again.

First, she'd had that strange premonition, and now she was seeing flashes of her lost memories. Why now? What had changed?

Regardless of every rationalization, she couldn't help but feel certain that whatever the Water had been warning her about hadn't yet come to pass. And she couldn't help wondering if the coming darkness was somehow connected to whatever business Salizar had at the market.

CHAPTER THREE

He spent the next month in a cage. Tall enough for him to stand and wide enough for him to spread his arms apart, its steel frame was built onto the base of a four-wheeled wagon. There were old scratches on the wood floor from claws trying to gouge an escape route.

This was not the first time someone had been kept in here. A man-sized cage designed for easy transport could mean only one thing:

His captors were flesh traders.

The realization made him crave their deaths all the more. He passed the hours dreaming of their painful demises and the creative ways he could deliver them. He came up with a great many scenarios, for there were a great many hours to pass.

He would crush the skulls of the men who sneered at him through the cage by forcing their heads between the narrow bars. Or perhaps he would impale them with various implements spotted lying around the camp. One who enjoyed whipping the animals a little too much would be strangled with his own weapon.

The leader of the group, a particularly nasty human called Cragar, would be delivered an especially gruesome death. Perhaps he would remove his limbs and watch him bleed out slowly in the dust, pleading for his life.

The images of purpling faces and struggling, bloodied bodies did not disturb him as much as they perhaps should have, but he couldn't find it in himself to care. He did not have mercy for those who showed him none.

The first day of travel was spent baking under the harsh sun with no way to shelter himself. The shredded sarong he was given as clothing provided no relief. His wagon-cage was pulled by an antagonistic camel that spat upon any that strayed near. He sympathized with the irate beast, forced into service against its will.

The hours stretched on, the sun climbing higher in the sky. He was given no food, no water. By late afternoon, the cumulative effect of his injuries, dehydration, and malnourishment began to catch up. Staring at the flat, lifeless landscape, he slowly succumbed to delirium.

He slipped into unconsciousness, hoping for death to take him, only to awaken later in darkness, shivering in the bitter cold. Moonlight illuminated the rolling desert and the tops of the travelers' tents a short distance away. A fire crackled between them, offering an inviting warmth that didn't extend to him.

Inside his cage, he discovered a small bowl of foul-smelling porridge had been left along with another jug of water. For better or worse, his desire for death was not stronger than his will to live, and he greedily consumed both.

The next morning, after dismantling the tents, the traders

threw one of the big sheets of canvas over the top of his cage for shelter. Evidently, they'd realized their prize wouldn't be worth nearly as much if it died of exposure. A shame, because said prize lost his only source of entertainment — watching his camel companion traverse the arid landscape.

Thus passed the rest of the month-long journey.

During the day, he saw nothing but the underside of the canvas. At night, the canvas was removed, and he lay on his back and stared at the stars, watching the moon wane and then wax again.

Faced with the never-ending monotony and the black hole that was his past, his intelligent thoughts began to deteriorate. Gradually, he became what the traders thought he was — a creature. A frightening, feral creature.

He made no attempts at communication. He crouched in his cage and snarled at any who approached. He left his claws unsheathed and his fangs bared. He lost his mind to visualizations of bloodshed.

Just when his sanity began to slip irrevocably, everything changed. The day after the moon completed her next cycle, they arrived at their destination.

The creature didn't see this. He could see nothing but the sun's glow on the underside of the canvas. But he could smell it. The scent of cooking spices, the smoke of countless fires, and the pungent reek of unwashed bodies assailed his sensitive nostrils.

Then, he could hear it, too. The shouting of hagglers, the clanging of ale tankards, the jingling of coins, the barking of stray dogs… It all blended into a cacophony of madness-inducing clamor, especially unbearable after weeks in the desert's penetrating silence.

They had finally arrived at the market where he was to

be sold, though he would have preferred death over that fate. But what could he do?

Wait, he told himself. *Watch and wait. Seize your opportunity when it comes. Kill anyone who stands in your way.*

That tiny shred of determination was the last remaining tether to his sanity, and he clung to it.

"I'm telling you, it was uncanny. Looking at him was like looking into a void. This"—Cragar cast a disgusted look at the cage—"is some new trick."

The creature in question had known he was valuable to the traders because of his supposedly strange appearance. So in the only act of rebellion he was capable of, he had altered it.

He had, in fact, discovered a new ability. Bothered by the attention he was receiving, he had briefly imagined blending in more.

And then his skin tone had changed.

All of a sudden, it had transformed to a golden brown, similar to that of some of his captors. He didn't have a clue how he'd done it but figured it was just another trait marking him as an unnamable oddity.

He had suffered greatly for his defiance—they had tried to convince him to revert with a savage beating—but apparently, he was a stubborn creature as well as a resilient one.

And watching his captors squirm now made every second of pain worth it.

"I don't know how he did it. We just blinked, and he

looked like this."

The buyer pursed his lips. Standing at a looming height, he radiated an unmistakable aura of power and authority. He held a staff with a small globe on the end, topped by a long spike, and a glint of loathing shone in his bright blue gaze, as though the creature's very existence was deemed a stain upon his world.

Well, two could play at that game. If the creature hated his original captors, within seconds of meeting that hostile gaze, he hated his future owner even more.

"You've no idea what he is?" the tall man asked.

"Well, after his little display, we're thinking he's a chameleon Hybrid, sir."

"A chameleon Hybrid." He seemed to be enjoying the exchange, almost as if he knew something the flesh traders didn't. "Then what about the wings?"

"Maybe some kind of flying chameleon Hybrid, then?"

"Flying. Like a bird?"

"More like a bat. A crossbreed or something. A bat-chameleon hybrid Hybrid."

Dark brows climbed high on his forehead. "A hybrid Hybrid."

"Must be, sir."

"I see. Well, he doesn't have wings now, nor is his skin changing colors. Why should I believe you?" But it was obvious by the light in his eye that he did and was just playing along as part of the bartering.

Cragar had obviously anticipated this. "Aye, but when he's unconscious, he'll change right back to black. Found that out earlier. I can knock him out if you'd like, but I figured you'd want to see him awake first."

"And the wings? How can you prove their existence?"

Again, the trader was ready. "We figured out that if you prod him in the back in just the right spot, he'll pop 'em out. They just appear out of thin air."

"Indeed." The tall man's voice was unimpressed, but again, his eyes betrayed him. He surveyed the creature with more of that cold loathing and...recognition? As if he already knew what kind of beast was before him.

"And you can see his eyes. No Elemental brute I've ever seen has eyes like that. He's dangerous. Lethal." This seemed to be a selling point rather than a hindrance. "Hasn't sheathed those claws once since we put him in that cage. Nearly killed two of my men with them."

The creature wished anew for the strength to slaughter them all. He wished to break free from his cage right then and kill them one by one with his bare hands. He would tear them to shreds with his teeth and bathe in their blood.

"We've been underfeeding him to keep him weak. I shudder to think what he'd be capable of at full strength. I doubt that cage would hold him, for one thing."

"I have ways of containing him. Loren!"

Another man ducked into the tent, this one with pale skin and hair the color of straw, stopping dead in his tracks when he saw the creature. His eyes widened.

"Prepare the horse. We'll be hauling the entire cage back to the grounds."

"Actually, sir," Cragar said, "the cage isn't incl—"

"Now, Loren."

"Y-yes, sir." The fair-haired man ducked back out of the tent.

"You can't have the cage. We need it."

"You won't be needing it any longer."

"But—"

"I will pay you three-quarters of your asking price after you prove to me he has wings."

The trader snapped to attention at the mention of money. "Pay it in full, and I'll prove his skin changes color too."

"Ah, but he fights back viciously when antagonized, does he not? Why take that risk? Three-quarters of your asking price, and we need only to poke him in the back, as you said."

"You've got to poke him hard or he just shrugs it off. It's dangerous work, getting close to him."

"Luckily for you, I came prepared." The tall man brandished his staff with a cold smile.

Cragar seemed to take a closer look at the staff for the first time. He took a step back, eyes widening. "That's not... You're one of them."

"Yes, I am indeed one of those Elemental *brutes*." His voice was cold, his smile colder. The human swallowed visibly. "Let's see if I can get our friend to show his wings."

Cragar waved a shaky hand toward the cage. "Be my guest."

Wielding the staff, the tall man approached the cage. Hatred burned bright in those blue eyes. The creature wasn't used to making friends, but he couldn't help but wonder what he'd done to inspire such loathing. Even the traders regarded him with only mild revulsion.

This man's hatred was deep. Personal.

Whatever it was, he wasn't cowed. He snarled into that proud face, preparing to fight.

The tall man thrust the staff into the cage.

Quicker than expected, the creature's hand shot out and seized it in an iron grip. He tried to snap it in half, but he underestimated the power of the weapon. The staff didn't break. Instead, what felt like a thousand bolts of lightning passed through his body, throwing him back against the bars. He landed on his stomach, stunned, though only for several seconds.

That was all the tall man needed.

The staff was thrust into the cage again, into his back. The second he was aware, he tried to roll over, but he wasn't fast enough. The lightning pierced him, right between the shoulder blades, and reflexively, his wings burst out. The leathery expanses didn't quite fit in the cage and crumpled painfully against the bars.

Immediately, he folded them back, and they disappeared as he sprang up into fighting position, head pounding from the aftershock of the lightning.

But the tall man stepped back. The pale, trembling human shrank away as he advanced, still wielding the staff. "I will pay you three-quarters of your asking price. Cage included."

Cragar eyed the staff. It seemed his fear of the enchanted weapon was all that was needed to strike a deal in the end. "Sold."

The canvas covering the creature's cage was yanked off with a flourish, revealing…another dark, empty tent. And two men staring at him.

He stared right back, imagining all the ways he might rend the flesh from their bones.

"What is he?" the blond human hissed at the tall man. He bent over the wagon harness, unhooking it from the horse, who stamped its hooves and tossed its head nervously.

"He understands you, Loren. He's a highly intelligent being, and his hearing is superior to either of ours."

Loren glanced back at the cage warily. "Why hasn't he said anything, then?"

The tall man shrugged, staring into the creature's eyes. "Why indeed."

After the deal was made, the tall man had tossed a sizable bag of gold at the flesh traders, thrown the canvas over the cage, and taken his new possession away to…somewhere. Wherever they were, it was still in the city. The trip had taken only twenty minutes or so, and the smells in the air hadn't changed much.

"If he's so intelligent," the human asked, "why are we keeping him in a cage?"

"Because he's evil. And he would kill us all given the chance."

The human snorted an incredulous yet nervous laugh. "How can you know he's evil? Sure, he looks frightening enough, but he hasn't done anything but stare at us."

The creature listened carefully for the tall man's response. He didn't trust a word out of his mouth, yet he had seemed to know more than he let on during negotiations.

"How much history do you know about the conflicts between the Queens, Loren?"

"A bit. Supposedly, after Furie's warlord mate was killed in a raid on Darya's borders, the Fire Queen lost her mind. She blamed Darya and retaliated, and then the other Queens joined in the fighting until humans got sick of it and turned against them. The Queens were forced to retreat and hide in their castles, and their once-noble Elementals became shunned outcasts of society."

"An abbreviated version, certainly. More specifically, do you know *how* Furie retaliated against Darya?"

"Sure. By killing every one of Darya's Seers."

The tall man stared into the creature's eyes as he spoke. "And how did she manage to wipe out an entire thriving group of Elementals?"

"Well, that part's a bit controversial. Everyone has heard of wraiths, but most people agree they're just a myth because Furie never created any Fire Elementals. I've heard they were Enchanter assassins skilled at fire illusions or some kind of winged Hybrid."

The tall man smiled.

Loren did the opposite of smile. "It is a myth, isn't it?"

"Is it?"

"*Is* it? By the Goddess, it isn't, is it?" He stared at the creature, his voice a breathless rasp. "Surely he's not... No. They're supposed to be like ghosts. You can't touch them, but they can touch you. They're invisible. Practically invincible. He can't be one of them."

"He is."

"But you can't trap a wraith in a cage. According to the myths—which you're saying aren't even myths—they're completely intangible unless they choose not to be."

"All true. Except for this poor wraith, who got permanently stuck in his corporeal body."

Loren stared. "How?"

But the tall man had shared enough for one night. He dismissed the question with a wave of his hand. "We'll use him as a side attraction at the circus for the final week of performances in Allegra."

If anything, this bewildered the human even more than the possibility of a corporeal wraith. "How!"

"We'll keep him in this cage. Paint a sign. It will say 'WRAITH' in big letters across the top." The tall man spread a hand through the air as though creating the sign right then.

"'Invisible. Invincible. The most dangerous killer in existence. Myth or reality? The answer lies within...but enter at your peril.'"

"Wow."

The tall man's eyes glinted again, full of loathing as they stared into the cage, and the creature took deep breaths to fight down the violent killing urge surging inside him. It did him no good in his state, and if he were to fly into a rage while trapped, he'd only hurt himself.

"Get started on the sign tomorrow. Tonight, I need you to make a trip back to the Underground. Find someone from the Ouroboros gang and get word to their leader that there are Elemental flesh traders in their district. The snakes will deal with them accordingly."

"The Underground is Elemental territory. Are you sure they'll talk to me?"

"Tell them I sent you. They'll talk to you." The tall man flung a hand toward the tent's entrance. "Now go. I need to get to work enchanting the cage. It'll take me all night to make it impenetrable."

"Sir...what if he escapes?"

At this, the tall man smiled again. "Then he will surely kill us all. Best hope I know what I'm doing."

The enchantments on the cage were completed the following day. The tall man had spent the night and half the morning working on it, careful to remain out of his prisoner's reach while his concentration was engaged.

Plans for his enemies' painful demises kept the creature occupied. Before the enchantments had foiled him, he'd begun weakening one of the bars at the top of the cage during the long trip. Soon it would have been loose enough to pry apart, and then, while the traders slept, he would have moved among them, as silent as a shadow, slitting their throats with his claws as he'd done before when—

When...what? When could he have done such a thing, and why?

He mulled over what the tall man had said the night prior. He'd called him a wraith. Some type of powerful, incorporeal being trapped in his physical form.

He tried the word out, but it seemed as unfamiliar as his own body had felt when he first awoke in the desert. But that feeling was distant now too. His body felt like part of him, not burdensome or confining.

By nightfall, he'd been fed three full meals and given access to as much water as he wanted. His shredded sarong was replaced with a pair of loose trousers—hardly respectable attire compared to everyone else, but certainly an improvement. A bucket, rag, and towel were provided for him to wash, and he dragged his fingers through his tangled hair.

After the evening meal, when the scents of food coming from the nearby meal tent had faded, the blond human came back into the tent. He was carrying an oil lamp and a bucket of painting supplies, dragging a big piece of wood behind him. He leaned it on the edge of the tent and spread out his brushes.

"Here to make your sign," he muttered. "Boss's orders."

The creature tilted his head but didn't rise from where he sat, leaning against the bars in the corner of the cage.

Loren glanced up and then recoiled. His face was a mask of repugnance, but he couldn't seem to look away. "By the

Goddess, your eyes are unnerving."

The creature growled low. It wasn't like he could do anything about his eyes. He'd already changed the rest of his appearance for the loathsome humans. If this one didn't like it, he could leave.

"Have to paint the sign in here," the human said as if hearing his thoughts. "Salizar doesn't want people to know about you yet, though I doubt he realizes how much gossip there's been already."

Salizar. So that was his enemy's name. Perhaps he would whisper it in his ear before he slaughtered him. Would he snap his neck, quick and quiet? Or would he draw it out and make it slow and bloody?

He gritted his teeth. He didn't like the thoughts in his head. They seemed to come from somewhere outside of him, as if the inclination to violence had been developed by association rather than by choice. His wrath was tinged with revulsion, and he got the sense that the power he recalled possessing when he'd first awoken had been a lie.

Ignorant of the creature's confusion, Loren went back to his task. Selecting a bottle of red paint, he dumped some onto a small tray and selected a brush. "What is this stupid sign supposed to say again?" He pitched his voice in obvious imitation of his boss. "'Wraith. Invisible. Invincible. Scary as piss. Will slit your throat without a second thought.'"

The creature frowned. If those were characteristics of a wraith, perhaps he didn't mind the association after all. Would it be so bad to use such powers to obtain his freedom?

Loren glanced up again. "Yeah, I bet you like that description, don't you? Bet you'd love the chance to slit all our throats."

The creature bared his fangs. Indeed, he would.

Loren recoiled once more. "Bloody Shades." He looked quickly back at the sign, dipped his brush into the red paint, and then began outlining the shape of an *R* on the board.

R? Wasn't it supposed to be the word "wraith?" He watched, curious.

The *R* was completed. Another dip of the brush, and the next letter commenced. *A*. Interesting. When the *A* was finished and the next letter began, he realized what was happening.

A hint of a smile lifted one corner of his mouth. He remained silent. Why wouldn't he? If he told the human, it would spoil his fun, and this was the only fun he ever remembered having.

Soon, the word was complete. Loren dropped the brush in the water and stood, murmuring something about needing whisky to get through this. He trudged out of the tent, leaving his work behind him in all its glory. The creature looked at it with amusement.

Along the entire top of the board, written in stylized block letters, was the word RAITH.

His good humor faded quickly. Whether he was a monster of myth or not, these people believed he was. And after his ordeal traversing the desert, he had little faith in the kindness of others.

What atrocities were his new captors capable of in the name of their fear and greed? And perhaps worse... what atrocities was he capable of inflicting upon them in retaliation?

Because if given the chance, he already knew he wouldn't hesitate.

CHAPTER FOUR

Harrow was swimming in tranquil water. Fresh, not salty. Her eyes were open. Above, rays of glorious sunlight penetrated the crystalline waves like light striking diamonds. Below, the turquoise deepened into blackness. There was no sign of the bottom.

Perhaps she ought to surface and surround herself with a more familiar environment? The surface was where she belonged, after all. It wasn't far. Just a couple of kicks and her head would break through the waves.

Then she glanced down at the deep where the light couldn't penetrate.

What was down there? What secret knowledge lurked in those lightless depths? Surely it would be frightening to swim through the deep with no sunlight to guide her, yet she felt drawn to the darkness in a way she couldn't describe. She craved to know the stillness of the indigo abyss, to be cradled by an unseen embrace.

But it was so dark. Dark enough to swallow her

completely. Somehow, she knew that choosing to dive would force her to confront things she wasn't ready to face. Things she might never be ready to face.

Indecision plagued her, churning her insides with increasing urgency. She struggled in the water, feeling as though her life depended on her choice, yet unable to make one.

But she had to, and quickly. She was running out of time. Up or down? Dark or light? Familiar or foreign? Why in the Goddess's name was it so damned hard to just pick one?

Enough! Harrow screamed in her head.

Without thinking of the consequences or weighing the options any further, she folded at the waist and executed a perfect dive straight into the lightless depths.

As she swam, it grew darker. The deep turquoise became the navy blue of the night sky. And then darker. Until suddenly, it was utter blackness. A colorless chasm of emptiness.

Her heart would have been pounding if it had needed to beat. The pressure was so immense, it would surely have burst her lungs had they held any air. She swiveled around, searching the lightless void.

Which way was up? Which way had she come from?

Panic filled her. She wasn't ready for this.

This was too intense, too exposing, too painful.

I made the wrong choice! I want to go back! But it was too late to go back. She had no choice but to be consumed entirely by shadows as her mouth opened in a silent scream—

She sat bolt upright in bed.

Chest heaving, she stared around the inside of her dark caravan and had never been happier to find herself there. With shaking fingers, she snatched up the matchbox from beside the bed and lit the candle. *Light.* She needed light to remind herself she wasn't in that inky void any longer.

What was the Water trying to tell her? Was it even the Water, or just an ordinary dream? It certainly didn't feel ordinary. It felt...loaded, somehow. Full of meaning she couldn't decipher.

She had been sure in the dream she'd made the wrong decision. If so, what were the consequences? And if it was wrong, why had she been drawn to the darkness in the first place?

First, she'd seen flashes of her lost memories. And now this. There had to be a connection.

Though she hadn't remembered anything from the night of her clan's deaths until recently, such a traumatic event couldn't help but shape a person forever, no matter how much love and care they received afterward. And Harrow had been cared for — by Malaikah and even by Salizar, who had taken her into his circus without question, feeding and sheltering her before she'd been able to work to pay for her keep.

And now? She'd thought she was all right. She slept soundly through the night, free from troubling dreams. Well, she had...until tonight.

Throwing off the covers, Harrow grabbed a silk robe from the wardrobe to put over her nightgown and then folded a patterned scarf into a band and tied it over her ears. A walk would help her regain calm.

Shutting the caravan door behind her, she crept down the steps on bare feet, through her fortune teller's booth and out into the open. The moon was glowing brightly, at the phase in her cycle when she looked as though she'd been cut in half. What remained of her naked face cast the rounded sides of the caravans in a bluish glow.

Allegra's fairgrounds had room enough to fit all their wagons and tents, yet they were still only steps away from the chaotic central market. Silhouettes of dark buildings surrounded them. Tonight, it felt like being trapped.

Harrow headed toward Malaikah's caravan. She would wake Mal up and tell her about the dream. Mal would listen and offer advice. It was always what they did for each other.

Except something made her stop abruptly.

On a whim, she turned toward the big top and started walking. Why? Because she had a feeling that was the way she needed to go.

She ended up around the side, standing outside Salizar's tent, of all places. She'd never been inside the area where the ringmaster conducted most of the circus business. No one had, except Loren and the kitchen staff. Salizar's private workspace was of little interest to her. She had everything she needed, and risking falling out of her boss's favor wasn't worth it.

But suddenly, she was fighting an urge to go in so strong she had to clench her hands into fists.

The tent was tied shut by little strings hanging down the edges of the entrance flaps. There was a lantern on the ground with a box of matches beside it. She would just light the lantern. That should satisfy her strange compulsion.

She struck the match, lit the lamp, and then stood, facing the canvas. Unfortunately, candlelight shining upon those neat little ties didn't quell the urge to enter in the least. Yes, a Seer listened to her urges, but she also needed to have a good sense of self-preservation.

So what did Harrow think she was doing?

She would just undo the ties and peek in. That would

satisfy her. She was probably just bored, seeking a little rush of uncertainty.

Her fingers worked the knots until, soon enough, the tent was open. Immediately, she knew peeking in wouldn't be enough. She needed to go inside. What could it hurt, really? She'd go in just for a split second, look around, and then leave and forget this entire incident ever happened.

Before she consciously made the decision, her hand was lifting the canvas and her head was ducking as she stepped inside.

It wasn't at all what she expected. There was no work desk or papers. From what little she could see in the dark, the tent was empty save for a large board leaning against one wall and what appeared to be an enormous cage. From its base on a four-wheeled cart, thick steel bars ran vertically upward, nearly as tall as the ceiling.

Dear Goddess, a man could fit comfortably inside that monstrosity. What was Salizar doing with it?

Cautiously, Harrow approached, holding the lamp out to see better.

A pair of eyes suddenly reflected the light from the darkness.

She lurched back, nearly tripping on her own feet. Swallowing the scream that stuck in her throat, she froze and waited for whatever monster lay within to attack.

It didn't attack. It just watched her.

The eyes were impossibly bright, like two rings of fire burning. A sudden urge struck Harrow from within. *Go closer*, it said. *Investigate.* She obeyed.

As she stepped forward, without warning, several lamps flared to life around her. The lanterns stationed throughout the tent seemed to have spontaneously lit themselves.

She jumped at the sudden illumination, but she quickly forgot all about that when she took in the scene before her.

Inside the cage…was a man. But he wasn't like any man she had seen before.

Like a great cat, he crouched in the center of the cage as if ready to pounce, his lip curling in a silent snarl. He was naked save for a pair of faded, worn pants. Golden-bronze skin rippled over sinewy strength, every inch of his body corded with powerful muscle. The tips of his pointed ears parted strands of sleek black hair that fell to his broad shoulders.

And his eyes…

The whites of them were not white at all but utterly black. The same inky black as his pupils. Two rings of flame comprised his irises. It was the only way to describe the reddish orange glow that seemed to flicker and churn like living fire.

Looking at those eyes, some chord of familiarity was struck within her, but it faded too quickly to grasp.

It was replaced with trepidation.

Every self-preservation instinct she possessed screamed *DANGER*. He was an Elemental, that much was obvious, but beyond that, she didn't have a clue what he was. But she didn't need to know to see that he was deadly. It was plain as day in the way he held himself with the poise of a predator, the menacing glint in his eyes, and the long, sharp canines revealed by the lip peeling off his teeth.

Her heart tried to crawl up her throat. Her lantern shook with the trembling of her hands.

And yet, as if from far away, she heard herself say, "Hello."

HELLO? a voice screamed inside her head. *What do you mean, hello? Don't stand around making small talk! Get out of there! Run for your life!* It was probably the voice of her survival instincts.

She ignored it.

"I'm Harrow. What's your name?"

The male blinked. Once. Twice. As if he was as confused by her sudden sociability as she was. His head tilted, sending silky hair sliding over one shoulder and shifting the shadows on his face.

That tiny movement was so menacing, she had to swallow the scream that rose in her throat.

Without a doubt, he could kill her as easily as breathing. She ought to be listening to that petrified voice in her head. She ought to be backing out of there slowly and running for her life.

As she entertained these thoughts, the strange, lethal man rose from his crouch, the powerful muscles of his thighs levering him gracefully up. Heart thundering, she tensed, ready to flee, but his liquid movements were just slow enough not to startle her.

Like a predator stalking prey.

He took a step forward.

She lurched back but froze again as his face came more clearly into the lantern light. He was no longer snarling and looked more inquisitive than murderous—if any expression could be said to be on his face at all.

She stared at him, fear momentarily forgotten. High cheekbones, a strong jaw, and a sensual mouth somehow softened the intensity of his piercing stare, though only slightly. But it was enough for her to realize…he was striking. His features were arresting. Regal. Proud.

Connection, the Water whispered. *Important.*

As if he sensed it too, he took another step. Still

mesmerized by his presence, this time, she didn't have to fight the urge to flee.

This time, she took a step closer, too.

If he was a predator stalking prey, then she had been lured into his trap. Her palms were clammy, and her heart was trying to burst from her chest, yet she couldn't have backed away to save her life.

"Can you understand me?" she whispered.

He blinked once. Somehow, it was answer enough.

She took another step toward the cage until she was close enough for him to reach her through the bars if he wanted to harm her. Yet fear for her safety was the furthest thing from her mind.

Who are you? she wanted to ask, half torn between terror and heartbreak. *Where did you come from?* The Water continued to whisper to her that this was important. Somehow, this moment mattered more than any other.

"What's your name?" she asked again, because it had become crucial that she knew.

The woman on the other side of his cage was close enough to touch. From the height of the wagon, he positively loomed over her, but she didn't shy away, which surprised him. He could practically smell her fear, it was so strong. She ought to be recoiling from the sight of him as others had done.

Instead, she'd asked what his name was. And suddenly, it mattered to him that he had one.

He cast about the room for inspiration, and his eyes landed upon Loren's misspelled sign. A sense of rightness sparked inside him, and before he knew it, he was opening his mouth and speaking for the first time in his memory.

"Raith."

His voice was hoarse and quiet from disuse, but the woman heard him anyway.

"Raith?" Her eyes huge in the dim light, she followed his gaze over to the sign before looking back at him. "That's your name?"

Yes, he thought. He supposed it was.

He was no longer nameless, no longer just a "creature" or an unclassifiable abomination. He was Raith. Not a wraith, but something else. The misspelled version, the mistake with no past or future.

The woman continued to stare at him. She seemed torn between fear and intrigue. He wondered why she bothered fighting her instinct to flee, and he studied her, trying to understand.

She wore a loose white gown with a colorful robe on top. Bare feet poked out from beneath her dress. Her hair was a wild mess of black curls, tied back by a colorful band of silk. Her skin was deep tan, several shades lighter than his current color, her eyes a luminous silver reminiscent of the moon's glow.

She was...beautiful.

It almost surprised him to be aware of this. Everyone he had come across since awakening in the desert had been ugly, of face or personality, but not her. He supposed he must've had some unconscious knowledge that beauty existed, but until he'd laid eyes upon her, he'd been unaware of what it looked like. Now, he knew.

He hadn't verbalized his response to her question, but she seemed to understand anyway because she said, "Nice to meet you, Raith. I'm Harrow."

Though he knew he hated to speak for some reason, he opened his mouth and used his voice once more.

"Harrow." Her name.

To his great surprise, her silver eyes suddenly filled with tears.

As if shot from a bow, she sprang into action so quickly he instinctively retreated to the middle of the cage. She seized the steel bars and shook them violently, rattling the door and lock that held it shut. The sudden clanging of metal pierced his sensitive ears.

"We have to get you out of here." She sounded so distraught, he found himself scanning for some unseen foe to save her from. But the tent remained empty save for the two of them, and he sensed no one else nearby. His brow furrowed as he fought to understand.

"Why are you in this cage? How do we open this door? The lock!" She seized the padlock and yanked on it. Her eyes shot back to his. "How did you light those lamps? Maybe you can open this, too."

He stared at her. He hadn't done anything to light the lamps. He'd just wanted them to be lit so he could see her better, and then they had been.

"You have to try. I can't just leave you here."

Finally understanding the source of her distress, though scarcely believing concern for him was the cause, he crouched again to her eye level. Slowly so as not to startle her, he reached out and touched the back of her hand, still gripping the bars tightly. She froze, silver eyes fixed on the point of contact.

He didn't try to cut her, strangle her, or rip her arms off as he would have done to anyone else who got this close. He just...touched her.

She had no idea the level of trust such an action showed, but he didn't mind. Every soul he'd encountered since waking had used him in some way—imprisoning him, selling him, forcing him to be a circus act.

But not her. She had asked for his name. She had fought her fear instinct to speak to him.

He wasn't sure he trusted her—wasn't sure he even understood the concept—but he did know he didn't want to kill her. He wanted to kill everyone he'd met so far, but not her. That had to mean something, right?

To express his conflicting feelings, he did freely for her what others would torture him into doing. Perhaps it was in some vain attempt to connect, or perhaps it was so he could understand her better. He wasn't sure which. He didn't think too hard about it.

Still touching the back of her soft hand, he changed his skin once again. This time, he studied the subtleties and shades of Harrow's skin and matched his own to it. He could have reverted to his original colorless void, but for some reason, he didn't want her to see him that way.

The change trickled over his body, starting from the point of contact at their hands and spreading down his arm to his torso until their skin matched exactly.

"Sweet Goddess," she breathed, staring at him with shock. "You— What are you?"

He glanced at the sign again.

She followed his gaze. "Raith... I don't understand—" She gasped. "*Wraith*? Does Salizar think you're a wraith? But that—"

Suddenly, she froze. As still as if she had been transformed into stone.

It seemed a counterproductive survival instinct, he thought distantly. If any part of her could have been said to move at all, it was her eyes. They grew wider and wider until they were tiny circles staring at him with horror.

A strange ache clenched his chest, not dissimilar to how it felt to be stabbed with Salizar's lightning stick. He didn't like the idea of her being afraid of him, which was strange, because it was much easier to protect himself when others feared him.

He changed his skin back to the darker golden brown, wishing he hadn't shown her his trick. It was foolish to think she wouldn't recoil from him as everyone else had—

"That's ridiculous," Harrow announced suddenly, and he watched in fascination as, one by one, her muscles relaxed and she regained normalcy. The fear melted from her eyes, and she shook away any remaining vestiges of it with a jerk of her head. "There's no way you're a wraith."

He cocked his head. *Why not?* he wanted to ask. *How do you know?* But the sound of his voice disturbed him, and he preferred not to speak unless he had to.

Luckily, she seemed to interpret his body language. "Because wraiths, if they even exist, are supposed to be incorporeal, like ghosts, and they can't be imprisoned. They're shadows of death, mindless killers that serve the Fire Queen. They're terrible, evil monsters."

Raith wondered again why wraiths were automatically considered evil, but he was also glad Harrow didn't think he was one.

"So why would Salizar make this sign? It'll be obvious to everyone you're not a wraith by the very fact that you're stuck in that cage. Unless...maybe he's going to lie? But how to convince people? You don't seem very wraithlike to me.

I mean, sure, your eyes are…well, they're very unusual, but that doesn't mean—"

The sudden murmur of voices outside the tent caught their attention. Their gazes locked in mutual panic at the approaching visitor.

For the third time in his new existence, he overrode his aversion to speech and used his voice. "Go."

"But what about you?"

He wasn't going anywhere—the enchantments on the cage were done well. There was no way he could break out.

Harrow seemed to understand this. "I'll come back. Tomorrow, after the circus shuts for the night."

He shook his head. It wasn't safe for her. She could be inadvertently harmed by her association with him, and he had already decided he didn't like the thought of that happening.

The voices were louder now. He pointed at the tent entrance, urging her to go.

Giving him one last look, she hurried toward the exit but stopped suddenly, realizing it was too late to leave that way. The voices were right outside now.

"Why are the lamps lit?" he heard Salizar demand.

Raith clutched the edges of the bars so tightly, the steel groaned under his strength. His inability to act threatened to send him into a mindless rage.

Harrow proved she could take care of herself, however. Spinning around, she ran toward the back wall of the tent, dropped to the ground, and rolled forward on her side. A second roll took her under the bottom of the canvas at the exact moment that the tent flap was ripped open and Salizar ducked inside.

"Who lit the lamps?" he demanded of Raith, who, of

course, said nothing.

Loren rushed in behind him. Salizar turned to him. "Did you leave the lamps lit?"

"No, sir."

Salizar glared at the human. "Someone's been in here." He transferred that glare to Raith. "Who was it?"

Raith just stared at him.

"Still being silent, I see." He approached the wagon, brandishing his lightning stick, hatred for his caged monstrosity shining clear in his blue eyes. Raith glared back, unafraid of pain, unafraid of any wound the lightning stick could inflict.

Without breaking eye contact, Salizar said, "Loren, post a guard on the tent at night." He turned to go. "I don't have time to monitor him myself, and— What the fuck is that?"

His eyes had landed on the unfinished sign. Raith almost laughed.

"Sir?"

"'Raith'? You've got to be kidding me."

"Sir, I don't—"

"There's a W. Wraith. W-R-A-I-T-H."

Loren spat a low curse.

Salizar briefly pinched the bridge of his nose. "Start a new sign first thing tomorrow. And by the Goddess, spell it correctly this time."

Loren bowed out of the tent. Salizar shot a look at his prisoner and then followed him out without another word.

Harrow sat on the ground, her arms wrapped around herself, breathing hard. That had been way too close. If her boss had caught her snooping… Not good. But now that she had snooped, there was no way she could forget Raith was in there.

Because of Salizar. He was supposed to be a protector of Elementals, as Malaikah saw him. How could he treat an innocent man that way?

Okay, so maybe Raith wasn't innocent. She wasn't that naive. Who knew what sorts of things he'd done? If she wasn't mistaken, he'd come up with his name on the spot, and he didn't appear to have any more idea about what he was than she did.

He certainly wasn't a wraith, however.

No one knew the true origin of wraiths, or if they existed at all. The rumors about them ranged from horrifying to downright ridiculous. Some thought they were evil spirits from the Shades that Queen Furie had found a way to summon. Some said they were actually mythical dragons that breathed fire, while others claimed they were nothing but Enchanter illusionists or Hybrid assassins. Others believed Furie had created them with Fire magic and the bottomless hatred that had consumed her since the death of her mate.

Whatever their origins, Furie had sent the wraiths on the most notorious killing spree in known history. A genocide that had wiped out an entire group of once-thriving people, whose worst offense against the Fire Queen was their connection to her enemy and sister, Queen Darya.

Despite the name he'd chosen, Raith was not a wraith. Harrow almost wished he'd picked a different name, but it suited him somehow, and when she thought of it now, it didn't bring the same fear as the word spelled with a *W* did.

Perhaps it was because of that unguarded surprise in his eyes when he'd opened his mouth and spoken it aloud. As if he hadn't realized until that moment that he was worthy of a name.

Harrow had looked into those eyes and had not seen evil. She was a Seer. A Seer knew how to read people. A Seer trusted her instincts. Her other, baser, instincts had told her loud and clear that she was in the presence of something deadly, and she wasn't fool enough to forget that. But the Water said otherwise.

Important. Connection.

Why? She didn't know, but she had a feeling she was going to find out. Now that she knew Raith was in there, there was no way she was abandoning him to whatever cruel plan Salizar had to earn money off his misfortune.

Her eyes stung with regretful tears. How could she have been so oblivious to Salizar's true nature? Sure, she had good reason to be grateful to him. As an orphaned Elemental female, she likely would've ended up somewhere far worse if not for him, but she still ought to have seen the cruelty he was capable of.

Harrow waited until she heard Salizar leave. She longed to go back inside and make sure Raith was okay but didn't dare. Not tonight, at least.

Nothing could keep her away tomorrow.

The urging of the Water was never without reason, and she intended to find out exactly what the mysterious Elemental had to do with her.

CHAPTER FIVE

The following night, Harrow peeked around the last caravan in the row, stomach churning with nerves. Sure enough, a guard was sitting outside the tent. She squinted to see clearer.

She was pretty sure it was Oli. The fox Hybrid was slumped forward in his chair, chin to chest, and she could hear his snores from where she stood.

She smiled to herself. Sure, Salizar was scary, but nobody else in their circus was, and they certainly weren't trained for enduring a grueling night watch.

She wasn't complaining. In fact, this was exactly what she'd been hoping for.

Hefting the heavy bag higher on her shoulder, she double-checked the coast was clear and then ducked out from her hiding place and strode quickly toward the tent. Though it was difficult to fight the urge, she didn't run—if someone did spot her, it would look far less suspicious if she was walking like she had every right to be there.

Which she did, she assured herself. The circus was her home, and Salizar hadn't told anyone what he had hidden in his tent, so there was no reason for her not to take a midnight stroll nearby.

With a bag full of food on one shoulder?

Whatever. If she was caught, she would bluff her way out of it.

Rather than going through the front entrance and risking waking Oli, she crept around to the side closest to the big top and slipped into the gap between the two tents. From there, she dropped to her knees, shoved her heavy bag under the canvas, and then rolled inside much the same way she had escaped the night before.

It was pitch-black.

Heart in her throat, she fumbled in the dark until she found her supply bag and loosened the ties, feeling around inside until her fingers clasped the candle. Next, she dug out the matches. She struck one, and a tiny flame illuminated the tent.

Raith was crouched at the edge of his cage grasping the bars, staring right at her.

It was obvious he'd known it was her all along, and she wondered if he had heightened senses like Hybrids. Perhaps he could see better than her in the dark or he had recognized her scent.

"Hello," she whispered into the heavy quiet. Her stomach was positively writhing with nerves, but the Water continued to whisper to her that he was important. That she needed to be there. That she needed to learn more about him.

It was those urges that pushed her to heft the bag and cross the tent to stand before him, holding the candle aloft between them. The bottom of the cage was at her waist height, so her standing and him crouching put them at eye level. She was glad because she could tell he was big. If they were to stand on even ground, he would tower over her.

"Hello," she said again, though it made her feel bumbling and awkward.

He blinked those strange eyes and said nothing. She hadn't expected him to. For whatever reason, he didn't seem used to speaking, and she wondered why. She wanted to ask but didn't dare.

"Are you hungry? I brought you some food."

He blinked again.

"Does Salizar feed you? You're not starving in here, are you?"

Still he said nothing. She hoped that meant he wasn't.

She shifted on her feet. His silence was unnerving, to say the least, but she forced herself not to be cowed. "I would have brought you a plate from dinner, but it's a little awkward to fit that in a bag. But I did bring you some dessert. It's hardly a balanced meal, but…"

Trailing off, she set the candle and the bag on the ground and then stuffed a hand inside. After some digging, she pulled out the cookies she had carefully wrapped in a cloth napkin, holding them out to him. Her hand shook slightly, and she was well aware that if he wanted to grab her, he could. He could snatch her arm, yank her against the cage, and kill her before she even had time to blink.

But she didn't think he would.

His head cocked, that silky hair falling into his face.

"They're just cookies," she told him in case he wasn't sure. "Have you had cookies before?"

His head shook once.

"Well, you can try one if you want. You might like them."

Slowly, one hand released the bars and stretched toward hers. He never took his eyes off her, as if he didn't trust her not to attack. Funny, because she never took her eyes off him for the very same reason.

As a result, they stared directly at each other until it felt almost too intimate. Her heart was lodged in her throat, and it was hard to breathe, but her eyes were fused to his and there was no way she could look away.

His hand closed around the napkin bundle, and he pulled it back into the cage. Unwrapping it carefully with graceful fingers, he studied the cookies as if he'd never seen such a thing in his life and found them utterly fascinating.

A nervous chuckle escaped her. "They're just cookies. They're not that exciting."

He set the bundle down and selected one, lifting it for closer inspection.

"Try a bite."

His eyes narrowed, and he glared distrustfully at her. Did he think she would poison his food? Goddess, what had happened to him? What kind of cruelty had he faced to end up where he was? A determination rose within to show him that was not all that existed in the world.

As if he were following her thoughts, that distrustful look slowly bled from his features.

And then he took a bite.

She froze, holding her breath. Somehow, waiting to see his reaction to that silly cookie was the most exciting thing that had happened to her in years. He chewed, a frown creasing his brow.

His eyes widened slightly and shot back to hers as he swallowed.

"Do you like it?" She was beside herself. She had to know.

He looked down at the cookie and then back at her.

And then he smiled.

His mouth curved upward, creasing his cheeks. And his eyes… The real smile was in his eyes. The flames in them seemed to burn brighter, and they crinkled in the corners and took her breath away all over again.

Her own face split into a smile so wide it hurt. "You like it?"

He nodded.

She grinned. Ridiculously. "Me too. They're my favorite."

Raith picked up another cookie from the napkin and held it out to her.

Her smile dropped, and she stared at that outstretched hand as emotion choked her. He was being kept in a cage like an animal, yet his first instinct was to share with her. His smile was so genuine and guileless, looking at him felt like a fist squeezing her heart. How could Salizar do this to him? How could anyone ever want to hurt him?

He shook the cookie at her, reminding her to take it.

She accepted his gift and spoke around the sudden lump in her throat. "Thank you."

They ate together in silence, holding eye contact the entire time. Her skin felt hot from the intensity of his attention, yet she had no desire to escape it. When the cookies were gone, they ate the fruit and the muffins and the scones and the cheese.

She passed them all to him to inspect, and after he tasted them and deemed them worthy, he passed some back to her to share. He didn't speak a word the entire time. He didn't need to. Somehow, she understood him perfectly.

After the food was gone, she pulled out an old book of Seer folktales and, though she felt silly and nearly lost her nerve, she offered to read him one. He nodded, and she ended up reading half the book. She stayed there until her candle burned down to a waxy stump and the walls of the tent started to turn a pale gray as the sun rose, and she knew it was time to go.

Climbing up from where she'd taken up residence on the ground, her back against the cage so Raith could follow over her shoulder, she stuffed everything back into her sack.

Turning to face him, she offered a smile. "Would you like me to visit again tomorrow?"

He looked hesitant, and her heart sank a little. She'd thought he'd enjoyed her company, but perhaps he would rather be left alone?

But then he said, "It's not safe."

The sound of his voice sent a shiver running through her. "Don't worry about me. I know how to be sneaky, and I won't get caught."

He said nothing, and she decided that meant he had enjoyed her company after all but was concerned for her safety. The relief she felt was stronger than it perhaps should have been.

"I'll see you tomorrow then, Raith." Smiling, she swung the considerably lighter bag over her shoulder. It was strange how badly she didn't want to go.

He smiled back, and her heart raced.

She was definitely returning tomorrow.

Raith sat on the floor, leaning against the cage bars, and watched Salizar conversing in low tones with Loren. The new sign had been completed several days ago, spelling mistake-free, and the two men now discussed the terrible monster it described and how they would force it to entertain humans in the days to come.

Raith tuned out their conversation, uninterested in their constant plotting. Instead, he thought about the woman who visited him at night.

He thought about her a lot.

He pictured the rich tan of her skin and remembered how soft it was to touch. He tried to imagine whether her thick hair felt silky or coarse. He wondered if her scent, the soothing fragrance of lavender, would be stronger if he breathed it against her skin.

Every night, Harrow would sneak past the sleeping watchmen and bring Raith food and sweets and read more stories to him. His favorite was a tale of a terrible dragon who guarded a princess in a tower, slaughtering every man who came to rescue her and earn her hand in marriage. At the end of the tale, however, it was revealed that the princess and the dragon were actually the best of friends, and she thanked him daily for saving her from a loveless marriage.

Though Raith hadn't found the courage to speak much, Harrow chatted away enough for both of them, telling him about her life at the circus, her friend Malaikah, and all the things they did together. She asked him questions about himself that he couldn't answer, but she never pressed or seemed disappointed if he remained silent.

He lived for those late-night encounters, and during the day, he had caught himself forgetting to visualize killing Salizar, wondering instead what Harrow was doing at that moment. Was she reading fortunes for circus patrons? Spending time with Malaikah? He was desperate to understand her better but couldn't quite bring himself to use his voice to inquire.

Salizar dismissed Loren from the tent and approached Raith. "Tonight's show is beginning shortly, but before I go, you and I are going to have a chat."

A week ago, Raith would have already been on his feet, snarling at his captor. Now, he was just bored. He wasn't scared of Salizar or his magic stick, and he was sick and tired of being in a cage.

He lifted a brow, not even bothering to stand.

"Two weeks remain of our time in Allegra. For the final week, your sideshow will be open to the public. People will be admitted to your tent to glimpse the wraith. There are two things I need from you to complete our performance."

Raith just looked at him blandly.

"If you perform without complaint, it will be painless. If you do not, I will force you. It makes no difference to me which you choose, and I daresay, a good fight will make things more entertaining. As part of the performance, I expect you to show off your wings and wraith skin."

Raith's lip curled. Over his dead body. Or, at least, unconscious body—which was probably exactly what was going to happen.

Salizar smiled thinly like he knew it, too. "If you don't perform willingly, as I said, I will force you. Your wings come out when I prod you in the back"—he brandished the staff—"and your appearance reverts when you're unconscious. Easy enough to arrange."

He began to stroll back and forth across the tent. "This is how it'll work. When the time comes, you will shed your disguise and show the humans your true wraith form. I'll give you a chance to do it voluntarily. If you don't, I will take measures to make it happen."

A growl started low in Raith's throat, hatred boiling his blood like lava.

"It will be humiliating for you. Even more humiliating than choosing to cooperate."

Raith's relaxed posture became rigid. Slowly, he shifted forward until he was crouched in attack position.

Salizar's eyes shone with equal loathing as he took a bold step closer. "Oh, I know how much you hate me. Know that I hate you in equal measure. You might think I'm the villain here, but you're forgetting the most important thing." He took another step. "I know what you are."

Raith growled louder, lip curling off his teeth.

"You're a vile creature, responsible for the worst massacre in known history. And what's to stop you from doing it again? If Furie gets an itch, you'll be doing her bidding in a heartbeat."

The growl died in Raith's throat. Salizar really believed he was one of these wraiths. If they truly were responsible for a genocide, no wonder Harrow hated them. He hoped he wasn't one.

"And now, for the first time, a wraith has been captured. Trapped in his physical body. Vulnerable to attack. But eliminating you isn't my place. I'm simply the deliveryman."

Salizar stepped back abruptly, staff at ease by his side. "Can you blame me for capitalizing off it in the meantime? If I'm going to expend such effort keeping you, I might as well make some money doing it. Money that will go toward providing for other Elementals who have lost their homes and the respect of humans because of Furie's fucking war."

He rapped the staff against the steel bars, and sparks shot out from the tip. "Fight me all you want, because I enjoy watching you suffer. I enjoy witnessing your pain, while still knowing it will never equal the pain your kind inflicted upon the Seers before you killed them all."

He added in a low voice, "All but one."

Raith barely understood what Salizar was accusing him of, but it seemed Salizar thought he did. There was no point explaining it or reasoning with him, and besides, with no memory of his past, Raith couldn't guarantee he hadn't done those things. The part about being trapped in a physical body seemed to fit, at least; he remembered the odd sense of confinement he'd felt upon first awakening in the desert.

Perhaps Salizar was right. If he truly was the monster described, he was better off in a cage.

Salizar circled the outside of the bars until he was within striking distance. Consumed by thoughts of guilt he wasn't sure were his to shoulder, Raith didn't move. What was wrong with him that he didn't care to defend himself from the attack he knew was coming?

"This is for Harrow."

What did Harrow have to do with it? He was too caught up in his confusion to move when Salizar stabbed the staff into the cage.

Or maybe he just didn't want to.

The sharp tip stabbed him in the chest, and lightning struck.

Harrow was more distracted than she'd ever been. And to make matters worse, her fortune-telling booth was busier than she'd ever seen it. Hours before the gates opened for evening performances, there were customers lingering outside—mostly women. Every one of them had come to consult the psychic. The very distracted, overtired psychic.

All week, Harrow had been consumed by thoughts of Raith.

She thought about his bronze skin and silky hair, how he cocked his head when he didn't understand her, and how she'd discovered he had a sweet tooth and loved any sugary snack she brought him.

She thought about the times she'd made him smile. She thought about the fewer times she'd heard him speak. She recalled the intensity of his stare, and her stomach would flutter and her heart would race, and it would take all her control not to rush and see him right then.

Every night, she visited Raith instead of sleeping, and it was starting to catch up with her. She would zone out mid-conversation with others, and people had started asking her if she was feeling unwell.

She looked forward to those visits too much to care. She planned them all day, hoarding extra food she thought he might like and finding stories to read him and even planning what she would wear, for the Goddess's sake. She worried constantly about him sitting alone in his cage, at the mercy of whoever found him there.

She was...obsessed.

And right now, readings were the last thing she wanted to do. But she did them anyway, as was her duty as a Seer. And her customers were so eager and receptive to her guidance that she began to get suspicious.

As her sixth client in a row ducked into the tent, wringing her hands nervously and staring eagerly at Harrow, she began to piece it together. The woman's pale skin and elegant costume were remarkably similar to another customer she had served on one of her first days in Allegra.

The newcomer perched on the edge of the chair. "How much for a reading?"

"Ten pieces."

The woman didn't even blink before she dropped the coins on the table.

After stashing the money, Harrow held out her hands, indicating the woman place her own in them. She turned them over, studying the lines on her palms. A Seer saw those lines like rivers from a bird's-eye view, snaking their way through the land to merge with the great ocean. "What's your name?"

"Brianna, ma'am."

Ma'am? A wealthy human did not offer titles of respect to an Elemental. "Why did you consult me today, Brianna?"

"Well, someone told me how you helped them, and I was hoping you might do the same for me."

"Someone?"

"My friend Rosemary. You told her she was going to have a son. She's so happy. She's talked of nothing else since."

Harrow sighed. Attracting attention was not smart. Humans that told fortunes mostly dabbled in the art, stumbling upon the occasional grain of true intuition. People visited them for the fun of it, perhaps hoping to receive some outside assurance their life wasn't as meaningless as it felt. They didn't line up outside the gate before opening hours, happy to pay anything, receptive to any advice they were given.

No—they did that only for Seers. Or had done that.

Harrow hadn't been able to withhold vital information about her pregnancy from poor Rosemary. But now, here was Brianna and every other woman from the city, lined up and desperate for Harrow's knowledge. Would they suspect what she really was?

Would they care?

These women were likely wives of wealthy, entitled businessmen—not the easiest of roles to fill. Such men expected their wives to be like delicate shadows, flitting around behind them, cleaning up their messes, offering their bodies at their husbands' convenience. If Harrow could inject a little hope into their empty lives, maybe it wouldn't matter to them who she was.

Deciding to trust Brianna, she shuffled the cards and laid out a reading. She told Brianna that her husband was unfaithful, but her youngest daughter would make a full recovery from the illness she currently suffered from, and if Brianna chose to leave her husband, she would face several years of struggle before finally finding a new life for herself and her children.

When Brianna left, an extra five pieces left on top of the ten she already paid, another customer came, and Harrow did a reading for her, too. And then another, and another.

But all the while, she never stopped thinking about Raith.

Finally, the main event in the big top commenced, and Harrow closed up shop for the night, eager to make it there in time to catch Malaikah's performance, the finale of the show. But first, there was something she needed to do.

Picking up her Seer cards, she shuffled the deck and pictured the otherworldly eyes of the man who was becoming a permanent fixture in her thoughts. Aloud, she whispered the name he'd chosen. And then she laid out a reading, though he wasn't there to see it.

Ice. Wetland. Waterfall. River. Ocean. And...

The Deep.

As she turned over the last card, images of that strange

dream from the other night flashed before her eyes. Diving straight down, feeling the darkness surrounding her, certain she had chosen wrong...

She couldn't deny the connection. But what did it mean?

She stared at his cards, trying to make sense of them. Ice. She closed her eyes and felt cold. Empty, isolated. Helpless. And *pain*. So much pain.

The next card... Wetland. That was a tricky one. Wetlands could be rich places of fertile soil, or they could be lifeless bogs. In this case, she sensed the latter. An image of a battlefield came to mind—after the fighting had concluded and bodies lay strewn about. Carnage and chaos.

Then, Waterfall. Waterfalls were the opposite of wetlands, full of energy and power, a sign of unpredictable and uncontrollable change.

Ocean was the most powerful card in the deck. Vast. Unfathomable. The source of all life. Often, but not always, benevolent.

And lastly...the Deep. The silent depths, where no light could penetrate, where stillness was absolute. Dark, silent.

And terrifying.

Why was it terrifying? The Deep had never scared her before, but it wasn't a card she drew often. After that dream, however, she felt differently.

Unfortunately, she couldn't do for Raith what she had done for the women who visited her today. There was no simple declaration of fate, no "do this and don't do that." For Raith, everything was hazy.

Was it because he wasn't participating in the reading? Or was it because of Harrow's involvement? Seers could never clearly read their own futures or those of the ones closest to them. That was the more likely scenario.

For better or worse, Raith's fate was closely linked with her own.

More questions bubbled up until she thought her head might explode, and she couldn't stand it anymore. Stacking the cards, she left her tent in a hurry. She didn't stop rushing until she reached the big top, slipping through the backstage entrance.

Inside, the show was going full swing—quite literally, as Malaikah was currently swinging back and forth on a trapeze high above, preparing to make the precarious leap to the next one.

She sprang, her lithe body arcing with perfect poise as she sailed through the air to catch the next swing. But, oh! She feinted a fall, only to catch herself with one hand and swing with incredible strength around the trapeze, holding on with only one palm.

At the top, she steadied and balanced in a perfect one-armed handstand, spreading her legs into splits. Her panther's tail whipped back and forth around her, aiding her balance. The crowd roared with applause.

Harrow shook her head in amazement. Malaikah never ceased to impress.

Salizar entered the ring below, wielding his pointed staff, demanding applause for the Amazing Malaikah, "exotic beauty of the Southern lands," in a booming voice.

Harrow cringed. Both she and Malaikah hated that damn line, though Mal had begrudgingly learned to cope with it over the years, unable to deny its effectiveness in encouraging the humans to give up their money. It had always been a point of contention between her and Salizar, however.

While the extra volley of coin now raining down from the bleachers was unmistakable, to Harrow, calling Mal that was degrading to the brilliant woman who had reached a level of mastery few ever achieved, and that wasn't worth any amount of gold.

Sure, Hybrids would always hold a level of fascination to humans, but it was born out of ignorance. Malaikah certainly looked different compared to everyone else in the audience, with her panther ears and tail and claws, but she deserved to be celebrated for her accomplishments and not for her appearance.

This was an old debate, but something made her think of it anew today. It didn't take long to discover why—Raith. Salizar was planning to do the same thing to Raith, but worse. Keeping him in a cage like an animal, making him out to be a terrible monster when he wasn't. It was sickening. Especially because it was *Salizar* committing these atrocities, a man she had always believed to be inherently noble, despite his ruthless reputation.

How could she have been so wrong about him?

Suddenly, she couldn't stand there another second. Couldn't watch the crowd cheering for the "exotic beauty" who landed perfectly on her feet, executing a graceful bow before them. Couldn't stare at the back of Salizar's head, at the top hat he wore to disguise pointed ears that made him just as *exotic* as the rest of the creatures in his circus. Couldn't stand there thinking about how she was just as bad as him for hiding her own ears beneath a scarf every day and pretending she was human.

Without another word, she left the big top and went straight to the only place she wanted to be. She assured herself that Salizar would be busy with the show for another half hour or so.

There was no way he'd catch her.

CHAPTER SIX

Harrow lit the lantern outside Raith's tent and ducked inside. It was dark, even with the light. However he'd done it the first time, Raith didn't light the other lamps. She heard nothing and saw no movement in the tiny space of illumination surrounding her.

"Raith?"

Nothing.

"Raith?" Panic seized her. Was he gone?

Then, a shuffling sound and a muffled groan, instantly stifled.

But Harrow heard it and knew instantly what it was—a sound of pain.

Caution abandoned, she raced to the cage and peered through the bars. A dark shadow on the far side had her running around to the back. He was there, painstakingly sitting up but trying to hide it from her.

Someone had hurt him.

Helpless fury choked her as she reached through the bars

to help him. Something warm wet her hand when it touched his chest, and she withdrew her palm to the lantern's light to see. It was blood.

She gasped. "What happened? Who did this?"

Raith, of course, said nothing. His fiery eyes met hers in the darkness.

Harrow pieced it together anyway. "Salizar."

She stared at the blood on her hand and at the man behind the bars, and suddenly, she felt the Water rise within her.

"I have to get you out of here," she whispered as the realization hit like a waterfall crashing overhead. He was in danger. And not just from more beatings.

Her power told her clearly that if she left him here, he would die.

His eyes snapped back to hers. "No, Harrow."

"I have to."

"No."

"You don't understand, I—" She swallowed, trying to make sense of the feelings of panic and fear for his life that suddenly boiled up inside her like a geyser. This was bigger than her own feelings of protectiveness or the way she'd been so helplessly drawn to him from the moment they met.

This was a matter of life and death.

The Water had led her to him from the start, she realized. He was the source of the premonition she'd had months ago, the person she'd needed to find. The Water had urged her to seek him out and help him, before she'd even known of his existence.

She had every intention of listening to it now.

"No," Raith said again, clasping the bars on either side of her face and leaning toward her, a firm line drawn between his brows. "It's not safe."

His adamant refusal out of concern for her only made her more determined. How could she explain that the moment the Water had spoken, the decision was taken out of her hands? It wasn't about what was safe for her or what either of them wanted at this point. All she knew was that he was in danger, and it was her duty to help him. The Water had declared it so, and she agreed.

"You don't understand," she said again, reaching up to clasp the same bars as him, their hands brushing as she did so. Despite the turmoil inside her, the contact sent tingles up her arms. "I have to do this."

At their touch, he flinched visibly, but he didn't pull away. He leaned in closer. "Why?"

So did she. "I just...have to."

His hands tightened around the bars, causing the veins tracing his powerful arms to stand out, and suddenly, she wasn't thinking about the Water anymore. Unable to help herself, her gaze followed them up his biceps to the breadth of his shoulders, traveled across his collarbone, and trailed down the line of his pectorals.

When she finally met his eyes again, she knew he was aware of her attention and what it meant. His pupils expanded until the flames were nearly swallowed, turning his eyes fully black save for the thinnest orange ring.

Their faces were so close. She couldn't blink, and she definitely couldn't breathe. Her stomach was doing backflips that would put Malaikah to shame.

The tent flap was thrown open. "Get away from him!"

Harrow lurched back from the cage with a yelp of surprise. "What in the Shades are you doing in here?"

"I—"

Raith started to growl.

To make matters worse, Loren raced into the tent with a lantern, nearly running into Salizar's broad back. He saw Harrow and blanched. "Harrow? Wha—"

"Quiet." Salizar advanced, causing Raith's growl to rise in volume. He was furious; it was plain to see. "Do you have any idea what he is? I would have thought the sign would be a pretty good indication."

Harrow found her voice. "He's not what you think."

"He's exactly what I think."

"You can't keep him locked up like this! You make me sick!"

Raith's growling grew louder.

"I'd have thought you, of all people, Harrow, would have a vested interest in the capture of one of the creatures responsible for the extinction of an entire line of Elementals."

He knows, Harrow realized, eyes wide. *He knows exactly what I am. He's probably known it since the day he took me in.* She'd always suspected but had never known for sure.

Now she did, and she didn't know what to make of it. Salizar had cared for her and protected her identity all these years, ensuring word of her survival didn't reach Furie and her supporters.

"He's not one of them," she said. "Trust me when I say, I would know."

Raith quieted at Harrow's words, watching the interaction intently.

Salizar's eyes narrowed. "How would you know?"

"What's going on?" Loren asked. "What are you talking about?"

They both ignored him. Harrow tried to think of a way to explain the Water's guidance without giving away her identity to the human in their company. "If he was evil, I would have sensed it. I'm telling you, he's not what you think he is."

"That you don't sense evil proves nothing."

"It proves everything. Wraiths are evil. And I would have sensed if Raith had killed. I can always sense those who have taken life before, and he hasn't."

It was true—and another thing Harrow sensed? Salizar *had* taken life before. More than once. She'd always known this but had believed he must have had good cause. She had trusted him. Now? Not so much.

"Wraith? Why call him a wraith if you don't believe he is one?"

"It's his name. Raith with an R." She glanced at the still-silent Raith. "After Loren's silly sign."

Despite the circumstances, Salizar snorted a laugh. Loren scowled. Then, the ringmaster shook his head. "You're mistaken, Harrow. There are things you don't know—"

"I know enough!"

"Don't push me," he snapped. "I'm telling you he is exactly what he appears to be. Of that, I'm certain. He will remain in that cage, and in one week, the chance to view a corporeal wraith will be offered to the good people of Allegra. The money earned will go toward keeping this circus afloat and providing for Elementals who have nowhere else to go. He will cooperate with my plans or suffer the consequences."

"You can't do this. You can't force him to be in a show like an animal!"

"Can't I? This is my circus, after all. If you know of another way to make him behave, I'm all ears."

Harrow stared at him. He genuinely believed he had captured a wraith. There would be no changing his mind or making him understand the error of his ways.

It couldn't happen. She wouldn't allow it to happen.

So she said the only thing she could think of to stop it.

"Let me do it."

Salizar blinked. "I beg your pardon?"

"Let me do it. Let me work with him and get him ready. Cancel next week's show and give me some time. We're heading to the West after Allegra, right? I'll have him ready before we reach the border city. He trusts me. I'll convince him to do whatever it is you want him to do."

Raith stared at her from the cage, his face unreadable. She could guess what he was thinking, however, and it made her feel terrible. But it was the only way.

"*You* want to work with him."

"Yes."

"Even knowing what he is, you want to do this?"

"He isn't what you think he is."

Salizar shook his head. "But what if he is?"

"He isn't."

"Humor me. On the off chance that he is actually a wraith, no matter how small or unlikely"—his disbelief was evident—"would you still wish to care for such a creature?"

"Never," Harrow stated, revulsion filling her at the mere thought. "I would die first."

"And yet you still want to do this."

"I trust my instincts. He isn't what you think he is. I'd bet my life on it."

Salizar considered this for what felt like forever. Finally, he nodded, and relief crashed through her. "Very well. It seems nothing can sway you. I admire your tenacity and can only hope you aren't forced to learn a very painful lesson." He flung a hand in Raith's direction. "He's your responsibility."

"Thank you." She could scarcely breathe, let alone speak.

"For the performance, he has two tasks—present the audience with his wings and change his skin back to its original shade. You can work with him, but only during daylight hours."

Raith had wings? That was news to her. "Yes, sir."

"I will not be canceling the shows next week. Don't even try arguing with me on that," he said when she opened her mouth. "He performs in one week."

"Yes, sir." Though it wasn't a total win, she was still reeling from her good fortune, scarcely believing she had convinced Salizar to listen to her.

The ringmaster spun on a heel but stopped at the exit. "Don't make me regret this, Harrow."

"No, sir."

"I've always been lenient with you because of the unfortunate circumstances that landed you here. That leniency does not apply here. I have no sympathy for that creature. If your plan fails, I'll treat you no differently than I would anyone else who crossed me. If you want to keep your home in this circus, I suggest you do not fail."

"Understood, sir."

"Good luck then." And he was gone.

Loren immediately rounded on her. "What were you thinking, Harrow?"

After facing off with Salizar, she was not even remotely intimidated. "Go away, Loren."

"No, you need to—"

A low growl filled the air once again. Raith was gripping the bars of his cage with clawed hands, lip curled off his teeth, black gaze locked on Loren.

"You aren't safe with him. You can't seriously think you are."

"Go away, please."

"You need to listen to me. He's not human—"

Harrow's patience finally snapped. Her power rushed to the surface, static charge filling the air.

As a rule, the Seers had been peaceful, respected by the inhabitants of the places they traveled. They were neutral in political conflicts, and wise leaders left them to their own devices, trusting that they could lure them to their domains for counsel with gifts. The not-so-wise leaders who tried controlling the Seers or forcing them to pick sides soon found that they were not quite so peaceful when provoked.

When threatened, a Seer could defend herself—quite well, in fact.

At the first stirrings of Harrow's power, Loren fell silent, eyes widening as he stepped back. He thought she was human. Everyone did, except Malaikah and, evidently, Salizar. Harrow had always gone to great lengths to hide the truth, but suddenly she was done. She was sick to death of pretending to be something she wasn't. Sick to death of being afraid of her origins, secretive about her past, fearful of her future.

Reaching her hands beneath her hair, she untied the colorful scarf over her ears and watched the silk float to the ground. "*I'm* not human, Loren."

For fifty years, she'd hidden her identity. Even if she didn't believe in the existence of wraiths, something had killed the Seers, and there was a chance it would come for her if word spread that a Seer had survived. As well, human descendants of Ferron the Conqueror's armies still lived in the South. Loyal to Queen Furie, they blamed Darya for starting the war, and Harrow had always feared they would use her as a chance to seek vengeance for their losses.

She didn't know what the ramifications of her choice to reveal her identity would be, but soon, it wouldn't matter anymore anyway.

Loren blanched at the unmistakable sight of her pointed ears. "You're... But you... What are you?"

The Water rarely expressed itself through any physical display, and tonight was no different, save for the sudden charge blasting through the tent and the mist collecting in the air. Harrow knew her eyes had started to glow, and she could feel her hair lifting in the phantom gusts.

"Get out."

It was all she needed to say. The words were pitched lower than her normal speaking voice and loaded with power.

Loren turned and fled the tent.

Alone at last, Harrow deflated, power retreating within immediately.

But she wasn't alone—Raith was there. Raith, whose fragile trust she had betrayed by promising to discipline him for Salizar. The wary look he was giving her was proof enough of that.

Harrow buried her face in her hands. She had, in one night, made a promise to Salizar she couldn't keep and, consequently, brought about the beginning of the end of her life as she knew it. Malaikah was going to be furious.

Raith rattled the bars of the cage door to get her attention. She glanced up at him, finding a frown creasing his brow.

"Are you okay?" His voice was quiet, as it always was the rare times he used it.

"Yes, I'm fine." She nearly choked on the words. He was still concerned for her, enough to fight his aversion to speech, even after he thought she'd betrayed him.

Suddenly, making him understand was her top priority.

Somehow, in the short time she'd known him, he'd become one of the most important people in her life. The truth of that scared her, but it was too late to turn back now.

She approached his cage. "I'm sorry. I had to say whatever I could to get Salizar to leave you alone. I have no intention of training you for any ridiculous circus show, I swear."

Raith's fingers tightened around the bars.

"I'm not going to force you to show your wings, and I don't care about your other abilities. I promise."

Raith didn't move, didn't even blink, and Harrow's heart sank. He didn't believe her. And why should he? Everyone he'd ever met had hurt him in some way, so why should he think Harrow was any different—

His skin suddenly morphed into a brilliant orange.

It was so bright, she lifted a hand to shield her eyes from the dazzling onslaught. Noticing the stubborn set to his chin, it clicked.

A bubble of surprised laughter burst out of her. "Yes, you can even be that color, if that's what you want. It might help save some lamp oil, it's so bright."

He smiled. Or, at least, his eyes did.

His skin became brown again as Harrow turned and leaned against the cage bars. "We have one week before the show. We have to figure out how to get you out of here, gather supplies, and decide where to go. No one can know what we're planning." She craned her neck to look up at him. "I guess that's not a problem for you. You're not much of a talker."

Facing forward again, she sighed. "I'll have to tell Malaikah, though. She can help us, and besides, I couldn't leave her without saying goodbye."

A light touch on her shoulder had her twisting around to

find Raith crouched behind her, a frown creasing his brow. Somehow, she knew exactly what he was thinking.

"I do have to do this. Even without what the Water told me, there's no way I could pretend I didn't see what I did tonight."

He frowned at the mention of the Water, and she debated explaining but decided against it. There was no point upsetting him with dire predictions, and besides, there was nothing to worry about anyway. She was going to help him escape before anything could happen.

She faced forward again, leaning her head against the bars, and an image of Loren's stunned expression flashed through her mind. She couldn't believe she'd blown her human disguise. What in the Shades had she been thinking?

She smiled into the darkness. No more hiding. No more pretending. No more damnable headbands. She thought of how good it had felt to give true readings again, and a sense of rightness filled her. She was done playing human.

If there were risks, so be it. She would find a way to circumvent the dangers. She would find a way to survive and make her people proud.

As if Raith was following her thoughts, the tiniest touch on her exposed ear tip sent tingles racing down her spine.

She looked back. "Yeah, they're pointed." She reached up to touch the tip as he had. "Just like yours."

He frowned, tucked his hair back, and touched his own ear. His eyes widened like he hadn't realized until that moment he had Elemental ears.

Harrow's heart clenched amid a wave of tenderness. There was something so pure about him. Oh, he was lethal, there was no doubt about it, but he was also innocent in many ways. He was an enigma she was determined to understand.

She wanted to be the first to touch that secret side of him and protect it from harm. She wanted him to trust her with an almost desperate need. She wanted to be closer to him than she'd ever been to anyone. She just...*wanted*.

"We're different, you and I," she said. "People like us have to look out for each other."

"Why?"

"Because." Did he genuinely not understand? "It's the right thing to do."

He didn't respond, and Harrow faced forward again. "You have a nice voice. You should speak more." She quickly added, "But only if you want to." She didn't like the idea of pressuring him to do anything before he was ready.

He didn't speak. Apparently, he wasn't ready. That was okay. Hopefully, in time, he would trust her more.

"I should go. Tomorrow's a big day. We have to start working on our escape plan. First things first, I need to figure out how to get you out of that cage."

Luckily, she knew just who to talk to.

When Harrow was gone, Raith lay on his back in the center of his cage and stared at the tent's roof through the bars. He thought about Harrow's fierce conviction to liberate him and wondered where it had come from. And he thought about the strange urges that had risen in him when their hands brushed. Urges to touch. To taste. To possess.

He wasn't sure how he felt about that. It was intense, all-consuming, and therefore frightening. He wasn't sure yet if he preferred the numbness. It certainly felt safer and more familiar.

One thing he was sure about, however, was that he didn't like the sacrifice Harrow was planning to make for him.

Contrary to what his preference for silence might lead others to believe, he was not stupid or lacking perception in any way. Based on what he'd heard tonight, he had pieced a lot together.

Salizar had told him that wraiths were responsible for the deaths of the Seers. *I enjoy witnessing your pain*, he'd said, *while still knowing it will never equal the pain your kind inflicted upon the Seers before you killed them all.*

But then his voice had dropped as he added, *All but one.*

And then, before Salizar had stabbed him with the staff… *This is for Harrow.*

The Seers had been destroyed by wraiths. All of them were dead, except one. One survivor.

That survivor was Harrow.

What if Salizar was right? What if Raith really was a wraith?

Harrow was positive he wasn't. He'd seen the certainty in her eyes and heard it in her voice when she swore it to Salizar. But how did she know? He certainly couldn't confirm or deny it either way. He had no memory of anything, which in itself was suspicious.

He couldn't allow Harrow to help him if there was even the slightest chance he was one of the monsters that killed her family. She was planning to free him, sacrificing her safety and security to do so. He didn't think he deserved it and didn't want her to throw her life away anyway.

But what could he do?

He briefly entertained the notion of finding a way to escape without her, but he reluctantly dismissed it. If he escaped now, Salizar would blame Harrow. He'd promised her no leniency if she failed in her efforts to discipline him. No, if Raith was escaping at all, it had to be with her at his side.

But he couldn't take her from her life here unless he could guarantee another safe way for her to live, which he couldn't. He hadn't even been able to save himself from capture, and he doubted his ability to protect himself and another from ending up in the same situation...or worse.

That left only one option.

He could play along with Salizar's circus act, becoming nothing but a trained animal for humans to gawk at. He'd change his appearance on command, flash his wings and claws, do whatever that bloody bastard wanted him to do. He would rather die than do that, but now Harrow was involved, and it wasn't that simple anymore.

Would he sacrifice his pride to protect her? The answer was yes.

His heart sank as he realized that was what he would have to do. Harrow had unintentionally betrayed him, though he could never hold it against her.

But because of her, Salizar had won.

Raith would stay in Salizar's circus. He would behave. He would perform for the masses like a dog. He would become the soulless monster Salizar believed he was.

For all he knew, that was exactly what he was anyway.

CHAPTER SEVEN

The next morning, Harrow knocked on Malaikah's caravan door, casting wary glances over her shoulder as if afraid of being seen. Which was silly because knocking on Malaikah's door was something she did every day, and if there was anything *un*suspicious she could be doing, that was it. Still, her thoughts were churning with so many plans and schemes that she felt like everyone could see them.

The door opened, revealing Malaikah in a silk robe. Her hair was unbraided today, the coiled curls free to spring around her head. She smiled brightly and then froze. "Where's your scarf? I can see your ears plain as day!"

Harrow grinned despite herself. "I'm done hiding, Mal. The secret's out. Only time will tell if it gets me killed or not."

Malaikah gaped at her. "Why? What happened?"

"Way too much."

"Then come in and tell me everything. I just made coffee."

Harrow followed Mal into her caravan. A little pot steamed on the stove. Pillows were piled atop her unmade bed, and as usual, sequined bodysuits and costume accessories spilled out of the wardrobe.

"You want a cup?" Mal asked as Harrow slid into one of the bench seats at the table built into the wall. She shook her head. She was too nervous for coffee.

Malaikah bustled about at the stove, pouring her own cup. "Why'd you give up your disguise?" Her long tail swished behind her. "I don't like it, Harrow. Your anonymity kept you safe. You don't know what's going to happen if word gets out."

"I just got sick of hiding. I've been sick of it for years, to be honest, but it wasn't planned. Loren was yelling at me about how dangerous Raith was, and he said, 'He's not human, Harrow!'" She imitated his voice with a petulant tone. "And I just snapped. Who does he think he is? Declaring someone untrustworthy because they're not human? Look where he works, for the Goddess's sake. I couldn't stand it for another second."

Malaikah was staring at her, coffeepot still in hand. "What are you on about? Who's Raith?"

Harrow fidgeted. "I did something bad, Mal. I'm leaving the circus. In a week."

Mal slowly set the coffeepot back on the stove without looking at it. "Harrow, you're scaring me." She lowered herself into the other bench seat, cradling her mug to her chest.

"I made a promise to Salizar I don't intend to keep. At the end of the week, he's going to know it, and by then I have to be long gone. But it's not just me I have to worry about. I'm taking Raith with me."

"Who is Raith? What in the Goddess's name are you talking about?"

"A week ago, I went into Salizar's private tent. I had this weird dream—I don't know what it meant, but when I woke up, I just went outside and walked straight there like I was possessed."

Malaikah shook her head. "Okay, so then what happened?"

"I met Raith."

"For the last and final time, who the Shades is Raith?"

"He's...well, Salizar thinks he's a wraith."

Mal's mouth dropped open.

"But he's not! He's—well, I don't know what he is, but he's sweet, and he trusts me, and I can't just abandon him. Salizar has him locked in a cage, and he's been hurting him."

Malaikah dragged a hand down her face. "Salizar thinks he's a wraith? But...why? Are wraiths even real? And aren't they supposed to be like ghosts?"

"He's convinced, Mal. No matter what I said, he wouldn't change his mind. But Raith's not evil. I know he's not. I would have sensed it."

"Wraith? But I thought he wasn't...? Honey, I'm so confused right now."

"Raith with an R."

"With an R? What?" Poor Mal was barely keeping up.

"It's his name. When I asked him what it was, he told me it was Raith, but I think he just picked it out of the blue. Loren tried to make a sign for him, but the oaf spelled it wrong, and I think he just read it off the sign."

"Why didn't he have a name?"

"Because he has no idea who he is."

"Why not?"

"I don't know."

"Why didn't you ask him?"

"I tried, but he doesn't speak much."

Mal shook her head again and then gulped a humongous swallow of coffee. "I still don't understand why any of this means you're leaving the circus. And you'd better start explaining fast, or I'm going to lose it."

Harrow did, telling Malaikah everything that had happened the night before, including how Salizar had agreed to let her "train" Raith for the performance and her certainty about what would happen if she didn't help him escape. "He's going to die if he stays here, Mal. The Water told me clearly. I can't just sit back and watch it happen."

"Are you sure, though? I mean, Sal may be acting like an ass, but I don't think he would actually kill him."

"Salizar believes he's a wraith. I think he'd kill him without a second thought. If it weren't for the money-making opportunity, he probably would have already. Besides, I don't know for sure who Raith's life is in danger from, only that it's in danger. I have to help him, Mal. He has no one else."

Malaikah sighed heavily. "You and your wild urges, Harrow. I never know what you're going to throw at me next."

"This is serious," Harrow pleaded. She couldn't do this without her best friend by her side. "I swear I'm not making it up."

Mal reached forward and patted the back of Harrow's hand. "I know you're not making it up. I just wish you weren't telling me you're putting yourself in danger to help someone you barely know escape."

"Mal..." Harrow winced in anticipation of Malaikah's reaction. "I'm not just helping him escape. I have to go with him."

"What? No way!"

She rushed to explain herself. "Salizar told me that if

anything went wrong with Raith's training, I wouldn't receive any leniency. He's going to kick me out of the circus when he finds out Raith is gone, and besides, I don't think Raith has any clue how to get by in the real world. At least if I go with him, I can help him and make sure no one hurts him again and—"

"Harrow, listen to yourself!" Halfway through taking a sip, Malaikah slammed her coffee mug onto the table so hard that black liquid sloshed over the edge. "Who is this guy? You just met him, and you're going to throw away your entire life for him? It sounds to me like whatever was going on in that tent last night was between Raith and Salizar. It's not your problem. This life is all we've got. If you run, what will you have? Where will you go?"

"I don't know."

"You can't get involved in this, Harrow. This isn't your fight. It's horrible and tragic, I know. But we're part of this freak show, on display for the humans, because nowadays, there's no other place for us in this world. Every night I perform for them because I have to take care of myself first. Let the pathetic humans clap for the weird cat lady. Let them clap and then give me all their money. Who cares? I'm fucking rich!" Malaikah sighed, her voice getting quiet. "Outside this life, Elementals aren't accepted anymore. The bitch Queens made sure of that by choosing their never-ending squabbles over their own people. Now we have to find a way to survive on our own."

Everything Malaikah was saying was true, and yet... "His life is in danger, Mal. I have to help him. I couldn't live with myself if I didn't."

Mal studied her with narrowed eyes. "What about this guy is so special?"

"I don't know. But I feel like…" Harrow paused, trying to understand her feelings, trying to put them into words. "I feel like he's important. To me. The Water told me that we're connected and he's meant to be in my life."

Malaikah scoffed. "You cannot be in love already."

"I'm not in love. It's not like that." Was it?

"Uh-huh." Malaikah didn't sound convinced, either.

"I can't explain it, but I'm not abandoning him. I just can't."

"Why are you so certain he isn't a wraith?"

"He's not."

"But how do you know? I mean, if Sal—"

"He's *not*, Mal."

"Honey, Salizar's no fool. He's a centuries-old Enchanter, one of the most powerful alive. He's been places, seen stuff, knows a lot. If he's convinced he's got a real wraith on his hands, what makes you so certain he's wrong? It would take a lot to trick that wily man."

Harrow sighed. "You know how I can read people. If I meet someone evil, I know. And I can always tell if someone has killed before. Taking a life leaves a scar on the spirit. The Water senses it instantly."

"And you don't sense anything from Raith?"

She shook her head. "The inclination for violence is there, but he's innocent. His spirit is squeaky clean. It's almost *too* clean. The only other time I've seen that is in children."

"Children?" Mal lifted a brow. "But he's not…"

"No. No, definitely not. But he has this purity about him, and he's totally clueless to the world. I know it sounds irrational, Mal, but I just…*need* to do this."

Malaikah stared at her for a long time. Finally, when Harrow was about to jump out of her skin, she nodded.

"Okay. All right. You have your weird Seer urges that I'll never understand. I get it, and I respect you and love you no matter what. If this—this…wild plan is really what you think you need to do, then I'm in."

"Thank you." Overcome with relief, Harrow leaned forward and clasped her friend's hands. "You know I love you too."

"So what do you need me to do?" Now, Malaikah's eyes lit up with the sparkle of challenge. A woman accustomed to backflipping through space was not one to shy away from uncertainties.

"We need to make an escape plan. We've got less than a week before Raith's supposed to perform, or whatever you call being tortured in front of an audience. I want to be long gone by then."

"So what do you want to do?"

Harrow released Mal's hands and leaned back in her seat. "First, we need to break him out of the cage."

Mal gave her a look. "You know I'm a little rusty at this escape-artist stuff, right? It's been a long time since I was on the run."

"You're still the best, and you're the only one I trust. I couldn't ask for a better accomplice."

She flashed a grin. "Flattery will get you everywhere." That long black tail started to flick again. "Okay, fine. But it won't be easy. You know Sal will have enchanted that cage within an inch of its life."

"I'm guessing the bars are unbreakable or Raith would have broken them already."

"So he's super strong *and* sweet? Are you sure you're not in love?"

Harrow felt her cheeks flush.

Mal cocked a brow. "What's keeping the cage closed?"

"There's a padlock on the latch."

Mal made a face. "Definitely enchanted. Luckily for you, I know a guy."

"What? What guy?"

"There's an old Enchanter in the Underground who sells slightly criminal enchantments. For the right price, I can get us a lockpick that will open any lock, even an enchanted one."

Harrow's eyes widened. "You're a genius, Mal."

"Nah. Old Godric's the genius. But an enchantment that powerful will last only a day or two, so we have to time this perfectly. So what comes next?"

"I don't know. I haven't thought much further ahead than getting Raith out of the cage."

"You've never staged an epic escape before, have you?"

Harrow pursed her lips. "You know I haven't."

"Then it's a good thing you've got me, even if I am rusty." Malaikah clapped her hands. "Okay, here's what we're going to do. First, you need an actual escape plan. It needs to be unexpected but not so unexpected it becomes obvious. Sometimes, the obvious plan is so obvious, it becomes unexpected."

"What?"

"Never mind. Second, you need a fake escape plan. A diversion. You need to lay a false trail so that when Sal starts hunting you down, he has something to follow that will lead him astray. You with me?"

Harrow nodded, more than a little sad when she realized where Malaikah's expertise in this area originated.

Mal's parents had been leaders of the famous Kambu panther clan in the Far South before they'd been assassinated by rivals. As soon as her enemies realized the leaders' young daughter had survived the attack, they'd been out for blood.

It was thanks only to Mal's cleverness and adaptability that she'd escaped with her life. She planned to one day return to Kambu and take back her birthright, but for now, the circus life was all she had.

"Let's look at it this way," Mal said. "Pretend you're Salizar. Your fortune teller and your wraith have escaped, and you're ready to hunt them down. Where's the first place you look?"

Harrow frowned, considering this. "I guess I'd assume we'd hide in Allegra. It's a huge city with so many different people coming and going that it would be an obvious hiding spot. We could easily find somewhere to lie low for the final week the circus is in town."

"Right. Exactly."

"So that means we do the opposite. We take my horse, gather provisions, and then leave the city immediately."

Malaikah shook her head. "Wrong."

"What? But you said—"

"I said, the best choice is something so obvious it becomes unexpected. Your first conclusion of the smartest place to hide was in the city. Salizar will come to that conclusion too. So you double bluff. You purchase a horse from the market and steal provisions to make it look like you're planning to leave Allegra. False trail: laid. But instead, you stash the horse somewhere he won't find it, and then you *do* stay in the city. When Sal finds the missing supplies, he'll send people out of Allegra to look for you, thinking you went with the unexpected option."

"We can buy the horse from a less popular seller so it's not obvious," Harrow said, catching on, "but still easy enough for

Salizar to find once he starts making inquiries. I'll wear a distinctive scarf so the seller will remember me. Salizar will think he's clever when he finds the guy we dealt with."

"Now you're thinking smart." Malaikah grinned. "And we'll steal the food from the circus stores to get Sal on the right track. That'll be the first place he'll check."

Harrow nodded, starting to believe this could work. "But what do we do with the horse? If Salizar finds it, the jig is up."

Malaikah's eyes narrowed as she thought hard. Then they widened. "What if we don't hide it at all? We'll buy a plain one, and I'll go in disguise and leave it at the main stables in the middle of the central market, where every merchant leaves their horses. Even if Salizar did check, you wouldn't have been seen there, so how could he know it was yours?"

"Okay." Harrow stared at her friend, heart pounding. She could scarcely believe they were planning this outlandish thing.

"Okay." Mal was still grinning. She'd always gotten off on danger in a way Harrow never understood. "When does this all go down?"

"We have six days before Raith's show. I say we leave the final night, so we have ample opportunity to get ready. We'll need to buy the lockpick, find a horse, steal provisions, and secure lodging to hide in until the circus leaves town."

Mal's eyes bugged a little. "You make it sound so easy."

Harrow laughed nervously.

"So you're really leaving? Just like that?"

"I have to. Like I said, after I made that promise to Salizar, he'll throw me out once Raith escapes."

"It won't be the same without you."

"It won't be the same without *you*. You're the only family I have."

"You too, Harrow. Goddess, I remember when you first showed up here, just a little sprite of a thing."

"You were pretty little yourself," Harrow said. Malaikah was only five years older than her. The two of them had joined the circus in the same year, but Mal had arrived several months before her.

Malaikah chuckled and shook her head. "We were so messed up back then."

Harrow smiled sadly. "We still kinda are."

"True."

"You should come with us, Mal."

"I'm tempted. But you know it's not exactly safe for me in the outside world, and besides, I love the circus. I couldn't give it up."

If Malaikah actually had plans to return to Kambu one day, she would have to give the circus up anyway, but Harrow decided not to remind her of that.

"I just hate the idea of leaving you here with slimy Salizar."

Mal snorted. "I'm not scared of him. I'm his star performer. He needs me."

Harrow sighed. "I suppose you're right." She swallowed hard, fighting back tears. "Goddess, I can't believe this is happening."

"I'm proud of you. Coming out as Elemental? Choosing to help someone in need?" Mal reached across the table and seized her hands in a tight grip. "I wish you weren't leaving, but knowing you're following your heart, doing what you believe is right even if it means giving up your whole life… It's amazing. You're Goddess-damned amazing, and I love you."

Harrow's fight against tears failed miserably. She practically burst into them, shoulders shaking with tiny sobs until Malaikah came around the table to sit beside her. She wrapped her arms around Harrow and held on tight. "Stop that, you horrible woman, or I'm going to cry too. You know I hate crying."

Harrow managed a laugh, and the two embraced in companionable silence.

Now all they had to do was outwit their cunning ringmaster and hide an Elemental with a completely unique set of features in the middle of a crowded city. What could possibly go wrong?

CHAPTER EIGHT

The end of the week came too soon, but there was no hiding from it. Harrow spent the final day going through her usual routines in a daze. She read fortunes, spoke to fellow circus workers, ate her meals, and tidied her caravan, but she wasn't really aware of any of it.

Everything was ready. Malaikah had secured a room for them at a tavern in the Underground and purchased the enchanted lockpick to open Raith's cage. Harrow had narrowed down her possessions into two heavy bags and bought clothes from the market for Raith. He was so big that she'd ended up ordering them custom-made, and the tailor looked incredulous when she'd given his approximate measurements.

She'd also purchased a horse which, combined with the cost of the inn, had put a significant dent in her savings. It was a plain brown, unremarkable mare, but the seller swore it was well trained. Not that it mattered. Once she picked it up on Friday at midnight, Mal, hooded and cloaked, would be leading it straight to Allegra's main stables and leaving it in the care of the stablemen.

Harrow had stayed up the night before with Malaikah stealing food and supplies from the circus stores. That hadn't felt particularly good, but it was part of the decoy plan and had to be done. Luckily, Mal had leftover skills from when she was on the run, and they managed to liberate some loaves of bread, a wheel of cheese, a small sack of vegetables, and two water canteens.

Raith tried repeatedly in his silent, intense way to convince Harrow to give up on her plan to free him, but she wasn't budging. She also knew Salizar suspected her of something. She was pretty sure Loren had been trailing her all week, and the guards outside Raith's tent had seemed more alert than usual. But she and Malaikah had been careful on their separate forays into town, and their tails hadn't followed them there. She was certain Salizar didn't expect her to go as far as she was planning to.

To take care of the guard tonight, Harrow had brewed up her strongest sleeping draught. The tea wasn't enough to actually knock him unconscious, but it was an effective sleep aid. The odds were good he'd be out within an hour.

After finishing her last reading, Harrow closed up her booth, putting the day's earnings in her purse rather than taking them to Salizar. Afterward, she gathered up her crystals and cards and emptied the contents of her hidden Seer drawer in the wardrobe, stashing everything carefully at the top of her bags.

She'd put on as much jewelry as she could today so she wouldn't have to pack it, but also as a farewell to her old life. On her last day as a circus fortune teller, she wanted to look her best. Half her hair was wound into a messy bun atop her head while the bottom half hung loose. She wore her favorite silver earrings and had covered her wrists with bracelets. She'd laid out her thick cloak with the oversize hood for tonight, alongside loose leather boots that pulled on like stockings and tightened with soft leather ties.

After closing up her caravan, she went to the meal tent and tried to eat, but her appetite was meager, and she managed only a small bowl of soup. People would pat her on the shoulder or call out a greeting as they passed, and she had to fight back tears every time. She tried to act normal, all the while knowing that every interaction was actually goodbye.

No one in the circus had shown much reaction to finding out she was a Seer, making her wonder if they'd always suspected but had understood her need to keep it secret. It only made her love them more and made her leaving that much more bittersweet.

But there was plenty of gossip about Salizar's latest acquisition and who it could be. The ringmaster hadn't said a word about it to anyone, and neither had Loren. Even the ones assigned to guard duty didn't know what they were guarding, and the speculation was rife.

After dinner, Harrow went to the back entrance of the big top to watch Malaikah's show. Her beautiful panther swung between trapezes and balanced on her hands and backflipped through the air like the fearless, powerful woman she was.

When the show was complete, Harrow walked to Raith's tent with the sleeping draught and had a drink with Oli, who was on guard duty again tonight. Feeling guilty for deceiving him, she pretended to sip hers and then discreetly dumped it when he wasn't looking, though she likely could have consumed the entire pot and felt no effect. She was so nervous, she doubted she'd ever be able to sleep again.

After the tea was gone, she went into the tent for a little while, avoiding Raith's pointed looks as she read to him. He seemed to sense she was nervous, but she saw no sense in addressing it, knowing he would object to her plans out of concern for her. She excused herself earlier than usual so Oli would relax and have adequate time to get sleepy, and then she went to Malaikah's caravan to wait.

Mal didn't take long to arrive. She took one look at Harrow and said, "You okay?"

Harrow couldn't find the breath to answer.

"Give me five minutes. I've got just the thing to help."

Malaikah went back outside to wash and returned dressed in a pair of black trousers and a black tunic, her long tail snaking out from beneath the shirt. Trousers were rarely worn by women in these parts, but dresses were awkward garments for a woman with a tail, and Malaikah had never given a damn about following social customs anyway.

She reached up to the cupboard and pulled out a bottle of whisky and two glasses. "Ta-da." Pouring one for each of them, she sat down on the bench opposite Harrow.

They downed the whisky, and Mal filled the glasses again. They downed those, too. "Better?"

Finally, Harrow felt herself calming a little. She nodded.

"Two hours till showtime. Did you visit Oli with the tea yet?"

She nodded again.

"You visit Raith today?"

She nodded once more.

"Bags are packed?"

Another nod.

"Well, then there's nothing else to do but have another drink."

One hour past midnight arrived.

Harrow donned her cloak while Malaikah extinguished the lanterns in her caravan. Together, they slipped outside and surveyed their quiet surroundings. Harrow waited for Malaikah to give the all-clear before moving. Mal's Hybrid senses would pick up on any disturbances more effectively than Harrow's.

Finally, Mal nodded. "Let's go."

Harrow took her friend's hand, and the two women crept through the camp toward Raith's tent. They kept to the edge of the fairgrounds, sticking to the shadows and avoiding the main path. Malaikah's ears twitched this way and that, listening for signs of movement.

Finally, they reached the tent. From their cover, they could see the tea was a success. Poor Oli slumped in his chair, sound asleep. The tent's front flap was securely tied down, but Mal made quick work of the ties while Harrow glanced over her shoulder, expecting Salizar to jump out at any second. They'd opted to go in the front entrance because Harrow didn't think Raith would fit under the sides as she did.

Inside, as usual, was completely black. Malaikah cursed in a whisper. "Wish we had some light."

"We can't risk a lantern."

"I know."

They crept forward through the dark to where they knew Raith's cage to be. Hands out in front of her, she felt the cold steel of the bars slide into her grip. "Raith?"

A light touch on her hands sent warmth rushing down her arms. She peered into the darkness, trying to see him, but could make out only an outline. "You ready to get out of here?"

"Don't do this," Raith said softly.

"I'm not changing my mind, so save your breath."

From beside them, Harrow heard the metallic sounds of Malaikah working the lock with her enchanted pick. "This would be a lot easier if I could see the damn thing."

Raith withdrew his hands at that moment, so Harrow twisted hers together nervously.

A tiny flame suddenly illuminated the darkness, and she jumped in surprise. The first thing she saw was the flickering orange light. Then her eyes traveled over what that little flame illuminated, and she drew in a sharp breath.

Raith was holding a hand outside the cage beside the padlock. The flame hovered several inches above the center of his palm.

Malaikah stared at it, transfixed. "What the...?"

"How did you do that?"

"I don't know."

He didn't know? How could he not know? Harrow felt a lurch of disquiet.

But there wasn't time to speculate. Mal bent back over the padlock, wiggling the pick. The seconds passed agonizingly slowly, each of them precious and essential to their escape.

Just when Harrow started to have doubts that the enchantment on the pick would fool Salizar's on the lock, it sprang open. "It worked!" Mal whispered triumphantly, sliding the lock out and opening the bolt on the cage. "Oh, Sal's going to be so pissed."

Raith curled his fingers into a fist and extinguished the tiny flame in his palm.

He was free.

Heart pounding for an entirely different reason, Harrow pulled the steel door open.

Raith leaped out of the cage. She couldn't see it, but she could *feel* it, feel the moment he regained his freedom.

He didn't waste a second. She heard him taking rapid strides toward the exit of the tent. He threw open the flap and ducked outside, Harrow and Malaikah hurrying behind him. Outside, he stopped and took in the still camp and moonlit night.

It was a glorious moment.

Raith stood, bronze skin lit by the night's bluish glow, silky hair falling onto his bare shoulders. His powerful back expanded as he took a deep breath of fresh air and straightened to his full height. Rolling his shoulders back, he stretched his neck from side to side, clenching his fists and shifting the strength in his arms and back.

A tingle of power charged the air, similar to Harrow's own when she was provoked. She cautiously approached, stepping alongside him to see his face. The flames in his black eyes glowed, almost casting light into the night. He lifted his hands and stared at them, and suddenly, sharp claws lengthened from his fingertips.

Then, he raised his arms slightly, arched his spine as if stretching, and…huge leathery wings burst out of his back, so tall they nearly doubled his height.

Harrow jumped back with a gasp, and Mal cursed. Salizar hadn't been kidding about the wings, had he?

Raith looked over his shoulder at Malaikah and bared his teeth in an attempt at a smile, but he looked so formidable that Mal recoiled. Then he looked at Harrow, but she couldn't tell what he was thinking. She was still caught up on the wings, staring at the foot-long talons at the tip of them, arcing high above his head.

Folding them against his back, he strode off into the night, leaving them behind.

Both women stood frozen, not quite believing what they were seeing, but Harrow recovered first. She raced after him, turning her run into a sprint when she found he'd already made it halfway across the fairgrounds. How did he move so fast?

"Raith," she hissed, running as fast as her legs could carry her. "Raith, wait!"

He stopped reluctantly and turned back. His face was inscrutable, his eyes still glowing. Those enormous wings surrounded him like a cloak of shadows.

"Where are you going?" Goddess forbid someone catch them now. There was no telling what he would do.

"To kill him."

"Kill whom?"

"Salizar."

Harrow gaped at him. "What? No, you can't kill Salizar!"

His eyes narrowed. He obviously didn't like that.

"Raith, you can't. We're supposed to be escaping." Harrow looked desperately around, hoping no one was there to see them and raise the alarm. This was the last thing she'd expected, and she hadn't the faintest clue what to do.

Which was foolish, she realized. Of course Raith wanted to go after Salizar. He was a proud, powerful being, and Salizar had imprisoned and humiliated him. Of course he wanted revenge.

"You can't kill someone in cold blood," she explained. "If

he tried to hurt you again, you could defend yourself, but you can't just kill him."

"Why not?"

She grasped him by the forearm, the muscle like a rock beneath her hand. "Because it's wrong to take life. Only the Goddess gets to decide who lives and dies."

"If he's dead, there's no more danger to you. Then you don't have to leave." He shrugged like it was the most obvious thing in the world.

A desperate laugh escaped her. He was explaining—the most she'd ever heard him speak—why she should be okay with him committing murder as if *she* was the one being unreasonable. She figured a change of tactics was in order. Obviously, he didn't see the problem with killing, so she'd have to appeal to him another way.

Dear Goddess, she was glad Malaikah hadn't caught up yet. It wasn't long ago she was swearing to Mal that Raith was innocent. While she knew better than to doubt what the Water had told her, Mal likely wouldn't have the same unshakeable faith. Still, Harrow knew with certainty that he wouldn't hurt her.

"Look," she tried again, "Salizar runs this circus. He started it, and it needs him to function. Without him, none of the people here would have jobs or places to live, and that's a difficult thing for our kind to find these days. In the outside world, Elementals are shunned by humans, and there are very few places in the Territories for us to live safely. And some of us here, like Malaikah, are on the run, and their lives would be in danger. Salizar gives them protection and stability. You can't kill him, Raith."

Raith's head tilted. His eyes were distant, and he seemed to be looking through her rather than at her.

They were standing in the middle of the fairgrounds where anyone could see them. To anyone else, Raith would look terrifying. Like death incarnate.

To Harrow, even as she was caught up in her anxiety, he was fiercely beautiful.

Now that he was liberated from captivity, a wildness surrounded him that called to her like nothing else ever had.

Freedom, the Water whispered. *Destiny*.

She craved it like a dried-up lake basin craved rainfall, and the strength of that craving terrified her. She was being sucked into a whirlpool of something she didn't understand, the pull so powerful she had no desire to free herself.

Was this the dream? Was this why the deep had called to her? But what awaited her there? Salvation or her own destruction?

"Harrow. You and Malaikah can run the circus as well as he does. He is not irreplaceable." Raith tugged his arm gently from her grip, and it became obvious that she hadn't succeeded in changing his mind. Fiery eyes narrowed, he started forward again to fulfill his quest for vengeance.

She couldn't let him do this.

"Raith, *wait!*"

He turned back even then. Reaching up, she grasped one powerful shoulder, and then she did the only thing she could think of to keep him from trying to leave again.

She rose to her tiptoes and pressed her lips to his.

It was like kissing a statue.

If he'd been still before, it was nothing compared to this. His entire body went rigid, and he did nothing—didn't respond to her in any way.

A little embarrassed, she pulled back, lowering to her flat feet. He just stared at her, his face expressionless. Of course he hadn't wanted her to kiss him. He was thinking of revenge and wasn't—

His clawed hands shot out, wrapped around the back of her neck, and then he stooped and pressed his mouth back to hers. The breath left her in a whoosh, and it was her turn to go rigid against him.

That didn't last long, however. This powerful man was hauling her up against his hard body, his lethal claws inches from her tender throat, yet they held her with care.

She melted.

She gripped his forearms weakly, unable to think, unable to do anything but give herself into the kiss. Her eyes fell shut, and she forgot everything except the feel of his lips against hers, firm and unyielding.

Amid the consuming tsunami of sensation, she felt the Water rising.

The power was responding to him the same way it did when she felt threatened, which didn't make sense. She wasn't in danger in any way, and yet it was surging within as if ready to defend her.

Was she in danger? Was Raith the threat?

But it certainly didn't feel that way. His mouth on hers, his hands holding her so firmly... All she wanted to do was surrender and be swallowed by his strength. That didn't feel like danger.

"Harrow!" a voice hissed from the darkness.

Reality returned. Raith released her quickly, drawing back, his black eyes wide. She stared at him, fighting to breathe, her heart beating erratically and her power swirling like a waking tornado gathering force. Never had she felt the like before. Raith had done this to her. But how?

"What are you?" she whispered.

The tortured look that flashed through his eyes could have torn her heart from her chest. He truly had no idea who he was.

Harrow was going to find out.

The conviction crystallized within her soul, and suddenly, as if pleased by her decision, the Water settled. The rising power retreated to the core of her, slumbering once more.

"Harrow!"

Malaikah was running toward them. "What in the Goddess's name are you thinking, snogging out here where anyone can see?" She kept her voice a whisper. "I tried to wait out of sight because I, for one, don't want to get caught, but I wasn't sure you'd ever stop! For the love of— Let's get going, yeah? Before Salizar peeps out the window of his caravan and sees you standing right there? And do you have to have the wings out, Raith? I mean, I thought we were trying not to attract attention to ourselves!"

Harrow looked at Raith, suddenly remembering why they'd ended up near Salizar's caravan in the first place. "We're coming." The words were a statement for Malaikah and a question for Raith. Their gazes met, and she silently beseeched him to give up his vengeance.

Raith looked anything but pleased, but finally, he nodded, and Harrow let out the breath she'd been holding. With one last flick and stretch of his leathery wings, he folded them into his back again, and they disappeared.

Crisis averted. At least for now.

She could only hope the next phase of their plan went smoother.

CHAPTER NINE

Raith allowed Harrow to lead him away from Salizar. The bastard was so close, Raith could smell him, practically taste his blood spilling. Vengeance had been within his grasp, and yet he'd allowed Harrow to distract him with her kiss.

But what a kiss it had been.

Her warm flesh beneath his palms, her silver eyes full of desire, her sweet lavender scent swamping his senses… It drew his mind from thoughts of blood and made him wonder why they seemed so important in the first place. Any other priority paled in comparison to tasting Harrow again.

Even now as she hurried ahead of him in the dark, he found it hard to worry about what they were doing or where they were going. He just wanted to pull her against him again and explore her further. Imagining it sent blood rushing down the center of his body, hardening him.

He knew what was happening. Though he had no memory of ever having done this with another, he knew what he wanted.

He wasn't sure he should want it, however. Not when his past was nothing but a black hole and he couldn't say for sure that he wasn't the monster Salizar thought he was.

But Harrow didn't think he was a monster, he reminded himself. Harrow had sworn he wasn't, and she believed it so strongly, she was giving up her home to help him — not that he wanted her to. Why shouldn't he believe what she did? She was the only person he'd met whom he felt something for other than cold indifference or a desire to kill.

He glanced at the back of her curly black head, and again he had to fight the urge to pull her against him. He didn't understand what he felt for her, but whatever it was felt…warm. Safe, yet exhilarating. It was intoxicating, and he wanted more of it.

"This has to be fast," Malaikah whispered. "We're way behind schedule, and I'm starting to get nervous."

"*Starting* to get nervous?" Harrow breathed a laugh. "I've been all the way there for a week."

Raith dragged his attention back to the present. They were approaching a large caravan with curved sides. An awning extended out from the back with colorful fabrics draped over the sides to serve as walls. A sign hung over them that read, FORTUNE TELLER.

This was Harrow's home, he realized. A home she was leaving behind for him.

Killing Salizar had been his final solution to stop Harrow from making this mistake. But now that that was off the table, he didn't know what to do. Aside from climbing right back into his miserable cage and refusing to leave — something he didn't think he had the strength to do — it seemed his only option was to give in to Harrow's plan.

Beneath the awning, Raith had to stoop slightly to keep

from hitting the canvas. There was a small table, a lounge, and a chair. Three steps led up to the caravan's door, and the two women quickly passed through. Raith followed them.

The caravan was cramped, especially with three people. He squeezed into the corner beside the door, fearful of knocking something over.

Harrow crouched beside the bed, pulling a heavy leather bag out from beneath. When she straightened, she saw Raith and smiled. "It's a little small for you in here, isn't it?"

Malaikah looked too and laughed. "Here, take this ridiculously heavy bag outside while we get the second one. What'd you put in here, Harrow? I thought we agreed that you didn't need four nightgowns."

While Harrow defended her packing job, Raith hefted the bag and squeezed through the tiny door, happy to be free of the confined space. Closed walls were not something he enjoyed so soon after getting out of that cage.

Outside, he set the bag down and was just about to return for the second when he sensed a presence nearby. Very near and approaching rapidly. He sniffed, recognizing the scent, and growled low.

Loren.

Either the guard had awoken and alerted the human, or Loren had checked Raith's cage himself and found it empty. What to do? Perhaps he should duck inside the caravan with Harrow and Malaikah. He could hide in the shadows, and Loren would never know he was there.

But Raith was free now, and he was angry, and hiding was for cowards.

And he wanted blood.

Loren had stood by while Salizar stabbed him with that damned staff countless times and done nothing. He deserved to pay for what he'd done.

Raith curled his hands into fists and faced the entrance to the tent.

Seconds later, the human burst through.

Jerking to a halt, Loren took one look at him and blanched, shrinking back. "Y-you…"

Raith bared his teeth.

To his credit, the human made a valiant attempt to recover his pride, straightening his spine and lifting his chin, though his hands shook. "How'd you get out?"

Raith said nothing.

"Harrow let you out, didn't she?"

Raith growled. He didn't like the human speaking Harrow's name.

"Harrow!" Loren suddenly shouted.

That angered Raith. Harrow didn't want anyone to discover them, and Loren wasn't trying to keep his voice down. If they were caught, who knew what Salizar would do to Harrow?

Raith had agreed not to kill Salizar tonight, but he hadn't agreed not to kill anyone else. Surely Harrow wouldn't miss this stain?

"Where is she?" the human snapped at Raith, bravado returning full force. "What did you do to her, you son of a bitch? I'll kill you if you touched her—"

Raith's hand shot out and snatched the man by his neck, lifting him and then slamming him down hard onto the table.

"I am the son of no one," Raith snarled in his face. "And you are a worm."

He lifted his free hand and unsheathed his claws, preparing to strike—

"Raith, no!"

Raith's head snapped up to see Harrow bursting out of the caravan and leaping down the stairs to grip his arm in her tiny hands and attempt to pull him off the human. Malaikah appeared, saw Loren, and then ducked back inside the caravan with a curse.

Harrow's strength was minute, and Raith could have resisted her without effort, but he allowed her to draw him away. He wasn't really sure why. The human sucked in desperate breaths, sliding off the table to the ground and scrambling away from Raith.

Harrow rushed to the man's side. "Are you okay?"

He wheezed, glaring at Raith with eyes full of hatred—a weakling's wounded pride.

"Bloody Goddess damn it all to the dark Shades," Malaikah was muttering repeatedly inside the caravan, too low for regular ears to hear.

"He...speaks." Loren's voice was hoarse from being strangled, and he pointed a shaking finger at Raith.

"Of course he speaks," Harrow snapped.

"You released him? What were you thinking? That thing needs to go back in his cage before he kills someone. He would have killed me!"

"He is not a 'thing.' And you probably would've deserved it for how you treated him!"

"Don't blame this on me. He isn't human and can't be trusted—"

"Nobody in this damned circus is human besides you! When are you going to understand that?"

Loren jerked out of her grip and lurched to his feet. "I'm sorry, Harrow, but I can't let you do this."

And he turned, ducked out of the tent, and sprinted away.

Malaikah cursed foully, poking her head out the door.

"We can't let him get away." Harrow's palms covered her cheeks. "He'll go straight to Salizar."

"How did you not sense him coming?" Malaikah hissed at Raith. "You were out here the whole time!"

Raith realized his mistake. He had jeopardized not only Harrow's safety but Malaikah's as well. This was his fault and therefore his responsibility.

Decision made, he shot out from beneath the awning in a blur, caught up with Loren in several seconds, and dragged him back by the neck. He tossed the human at Harrow's feet, awaiting instruction.

She stared at him with an open mouth.

Muttering more curses, Malaikah ducked inside the caravan once more.

The human started to rise again, so Raith flipped him over and pushed him into the dirt with a foot between his shoulder blades.

Harrow dragged her hands down her face.

"Should I kill him?" It seemed the easiest solution.

"No, Raith!" She looked horrified. "You shouldn't kill him or anyone!"

He frowned. He really didn't see the issue. Loren was a problem, so why not eliminate him?

"We need to—" She winced. "We need to tie him up so he can't run to Salizar. We'll leave him somewhere where someone will find him in the morning."

"Don't do this, Harrow," the human whined from the ground. Raith pressed his foot down harder, fighting the urge to crush his spine and rib cage.

"Should I put him in my cage?"

Harrow's eyes flicked to his, and he watched in fascination as her ire vanished to be replaced with that soft look she often gave him. It was a look he'd come to crave.

Her gaze hardened again as she looked down at Loren's struggling form. She glanced back up at Raith and nodded fiercely. "Do it."

"Harrow, you bitch, don't you dare!"

Raith growled, claws curling, but he waited for Harrow's permission to respond to the insult.

She met his gaze with a vicious smile that stirred his blood. "If he's going to make a fuss, I suppose we'd better gag him."

Raith hauled Loren up by the shirt, and the human started shouting. "Put me down, you Goddess-damned bastard! Harrow, don't even th—"

Raith struck him upside the head. At the last second, he pulled back the hit so as not to kill him. Instantly unconscious, the human dangled from Raith's grip on his shirt.

"Sweet Mother Goddess of the Veil," Malaikah said from the doorway.

Harrow didn't miss a beat. "Mal, grab a tea towel and one of my headscarves from inside."

Malaikah returned moments later to pass the items to Harrow. "Do you think he saw me?"

"He didn't see you." Gingerly, Harrow stuffed the tea towel into Loren's mouth and then tied the scarf around his head to hold it in place. It was a pretty piece of silk, and she tied a neat knot at the back with trembling fingers.

This was not a female accustomed to gagging a prisoner, Raith thought, and he decided that was a good thing.

"Can you carry him back to the cage and shut him in without being seen?" Harrow asked. He nodded, and her eyes narrowed. "Can I trust you not to kill him? And to come right back here afterward without going after Salizar?"

Raith made a face. She was far too clever for her own good. Reluctantly, he nodded.

She stared hard into his eyes. "Promise me you'll come right back here without killing anyone."

A vow.

Suddenly, he knew. A vow was enslavement.

He couldn't break his word once it was given, and though he wasn't sure what would happen if he tried, he knew it would be something extraordinarily unpleasant. He didn't know how he knew this, but he just did.

Did Harrow realize how binding such a thing was for him? Likely not. But he was coming to trust her, and he wanted to prove himself for the sole reason that she alone believed in him.

He met her gaze and said, "I vow to return immediately after depositing the human in the cage. I vow not to kill anyone before returning unless they try to kill me first." He added that last one as a measure of self-protection. Then, to be sure he didn't bind himself indefinitely, he added, "If I do not return for any reason or if our plans are interrupted, this vow will hold for the remainder of this night, and then I am free of it."

The binding settled around him like a vise, like a collar around his neck, squeezing the air from his lungs. A prison worse than the one he'd just escaped.

Whatever circumstances arose, he would follow those words unto pain of death—literally.

Because what he felt if he tried to break a vow was worse than dying.

He frowned. How did he know that? Hadn't he just concluded he didn't know what would happen?

The questions faded as he noticed Harrow staring at him.

"What was that? I felt... When you promised, it felt like—"

"Go," Malaikah hissed from the caravan door. "We're running out of time."

Raith tossed the human over one shoulder and hurried from the tent to fulfill his vow.

O nce they were alone, Malaikah stood in the doorway of the caravan and gave Harrow "the look."

Harrow could return it with only one thing: sheepishness.

"Innocent? Pure? Really, Harrow?"

"I know what I sensed."

"That man is so bloodthirsty, you'd think he lived off the stuff. I hope you know what you're doing."

She sighed. "I have no idea what I'm doing."

"Raith would have killed both Salizar and Loren if you hadn't stopped him."

"I know."

"Harrow, honey, that's messed up."

"I know, okay? I know."

Malaikah sighed too. "The good news is you were able to stop him. He listens to you. All I'm saying is, you're going to have your hands full."

Would Raith try to rip the head off anyone who looked twice at him? Was she going to have to be on full-time murder-prevention duty? Goddess, she hoped not.

He returned at that moment, silent and deadly as, well, a wraith.

"It's done?"

He nodded. After that strange promise he'd made, the air had been buzzing with some kind of power, and he'd looked strangely resentful of her, like she'd forced him into a trap. It wasn't her intention at all, but she hadn't been willing to budge without getting his promise. No one was dying tonight if she could help it.

Still, what had that meant? It was yet another mystery to add to the list.

She'd made her own mental vow to help him figure out who he was, but she hadn't a clue where to start.

The rest of the plan went off without a hitch. If Salizar had an enchantment to alert him if the cage was opened, it either didn't work in time for him to catch them or it was fooled by Malaikah's lockpick. Whatever the case, the fairgrounds remained quiet as they snuck into the city.

Harrow held tightly to Raith's hand. He'd donned the cloak she'd purchased for him, but even with the big hood obscuring his face, she could tell he was overwhelmed by the assaulting sights and smells, even in the relative stillness of the night.

Allegra was not a city that ever fully slept, and as they crept through the cobblestone streets between stone buildings, they passed staggering drunks, beggars, weary travelers, and the occasional hooded stranger of unknown intent.

They didn't bother anyone, and no one bothered them. It was the way of the city.

Malaikah led them through a labyrinth of narrow streets, taking so many different combinations of turns that Harrow quickly lost all sense of direction.

The central city had a few quirks one needed to be aware of when navigating. Rumored to be caused by an excess of magic leaking from the Ether Queen, entire streets were known to disappear from time to time, only to reappear later. Sometimes, a wrong turn would still deliver you to where you wanted to go, and a correct turn would get you lost completely. Though many maps of the city were sold, it seemed no two were exactly alike, nor was anyone capable of giving concise directions.

As such, Harrow was slightly amazed when finally, at the end of another nondescript dark alley, Malaikah motioned them to a stop and said, "We're here."

They were standing outside a tavern, marked only by a small swinging sign in the shape of a circle. Upon closer inspection, Harrow realized it was carved into an ouroboros—a snake winding around to consume its own tail. She had seen the ancient symbol before, but something about its use here gave her pause.

The orange glow of firelight shone through the tavern's narrow windows onto the cobblestones, and even at this hour, the hum of hearty conversation could be heard from within. The second-floor windows were equally aglow, but no noise spilled from the open shutters, and Harrow guessed that was where the inn's rooms were located.

She stopped in her tracks, suddenly nervous. "How did you find this place?"

"Told you," Mal replied. "I asked around for a seedy inn deep in the Underground, and ta-da. It doesn't get any more underground than this."

"Are you sure it's not run by that gang?" Everyone knew about the Hybrid gang that owned and operated most of the enterprises here.

"Oh, I know for a fact it's run by them. Hence the sign. They're called the Ouroboros."

"Then why are we going here?"

"Because, consequently, it's also the most discreet place to hide. If Sal comes looking for you, no one here will breathe a word about anything to anyone, especially to outsiders, and especially to Salizar. You know how Elementals here feel about Sal's circus."

Harrow looked apprehensively up at the sign. "But will they let us stay?"

Mal shrugged. "I already paid for the room. Come on."

They headed toward the tavern entrance, a wooden door with a rounded top, only for Malaikah to stop suddenly and spin around. She looked up at Raith and made a face. "On second thought, you should wait outside. You're going to stand out like a sore thumb in there."

Raith said nothing.

"How is he supposed to get to the room, then?" Harrow had to agree with Mal's assessment, however. Even from beneath his hood, his unusual eyes glowed, and his looming height meant he would tower over everyone.

Raith tipped his face up to the second floor. "I'll climb through the window."

"That's absurd," Harrow said at the same time that Mal said, "Cool."

"But it's too dangerous—"

"Hon, I could climb that stone with ease, and something tells me Raith can handle himself just fine." Mal shot him a pointed look. "Just stick to the shadows, and don't let anyone see you."

With a silent nod of agreement, Raith stepped into a corner and then seemed to dissolve into the darkness until he was nearly invisible.

"Damn," Mal whispered with a shudder. Harrow hid her

reaction, but she felt much the same way. She would be a fool to forget for even a second how dangerous Raith could be.

She and Malaikah entered the tavern together, and Harrow realized she had vastly underestimated the level of activity from outside. Every table in the alehouse was packed full of shouting, guffawing intoxicated people. The odd shadowy figure lurked in a dark corner. Servers with trays of ale wove their way through the crowds while a drunken fiddle trio dragged through a jig no one paid attention to.

Harrow had always avoided places like this. Too many eyes upon her made her nervous—her safety had always depended on her anonymity. She reaffirmed their decision for Raith to wait outside. If she was uncomfortable, Raith would have felt much worse.

Pushing her way through the crowd, Malaikah headed toward the bar, where a woman was filling tankards of ale. "I rented a room upstairs," Mal shouted over the melee. "Here to get the key."

The innkeeper nodded. "Follow me."

They were led up a narrow staircase to the second level. Upstairs was a long, narrow hallway lined with doors. The noise from below bled through gaps in the creaky floorboards.

The innkeeper unlocked a door at the end of the hall, ushered them inside, and passed the key to Malaikah. "Food orders are put in at the bar, but we can deliver to the room. I'll send the lads up with some firewood and water. Washroom is behind the curtain. Latrines are out back. You need anything else?"

"We're good, thanks."

"Enjoy your stay," she said unenthusiastically and then left. The bar sounds boomed through the floor. They dropped the bags on the bed and looked around.

Though quite small, the room was surprisingly comfortable. There was one double bed, a stone fireplace, two chairs and a table, and a small couch much like the one in Harrow's caravan. The curtain on the wall beside the fireplace covered the door to the bath.

The first thing Harrow did was hurry to the window, unlatch the panes, and push the glass open. "Raith!" she whispered to the silent street below. Leaning out, she scanned the lane for him but couldn't see a thing.

Just when she started to fear that he was gone, his flaming eyes looked up at her. Not from the street but already halfway up the wall, as his claws found purchase in the gaps between stones.

She jumped back to make room for him, and a moment later, he leaped lightly through the window and pushed his hood back. His features remained blank as he scanned his new surroundings.

"Right, then," Malaikah said into the growing silence. "We did it."

The victory felt hollow somehow.

"I guess I'd better head back before people notice I'm gone." Mal gave Harrow a sympathetic look. "You realize you're going to have to stay here, right? No wandering around."

Harrow winced. "I know."

"All right, then. I'll leave you to it. I still have to get your horse set up in the stables." She looked between Raith and Harrow, shifting on her feet. "Goodnight, then."

Harrow hugged her. *It's not goodbye yet*, she assured herself. She would see Mal again soon—possibly even tomorrow, if she could sneak away safely. "Night, Mal. Love you."

"Love you too." They broke apart. Malaikah gave Raith an awkward wave and then left, pulling the door shut behind her.

Alone, Raith and Harrow stared at each other from across the room.

A knock sounded at the door. "Water and firewood."

"Come in," Harrow called as Raith slipped into the washroom to hide. A big bucket of water for bathing and a jug for drinking were delivered by two lizard Hybrid males along with a bundle of wood. After directing them to leave it by the fireplace so they wouldn't see Raith, Harrow bid the men goodnight, and then silence reigned again.

"We made it," Harrow finally said, tugging her hood back.

Raith emerged and looked around. He didn't look any happier about it than she did, and it didn't take a genius to figure out why.

"From one cage to another," she muttered, seeing the room in a whole new light. For his size, it was cramped. The ceilings were so low, his head nearly brushed them.

He didn't reply.

"We should get some rest." She looked at the singular bed and felt her face heat.

Raith followed her gaze, and the silence suddenly felt charged.

"I will sleep on the floor."

The sound of his voice never failed to send a jolt through her, and she glanced at him. His was not an expressive face, and she had no idea what he was thinking.

"There's room enough for both of us," she replied.

He just looked at her.

She planted her hands on her hips. "The couch is too small, and you're not sleeping on the floor, so don't even suggest it."

His eyes narrowed, so she narrowed hers right back, refusing to budge.

It had nothing to do with the butterflies in her stomach when she thought about lying next to him. She refused to let a man who'd spent weeks in a cage sleep on the floor on his first night of freedom. Never mind that she had kissed him barely an hour ago, and the memory of his strong body against hers was so vivid it took her breath away.

The heat rose back to her cheeks. *That's not what this is about.*

Deciding two could play at the silent game, Harrow turned away and went about readying for bed. After washing up and changing into her nightgown in the washroom, she came back out and found Raith still standing there. She went to the bed and pulled back the covers on one side, fiddling with the pillows to give her something to do with her hands.

All the while he watched her.

Still pretending to be oblivious, she slipped under the covers, bidding Raith goodnight and leaning over to extinguish the lantern at her bedside. She closed her eyes and feigned sleep while she listened to him moving about the room.

Eventually, she felt the mattress dip as his considerable weight settled in beside her, and her heart began to race. But he didn't get under the covers.

Which was fine, she assured herself. It was only proper to keep some space between them, and just because she'd kissed him didn't mean she was ready for—

"Why don't you come under the blankets?" she whispered into the darkness, immediately wanting to smack herself on the forehead.

Why was she pushing this? Because she wanted him to be comfortable. She didn't want him to regret escaping with her. And maybe…because she wanted to be closer to him.

She felt his body shift, turning onto his side, so she turned too. Striking fiery eyes peered at her from the dark. Their faces were so close. She let her gaze trace the curve of his lips, the arch of his nose, wishing she could use her finger instead. He was so handsome, his features so proud and noble. Where had he come from? Surely someone out there knew him and felt his absence?

"Goodnight, Harrow."

His voice… A shiver went through her. *I guess he's not coming under the covers, then.* That was okay. Going from a cage to a soft mattress was a big jump, and perhaps the added comfort of blankets would be too much for one night. She could understand that.

Freedom was as much a state of mind as a state of being.

"Goodnight, Raith." She offered a sleepy smile and closed her eyes, taking a deep inhalation of his scent and allowing it to relax her.

She would ensure he remained free until he had enough time to believe in it.

Whatever it takes. Whatever lies ahead.

CHAPTER TEN

Raith lay atop the blankets, listening to Harrow's soft breathing, watching her chest rise and fall as her sweet lavender scent filled his head and clouded his thoughts. He waited in perfect stillness until her breaths deepened to the pace of sleep and then rolled over and sat up.

He would not rest while she lay defenseless. He should never have allowed her to free him from that cage, let alone followed her here.

But he had. So he would protect her.

He climbed to his feet and looked around. The room was dark, but his eyesight was good, and he could still see nearly perfectly.

His gaze was drawn back to Harrow as if she were all that existed in the world. She slept on her side still facing where he had lain, her arm stretched over the blankets as if reaching for him. Her nightgown was sleeveless, and he drank in the sight of her bared skin on the white sheets. Her hair was like a midnight storm, all curls and chaos, strewn across the pillow like billowing clouds.

He wanted to go back to the bed and slide beneath the blankets beside her, to hold her against him and breathe her scent until it was the only thing he knew.

Admitting that desire gave way to another. He wanted to kiss her again, to touch her bare skin, taste her—

Not right. He felt unclean, unworthy, and he thought he knew why.

He couldn't forget the look of horror on Harrow's face when she'd stopped him from killing Loren. Eliminating the human had felt as natural as instinct, and yet Harrow had been appalled. What did that say about him?

Whoever he was, whatever he was, he feared it was something ugly. He feared his presence in Harrow's life would taint it in some way. But what could he do? It was too late to return to his cage. Because of his weakness and strange, unquenchable desire to be close to her, he had endangered her.

He couldn't undo that mistake, nor could he procure for Harrow the life he wished her to have, but he could be her guardian. He could protect her at any cost to his body, mind, or pride until the moment he drew his last breath.

It was a small price to pay for what she'd given him, a nameless creature with no past or purpose.

The void of that forgotten past hung over him like a shadow, and his skin itched with the urge to crawl out of it. He had come from somewhere. He had done things. And the more he looked at himself, at his instincts and urges, the more he started to hope he never had to remember.

Maybe this could be a fresh start. Maybe he could use his new life to be a protector for Harrow and leave the past behind him, where it belonged.

Physical cleanliness was a good place to begin, he decided, so he moved silently away from the bed, lifted the heavy bucket of water, and ducked behind the curtain into the washing area.

There was a small wooden bathtub, a floor-length mirror, and two towels. He found a bar of soap on the shelf beside the towels of such a gritty, rough texture he thought it might be for laundry. He didn't care. He scrubbed every inch of himself until his skin burned, trying not to think about the inky shadows that skin could become and the fear and hatred he'd inspired in others because of it.

Using the cup provided, he scooped water out of the bucket to rinse off and then climbed out of the tub, wrapping one of the towels around his hips. Reaching for his clothes, he froze when he caught sight of himself in the mirror.

He tensed, turning slowly to face his reflection. Dim moonlight shone through the curtain—enough for him to see by. For the first time in his memory, he saw what he looked like.

And he finally understood why people were afraid of him.

His eyes were…black.

Everywhere, except for the thin rings of his irises, which were swirling orange like fire. No one else he'd seen had eyes like that.

He stared at the mirror, and those eyes stared right back at him. He could change his skin, hide his wings, and sheath his claws, but his eyes would always tell the truth.

He was a monster.

. . .

Harrow had fallen into a dream as soon as sleep took her. She was swimming through the turquoise waters in peace before the urge to make a decision took over, just like the last time. This time, however, she chose to dive easily, swimming down with defiant confidence like she knew the dangers of the deep and dared them to frighten her.

But once she was fully surrounded by blackness, that confidence seemed miles away. Still, she fought to retain her calm, focusing on understanding what she was seeing. Well, *nothing* was what she was seeing. Nothing but blackness. Still, she kept swimming downward, believing there had to be some meaning to this, some end approaching.

And then it came. A tiny orange light, flickering like a candle flame.

Excitement coursing through her, she swam harder, desperate to see what it was. As she approached, she realized it wasn't one light, but two.

Two candle flames burning in the dark.

But they weren't candles. They were rings. Two rings of fire. They seemed intelligent, aware, and as she drew still closer, she realized they weren't rings at all, but eyes—

The dream changed.

"Do I have to scry tonight?" Ten-year-old Harrow complained as her mother set a copper basin of water on the ground before her.

Taking a seat and crossing her legs beneath her skirts, Mellora stroked her daughter's hair, tucking an unruly curl behind the tip of her pointed ear.

"A Seer should practice scrying every day," Mellora

explained. "That way, her connection to the Water stays strong, and the element can work through her. It's important, Harrow, especially now."

The women of their clan were gathered around a crackling fire, their caravans a short distance away, their horses tethered to the trees nearby. The sky was black, the stars hidden by the light of the full moon. Across the flames, Luthera studied her casting stones upon the forest floor with deep concentration. The others shared cups of soothing lemon-ginger tea.

No one spoke, and the air was thick with sorrow and tension. Harrow knew her clan was worried. Her mother had tried to shield her from the worst, but she was old enough to put things together.

Something was hunting them.

Across the Territories, the Seer clans were dying...and it was only a matter of time before theirs was next.

"Now, where do we begin?" Mellora nudged Harrow, forcing a smile.

"Focusing on the water in the bowl," Harrow replied, no longer wishing to complain about the lesson.

"That's correct. Let your eyes be still, listen to your breath, and when you feel the Water rise inside you, surrender to it."

Forcing her tired eyes to focus, Harrow watched the ripples in the bowl reflect the colors of the fire until it appeared she was looking directly at the flames themselves. It seemed strange that water could appear so like its opposing force.

After a time, Mellora declared her effort satisfactory for the night. "You're falling asleep sitting up," she said with a chuckle. "Let's get you to bed." Climbing to her feet, she smoothed her dress and held out a palm.

Just as Harrow placed her hand in her mother's, Luthera let out a small cry from the other side of the fire. She looked up, her expression stark. A sense of dread overtook Harrow, and she stood quickly and pressed against her mother's side.

"It has found us," Luthera whispered. "It's too late."

Gasps sounded around the fire. Someone murmured fervent prayers to the Goddess.

Harrow tugged on her mother's hand. "Mama?"

Mellora looked down at her with wide, frightened eyes. "My love, I want you to run into the forest. Don't look back, no matter what happens."

"Mama, no—"

"It's already here." Luthera extended a shaking hand to point at the sky.

Above, the full belly of the moon cast her light over their forest clearing. The sky around it was pitch-black.

A shadow streaked across the moon's face.

Collectively, the Seers' magic rose in response to the threat until it crackled in the air like a lightning storm.

"Harrow, go!" Mellora pushed her daughter toward the trees.

"Death descends upon us," Luthera breathed. "The last Seer clan falls prey to the shadows."

"Now, Harrow!"

But in the end, she couldn't run.

Cowering beneath the wreckage of an upturned caravan, Harrow hid with her palms pressed against her ears, trying to drown out the screams.

Eventually, an eerie silence fell, and she slowly lowered her hands. Something was still out there; she could sense it. She held her breath, knowing better than to make a sound, though the urge to scream was overwhelming.

And then...*it* found her.

The monster floated down, directly in front of the broken beam of wood sheltering her from view. Her hands shook. Though she had never seen death before, she knew her mother and the rest of her clan were gone.

And she knew the monster would kill her, too.

Trembling, she forced herself to meet its gaze. It stared back at her.

It was completely black, like a void. Like a bottomless pit that sucked all color and shade into itself. Could such a being exist at all in daylight?

There was no defined edge to its form, but she could discern the outline of a powerful body, great wings arcing high above, long claws reaching forward to grab her. Its face was equally shadowy except for gleaming white fangs. And its eyes...

She stared into those fiery eyes and waited for death.

But it never came.

The creature stared back at her, its shadowy head tilting to one side and then the other. And then, without warning, it dissolved, its incorporeal form dissipating like smoke from an extinguished candle.

Scrambling to the edge of her shelter, she peeked out into the night. She caught a glimpse of a wisp of black shooting across the full moon before it whisked away and was gone.

Harrow awoke with a start and stared at the dark ceiling. The grief and pain threatened to choke her. Her heart was pounding, her eyes wide and unseeing.

The memories... She had relived them all. Her mother,

her clan sisters... At last, she had remembered the night of their deaths.

And what had killed them.

She'd always known what came after—she'd been found the next morning, cowering beside her mother's body, and then brought to the last remaining Temple of the Goddess in the region. There, a kindly priestess had instructed her to cover her ears and never tell a soul what she was.

Shortly after, the circus had passed through. She'd met Malaikah and formed an instant bond, and when Salizar had offered her a place among his people, she'd accepted easily. She'd always wondered if Salizar had come for her on purpose or if their meeting had been coincidence, but she'd never dared to ask him and wasn't sure he'd tell her anyway.

As for the night of the murders, well, everyone had heard the rumors of the Fire Queen's deadly assassins, but most doubted they were real. After fifty years, the mysterious extinction of the Seers and the monsters responsible had become the stuff of legends. And with her fragmented memories of that traumatic night, even Harrow had begun to doubt their existence.

But now, she knew.

She hadn't been able to remember what a wraith looked like. Now, she did.

She started to tremble. She heard Salizar's voice in her head saying, *I'm telling you he is exactly what he appears to be.*

But then she heard herself saying firmly, *I trust my instincts. He isn't what you think he is. I would bet my life on it.*

Raith was a physical being. She had touched his skin, kissed his soft lips. He may have had some of the characteristics of a wraith, but he was missing the most essential one—incorporeality.

She racked her brain, trying to remember what else she knew of them. Where had they come from? How were they created? Could it be possible that there were other wraiths—wraiths that hadn't assisted Furie in her brutal war? All she knew of wraiths was that they were mindless, soulless killers. She knew her Raith wasn't one of them.

Had what she'd seen him do tonight changed her opinion? Did her instincts tell her anything different now?

No, she realized. They didn't. He may have been a little more prone to violence than she'd anticipated—okay, a lot—but he wasn't evil, and he hadn't taken life before. The Water would have told her. The Water had never failed her, and she had to believe in it. To doubt her instincts about this was to doubt everything she'd ever believed, everything her beloved mother had taught her, and she wasn't ready to go there.

The sudden splashing of water jerked her back to the present, and it was only then she realized she was alone in the bed.

"Raith?" After her distressing dreams, she craved the comfort his presence brought her.

There was no response. She heard water splashing again and figured he must be in the washroom. It seemed a strange time to take a bath, but she could understand.

She waited for more sounds but heard nothing for a long time. So much time passed that she began to wonder whether he was even in there at all. But if he wasn't, then where was he? And what had been making the noise?

All sorts of scenarios flashed through her anxious mind until she couldn't stand the tension any longer. Throwing back the covers, she slipped out of bed, her toes landing on the cold floorboards. The noise of the bar was vastly subdued from earlier, but amazingly, it was still going. Did they ever shut for the night?

The low hum covered her footsteps as she crept across the room with a pounding heart. Outside the curtain, she hesitated, listening for any sounds within. She didn't want to disturb Raith if he was actually in there, but it sounded empty.

Finally, she summoned up the courage to lift the edge of the curtain and peek in.

He was there, standing in front of the mirror with a towel around his hips, leaning in and staring at himself. Specifically, at his face. The blue glow of moonlight cast shadows across the ridges of muscle in his broad back. He didn't seem to notice her at all.

She pulled the curtain back a little more.

At the sound of the fabric shifting, he spun around with a growl, flashing fangs and claws. She recoiled instinctively.

Seeing her, he quickly retracted his claws and turned away. But he didn't face the mirror again, either, as if he couldn't bear to see what was reflected in it.

"Raith?"

His gaze flicked to her, and she couldn't help it—her heart skipped a beat in fear.

His eyes... They were the very same eyes from her dream. First, the eyes that had come to her in the silent depths, and second, in the gruesome memory that followed.

But she forgot all about that when she saw the tortured look in them.

"Are you okay?" She stepped closer. Any fear she had of what he might be was quickly overridden by the strange protectiveness he drew out of her.

He met her gaze again briefly before glancing away. "My eyes."

"What about them?" He'd probably never looked into a mirror until now, she realized. She chanced another step. A few more and she'd be close enough to touch him.

"How do you know I'm not what Salizar thinks I am?"

"I just do. I know it to the bottom of my soul."

"But I look..." His mouth twisted.

"You look like a wraith." She couldn't deny it any longer.

"What does it mean?"

"I don't know, but we're going to find out."

"What if Salizar is right?"

She took another step. "The fact that you're asking that question proves he isn't. Don't you understand? Furie's wraiths were mindless, soulless creatures. You're not like that. You've been kind and sweet to me. You wanted to protect me from Salizar." By killing him. But it was the thought that counted, right? "I trust you to keep me safe."

And she did. She fully believed he would never hurt her. That was how she knew he wasn't a wraith.

Without really being aware of it, she took that final step. She could see him better from this close. Water droplets clung to his bare chest, dripping from his hair and trailing over smooth skin. His cheekbones were so defined, tiny hollows formed beneath them. His mouth... Her mind blanked, unable to do anything except think of how kissing it had felt.

He lifted a hand and brushed a lock of her hair. Tingles erupted down her spine. She swayed into him.

"Raith, I—"

His fingers traveled to her jaw, featherlight touch tracing bone. Her face tipped up, exposing her throat, welcoming more of his caress. She didn't know what he was or why he so closely resembled an evil being, but none of that mattered now. The connection between them was undeniable, and right now, it demanded acknowledgment.

She was powerless against it. She had no desire to fight it anyway.

He reached the edge of her jawbone and then trailed his fingers up the outside of her ear, pausing at the pointed tip. She couldn't suppress the shiver that ran through her.

His hand slid into her hair, long fingers sifting through the tangled strands until he was cupping the back of her neck in his big palm. The breath gusted out of her. He was so close. So close she couldn't think.

"Raith…"

The word was whispered against his lips. She couldn't remember straining up to reach them, nor could she remember curling her fingers around his forearms. The hard muscle had no give beneath her grip.

He leaned a little farther down, and their mouths brushed.

Again, her breath caught in her throat. He pulled back infinitesimally, but she chased him. They brushed again. They were frozen. Time was frozen.

And then he leaned the rest of the way down and fused them together.

His mouth was hard and soft at the same time. His body poured out heat like a furnace. His heady male scent swamped her senses. She wanted more.

Their lips parted, tiny gaps for air to escape forming between them before they pressed back together. One hand still tangled in her hair, his other landed on the curve of her waist, fingers clenching the silk of her nightgown.

Her palms slid up to the moist skin of his shoulders,

droplets from his wet hair slicking the backs of her hands. He kissed her firmly but didn't try to take it further, and she suddenly wondered if he had ever done this before. If not, it was up to her to show him.

Gathering her courage, she flicked her tongue against the seam of his lips, encouraging them to open. He stiffened for a second before parting them. She stroked her tongue inside his mouth, brushing it against his, careful to avoid his fangs.

His fingers tightened in her hair, tugging at the roots. Encouraged, she did it again, and this time, he mimicked her. They met in the middle, tangling together, and she was lost.

Apparently, so was he. Unraveling from her hair, both his palms spanned her waist. They slid down to her hips, pulling her firmly against him. His arousal, long and thick, pressed against her soft belly.

She moaned, rubbing against him, longing to feel more of that tantalizing friction. His fingers tightened almost painfully as they slid down to grip her ass.

He dragged his mouth away. "Harrow..."

She was too far gone to care about anything except having more. "Raith."

"We shouldn't..." His lips brushed hers again, not quite a kiss, and she tried to chase his mouth as he pulled back, but he held her firmly in place.

"Why not?" Still, she strained to reach him. Another time, she might be embarrassed at her boldness, but not now. Not with him.

"I want..." Another brush of his lips. Was he trying to drive her mad? "Things."

"What things?"

"Things."

"I want things too." She wanted a lot of "things." He had

no idea how badly.

"I shouldn't."

"Why not?"

"You're — I'm —"

His hesitation only stoked her passion higher. "There's nothing wrong. I want the same things as you." Maybe. If he was as inexperienced as she guessed he might be, he probably wasn't thinking half the salacious thoughts she was.

Then again, maybe he was.

That firm grip on her ass scooped her up as if she weighed nothing. Her legs wrapped around his hips, and their mouths melded together as he crossed the room and ducked under the curtain.

He dropped her on her back on the bed.

She stared at him, looming over her, braced by powerful arms, and she couldn't believe she was about to do this. She shouldn't have been surprised—if she was honest with herself, she'd wanted it from the first moment she laid eyes on him. And yet there was a part of her that still couldn't believe she was here, with this man. This quiet, intense, powerful, beautiful man. Her gaze followed the ribbed strength of his abdomen down, down...

"Take the towel off." Though the words were bold, her voice came out a whisper.

He stood, eyes never leaving hers. He tugged the towel off.

CHAPTER ELEVEN

The concept of modesty did not exist for Raith. And yet, as he stood there while Harrow's gaze traveled over every inch of his naked skin, he fought a bizarre impulse to shy away from her.

Did she like what she saw? All he knew about his body was that it was strong and good for violence, and that he looked frightening to others. He had yet to consider it from the standpoint of how it might give pleasure.

He wanted to give Harrow pleasure. He needed to. But how? He had no memory of anything beyond that first day in the desert, and not one of the moments he'd lived since then included anything remotely close to this situation.

Instinctively, he knew what to do—or at least what he wanted to do—but was that what she wanted? The things he was imagining... Surely there was no way Harrow would want that. Would she? Or was he wrong in wanting them?

"Come here." Her whispered words were seductive, yet a certain shyness lurked in her gaze.

He didn't even consider hesitating, was crawling onto the bed over her before she'd even finished speaking. As soon as he was within reach, her hands lifted to touch him. They hesitated, trembling slightly, and he went still so as not to startle her. Soft palms landed on his chest and slid up to his shoulders. Her fingers clenched slightly around the muscles at the top before traveling over to his back.

Her eyes fell shut as if it brought her great pleasure just to have her hands on his skin. He stared at her in awe. He hadn't even done anything, and she enjoyed it this much? Maybe he could do this after all.

"I want..." He trailed off as her hands traveled down his abdomen, the muscles jumping beneath her touch.

Her knuckles brushed the tip of his hardened sex.

He wasn't sure if it was intentional or not, but he couldn't hide his reaction regardless. His hips jerked of their own accord, breath expelling from his lungs as if he'd been struck.

"What?" She watched him with that sultry gaze. A combination of vulnerability and seduction.

"Touch you," was all he could manage.

She started to sit up, so he shifted back to let her, watching to see what she would do. Those slightly trembling fingers reached down and pulled her nightgown over her head, tossing it away.

His mouth went dry.

She glanced away, and her hands lifted to cover her breasts before she forced them back to her sides and met his gaze again. He couldn't stop staring. He never wanted to stop staring.

Supple skin was lit lovingly by moonlight. Her breasts were heavy, her belly a soft curve. Her naked thighs parted to welcome him between them, and he followed her down as she lay back, tracing the swell of one full breast, watching in fascination as she arched into his hand with a sweet sigh.

She liked his touch. She liked his eyes upon her. It was too perfect to possibly be real, yet he refused to waste a second doubting his good fortune.

The passion in her silver eyes gave him confidence, and he flattened his palm on her sternum, sliding it over to cup her other breast. The way the flesh overfilled his palm appealed to some ancient, primal part of him he hadn't known existed until now. Such a simple thing—womanly flesh overflowing his grip—made him want to growl with satisfaction. It lit a fire in him he had no idea how to control.

He wanted to be closer, as close as it was possible to be. And then closer than even that. He wanted to sink so deep into her warmth he lost himself completely.

Lifting her arms, Harrow wrapped them as far around his shoulders as she could reach and pulled him down to her lips again. His hands continued to travel hungrily over her body as they kissed. She kneaded the muscles of his back, digging her nails into his skin.

He wanted more. Something. Everything. Just *more*.

He nipped gently at the skin of her neck as she tilted her head back to expose her soft throat to him. So delicate. So vulnerable. She would snap like a twig under his fingers if he lost control for a second. He would die before that happened.

He dragged his mouth down her chest and paused at her breast, suddenly doubting his desires. Lifting his head, he met her gaze. "Kiss?"

She dropped her head back. "Yes. Kiss."

He sucked her nipple into his mouth, pleased at her responsive moan. He did it to the other one, too, and received the same reaction. Emboldened, he gripped her supple backside and squeezed.

"I want…" Did he even know what he wanted?

He wanted her. Her head thrown back, crying with pleasure as he tasted the very core of her.

"Yes," she breathed, though she couldn't possibly know what he was thinking.

He worked his way farther down her body until his mouth hovered above her abdomen. He ground his hips into the mattress, dragging his erection painfully over the scratchy blankets in an attempt to calm his fervent desires. Unable to deny the urge, he snaked his tongue out to trace the arch of her hipbone down until he reached the soft hair between her thighs.

He forced himself to stop, lift his head. Did she want what he did?

Their gazes met, and she nodded mutely.

Okay, then. Sliding the rest of the way down until his mouth was inches from her glistening core, he froze a moment, staring in awe at the wonder before him. His short memories had been nothing but misery until he'd met her, and now this?

She was laid out naked before him like a succulent feast, her legs spread wide, her hands fondling her own breasts as she watched him with naked desire. It was too good to be true, too impossible to be real.

She squirmed. "Raith…"

He used his fingers to part her folds, baring her even further to his hungry gaze. Hungry? No. *Ravenous* was perhaps a better description of how he felt looking upon her. She moaned at the exposure, writhing in his grip.

Lowering his head, he licked once up her center, assessing her reaction. It was a languid moan. A good sign. He did it again. "More, Raith— *Oh*." He kissed her, sucking her tender flesh between his lips. Repeating the motion, he was rewarded with more gasps and moans.

Her back arched off the mattress as he slid a finger inside her silken, wet heat. Beyond all compare. Sucking her flesh again, he added another finger, wanting her to lose control. He was amply rewarded by her cries, so he sucked again. And again, until she was moaning ecstatically and saying his name.

She begged him repeatedly not to stop, which was odd because he'd given no indication he had any such plans. It was the opposite. He wasn't sure he could stop at this point. He assured her of this by working his fingers in and out of her like he longed to do with his shaft, all the while sucking on that luscious nub of flesh. Her head thrashed about, her body trembling and writhing. She was so responsive, it was easy to discover how to pleasure her.

She cried out his name as she went over, the muscles of her inner walls spasming around his fingers. Finally, gasping for breath, she pushed his head away, unable to take more.

He obliged, content to let her lead this. For now.

She tugged on his shoulders, so he allowed her to guide him back up. Their lips met, and he shared her sweet, salty flavor with her. The idea that she was tasting the release she had spilled over his tongue made him feel such a sense of primal satisfaction that he pulled back from the kiss, withdrew his fingers from inside her, and then pressed them to her lips.

He watched in heady fascination as she sucked them inside. It was his turn to moan. The sensation on his hand went straight to his cock, until he was unconsciously rolling his hips and imagining her lips sliding over— No. He wouldn't think of that.

"Your turn," she murmured, slipping free of his fingers. Placing her palms on his chest, she pushed to roll them.

He ended up on his back, Harrow straddling his hips, her naked body gleaming in the moonlight. Shadows fell beneath her full breasts and below the softness of her belly. Unbidden, his hands lifted to grip her hips tightly. He was already imagining her sliding down his length from this position, her head thrown back while he sat up to suck her breasts—

She interrupted his fantasy by crawling down his body, trailing her mouth over him, much the same way he had done to her. Surely she didn't intend to...?

All thought vanished as her small hand curled around his erection. It was his turn to throw his head back and moan, hips thrusting involuntarily into her grip.

When he opened his eyes again, she was poised right over him, her eyes locked on his sex, mouth inches away.

She was going to use her mouth on him. No, she wouldn't possibly. But it really looked that way. She licked her lips, wetting them with a sheen of saliva. *Please*, he almost begged, but wouldn't dare say a word to coax her into this if it wasn't what she wanted. Surely she would never—

Her lips wrapped over the head and slid down his length.

A sound such as he'd never made before was torn from his throat, and his eyes rolled back, only to snap sharply into focus again. He couldn't bear to miss a second of this. She held him firmly at the base, palms rising to meet her lips as they worked their way down.

Another moan was torn from him. This was indescribable. She was perfection, and he would destroy anyone who touched her. He would rend the flesh of any who dared to threaten her to tiny, bloody shreds. He would eviscerate entire armies—

Her mouth popped off the top with a tiny suction sound, and his mind blanked.

Those sultry lips slid back down again. He thought he might die from pleasure. His hips flexed, hands clenching in the blankets. She was a temptress. Nay, a goddess. It took everything he had not to thrust hard into her mouth.

Her fingers tightened around the base, the bottom hand reaching down to cup his sack, massaging gently as she slid her mouth down and swallowed him deep. The tip of his cock hit the back of her throat, and she moaned, the vibration sending a wave of sensation down his shaft.

He couldn't help it. If she was trying to drive him mad, she had succeeded. All rational thought flew out the window, and he reached up, buried his fingers in her thick hair, and then thrust his hips into her mouth. Her cheeks hollowed as she sucked. He moaned. So did she.

He thrust again. And again.

Gripping her hair, he tightened his fingers until he knew it had to pull, but he couldn't make himself loosen his grip. He worked himself in and out of her mouth again and again until he soared over the edge into oblivion.

The climax burst out of him, catching him by surprise. Perhaps if he'd remembered ever climaxing before, he might have felt its approach, but he didn't. It was a new experience. A strangled shout tore from him. A surprised, strangled shout, because he'd never expected it to feel this incredible. Eyes rolling back, colorful lights bursting in the blackness, the orgasm pumped through him and released right into Harrow's perfect mouth.

It seemed to go on forever. He wasn't certain he didn't

pass out for a moment.

When he came back to reality, Harrow was climbing up his body to collapse on the bed beside him. He turned to his side and drew her into his arms, squeezing her against him. Maybe he clutched her too tightly, but he was shaking all over, and she seemed to be the only thing that could ground him. Neither of them spoke.

Then he remembered the way he had yanked on her hair and thrust so fervently into her mouth, and shame suffused him. He sat up on an elbow to study her face. "Did I hurt you?"

She smiled. Her eyelids were droopy, and her lips curved. She shook her head lazily.

He frowned, unconvinced.

She stroked a soothing palm down his chest. "You didn't. I swear. I liked it."

She had liked it. He allowed her to push him back down to the bed. But he didn't relax completely. "I haven't…before now… I don't remember—"

"I know. I figured that out."

"I wanted to please you."

"You did." He could hear the smile in her voice. "Not a worry about that."

He relaxed further.

"I wanted to please *you*." She pressed her cheek against his chest. "You haven't told me much, but I gather you haven't had much pleasure in a while."

"I have no memory beyond a month and a half ago."

It was Harrow's turn to sit up and stare down at him. "You don't remember anything at all?"

He shook his head.

"I figured you had some kind of memory loss, but I never

realized…" Her eyes were wide. "What happened? What was the first thing you remember?"

"I awoke in the desert at midday. I didn't know where I was."

"Must have been somewhere in the South. Then what happened?"

"I was near death when the flesh traders found me. I tried to fight back, but I was too weak. They chained me and put me in the cage and took me to Allegra, where I was sold to Salizar."

"Raith, that's awful. I'm so sorry you went through that." Her eyes were full of sympathy and softness. Somehow, her reaction comforted him. She was giving him solace he hadn't realized he needed.

"That's it?" she asked. "That's all you remember?" He nodded. "Has anything seemed familiar to you?"

He thought about this for a moment. "When I first awoke in the desert, I felt that my body was separate from me. And earlier, when you made me promise…"

Harrow's gaze softened again. "That promise meant something bigger to you than I realized, didn't it?"

He nodded, shifting his gaze to the ceiling. "I don't know how I know this, but once given, my word is binding. The promise felt like chains."

"Goddess, Raith, I never wanted you to—"

"I know. That's why I gave you the vow anyway. I trust you."

She smiled. "Thank you for your trust. I won't betray it."

"I know."

A crease appeared between her brows. "Your unbreakable word… Is that why you don't like to speak much? To protect yourself from saying something that might bind you?"

He nodded. "But I didn't know that until tonight."

"It must have been instinctive, then. I wonder what you were like before you lost your memories. Did you like to speak more?"

"I don't think I spoke at all unless I was forced."

"What do you mean? How do you know that?"

He hesitated. "I don't know."

"Did you just remember something?"

He shook his head. A head that suddenly ached as he tried to recall. "I don't—" He lifted a hand to pinch the bridge of his nose. "It feels painful to try to remember."

"Don't, then." Harrow pulled his hand from his face and threaded their fingers together. "It doesn't matter." She brought their joined hands up to her lips and kissed his fingers one by one.

"What if it does?"

Physically, he was much bigger and more powerful than her, and yet when she gave him that soft look or stroked her small hands down his body, it was as though she seized control over his entire being. His very soul lay curled and resting in the palm of her hand.

"We'll figure it out," she promised, meeting his gaze. "Together."

He nodded. He could only hope that whatever they learned didn't break her heart or shatter her trust in him.

Harrow lay back down and snuggled against him, breathing a contented sigh as he wrapped his arms tightly around her. As he lay there, full of more peace and contentment than he'd ever felt, a memory surfaced of the night Salizar had caught Harrow in his tent. A haunting wisp, it came as if to mar the perfect intimacy of the moment.

On the off chance that he is actually a wraith, Salizar had said, *no matter how small or unlikely, would you still wish to care for such a creature?*

Never, Harrow had whispered fiercely, eyes burning with sudden hatred. *I would die first.*

A gainst all odds, Malaikah made it back to the fairgrounds without incident. She even managed to pick up Harrow's horse and drop it off at the stables first. Their plan seemed flimsy, but she had to believe it would work. If Salizar caught Raith again…

He would what? Force him to perform at the circus? Kill him? She supposed it wasn't worth the risk of finding out, though she wished Harrow hadn't thrown away her entire life for a man she'd just met with a predilection for violence.

Never taken a life, my ass. Raith was a walking nightmare. Terror on two legs.

But he did look at Harrow like she'd hung the moon, and Malaikah believed he'd cut down an entire army and then himself before he let anything hurt her. It was the only reason Mal had helped with this plan and not gone straight to Salizar once things had started to go south earlier. As abhorrent as the idea of betraying her best friend was, she would have done it if she believed for a second that Harrow was in danger.

Pushing open the window in her caravan, Malaikah scented the air, and yep, there it was. The unmistakable scent of Enchanter sweeping the grounds. Salizar had freed Loren from the cage and would likely come straight here as soon as he confirmed Harrow's caravan was empty. He would suspect Mal's involvement, and he'd be right.

She stripped off her clothes and stuffed them into the wardrobe, throwing her nearly naked body into bed. She wasn't shy, and if strutting around in her underwear threw Salizar off his game, then all the better for her. Pulling the blankets up, she curled her tail around herself and shut her eyes, trying to slow her breathing.

About thirty seconds later, there was a raucous banging on her caravan door. She tensed, heart immediately racing again, but didn't get up immediately. She was a deep sleeper, and if she'd actually been asleep, it would take a lot more than that to wake her.

Further banging sounded. She winced. Okay, that would have woken her. It sounded as though he was using the end of his staff to break the damn door down.

Tapping into her best performer skills, Malaikah dragged herself out of bed and made a great show of yawning and stretching as she trudged to the door. Yes, Salizar couldn't see her yet, but the more she got into character now, the more believable she'd be. She opened the door, peering at the enraged man standing outside through squinted eyes.

"Where is she, Malaikah."

Yep, he was pissed. The threat of being struck by lightning with his witch stick was so thinly veiled, little sparks were shooting out the tip. He was so tall, their eyes were level though he stood at the bottom of the steps. His piercing blue gaze could instill fear into the hearts of the bravest men.

Good thing she wasn't a man.

"Who?" Malaikah yawned and stretched languidly, leaning suggestively against the doorframe, tail swinging lazily behind her. She wore only knickers and a bralette from one of her racier costumes.

Salizar's jaw clenched. *Affected by the exposed skin, Sal?* Maybe there was a hot-blooded male in him after all. "Harrow. Where is she?"

"Isn't she in her caravan?"

"Don't be coy. I know you're in on whatever she was planning."

"Sal, it's late, and I'm not even fully awake. You're going to have to give me more than that."

But Salizar wasn't buying it. Climbing up the steps to the threshold, he loomed over her, forcing her to step back as he let himself into the caravan.

Her eyes widened a little. Okay, he was seriously pissed.

"Tell me where she is, Malaikah."

"I don't know, Salizar."

He forced her back another step, reaching behind him to slam the door shut.

Damn. Maybe the lack of clothing wasn't such a great idea after all.

No, she refused to be intimidated by him. If he came at her, she'd use her claws if she had to. Take a page from Raith's bloodthirsty book.

"Where. Is. She."

"I. Don't. Know."

He banged the staff on the floor, and another shower of sparks shot out the end. "Don't fuck with me."

"Look, even if I knew where Harrow was, I wouldn't tell you. Especially with you barging in here waving that damned thing around."

"You do realize what she's done? Do you know what the creature she absconded with is?"

Mal shrugged, feigning calm. In reality, her heart was trying to crawl its way up her throat. "Harrow says she trusts him, so I trust him. If they took off, it was probably for a good reason."

"Harrow is deluded by her infatuation. I'm trying to protect her, not punish her."

"Look, I already told you I don't know—"

"Save it," Salizar snapped. "Instead, let me tell you why I'm confident I am—*was*—in possession of a real wraith."

"Wraiths are incorporeal. You can't hold them in a cage. If they even exist, that's the number one thing everyone knows about them."

"Yes. Unless someone found a way to trap one in its physical form."

"Which would take buckets of magic."

"The kind of magic possessed by, say"—he gave a telling lift of his brow—"an Elemental Queen."

Her jaw dropped.

"Let me tell you a story, Malaikah. Shall we sit?" Salizar spun, long coat whooshing around him, and took a seat at the table. He removed his hat and ruffled his dark hair. The tips of his pointed ears were distinguishable between the thick strands, and his vivid blue gaze tracked her intently. He sprawled sideways on the bench seat, long legs not even close to fitting under the table.

This tall, imposing man in her tiny caravan looked decidedly incongruous. Yet he sat there like he owned the place. Which he kind of did.

She gritted her teeth and bit back a snarl. Though she'd never tell him in a million years, Sal had successfully intimidated her, the bastard. Grabbing a robe from the closet, Malaikah wrapped it around herself and sat opposite him.

"As you know, the eradication of the Seers began a century or so ago," he began without preamble. "Roughly fifty years ago, the last remaining clan was making their way back to Darya's territory when tragedy struck. A wraith descended upon their camp at night and killed all, save one. A small girl, aged ten." There was a knowing in those piercing blue eyes, and it clicked.

"You knew," Malaikah breathed. "You've known who she was all along."

"Yes."

And he'd never said a word to either of them, had been content to protect Harrow's secret all these years without a whisper of acknowledgment. Malaikah could only stare at him.

"To this day," Salizar continued, "no one is quite sure why an unfeeling, incorporeal assassin disobeyed its mistress and spared the life of an innocent child. The story spread like wildfire, each retelling more grandiose than the last, until it was regarded as nothing but a silly rumor and faded into oblivion. But as we know, Harrow, the last surviving Seer, is no rumor."

"And neither are the wraiths. I get it. But how does this prove anything?"

One dark brow lifted. "I'm not finished yet. After the obliteration of her bloodline, Queen Darya set about exacting her own revenge. She was determined to find a way to destroy Furie's Elementals the way Furie destroyed hers."

Mal shook her head. "And the cycle continues…" The bloody Queens and their petty squabbling were the cause of so much death and suffering, and it wasn't fucking fair.

"Indeed."

"I thought wraiths were unkillable."

"Nothing is unkillable. The wraith that spared Harrow's life was savagely punished by Furie for its disobedience, which greatly weakened it, providing Darya the perfect opportunity to capture it. She spent the next fifty years searching for a way to destroy the wraith before she was finally successful."

"Which brings us to today, then."

"Yes. Darya discovered how to permanently bind the wraith to his corporeal form, making him vulnerable and, therefore, killable. Unfortunately, during the transformation, he was cast from her prison in a magical explosion and disappeared. She believed the wraith had escaped, until recently, when I received word of a creature for sale in Allegra that fit the description."

"You're saying...Raith."

Salizar nodded.

"Is actually a wraith."

"That's exactly what I'm saying."

Malaikah's blood went cold. "But how do you know this whole story with Darya is true? You can't have spoken to her directly. No one's heard from the Queens in years."

"I think it's time you understand who I am, Malaikah. I allow others to believe I'm nothing but a wandering Enchanter seeking his place in a new world where our kind has become outcasts. While that is partly true, I am also an emissary of Queen Audra, dispatched with orders to protect stray Elementals from subjugation and consequent eventual extinction. Running this circus is my royally decreed duty, not just a hobby I entertain."

Malaikah gaped at him, seeing the tall, imposing Enchanter in a new light. She'd always known he was powerful. Few Enchanters could create a weapon as potent as his staff. But she'd never suspected he was on a secret mission from the Air Queen.

"But that would mean…" She couldn't even finish the sentence. What did it mean?

"It means the Queens are still involved in our world and are trying to change things. As soon as Darya lost the wraith, she sent word out, asking for help locating her missing prisoner. Audra came to me. I was to find the wraith, contain it, and travel west to deliver it to Darya, where it would be destroyed."

Mal could only stare. "Sweet Mother Goddess."

Salizar stared right back at her, those brilliant blue eyes drilling his point into her head.

"But why…" She couldn't accept this. There had to be another explanation. "Harrow said she sensed Raith was innocent. That he hadn't killed before. If he's the one who killed her whole family, then how…?" The idea of Harrow running around with her mother's murderer was enough to make her sick.

"I don't know why Harrow believes what she does. Perhaps she is fixated on him because she instinctively senses the connection he has to her lost family. Perhaps her mind, broken by tragedy, has sought closure so desperately that it turned that connection into desire."

Malaikah stared at Salizar, hating how this made sense. Was it possible Harrow was wrong about Raith? But no, this was way too big. Her power, the Water, was supposed to be wise and all-knowing. It would have told her if Raith was dangerous, if Raith had *killed her family*, for the Goddess's sake. It would have.

Wouldn't it?

Salizar stood suddenly, causing Malaikah to jump. "I'll leave you to your thoughts tonight. I will continue my search for Harrow and the wraith and won't push you further for your cooperation. However, I warn you that I'll do everything in my power to uncover them. I've already sent word to Audra about their escape and have no doubt she will pass on the news to Darya, who will likely—"

"Wait. Darya knows about Harrow too?"

"Who do you think sent me to find the ten-year-old Seer orphan in the first place?"

Mal stared at him with her mouth hanging open.

"As I was saying, think about what I've told you. Is Harrow's life worth endangering for this? How devastated do you think she'd be to learn the truth? If you change your mind, come to me at any time."

He put his hat back atop his head and crossed the caravan, throwing open the tiny door and stooping to pass through. At the last second, he turned back. "I run this circus to protect Elementals and give them a chance at a better life. I know who you are and who your family was, Malaikah. I know who you're running from. Why do you think they've never caught up with you after all these years, though your face is plastered across every poster for our show?"

"I—I never thought…" She honestly hadn't considered it. She'd always thought Kambu was too deep in the South to be in contact with the other cities they traveled to.

"The truth is that those who wish you harm are very aware of where you are, but they don't dare target you while you're under my protection. I have killed more than a few would-be assassins found lurking around my circus, and I will continue to eliminate any threat to you or anyone here. I protect my own, Malaikah. Always remember that."

And he swept out the door, leaving Malaikah sitting at the table with her eyes wide with shock and her heart full of doubt.

CHAPTER TWELVE

The next morning, Harrow woke to the awareness of another's touch. She blinked slowly, humming with contentment. Raith was lying beside her, propped up on one elbow, trailing his fingers along her naked skin. As he circled her nipples, his strange black eyes tracked his ministrations with intense focus.

She purred with delight. "Good morning."

His response was to lean down and kiss her.

A warm sunbeam stretched across the bed, making Raith's skin glow. The sizable erection pressed against her hip made her burn with desire.

Memories of what they had done last night before falling asleep together washed over her. The way he'd watched her while she sucked him, fingers digging into her hair, moans vibrating his deep chest... She wriggled in delight, heat flooding her core. She wanted more of him.

Turning in the circle of his arms, she lifted her face for another kiss. As their lips danced, her palms landed on his chest and slid down over soft skin and hard muscle. He gripped the ample flesh of her backside and hauled her up against him with a growl.

She'd loved it when he lost control last night, when his desire had overridden his carefulness and he'd acted on pure instinct. And now he was kissing her passionately and pressing her hips against his with a firm grip, and she wanted him to lose control again.

Lifting her leg, she hooked it over his hip and worked herself against him. Another growl rumbled in his chest. His fingers slid down between her thighs to drag through her wetness, wringing a soft moan from her lips. There was no space between their bodies for her to touch him in turn, so she just gripped his arms, sighing with pleasure as she felt the strength in them.

She wanted more. She wanted…everything.

She let him touch her until she was soaking wet, their bodies still sliding together, battling for closeness. Then she reached down, stretching an arm around her hip to grab his erection. He moaned, hips jerking. She aligned the head of his cock at her entrance. One thrust and he would enter her. His hand landed on her hip, squeezing tightly.

Transferring her grip to the firm muscles of his ass, she tilted her hips to take him inside.

He was big—oh boy, was he ever. But she was so ready for him, so desperate, that she pushed greedily through the sensation of tightness, sliding over him, tighter, tighter, until he was nearly all the way in and—

He went rigid and jerked away. His eyes were wide and… spooked?

Harrow sat up, horror suffusing her. What had she done? She hadn't even considered asking him if he wanted this.

"I'm sorry." Just because he was a male did not automatically mean he was ready for sex. He'd been tortured, imprisoned, had no memories beyond a month and a half ago, and she hadn't thought twice about taking what she wanted from him. Of course he wasn't ready. Intimacy had to be terrifying for him after what he'd been through.

"I shouldn't have— I didn't even think—"

He just stared at her.

She couldn't take it anymore. "I'll just go to the other room to wash." Jumping out of bed, she all but ran straight for the washroom, her skin hot with shame.

She made it two steps away from the curtain when Raith appeared in front of her. How did he move so fast? He didn't say anything, just stood there blocking her path. He was still naked and very erect. It took every ounce of will she possessed not to stare, desire for him still pounding through her bloodstream.

Hence her plan to wash. Hopefully, the cold water would take her down a notch.

But Goddess, if he kept looking at her like that, she didn't think she'd be able to—

He grabbed her, moving so fast he blurred, and yanked her against him. A surprised squeak came out of her as she slammed into his chest. He took her mouth with ferocity the next instant.

He kissed her so hard, she stumbled back until her spine hit the wall. He pressed her into it, gently cradling her head though he was nearly crushing her otherwise, and she moaned in delight. He scooped her up and ground himself against her.

Okay, so maybe she'd read the situation wrong?

There was no time to think about it. She threw her head

back with a cry as he feasted on her throat, his cock hard and hot and stroking right against her soaking-wet center. She wrapped her legs tightly around him, begging him with her body to enter her. He tilted his hips in just the right way, and the head of his sex breached her.

They both froze.

Harrow didn't dare push him again, though it took everything she had not to move.

"You want this?" He was breathing hard, staring at her intensely.

"Oh Goddess, yes. Do you?"

"I would kill to have you."

A strangled laugh escaped her, causing her inner muscles to clench and turning the laugh into a moan. "You don't have to kill anyone, Raith. I'm right here. I want you too."

Still, he didn't move. How did he have such control? She was nearly passing out from anticipation. *Get a hold of yourself, Harrow!*

"Raith, do you trust me?"

He nodded instantly, and her heart swelled.

"Then hear what I'm saying now and trust that I'm telling you the truth. I want to be with you. More than I've ever wanted to be with anyone. So just tell me what you want and don't be shy, because the odds are good I want the same thing."

"I want to be inside you."

"Then thank the Goddess, because I think I'll die if you don't— Oh *yes*…"

Her thoughts scattered as he slowly penetrated her. Goddess, he was big. She was no virgin, but he made her feel like one. Slowly, he worked himself in until he was buried to the hilt, and she clutched him tightly, her whole body trembling.

"Harrow?"

"Yes!" A response or a plea for more? It didn't matter.

Apparently, he didn't need instructions on this, which didn't surprise her. Slowly, he slid back out, giving her time to adjust before he pushed back in. He did it again, hips flexing beneath her legs, her heels digging into his lower back.

The speed of his thrusts increased, and she sensed he was on the verge of losing control. There was no discomfort now. Her wetness coated his shaft, and her muscles had relaxed to accommodate his size, and now she was just...ravenous. The idea of him losing control was very appealing indeed.

"Harrow," he moaned again, burying his face in her hair.

"More, Raith." She knew what he needed. He was rigid with tension, muscles shaking beneath her hands. Rigid from holding back.

Lose control, she silently begged. *Let go.*

His next thrust was harder. But he stopped again when he was buried deep, still fighting himself. "Again," she moaned, and he moved again, wringing a cry from her lips. "More."

"Don't want to hurt—"

"Feels so good. More." She inwardly groaned. She was trying to be patient with him.

But he seemed pleased. He lifted his head and met her gaze. "More?" It almost sounded like a threat.

"Yes!"

He lifted her suddenly, took two steps, and then dropped her on the mattress. Crawling onto the bed over her, he pushed her legs open and thrust back inside. She cried out as he went so deep she saw stars.

And then he wasn't holding back anymore.

Grabbing her wrists, he pinned them beside her head

and then rode her hard. With each thrust, his pelvis pressed against her clit while his sack hit her ass.

It was divine. It was so glorious, she started to laugh between cries of delight.

He released her wrists to grab her ankles and hook her legs over his shoulders. Now, she had no breath left to laugh because she was too busy moaning. She stroked him anywhere she could reach, and his low growling filled the spaces between her cries.

She dropped her ankles and wound her legs around his hips, reaching up to pull him down to her. Their mouths met, tongues tangling so fiercely, his fangs pierced her lip and drew blood. Neither of them noticed. His arms dug into the mattress under her back, wrapping around her so tight she couldn't breathe.

She started to climax but couldn't make a sound, couldn't do a thing except shudder violently beneath him while he clutched her so close, it was like he was afraid she would shatter. If he let go, she wasn't sure she wouldn't.

"Harrow..."

He was close; she could tell. "Yes, Raith!" She wanted him to come, wanted him to sail over the edge moments after her.

He did. His whole body locked up, and his deep moan sounded in her ear as he buried his face in her hair again. Suddenly, she was the one cradling him, arms and legs wrapping tight around him as his orgasm went on and on, his powerful body trembling above her.

Finally, he collapsed atop her, crushing the breath from her lungs. It was all right. She didn't need to breathe anyway. She'd hyperventilated so much from crying out that her head was spinning.

She lay there, staring at nothing, stroking his silky hair and feeling something so strong that her heart was bursting.

Eventually, he lifted his head. "Okay?"

She could only nod numbly.

His concern softened to warmth as he rolled them to their sides, where they lay, staring into each other's eyes, their bodies still joined. It was incredibly intimate—almost too intimate—but to turn away would be to shatter something precious.

They lay like that for so long, she lost track of time. It could have been ten minutes; it could have been an hour. It didn't matter anyway. It wasn't like they had anything else to do. If she spent the next week just staring into his eyes like this, she'd consider it time well spent.

But her stomach rumbled loudly, and that was it.

Raith glanced down and then back up, and his lips curved. A smile. It was so pure she nearly burst into tears.

"You're hungry," he said.

"I guess so." She smiled back like a silly, smitten girl. "You must be too."

He shrugged like he wasn't overly concerned about his own needs. "I'll bring you food."

"You can't. You have to stay in here, remember?"

He frowned.

"I know. But you're very recognizable." One look at those eyes and they'd be burned into a person's memory forever. "Remember what Malaikah said? I have to go downstairs alone to order food and then wait up here for them to bring it to us. I'll wear my big cloak so no one can see my face. You can hear everything from up here anyway. You'll know if there's any trouble."

His eyes narrowed. He didn't look convinced.

"If anything happens, I'll scream at the top of my lungs. You'll hear that, no problem." It suddenly occurred to her that not long ago, she'd been doing just that, but for pleasure. How many people had heard her? Probably everyone. Oh well. "You can break through the floor to get me." She had no doubt he was strong enough.

He sighed in defeat.

"Thank you." She smiled and leaned in to kiss him. "First, I want to take a bath. Join me?"

They made love twice more before she finally managed to leave the room.

M alaikah waited until well past midnight to sneak out of the fairgrounds. She didn't delude herself into thinking Salizar wouldn't be watching her, but she did count on him underestimating her sneaking abilities.

Salizar was good. But Malaikah was better.

Sure enough, she made it out of the circus grounds and into the city without incident, but it remained to be seen whether she'd been followed or not. Taking care to remain hidden in the shadows, she took a roundabout route to her destination, turning unexpectedly down side alleys only to double back the next block.

She was careful to keep her cloak's hood over her face and her tail tucked beneath the fabric, and she kept her senses on high alert. Salizar's revelation had shaken her more than she cared to admit, and she kept expecting assassins sent to kill the clan leaders' daughter to jump out around every corner.

No one attacked her, however, and she made it to the

stables without incident, her first task of the night to check on Harrow's new horse. The mare, named Fiona, was a gentle beast, and though Mal didn't have much experience with horses—Salizar owned all the ones at the circus, and their care was managed by the laborers—it was easy for her to befriend this one.

Fiona gave a chuff in recognition when she approached, which Mal took as a compliment, considering she'd met her only one other time. "You'll get out of this stuffy stable soon," she promised. Six more days and the circus would hit the road, and then Harrow could collect her horse and leave with her new beau.

Except her "new beau" was actually a deadly killer who had murdered her entire family.

Malaikah's stomach clenched so hard she nearly threw up. Gripping the top of the gate, she folded in half and breathed through the wave of nausea. Her best friend, her sister, was shacked up with a lethal assassin complicit in a genocide.

"Fuck, fuck, fuck." A cold sweat broke out across her brow.

She straightened, forcing herself to shake it off. She'd had this internal debate before. All night last night, and then all day, too, including during her damned performance, which had resulted in her missing the one-armed handstand at the finale. She'd flung herself off the trapeze into a triple backflip instead, sinking a perfect landing, which had actually been pretty cool, but still.

The fact remained that she was sick with worry.

But she'd also concluded that she wasn't doing anything without speaking to Harrow first. Their friendship was too solid for Malaikah not to give her the benefit of the doubt. She owed that to Harrow and knew Harrow would do the same for her.

So here Malaikah was, sneaking out to visit Harrow the night after her successful escape, though it was exceedingly risky. What was the most obvious thing she could do after Salizar had dropped that bomb on her? Visit Harrow. And what was she doing? Visiting Harrow.

But she had to. What Salizar had told her was too serious to delay.

She just had to be extra, extra sneaky.

After a few pats and handfuls of hay, Malaikah snuck back out of the stables. As far as her senses told her, no one had followed her. Keeping a watchful eye out, she set off toward her next destination, doing her same double-back-and-hide routine all the way to the Underground.

There, even at this hour, the hum of voices was discernible from several nearby locations. If she ran and darted about as she had in the other area, she would only draw attention to herself. Instead, she walked purposefully, hood still hiding her face, and tried to look uninteresting.

Ahead of her was a bustling tavern, though not the one she was aiming for. She stopped abruptly, scenting the air. Something felt off. The hairs on the back of her neck rose. She spun around, ears twitching beneath her hood, and heard the slightest movement behind her.

Claws out, she spun back around and came face-to-face with a huge man with a shaved head, a long leather jacket, and a mean face. Immediately, her paranoia about what Sal had told her flared back to life. Was he hired by the Kambu usurper to kill her?

Fight first, ask questions later. If he was, it was too late to hide her identity, and the hood would impair her vision, so she whipped it off a second before slashing her claws out.

Her assailant ducked back, moving like liquid.

She swiped again. He dodged effortlessly, and the bastard actually had the nerve to grin at her. Long fangs poked out of his menacing smile.

Taunting a panther? Bad idea.

She growled again and slashed out, going for his side, though it was well protected by his thick jacket. He flowed out of reach once more, so fast that he nearly managed to go in a complete circle around her before she even realized he'd moved. Who *was* this guy?

She swiped again anyway, trying to predict where he'd end up, but the motherfucker anticipated that and went the other way. He was fast, perhaps too fast, and he still hadn't tried to strike her, which pissed her off.

"Fight me, asshole!" She swiped violently in all directions with her claws. Any other opponent, she'd have slit their throat seven times over, but not him.

The next time she struck, he snatched her wrists in midair.

Fuck. She struggled violently in his grip, but it was unrelenting. He loomed over her, his clenched jaw the only indication he was exerting himself at all. She kicked up her knee, aiming for his crotch, but he twisted out of reach. So she did it again. And again.

Finally, he started to look annoyed, like he was wondering why the little female wouldn't shut up and submit already. Releasing one wrist, he yanked suddenly on her other one, hard. The tug sent her stumbling forward, where he spun her with another violent jerk and then grabbed her free wrist again before she could retaliate.

She ended up with her back to his front, arms caught uselessly behind her. Trapped.

She threw her head back, colliding with his skull. He

grunted. His grip loosened infinitesimally, and she was seconds away from freedom, but then a heavy boot crashed into the back of her knees, and she went down, kneecaps screaming from the hard landing on the cobblestones. From there, she tried a throw, using her weight to unbalance him, but the bastard was way too big and too skilled a fighter, and she couldn't get any momentum from here anyway.

Finally, she stilled, accepting defeat. For now. The second he relaxed, she'd be on him. Until then, she'd conserve her strength.

"You finished?" He was twisting her arms and pulling them upward enough that the threat of an easy break loomed. She was pleased to hear he sounded out of breath, considering she was gasping for it.

"Fuck you!"

"Look around. You're surrounded by my men. Try to fight again, you won't get anywhere."

She did look, and sure enough, a tight circle had formed around them, each guy as nasty-looking as the first. They were all tall and built and clad in black. All Hybrids, she realized. She scented the air, and then it hit her.

All *coldblooded* Hybrids.

This was the Ouroboros gang. The gang that ran the entire Underground.

"What do you want with me?" She played it cool, though she was starting to freak out. Even if they weren't assassins, they were a criminal gang, and Mal had a price on her head. What were the odds they hadn't heard of her?

"I don't want to fight you," the man almost breaking both her arms said calmly. "I want to release you so we can talk, but if you even think about—"

"I'll slit your fucking throat!"

"Not a good start, kitty cat."

He had *not* just called her that. "I'll slit all your fucking throats!"

"Better hurry this up, boss," one of the men muttered. From the corner of her eye, she caught a glimpse of broad shoulders, turquoise eyes, and a long lizard's tail. "We're in the middle of the street, and this looks way worse than it is."

The "boss" sighed. Malaikah prayed he wasn't *the* boss. Hopefully just some lackey in charge of this ragtag band of thieves. "Look, I will knock you out if you don't cooperate. Then I'll throw you over my shoulder like a sack of potatoes and take you somewhere quiet to talk. Or you can stop shouting threats, and we can talk here. What's it gonna be?"

The idea of being carted around unconscious to an unknown location was not appealing. She grumbled and growled and then finally mumbled, "Fine. Let me up."

"You won't fight?"

"I won't fucking fight."

He released her, and she jumped up and spun around to face him, rubbing her aching arms. She glared at him, and he smiled back with fangs. Unlike the other guy, he had no tail or claws, meaning he was a snake Hybrid. The fangs were a dead giveaway anyway—of all Hybrids, snakes always had the longest, most impressive canines, and his were no exception.

If he hadn't just beaten her in a fight and sorely wounded her panther's considerable pride, she would have found him attractive. She liked a male with a good, lethal set of teeth.

His shaved head made it impossible for him to disguise his pointed ears. And why would he? Like Malaikah, there was no way he'd ever pass for human. His pupils were thin, vertical slits over startlingly green irises that filled his entire eye—no white at the outer edges. His golden-brown skin was textured by a pattern underlay of scales. Somewhat iridescent, they would flicker with color in the light.

"What's your business in my district?" He didn't sound cocky when he claimed the entire Underground as his.

Malaikah decided her best chance was to lie through her teeth. "Getting a drink at the tavern." She jerked a thumb at the random bar behind them.

"At two in the morning?"

"Why not?"

"I heard there was a circus in town," the snake said casually. He was half smiling as if this whole thing was a big joke. Except on his mean face, a smile just looked like a death threat.

"That so?" Malaikah cocked a hip. She could play it vague with the best of them.

"Yeah. You check it out?"

"Can't say I have."

"Well, I did. Saw a really pretty kitty cat doing backflips, if you can believe it."

Fuck. He definitely knew who she was. But did he know she was a wanted woman? "Sounds amazing."

A few chuckles sounded from the wall of muscle surrounding them.

"It was." The snake crossed his arms, the breadth of his shoulders straining the fabric of his jacket. "But get this. Ever since the circus came to town, I've been hearing wild stuff. Backflipping kitty cats ain't even the worst of it."

She balled her hands into fists. If he called her *kitty cat* one more time… "That so."

"Yeah. It is."

"And what's all this got to do with me?"

His little smile was gone, replaced with a look of cold intent that told her he wasn't playing games anymore. "A few weeks ago, I heard a rumor about an Elemental being sold by flesh traders. Huge thing, void-like skin that could take on other colors, big-ass wings."

Double fuck. He was talking about Raith. What did this guy want with Raith? To kill him? To use him as a weapon? Whatever it was, it couldn't be good. Remembering how she'd convinced Harrow to hide at the Ouroboros tavern made her want to kick herself. She should have known Salizar wouldn't be the only one who wanted to get his hands on the rogue wraith.

"That so," Malaikah said again, though her attempt at being casual was considerably less convincing.

"Yeah. But you see, I don't allow flesh traders in my city, especially not when it's Elementals being sold. So I caught up with the sellers. Dealt with them. And with a little motivation, they were happy to tell me who the purchaser of their item was. Imagine my surprise when I found out it was the Fiend Collector. Apparently, he raced here all the way from Beirstad to claim his prize. But strangely, he was also the one who tipped me off to the traders' presence in the first place."

"Funny."

"Yeah, he's a real funny guy. Helps me clean up the rubbish, but only after making use of their services. Seems a little hypocritical, don't you think?" The snake cocked a brow. "But I've heard the great Salizar will do pretty much anything to get his hands on more curiosities for his collection."

Mal gritted her teeth. Other Elementals didn't exactly view the circus workers in the best of lights. A lot of them considered performing for humans' entertainment akin to prostitution. Salizar wasn't well-liked in the Elemental communities, nor was he fully accepted in the human ones.

He was an enigma, living between two worlds, making his way with his chin up and a staff in his hand that could zap you straight to the Shades if you messed with him. Mal had to admit she respected him for it, especially after recent revelations. She felt protective of him, even.

"Don't suppose you heard anything about that, have you?"

"Can't say I have."

The snake gave her a look like he knew she was lying, but strangely, he didn't seem fussed about it. "The story gets weirder. You see, just last night, I get wind that Salizar's new acquisition has escaped. With his fortune teller, of all people. A fortune teller who's been making quite an impression on the city in the last few weeks. People are saying she changed their entire life with just a few words of advice. An amazing feat for a phony Seer, don't you think?"

Malaikah inwardly cursed. *Goddess damn it, Harrow, did you have to do your job so bloody well?*

"So the fiend and the fortune teller vanish in the night together, and now Salizar's turning the city upside down looking for them."

"That's a pretty wild story."

The snake nodded. "All true, too. Just ask one of the horse sellers in the main market. He's telling everybody how Salizar showed up the next day to interrogate him about a horse he sold. Apparently, the fortune teller arranged to pick it up at night, all ready for the long road ahead."

Salizar had already found the horse seller? Damn, he worked fast.

"Only get this. The horse never even left the city."

"W-what?"

Sweet Mother Goddess, they were doomed.

"Yep. Salizar had the bright idea to take the horse seller to the stables to look for the animal, and sure enough, it was there, just waiting in a stall. Which means…" The snake paused for dramatic effect. "The fiend and the fortune teller never left Allegra."

Fuck, fuck, fuck.

Malaikah stuffed her hands in her cloak pockets to hide their sudden trembling. She'd visited that damn horse *tonight*. Anyone could have seen her. For all she knew, Salizar had been squatting in the stall next to hers, using a damned enchantment so she wouldn't sense him. He never used them against the circus folk, but she couldn't be sure he'd stick to that principle now. Could he have somehow followed her here?

Change of plan. No visiting Harrow tonight. She was going straight back to the fairgrounds.

The snake was studying her closely. How much did he see? When it came to her survival, Malaikah could lie, cheat, and steal with the best of them. It was the only reason she'd made it out of Kambu alive.

But this guy lied, cheated, and stole for a living. He was quite possibly the boss of all the liars, cheats, and thieves in the city.

"So what does all this have to do with me?" she asked innocently.

"I'm looking for the fiend and the fortune teller." He chuckled. "Sounds like a fairy tale, no? The Fiend and the Fortune Teller. It's a romance, I think."

Malaikah stared at him. *How much does this bastard know?* His poker face was inscrutable. "Why are you looking for them?"

"Good question, kitty cat. You see, there's someone special in this city. She lives in my district, and she's under my protection. In exchange, she protects us too. We call her the Oracle."

"Uh, right."

"The Oracle wants to meet the fairy-tale couple badly enough that she asked me to find them and bring them to her. So I'm out here, doing just that."

And he'd found Salizar's star performer sneaking around his territory.

Malaikah could only thank her lucky stars she was still a ways from the tavern. If he'd caught her outside, it wouldn't be hard to piece together that Harrow and Raith were staying upstairs. She was doubly grateful she'd had the foresight to have Raith climb through the window rather than go in through the bar, because at this point, that was probably the only reason these guys hadn't figured out where they were. Raith didn't exactly blend in with a crowd.

But perhaps the even bigger questions were: Who was this Oracle? Did she know what Raith was? Whose side was she on? Would she want to kill Raith to protect the Seer, like Darya, or would she want to weaponize him, like Furie? Or just sell him right back to Salizar for a shitload of money?

There was no way to know. All Malaikah knew was that she wasn't inclined to trust gangs that waylaid lone females in dark alleys. She hadn't been willing to give up Harrow to Salizar, even when Harrow's life could be in danger, and she definitely wasn't willing to give her up to a random stranger she'd just met who'd given her no reason to trust him.

"Wish I could help you find your fairy-tale romance," she said with a fake sigh of disappointment, "but I can't. Sorry about that. Can I go now?"

The snake didn't answer for a long time, just studying her with those bright green slitted eyes until her palms started to sweat. Finally he nodded. "All right, kitty cat. Play your games for tonight. You're free to go. But I want you to pass on a message."

"To whom?" she asked innocently.

"Tell them the Oracle has information they need. Need as in life-or-death need. Tell them she means no harm. If you decide to trust me, go to the tavern in the center of the Underground. There's a sign out front with a snake eating its tail. Ask for me."

"Who are you?"

He flashed a fanged smile at her. "Ouro."

"As in ouroboros. As in *the* Ouroboros." He *was* the leader, damn it.

"The one and only."

Why, oh why, had she thought it a good idea for Harrow and Raith to stay at that damn tavern? Well, it would have been a good idea if Raith hadn't suddenly become such a hot commodity. It was the perfect place to remain anonymous, but if you weren't anonymous to begin with, well, then it sucked.

Malaikah needed to speak to Harrow more than ever, but there was no way she was going there tonight. It was time to retreat.

"Okay, Ouro, I'll remember your message. Though I don't know what good it'll do, since I'm just an innocent little 'kitty cat' on her way home from a harmless drink with friends." She shot him a glare, still not pleased about the nickname.

"Much obliged, kitty cat." He flashed his fangs again and flicked a hand at the wall of muscle. "Let the lady pass, gentlemen." The men parted, and Malaikah sauntered out of the circle, pretending her heart wasn't still slamming in her chest.

"Take care on your way back," Ouro called after her. "Lots of unsavory people in these parts."

She couldn't resist saying over her shoulder, "Yeah, I'm really starting to get that."

His low chuckle met her ears though she was already halfway down the alley.

"Goddess fucking damn it," she muttered under her breath as she stalked away. Harrow and Raith were in deep shit, and by association, so was Malaikah. This attention did not bode well for a woman whose entire life consisted of hiding from would-be assassins.

One day she was going to march right back into Kambu, cut every one of those traitors down at the knees, and take back her family's lands once and for all. Then there'd be no more hiding.

But for now, she just needed to protect Harrow. And pray to the Goddess that the Ouroboros gang didn't think to look upstairs at their own damn tavern.

CHAPTER THIRTEEN

Five days later...

Harrow sat naked astride the most gorgeous male she'd ever seen, his hard length buried inside her. Tilting her head back, she fondled her breasts, her hair swaying across her back. Below her, Raith dug his fingers into her thighs and fought to keep from taking control. His jaw was clenched, and his arms were so tense, veins bulged along the thick muscle.

Over the days they'd spent locked together in this room, she'd learned that Raith liked to be in control during sex. At first, his touches had been gentle, exploratory, hesitant. Then, as they learned each other's bodies, he'd grown fiercer and more demanding. As he gained confidence and realized how responsive she was to him, he'd begun taking control more, deciding where they would go in their play and even initiating it when Harrow wasn't expecting it.

She loved it. She loved everything. She loved h—

Nope. She blocked the rest of that thought out for now. Five days was not enough time to go there, even if those five days had been some of the most wonderful of her life.

Raith sat up, gripping her waist with big hands and forcing her to lean forward so he could suck her nipples. It felt divine, but she shook her head with a playful smile and pressed him back down with a palm on his chest. Yes, Raith loved to take control, but this time Harrow was supposed to be the one leading, just because. Because it was fun, and they were playing together. And her Raith loved to play, so he'd agreed to her game.

Needless to say, he wasn't doing so well.

Growling in frustration, he went back to gripping her thighs, arms straining as he still fought to control her movements. She fought him right back. He wanted her to go fast and hard; she wanted to go slow. Oh, Harrow loved fast and hard, too, but this was her game, and she was going to make him work for it.

"Harrow," he growled in warning.

"Not yet," she teased. His grip tightened again, but he stopped fighting her. She laughed, realizing how incredibly difficult this must be for him. He deserved a reward for trying so hard and would get one soon.

But first...more teasing.

Running a hand down her body, she began to stroke herself lazily while sliding up and down his decadent length. Goddess, it felt incredible. Head tipping back and eyes closing, she moaned languidly, rising and falling onto him, forcing the poor male to lie there and watch her.

"More," he growled.

She granted his request, increasing the pace of her

stroking and riding him a little faster. The pleasure increased, the sensation setting off spotlights of rapture behind her closed eyelids. "Raith," she heard herself moaning. "I'm so close."

"Faster."

She stroked herself a little faster.

"Harder."

She rode him a little harder—

Wait. When had he taken over again? Sneaky man.

Her eyes cracked open. "I'm in control, remember? What if I don't want to go harder?"

Raith's black eyes narrowed in challenge, and she knew the game was up.

In a flash, he sat up and tossed her beneath him. But he didn't stop there. He flipped her once more, and she ended up on her belly with the hand still at her core trapped between her body and the mattress. He yanked on her hips suddenly, and her ass flew up into the air. She tried to raise onto her hands, but he palmed her shoulder blades and pressed her upper body down.

She moaned ecstatically into the pillow her face was crushed against, shivers racing along her naked skin. The feeling of exposure on her bare sex was invigorating. A sinful delight.

"Stroke yourself," Raith said.

She moaned again at the commanding tone of his voice. She loved it when he got like this, all dangerous and threatening. Her hand went right back to her center, and she obeyed, feeling his eyes on her. Her inner muscles clenched in response, in readiness for him to enter her again.

"Raith," she begged into the pillow. "Want you…inside."

The head of his cock breached her entrance, his hands

landing on her hips. She tried to thrust back onto him, to take it all, but he held her away. "Keep stroking," he bit out.

She kept going, pleasure rushing all over her like warm water on cool skin. "Raith, I'm close. Please…" He knew she could come faster if he was inside her. That was why he was holding back, the diabolical man.

He gave her a little more but not enough. She tried once more to push back, but again he held her off.

"Raith!"

Her thighs were quivering, the fingers at her clit working faster and faster, but she couldn't quite get there, couldn't quite go over the edge without his thick length inside her, stretching her, filling her, taking her. She needed it, needed him desperately—

He finally pushed back inside her with a firm thrust.

The climax hit like stepping under a waterfall—a powerful explosion crashing over her—and she screamed with abandon. Forgetting the patrons of the tavern below who might hear, she was helpless not to surrender completely as he penetrated her, the thick end of his shaft hitting her right in that perfect spot. More colorful lights flashed behind her closed eyelids as her orgasm went on and on.

Overwhelmed, she tried to pull away the hand still stroking herself, but Raith leaned forward and wrapped an arm around her, covering her hand with his, forcing her to keep going. It was too much, too much—

Another orgasm hit on the still-cresting waves of the last, and as she continued to cry out, she felt Raith reaching his climax with her. His powerful body tightened, his thrusts becoming faster and more forceful, and then he locked up, clenching her against him, groaning into her hair as he spent himself inside her.

They collapsed forward onto the bed together, gasping for breath.

Raith rolled them to their sides, gathering her tightly in his arms. Another thing he did that she loved—cuddling her from behind, he used his arms and his legs, throwing his thigh over hers and covering her completely, like a gorgeous, hot blanket of manliness.

She purred in his embrace, so happy she could burst. Everything felt so right. So aligned. Her anxieties about the future and her restlessness at being stuck indoors had faded into the distance, and she felt nothing but bone-deep contentment. Just the thought of Raith made her feel full to bursting, and whenever she looked at him, she was so overcome with emotion it was almost unbearable.

The urge to voice her feelings arose, and she gave into it without thought.

"I love this, Raith. I love yo—"

She choked. Her eyes snapped open.

"—it when you hold me like this," she corrected, her stomach flipping over at how close she'd come to blurting out a declaration she wasn't ready to make.

It's too early, she told herself. No one could fall in love in five days.

She'd never been in love before. She'd had lovers—she was a confident woman with a healthy sexual appetite who didn't believe in self-denial—but never had she felt the urge to declare her love for them.

It was doubtless she and Raith had a deeper connection. Something had drawn her to him from the moment they met. But love? After five days?

Surely she was simply intoxicated by the endless tender care and affection he showered upon her. Surely she was simply being sucked into the whirlpool of their constant lovemaking, awash in a dream where nothing existed but the two of them, locked in an embrace so tight, the rest of the world faded away.

But the rest of the world was still out there, and they had only two more days before they had to face it again. When it was time to do so, Harrow was sure she'd be glad she'd held the words back.

Besides, how could a woman be expected to know for sure if she was in love without first consulting her best friend?

Nearly a week had passed since their escape, and Malaikah still hadn't visited, which was worrying. Not for Malaikah, necessarily. Harrow trusted Mal to take care of herself. But she also knew Malaikah would've needed to be confident she could shake off anyone tailing her as she left the circus grounds. If Malaikah hadn't come, it must have meant the pressure on her was great indeed.

As well as needing Mal's advice, Harrow was dying for information. Had Salizar followed their false trail and been led off course? Was Malaikah in trouble with him, or had he believed that she wasn't involved? Was the circus still leaving Allegra on schedule, even if Harrow and Raith were missing?

Just then, Raith placed a gentle kiss on the side of her neck, drawing her out of her thoughts. Anytime she started to worry about Malaikah and what was happening in the outside world, Raith would kiss her or look at her sidelong, or she'd catch a glimpse of his body in the sunlight, and it would be oh so easy to forget everything again.

And she *wanted* to forget. Who wouldn't want to get lost in the little fantasy bubble they'd created in their tiny room at the tavern? It was easy not to worry about the present or think about the future.

They had each other. What more could they need?

For now, at least, it was enough.

"How do you know?" Raith heard himself ask. The question slipped out of him unbidden.

"Know what?"

"That you love something."

Harrow stiffened in his arms.

"You said you love how I hold you. And when you embraced Malaikah before she left, you told her that you loved her."

"Yes, I—" She closed her eyes briefly before rolling onto her back and meeting his gaze. "You don't know what it means?"

"I know the definition, but I don't know what it feels like."

Her eyes softened. "Well, I know you know how it feels to want something. To desire. It's like that, but stronger."

"Like attachment?" For some reason, it was important to him to understand this.

"Kind of...but not really." Rubbing her eyes, she sat up suddenly, stretching her neck from side to side like she was preparing for a battle. "There are different types of love and varying depths. The love for another person is the strongest, and you love a friend differently than you love a mate."

She fixed her gaze on her hands twisting in her lap. "When you love someone, you want what's best for them, no matter what. It's selfless and, ideally, unconditional." She searched his gaze and then rubbed the back of her neck, likely frustrated by his lack of understanding.

"You feel attached to them," she continued, "and you want to be close. But if it's truly love, you're also willing to make sacrifices, even if those sacrifices aren't what *you* want. You put their needs before your own. And there's also trust. No matter what, you trust the other person to be on your side, to never betray you, and you offer them the same. It's a beautiful, wonderful feeling."

Raith had never experienced such a thing before and could only imagine what it would be like. He trusted Harrow, but he wasn't sure he was capable of it to that level. But when he looked at her, he realized that he wanted to be. He just didn't know how.

He did know, however, that he felt some unidentifiable, intense emotion for her that frightened him because he was powerless against it. Against her. It was why he'd asked about love in the first place—he wanted to know if there was a name to give the feeling.

But this did not feel beautiful or wonderful. It felt dangerous. Like he was standing on the edge of a precipice with his wings bound, about to fall.

Perhaps that was why he craved control over her in sex— because he needed to feel in control of something. She didn't have a clue how much power she had over him in every other way. In fact, even when he dominated her in sex, she still controlled him.

He would kill anyone who threatened her. He would do unspeakable, terrible acts to defend her. He would annihilate anyone or anything to possess her. It consumed him.

He lay awake each night, Harrow asleep in his arms, and stared at her, wondering what she had done to take such a hold over him. He feared what he would become if anything happened to her. He feared what he would become if he was ever forced to live without her.

Whatever it was would be dark and deadly. A scourge upon the world.

He could only pray to the Goddess he never had to see it happen.

The last five days had been by far the most enjoyable of his short memories—something so obvious it hardly warranted acknowledgment. But those five days had also, in a way, been worse than any torture he had endured because they had done what torture could not—given him a glaring weakness. A breaking point. A definite end to his sanity outside his control.

Harrow had made him feel whole, with her radiant smile and compassionate heart and her perfect acceptance of him, and now, she could so easily break him.

"Does that make sense?" she asked.

He nodded because he sensed she would prefer not to discuss this any further, not because he was satisfied with his understanding. But it seemed this was a matter that could not be grasped after one conversation.

Indeed, his response seemed to relax her, and she lay back down. He drew her into his arms while she pressed her cheek to his chest, and he had to fight the urge to crush her against him. Sometimes he felt as though she would slip away like fine sand between his fingers if he didn't clutch her tightly enough.

"What are you thinking?" she murmured after a prolonged silence. She often asked him that—he supposed he didn't speak his mind enough. He was trying to do it more to please her. He would do anything to please her.

"I'm thinking that I would do unspeakable things to protect you," he replied honestly because she'd told him she appreciated that quality, "and that frightens me."

"Raith." Her silver eyes softened as she tilted her head back and placed a hand on his cheek. "I feel the same way about you."

Though he believed she did feel some kind of protectiveness toward him, he doubted she understood the full weight of his words. He didn't think she'd believe the level of violence he was capable of in her name.

Again, he could only pray to the Goddess she would never need to know.

Eventually, they rose from the bed to wash and dress. They'd already eaten their evening meal—feeding each other bite by bite was what had commenced that night's round of lovemaking in the first place—and Harrow placed the dirty dishes outside in the hall for the staff to collect.

When he emerged from the washroom, he found Harrow staring out the window. Her brow was furrowed, her fingers clenched on the frame, a small frown turning down the corners of her mouth.

"What are you thinking?" he asked, because two could play at her game.

"I'm worried about Malaikah. Wondering why she hasn't visited us yet. And to be honest, I'm feeling a little claustrophobic. We haven't been outside in days. I want to see the stars, the moon. Breathe fresh air."

Disliking the idea of her being unhappy, Raith immediately tried to think of a solution. He couldn't do anything about Malaikah—he'd promised Harrow not to leave without her agreement unless it was an emergency. But perhaps he could help with her second problem.

"We could go onto the roof," he suggested.

"How? We can't go out to look for stairs up there, and I'm

not even sure they exist anyway."

"I could climb through the window to the top with you on my back."

Harrow turned from the window to stare at him. "You could? I mean, I already know you can climb, but wouldn't it be too much with my added weight?"

He shook his head. "You're not heavy."

She started to smile, and a laugh bubbled out of her. "Okay. Let's do it."

He opened the window wide and then crouched before her, facing away. "Climb on."

With another giggle that made that ache in his chest twinge, she did, and he climbed through, moving carefully so as not to hit her on the frame. Once through, he perched easily on the sill, unsheathing his claws before scaling the building. The rough stone surface had many easy handholds, and, just as before, he climbed without difficulty.

He might have suggested flying, but he remembered the look on her face when she'd seen his wings for the first time, and he decided against it. He didn't want to remind her of traits he had that made her wary of him.

The climb was a nearly effortless task, yet when he let her down on the roof, Harrow was wide-eyed with excitement. "That was amazing!"

He allowed himself a satisfied smile.

They lay side by side on the flat surface and stared up at the twinkling stars. The sky was clear tonight, and even the nearly full moon failed to dim their brilliance.

"Do you know how to read the stars?" Harrow asked, snuggling against him as he wrapped an arm around her.

He shook his head.

"The Seers used to navigate by them. See that bright one

there?" She pointed, and Raith leaned in to follow her gaze. "That's the tip of the Tidal Wave." She traced the stars with her finger. "That's the top curve of the wave. And there's the bottom. The Wave always faces the west. If you can find the constellation, you can always orient yourself. My mother taught me to look for it so that if I was ever lost, I would know the direction of our homeland."

"Your mother loved you," Raith guessed, still trying to understand the concept.

"Yes, she did." There was such a pang of sadness in her voice that Raith felt that pain in his chest again. "She used to tell me what a blessing I was. Elemental children are very rare, you see. I think because we live for so long, nature has made it so we don't reproduce the way humans can, or we would overpopulate the world. I was the first Seer child in a century."

"She wanted to protect you because she loved you," Raith guessed again. This seemed to be a quality of love.

"Yes, she did." There was even more sadness in her words now, and Raith almost regretted encouraging her to speak about this when it seemed to pain her so. Yet there was nostalgia as well, as though she enjoyed the topic despite the grief it caused her.

"I feel very blessed to have had a mother who loved me so much," Harrow said, "even if I had to lose her too early."

"Your father?"

"I never knew him. My mother told me she had a fling with the odd man here and there, never expecting she'd actually get pregnant. Though she never determined who my father was for sure, she always suspected it was this one man from the South, since my skin was darker than hers. She used to tell me stories about him and said he was the

kindest man she'd ever met. I think she secretly loved him."
Harrow sighed wistfully. "I wonder if she would have looked
for him once I got older. I was only ten years old when she
was killed."

Killed. Along with her entire family, leaving little Harrow
all alone in the world. Raith's arm tightened around her. "I
want to destroy whoever hurt you."

"Me too," Harrow said, but there was no wrath in her tone
as there was in his. As if she'd long ago accepted defeat and
now considered it a futile desire.

Raith begged to differ.

"You have no memories of your mother?" Harrow asked,
changing the subject as if she sensed the violent direction
of his thoughts.

"No." But he was suddenly certain that if he did, they
wouldn't be good ones.

"What about your childhood?"

"No." The concept of childhood felt foreign, even more
vague than the concept of love. He doubted he'd ever
experienced such a thing.

"I'm sorry. Everyone should have those memories to help
them get through difficult times."

"I don't think they would be good memories for me."

"Why not?"

"I don't know."

She sighed. "I don't know" was always how Raith
answered inquiries into his past. He couldn't help it. He
genuinely didn't know. He only had certain impulses or
senses that things had once been a certain way. Just as his
aversion to being bound by his words made him certain he'd
been trapped before, he was also certain he'd had no mother
or childhood—or at least not the classic definition of the two.

But he didn't know anything beyond that.

In all honesty, he didn't care to know, either. He was...
happy now.

Though he'd never imagined he could say such a thing, it
was true. He was happy and didn't care to mourn what might
have been denied him in the past, just as long as his future
continued in the current trend of the present.

In the present, he lay with the most beautiful woman
in the world in his arms. He was strong and capable and
confident he could defend her from any threat. At night, and
during the day, too, she welcomed him into her body, crying
out his name—a name he'd chosen for himself—as she found
her release.

He decided he could go anywhere, do anything, as long
as he continued to have those blessings. If he could always
be Harrow's protector, he could always find happiness.

Maybe that feeling was love after all.

What did it matter who he'd once been when he had
a new identity now? As far as he was concerned, the past
could stay buried forever.

CHAPTER FOURTEEN

That night, Harrow couldn't sleep. Neither could Raith, apparently, since he'd given her a kiss a while ago and then climbed back up to the roof by himself. But that was nothing new.

Raith rarely slept. He liked to guard her at night yet never rested when she was awake. She didn't think she'd once seen him actually asleep. Every morning when she woke, he was already awake, watching over her. And he would lie beside her and hold her as she fell asleep at night, but he never slept before she did.

Was it some kind of leftover habit from his weeks as a prisoner? Never relaxing enough to fall asleep in the presence of another? She hoped not. She wanted him to feel safe with her—wanted him to trust her the same way she trusted him.

Goddess, she cared for him so much, but there was always this part of him that was unreachable to her, a vast distance in his eyes like a great ocean she couldn't cross. She longed to, but she didn't know how, nor did Raith understand it enough to show her the way.

More and more, she was beginning to suspect the answer to crossing that ocean lay in his lost memories.

Unfortunately, from what she'd seen so far, those memories weren't pleasant. Whenever Harrow asked him questions about his past, he usually responded with "I don't know," but occasionally, something would slip out, surprising even him, revealing some insight into what his life had been like.

Not once had those slipups revealed anything good.

Her beautiful, sweet Raith had scars that ran deep. Maybe it was better for him that he didn't remember. Maybe it was a blessing, a chance to start a new life without being burdened by the traumas of the old.

But she couldn't shake the feeling that his memories were important. The Water was stirring in her, telling her to *dig*, *dig*, *dig* until she found answers. It kept her restless and agitated.

Which was why she currently sat at the table by the window, shuffling her cards. Only now could she finally admit to herself that she'd been fighting the urge to do another reading on Raith. The last reading she'd done on him hadn't bothered her much, but now she was dreading it, afraid of what she might learn. Was Raith's past really that horrible?

But no matter what he'd been through, she was certain it wouldn't change her feelings about him. Uncovering whatever the Water was nagging at her to uncover was a potentially painful but necessary step forward.

So why was she so resistant to it?

Frustrated with her indecision and her own behavior— fighting the instinct was the number one no-no in the Seer rule book—Harrow pictured Raith in her mind and allowed the Water to rise within. As it often did in his proximity, as soon as she opened its cage a tiny bit, it rushed to the forefront. The air crackled around her, the curtains blowing and condensation forming on the windowpanes. She didn't feel any threat was near, so why did her power respond in that way?

Yet another reason she needed to do this reading.

With shaking hands, Harrow flipped the first card off the deck and set it faceup on the table.

The Deep.

Heart pounding, she stared at it. The black card with those two words scrawled in her own calligraphic writing seemed to taunt her, luring her into some abyss. Chair scraping back, she leaped to her feet suddenly, setting the cards away from her on the table as if they contained some dark magic.

Whatever the Water wanted to tell her…she wasn't ready to hear it.

Stuffing the Deep somewhere in the middle of the deck, she went to the bed and lay down on her side. Suddenly cold, she yanked the blankets over her and stared blankly at the wall, still seeing the Deep in her mind's eye, beckoning her to finish the reading.

The room was dark—her candle had been extinguished in the burst of magic. Raith was still on the roof, and she knew he wouldn't leave without telling her, because he'd promised in that quiet, intense way of his, and his word bound him. He had willingly fettered himself because he wanted her to trust him.

She wished he would come back inside to hold her but didn't want to call him in. If he wanted to be alone, he deserved to have the freedom to choose.

Her heart ached. Her eyes blurred with tears. All the while, the image of the Deep wouldn't leave her head.

Finally, she drifted into an uneasy sleep, hoping to find some peace there.

H alf an hour or so later, Raith crept back inside through the bedroom window. He felt strangely apprehensive, like some great threat lurked around the corner, but he couldn't figure out what it was or when it would strike.

Earlier, he'd gone back to the roof alone, feeling some kind of impending isolation about to strike and needing to prepare. Which made no sense because Harrow had kissed him as he left and told him with a beautiful smile that she would await him in their bed. It was all so good, so pure.

Too good and pure for one like you.

The thought came with no explanation, and yet it filled him with doubt. Surely something like this couldn't last. Surely the end was nigh, and all was about to fall apart.

Harrow was asleep when he returned, but it looked as though she, too, rested uneasily. A frown creased her brow, her hands gripping the blankets too tightly. He decided he would climb into bed and take her in his arms to soothe her. It amazed him that he could do this for her. He cherished it as the greatest of gifts.

Turning from the bed, he headed to the washroom to get ready. Halfway there, he stopped, eyes catching on something on the table.

Harrow's stack of Seer cards.

She'd explained to him how each of the twenty-four cards represented a different form of water. Each meant a different thing according to how it was drawn from the deck and, more importantly, what the Water told her as she drew it. Raith was curious to learn more, but when he'd asked her to show him the cards or do a reading on him, she'd demurred, so he hadn't pressed.

But now the cards lay unattended on the table and Harrow lay sleeping in the bed. Would she mind if he touched one? Surely not. He would tell her first thing in the morning. But for now, he couldn't shake the curiosity.

He picked up the card on the top of the deck, laying it faceup on the table. It was solid black with an intricate gold frame around the edges. In the middle, written in scrawling calligraphy, were two words:

The Deep.

A shiver of awareness raced down his spine. Something inside him stirred in recognition. He stared at the card, feeling on the verge of understanding something important.

The Deep was darkness, like him. But for once, staring at that card, the dark didn't depress him. Instead, it felt... peaceful? Necessary? Like it had its own essential role to play in the world, and without it, something important would be missing.

He peered closer, fighting to understand, but the harder he concentrated, the more the feeling slipped away. Eventually, he was left just staring at the card, wondering if he'd imagined it in the first place.

From across the room, Harrow gave a tiny moan in her sleep. He would go to her and protect her from all threats. That was a role in the world he could fulfill with pride.

Discarding his shirt, he washed quickly and slipped into bed beside Harrow, pulling her into his arms. She mumbled something unintelligible in her sleep, so he stroked her hair and held her tightly until she calmed.

He didn't plan on sleeping. He rarely slept. Part of it was his need to protect Harrow, but another part was his desire to hide his true nature from her. He knew that if he lost consciousness completely—either from injury or by falling into a deep slumber—he would automatically revert to his real nature: pure celestial darkness, devoid of all tone and texture, absorbent of all light.

Like a wraith. He never wanted Harrow to see him like that.

Unfortunately, something about this night was different. Within moments, he was blinking heavily, longing to slip into oblivion. He fought it as long as he could, all the while thinking of that mysterious card and trying in vain to understand what it had been trying to tell him.

He was sucked into sleep minutes later.

Immediately, the memories began.

Harrow was swimming in the dream again. But it had shifted once more. She was back in the shallow water, but this time, she was desperate to dive down, somehow knowing the deep represented Raith. Her earlier fear of it had simply been fear of the unknown.

Now, that unknown was known, and it was loved. She loved him.

In the dream, the shoulds and should-nots didn't matter. In the dream, he was hers, and she loved him enough to dive into the darkness to save him. He was down there waiting for her, and she had to get to him.

But she couldn't. Because something was trying to pull

her to the surface.

Like an invisible tether tied to her waist, it tried repeatedly to yank her up. She fought violently, trying again and again to execute her dive only to be thwarted with another tug around her middle.

She thrashed anew, diving, only to be yanked backward yet again. Feeling her back breach the water, she fought harder, somehow certain that if she allowed whatever it was to pull her up, she'd never be able to get back to the deep where Raith was waiting.

"No!" She fought harder, though her muscles were tiring and her vision swam with spots of exhaustion. "Don't make me leave him. He needs me." Somehow her words carried perfectly in the underwater dream world. "I have to get to him. He's mine! I love him!"

The tugging stopped. For a moment, Harrow thought she had succeeded. She gave a triumphant shout and started to dive. She was doing it! Diving deeper, the light disappearing—

The tether yanked, harder than before, catching her by surprise. It pulled her up faster than she could fight, though she certainly tried. She broke the surface in an explosion of thrashing limbs and spraying water.

And landed in a room.

Completely dry, dressed in a simple white gown, she glanced around in shock after noting her own appearance. She was in a spacious sitting room. Ahead, a stone fireplace lay empty of wood or any signs of a recent fire, though the air was cold. A heavy piece of metal had been welded around the hearth to block the chimney, and a thick layer of dust coated it, though the rest of the room was spotless.

As if whoever lived here wouldn't dare touch the fireplace...

Beside the empty hearth were tall bookshelves packed with colorful volumes. Fountains adorned every available space, their pleasant trickling filling the air. Normally, Harrow would have loved to investigate, but other things caught her eye now. Particularly, the view through the large windows to her left. She crossed the room to peer outside, bare feet padding noiselessly on the hardwood. When she reached the glass, she sucked in a breath.

The ocean stretched to the horizon and beyond, farther than the eye could see. For eternity, it seemed. It was gray and stormy, the powerful water tossing and turning in frightful whitecaps that would overturn even the most stalwart of ships. The sky brooded, flickering with lightning that didn't yet reach the surface, unloading a steady stream of rain on the vast seascape.

"You look just like her," a soft voice said, and Harrow spun around with a gasp.

A woman sat in an armchair in the far corner. Another empty chair was angled beside it, an oil lamp atop the small table in between.

She was beautiful, her every feature flawless. Her skin was brown, like Harrow's but lighter. Wavy black hair fell in glossy waves past her breasts. Her bone structure was delicate, her lips contrastingly full. Also just like Harrow, her eyes were sparkling silver, and behind the bewitching color, they were full of old pain.

Though she'd never seen her before, Harrow knew instantly who she was looking at.

"Queen Darya."

The Queen of the Water inclined her head and gestured to the empty chair. "Please sit."

Numbly, Harrow crossed the room and lowered herself

into the armchair. "Y-your Majesty." She had no idea how to greet a queen, let alone an immortal, Elemental one.

Darya waved away the formal greeting with a flick of the wrist. "The similarity is striking. You truly look just like her."

"Like whom?"

"Your mother, Mellora. She was a great beauty, and you take after her."

"You knew my mother?"

"Of course, child. I knew every one of my precious Seers like my own children, for that was what I considered them." Her silver eyes flickered with emotions—ones Harrow was very familiar with. Grief. Loneliness. Loss. "You're the only one left."

"You know me?"

"Of course I know you. You're my last remaining Seer. I have followed your life closely."

"But Salizar—"

"Was under orders from Audra to protect you. Audra and I keep in contact. She's the only one of my sisters I still consider an ally, and I owe her much. She has worked with me every step of the way to keep you safe and protected."

Harrow struggled to keep up. "So you knew— When Salizar took me in—"

"Salizar is Audra's emissary on a mission of great importance to protect the dwindling Elemental populations. His circus is a way for him to do that while remaining in the public eye. It's for safety, you see. With his famous troupe of Elementals beloved by the human populace, they are protected. Salizar is powerful and well-known. No one would dare strike at him or those in his care. He has done his duty well."

"But why protect Hybrids? If they're Tierra's, and you

don't consider her an ally…"

"I don't consider Tierra or my other sisters as allies, but Audra has long worked at bridging the conflicts between us. Though I consider it a fruitless endeavor, I admire her perseverance."

"Why not try to make amends? You could end the centuries of fighting and win back the love of your queendom. You could bring the world back to how it used to be."

But Darya waved a hand. "Some feuds are so ancient, they have lost all chance at redemption. And some wrongs that have been done are simply too great to ever earn forgiveness."

Harrow frowned, not sure she agreed with that.

"In any case, I didn't bring you here to speak about the past. Or at least not the distant past."

Suddenly, Harrow remembered where she was. Or rather, where she wasn't—asleep in her bed. "How did I get here? Where am I?"

"You're currently resting somewhere in the belly of Allegra. You were dreaming, and I stepped in and whisked you away to Castle Vari so we could have this conversation."

"I— How?"

"I am the Queen of Water. I can do whatever I like. But fear not. When I release you from the dream, you'll awaken safely in your bed—" She frowned suddenly. "Well, as safe as you can be at present, which is why I brought you here."

"Why talk to me now? You were never interested in me in the past."

"On the contrary, following your life has been one of my greatest pleasures in the last century, if not my only. I'd long forgotten the simple joys of mortal life. Watching you has shown me much."

Harrow wasn't sure how she felt about the sudden interest from the mysterious Water Queen. Where had Darya been the night of Mellora's murder, while Harrow cowered beneath the wreckage of her caravan, staring death in the eyes?

She knew better than to voice her doubts, however. Instead, she asked, "Why am I here? I don't understand."

"I have much to explain and little time to explain it, but I'll do my best. To begin, we must go back to something that happened long ago. It was the very event that triggered the conflicts between us in the first place. It was the night I killed my sister's beloved."

CHAPTER FIFTEEN

"I know this story, I think." Harrow shifted uncomfortably in her seat. "Everyone does. Furie's mate attacked a village in your territory, and when you retaliated, he was killed."

Darya looked away. "That is what happened. To a point." Was that guilt in her expression?

"Was it on purpose?"

Her silver eyes flashed. "What do you think?"

Harrow studied her closely. The Queens could be benevolent goddesses one day and fickle, ruthless tyrants the next. "I've heard tales that Furie's mate was blood-crazed, obsessed with warring. I was told that Furie was the senseless one, who hungered for power and preyed on innocents. But that's not true, is it? I think you were sick of defending your borders from the constant threat of invasion. You killed him on purpose and tried to make it look like an accident."

As the truth sank in, her heart broke all over again. This was the real reason she'd lost her people. Darya was not a protector, but the aggressor in a war that had plunged the world into a dark age.

Again, Darya's gaze wandered away. "Think you so little of me, daughter of the Water?"

"Am I right?"

Reluctantly, she nodded. "Furie was incapable of denying Ferron anything. She lured him in with the promise of immortality, but that wasn't enough. He wanted every soldier in his army gifted with Fire magic, and I feared what would happen if she allowed her powers to spread too rampantly. Her queendom was growing too powerful, and I had to put a stop to it.

"So when Ferron and his men attacked my borders, I dispatched a secret cadre of soldiers with special orders to assassinate him and make it appear to be an accidental casualty in the skirmish. He was a legendary warrior, but even he could not defeat two dozen men at once. The assassination was a success, but my plan failed. Furie knew her mate was too skilled a fighter to ever be killed in a mere raid. She didn't believe my ruse for a second." Darya sighed heavily, appearing her ancient age for a brief moment. "Needless to say, I paid for my betrayal many times over."

Harrow couldn't speak. That old grief had risen in her throat like bile, transformed into helpless anger. Her mother's death, her clan's death, all the Seers' deaths... They were all because Darya had betrayed her sister and Furie had retaliated tenfold. In their struggle for power, they had broken the land and their own people.

Countless lives had been lost. Centuries of wars had ensued. The losses were staggering.

"I know what you're thinking, dearest, and it's nothing I haven't thought myself a thousand times over."

"Then why are you still fighting? Why not end this?"

"How can I? After her warrior's death, I tried my best to reconcile with Furie, but there was no reaching her. Her grief consumed her, changed her utterly. I had no idea she cared for the man that much." She shook her head. "I never could have imagined. My own mate passed away eight centuries ago—he was tired of immortality, so I released him from my life-prolonging magic. I still think of him on occasion with fondness, but Furie... Once she was light and life and progress, the favorite of the people. She was never the same after Ferron's death. She never recovered. She spent centuries stewing in rage, plotting her vengeance, and when she finally exacted it..."

"She wiped out an entire group of Elementals."

Harrow knew this story, had heard it over and over, and she didn't want to hear it again. She didn't want to think about it anymore, didn't want to dredge up that old grief that never went away. Nothing anyone could ever say or do would make it right or take away the pain.

"Yes. Furie unleashed her vile creatures upon the world and destroyed my Seers in the span of but fifty years. I had no time to muster a defense and no way to protect them when they were spread across all five Territories. I lost everything I'd ever loved."

Harrow sighed. "Why are you telling me this?"

"Because it's necessary to understand what I've spent the last several decades doing. Most people think that after the death of her Seers, poor Queen Darya slunk away behind the walls of Castle Vari and was never heard from again. In reality, I was searching for a way to ensure Furie could never again unleash that kind of destruction upon the world. She was satisfied with the blood spilled then, but what's to stop her from doing it again? Until recently, no one had ever found a single defense against her wraiths, for how can one harm that which is but a ghost? I was determined to find a weakness in a creature that apparently had none."

Harrow's eyes widened. "All this time, you were searching for a way to kill a wraith?"

"Precisely."

"And...?"

"And"—the Water Queen smiled triumphantly—"I was successful."

"How? What did you do?" Harrow sat up straighter in her chair. She was not a violent person, but one whose entire lineage had been eradicated could not live without desiring some kind of justice. It was the only way to stay sane after such a tragedy. She'd always longed to strike back but had dismissed the idea as impossible.

But this changed everything.

Except Darya's smile twisted. "Well, I was successful... to a point."

"What do you mean?"

"First, let's discuss wraith physiology. A wraith is a specter. Incorporeal. A spirit cannot meet a physical death, for it is not of the physical world to begin with. But wraiths can form a corporeal body for several hours at a time. When a wraith settles into a physical body, he becomes as vulnerable as any other Elemental species."

"Are wraiths Elementals, then? I'd heard they were evil spirits from the Shades that Furie found a way to capture."

"No, they are her creation. But, since Furie's magic was twisted and depraved by her grief, her Elementals were formed twisted and depraved like her. Her sorrow warped her mind, and it made her creatures abominations."

"So you found a way to kill them? Did you force them to take a physical form?"

Darya shook her head. "There is no way to force them without Fire magic. Furie can make them do whatever she wants, for their very essence is Fire, and she controls that Element. My Water magic is the antithesis of that and was therefore almost useless against them. That was why it took me half a century to have any results with my test subject."

"Test subject? What test subject?"

Darya folded her hands neatly in her lap and gave Harrow a long look. "Wraiths were created to be enslaved to Furie's will. Their very word, once given, binds them."

A trickle of foreboding ran down Harrow's spine, but she suppressed it.

"Since she created them, Furie was able to control their speech and force them to vow to do her bidding. Her wraiths were bound by her to kill the Seers. One wraith in particular was sent to eliminate your family."

"But it left me alive." Harrow knew this. "How?"

"Because it disobeyed her."

"But I thought they were bound and couldn't disobey?"

"They couldn't," Darya agreed. "It should have been impossible. But for this one wraith, it wasn't. To this day I don't know why, and I don't think Furie does, either. The wraith spared you for whatever reason. Perhaps it didn't deem you a worthy opponent. I doubt it was from any place of compassion. They are heinous things, formed by a heinous being, and aren't capable of it. But whatever the reason, Furie was livid. She punished the wraith responsible for the failure severely."

"How do you punish a ghost?"

"She can manipulate them with Fire magic, do whatever

she wants to them. They are like golems, molded from the clay of her evil nature into powerful, unstoppable beings that obey only her. When displeased with this one, she dispatched a foul punishment. Agonizing torture lasting for months."

"Dear Goddess."

Darya wagged a finger. "Don't make the mistake of feeling sympathy for those creatures. Excruciating pain is the only experience such a beast deserves to have. Its existence is a stain that taints the very fabric of our reality. They are abominations."

Harrow smothered her disquiet. "So why does it matter if Furie tortured the wraith that left me alive, then?"

"Because, child, Furie made a mistake. Torturing her wraith weakened it to a mere wisp, rendering it powerless for a time. To begin experimenting on how to kill these creatures, I first needed to trap one. But they were far too powerful, and my Water magic didn't work against them the way I needed it to. After several years of attempting in vain, I was presented with the perfect target by Furie herself. Weakened by the torture, the creature stood no chance against me. I captured it easily.

"From there, it was a simple matter of changing how I wielded my magic so I could find a way to trap it permanently by myself. Studying how Water magic had almost the opposite effect of what I intended, I soon found ways for my power to work and devised a prison for it. The wraith eventually healed and regained his strength, but by then, the cage I'd fashioned was inescapable. I spent the next fifty years trying to find a way to kill it."

"Fifty years," Harrow echoed.

"Yes, well, did I not just say they were considered unkillable?"

"What did you do?"

"First, I tried convincing it to assume a physical form so I could kill it that way. But, as it was a creature of hatred that had endured years of torture, nothing I did could break its will. It resisted my efforts with remarkable tenacity. So I changed my tactic. If I couldn't persuade it to change by itself, I decided there had to be a way to force the change."

"Was there?"

"Yes, though it took decades to uncover it. I won't go into the science of it, for that level of magic is too complex for any mortal mind to grasp—even yours, dear daughter, with your Elemental lifespan."

It was nice to know Darya had such a high opinion of her intelligence. "What was the result?"

Darya leaned forward, almost eager now. "I lingered in Castle Vari with my test subject for many years until I finally uncovered the secret formula. At last, I discovered the perfect balance of Water magic with the wraith's inherent Fire nature. At the moment of application, there was a massive explosion. It took out the entire west turret of the castle, in fact. When the dust settled, I knew I'd been successful, but unfortunately, the creature was gone."

"Gone? Where did it go?"

"It was sent back within the Fire Territory, since that was the place of its original creation."

Deep inside Harrow, the Water started to churn, as if encouraging her to make some connection. "I don't understand."

"I created a body for a creature that didn't originally have one and then forced it to occupy it, similar to the way our souls are bound to our physical bodies at the moment of conception."

Harrow stared at the resplendent Queen, trying to wrap her head around this madness. "You actually *created* a physical body for the wraith?"

"Precisely. The body I created was a replica of the physical body he would have formed temporarily as a wraith, but it was formed by my magic. All I did was apply the skill Furie used to create wraiths in the first place, but in reverse, with Water instead of Fire."

Harrow gave up trying to understand. Perhaps Darya was right, and her puny, mortal mind couldn't wrap itself around such concepts. "So…where is the wraith? Did you finally kill it?"

"It escaped, as I said, transported to somewhere in the Southern Territory."

"How do you know for certain?"

"I am the mother of all Seers. Do you not think I possess your abilities? Have you never used your powers to locate someone before?"

"Oh. Yes, of course."

"I found the approximate location of the wraith and then contacted Audra, requesting her aid in retrieving it and returning it to my territory. A few weeks later, I received word that Salizar had successfully secured possession of the creature."

"Salizar?" Harrow frowned in confusion. The Water was frothing with agitation inside her.

"Yes. As I said, he is an emissary of the Air Queen."

"But I thought Salizar went to Allegra to—" The words stuck in Harrow's throat, and she choked on them.

Suddenly, it all slid into place.

"No."

Darya's eyes softened. "I'm afraid so."

"No. It's not— Raith— He's not—"

But suddenly, the Water inside her was telling her it was so.

The writhing, boiling waves settled into perfect stillness, and everything became crystal clear.

Why now? Before, she'd been so positive. She'd told Salizar she would bet her life that Raith wasn't what he thought he was. And now this? Had her power deluded her on purpose? The Water didn't scheme or trick.

But the ringing of truth inside her was unmistakable.

Still, she fought it, unable to accept that she could have made such a terrible error in judgment. Suddenly short of breath, she jumped to her feet, clutching her throat. Where was all the air? She needed to breathe. The room was spinning.

"I'm so sorry, dear."

"He can't be— I would have sensed—" But her feeble protests held no sway over the power ringing true inside her. She bent at the waist, gasping for breath.

"As I said, I created a new body for him. It's akin to being reborn from a mother's womb. Just as we don't remember what our souls were doing before we arrived in this world, the wraith didn't have memories of what he'd done before his rebirth."

"But he hadn't— I sensed that he hadn't killed."

"He hadn't killed in his new body. His kills were done in his previous existence as an incorporeal being. That's why you can't sense the many stains upon his spirit. He was reborn as my creation. He is, in effect, a new species. A physical wraith. A perfect merging of Fire and Water. A possible impossibility."

"That's why he doesn't remember anything?" She could

scarcely get the words out.

"Yes. The moments after the magical explosion that transported him back to the South will be the first memories he has, as they were the first moments of his new existence."

"He's the one...who killed..."

Darya nodded solemnly. "Your mother. Everyone in your clan. It was him."

"Raith...*killed*..." Harrow's stomach heaved. Her knees gave out, and she sank to the floor, wrapping her arms around herself, suddenly unable to stop shaking. The room felt like it had entered a blizzard, the origin of which was her frozen heart cracking in two. "No..."

"I am truly sorry, Harrow. As soon as Salizar sent word to Audra of your interest in the wraith, I began efforts to contact you and warn you. I knew you wouldn't believe Salizar if I entrusted him to break the news."

"Why didn't you get to me sooner?"

"I couldn't. I am powerful, but it takes advanced magic to weave a dream spell this deep for two people, especially when you were fighting me so determinedly. Every time you ignored my call from the surface and chose to dive into the deep in your dreams, I had to start all over again."

"T-two people?"

"As we have this conversation, I've also trapped the wraith in memories of his past existence. He is currently reliving every pain he endured and every death he dealt in vivid detail. Living life without memories of his torture was a gift he did not deserve, so I have relieved him of it."

Even now, a tiny part of Harrow's heart ached to imagine Raith reliving such torment. How those memories would hurt him.

Protect him, the Water suddenly demanded inside her. *He*

needs you. Go to him.

No! she screamed mentally, pushing the power back down.

Or had she screamed aloud? Judging by Darya's flinch, she had.

Raith was a wraith. And not just any wraith. The very wraith who'd killed her beloved mother and her entire clan. The very wraith who'd floated down amid the carnage and stared into her eyes, head tilting as he studied her like a bug beneath a magnifying glass.

Those eyes... *Fire and shadow.* They were the eyes she had stared into as they made love just hours ago.

Harrow scrambled across the floor on her hands and knees and threw up into the potted plant by the window.

How in the Goddess's name had she been so resistant to the truth? Why hadn't she pieced it together sooner? Why had she been so bloody stubborn? Salizar had warned her, all but telling her exactly what Darya just had, yet Harrow had refused to believe him. Why?

She remembered Raith's inclination to kill Salizar, the blank look on his face when she'd told him he couldn't go around murdering people. He'd genuinely not understood why killing was wrong.

Because he was evil. Because he'd killed her mother and her entire family.

GO TO HIM. The Water rose like a flash flood. *PROTECT HIM.*

I will never go to him! Harrow screamed back at it, shoving her power back down, this time slamming the door behind it.

Eventually, she rose from the ground, wiping her mouth with her sleeve, uncaring if she appeared disgusting to the beautiful Queen sitting in the armchair. Everything felt numb.

Her heart had shattered into a million pieces. Her mind had switched off, unable to comprehend any more pain or sorrow. All that remained was numbness.

And cold, deadly purpose.

"What do I do?" Her voice was flat, strange to her own ears. Inside her, the wellspring of her power had become a silent, empty pit, as barren as the Southern deserts.

"You have to get away from the wraith immediately. Salizar is under orders to retrieve him and bring him back to my territory. As soon as the wraith is within my boundaries, I can dispatch him. As long as he remains in the Ether Territory, he is under Queen Nashira's protection. We can't act there without risking war."

"Why—" Harrow swallowed hard, her raw throat scraping. "Why would Nashira protect him?"

"I don't know, but she has made it abundantly clear that there are to be no executions in her territory without inviting her retribution. I can't afford to start another conflict. The wraith must be brought here."

"E-execution…"

Executing Raith. Killing him… The thought horrified her.

"It has to be done, child," Darya said softly. "It's the only way. He isn't what you thought he was. Do you understand that now?"

Harrow could only nod numbly. Could only feel emptiness, aching in her chest, burning, stabbing pain. Confusion. Loneliness. Betrayal.

"I need you to tell me where you're hiding, Harrow, and I'll pass on the information to Salizar. You'll be released from the dream and awaken. I'll continue to hold the wraith under. He won't wake until after you've left. Head back to the circus grounds directly, and Salizar will go to the Underground and recapture the wraith."

Harrow just nodded.

"Where are you staying, child?"

"You can't just use magic to find me?" Why did she even care? Why was she hesitating?

"Your escape plan worked well. Using the Water to divine your location has given me some results, but the Underground is a vastly populated area and Allegra is so doused in Ether magic, it's nearly impossible to track anything within it. Half the streets disappear as soon as I start to get close in my scrying, as if the city itself is trying to hide you from me."

Finally, Harrow forced herself to say it. "I'm upstairs at the Ouroboros tavern."

Darya shut her eyes briefly. "That complicates things. However, if you are quiet and careful, you should be all right. When you leave, no one must see you. There are people searching for you—people who do not want you to rejoin Salizar. If they find you, they will take you. Do you understand?"

Harrow nodded numbly again. It didn't occur to her to ask more questions. She only wanted to be alone where she could hide from the world and try to make sense of the mess that was her entire life.

"Do you understand what you need to do?"

"Wake up. Leave the tavern without Rai—without the wraith seeing me."

"Without the wraith *or anyone else* seeing you."

Another nod. "Return to the circus grounds."

"Exactly. We'll get you out of Nashira's territory as soon as possible."

"I don't— I can't be near—"

"You'll be nowhere near the wraith, I promise. I'll do

everything in my considerable power to ensure you never again have to set eyes upon him after leaving that tavern. And soon he won't be able to hurt you ever again."

Hurt? Did Darya think Raith had violated her in some way? If only the truth were that simple.

"I went with him," she admitted, the shame burning her skin like fire. "Willingly."

"I know, dear, but you mustn't blame yourself."

"I thought we were connected. I thought the Water was telling me we were connected. I thought I l-loved—" Her stomach heaved again, and she swallowed hard.

Darya's voice was soft. "You were confused, child. A gentle heart like yours was never equipped to handle such a devastating loss. Your longing for family distorted the connection you felt to the wraith."

"I didn't— I was so certain he wasn't—"

"It doesn't matter, dear. No one is blaming you. Wraiths are beautiful, alluring creatures for a reason. Furie created the perfect killer. Death that arrives at one's doorstep in an appealing form is much more likely to be invited inside, don't you think?"

Death at her doorstep. That was exactly it. Beautiful, sweet Death had come knocking and tricked her into inviting him in. *Desperate for love*, Darya had all but said. It was true. All Harrow had ever wanted was to belong. All she'd ever wanted was to feel loved.

Death had taken that longing and twisted it into something foul. Even now, her body was back in the tavern in Allegra, no doubt encased by Raith's strong arms, lulled into a false sense of security.

She had to get away. Far, far away. She had to run until her legs gave out and she collapsed in exhaustion. She had to scream until her voice broke. She had to wash herself for days. No, she had to burn all her skin off and regrow it anew so not a single cell in her body remained that had ever touched him with love in her heart. Love for the very thing that had murdered her mother.

False love. Love that was a lie.

For Mellora, she had to do this.

Steeling herself, she turned to Darya. "Send me back now. I'm ready to wake up."

CHAPTER SIXTEEN

Harrow blinked her eyes open. The stress responses she'd felt in the dream—shaking, sweating, nausea—didn't transfer over to her reality. At first, she felt sleepy, relaxed. The warm weight of another body was curled around her from behind, a heavy arm wrapped around her middle. The room was quiet. Dark, save for the blue glow of moonlight.

Everything came back in a rush.

The shaking started immediately, but she froze in place, terrified. At any moment, Raith could awaken and...

And what? Kill her? Or just look at her in hurt confusion because he didn't understand why she suddenly feared him? Goddess, that would be harder to face than him attacking her.

He truly remembered nothing. Darya had confirmed it. He hadn't been lying about that, but had he lied about anything else? How much of what they'd shared was real? All of it? None of it? It didn't matter anyway.

She could never meet his eyes again without seeing him for what he was.

A killer. An abomination.

Tears spilled down her cheeks to soak the pillowcase. She trembled with fear in his embrace yet still hesitated to leave it. What was wrong with her? She was lying naked in bed with the monster who had murdered her family. It was sickening. She would never recover from the shame.

Worse, she couldn't just turn off her feelings for him. Her body wanted to snuggle back against his, burrow into his embrace, breathe his warm scent, savor that safe bubble he always made her feel she was in.

False security. False intimacy.

Killer. Murderer. Abomination.

With shaking hands, she lifted his arm and crawled out from under it. Sliding her bare feet to the cool floor, she rose from the bed, turning back around to face the man she left behind.

His body was a pure, inky void.

A scream caught in her throat. His hair, skin—even his lips—were utter darkness. No hint of his former brown, no depth of tone. It was like he was an absence in the room, rather than a being who occupied space.

Just flat black. Pure shadow.

He looked…wrong. Like an apparition that should not have existed in the world.

Salizar had told her about this, hadn't he? And she'd just brushed him off, thinking him a cruel madman at the time. Raith had fangs, leathery wings, unnatural eyes, and skin made of shadows, and she'd thought *Salizar* the madman? How had she been so oblivious to the obvious?

Raith really was a wraith. The very wraith who had killed her family.

The unbearable weight of the truth settled over her, and

a new pang of agony sliced across her heart—grief. Grief for her lost love. Because she had truly loved him, only to discover he wasn't even close to what she thought he was.

The tears spilled down her cheeks freely, obscuring her sight. Not that she could see much of him. In the night, he nearly disappeared completely, disguising himself in the slightest shadow like a ghost.

A shadow of death passing over the full moon's face.

Even now, she still loved him, or at least she loved who she'd thought he was. That was the hardest thing of all. As she backed slowly away from the bed, grabbing a dress and robe from her bag and donning them with shaking hands, one part of her was desperate to escape while another part longed to climb back into bed beside him. Knowing he was trapped in that dream reliving his memories didn't help. Was he hurting? Afraid?

No. She steeled herself. He was a killer, and not just any killer. The very one who killed her beautiful mother and her entire clan. He was an abomination, as Darya had said. He needed to be put down.

Just then, Raith moaned low and twisted in the bed as if in agony. Oh Goddess, he was in pain right now, trapped in the horrors of his past. Her breath hitched. Her hands ached to reach for him. Her heart broke just looking at him. Her old wounds of grief for her family were torn open anew at the sight of him.

She could never look at him again without seeing that blood on his hands.

It was that thought that finally got her to turn away. She crossed the room to the door, eyes so blurred by tears she couldn't see it. Reaching a shaking hand out to unlatch the lock, she pulled the door ajar and then hesitated. The urge to turn back was nearly overwhelming, but she fought it hard.

In the end, she prevailed.

Gritting her teeth against the searing pain in her chest, Harrow stepped through the door and pulled it softly shut behind her. Without a backward glance, she took the stairway out to the back courtyard to escape into the night.

R aith fought the dream prison with everything he had. Images of his violence and the violence done to him flashed in rapid succession, interspersed by the screams of his victims and the screams of his own self. Still, he fought to break free.

Agonized screaming. His own. Others'. Blood and death and destruction. Enslaved, bound to another's will, forced to commit unspeakable acts...

Darya intended to keep him trapped here until Salizar arrived and captured him again. But the Water Queen had spent fifty years underestimating him, and it seemed she still hadn't learned her lesson.

With a monumental expulsion of willpower, Raith finally managed to pull himself out of the mire of horrific memories. He jerked upright in bed, whole body shaking, skin slick with sweat. The sheets around him were torn to shreds from his claws. The images continued to swirl around his head.

The atrocities he'd committed... Centuries serving as one of Furie's assassins. The pain he'd unleashed upon the innocent. Torture at his mistress's hand for his disobedience. Fifty years in a mythical cage as Darya's kill experiment.

He lurched out of bed, head spinning, heart pounding. The memories kept coming. Staggering forward, he crashed into the wall, knocking a picture to the floor. He stumbled back into the bed, then the table, then the couch, before finally ending up on the ground. On his hands and knees, he shook his head violently, trying to force them away.

But they persisted.

Captured by Darya in his weakened state. Blasted by wave after wave of magic, trying to break him. Darya's frustrated screams at his continued defiance.

The images traveled back in time.

Furie screeching at him in rage. Why had he spared the Seer child? How could he have defied her? How had he been able to break his vow? Then, burning. So much burning. Beyond skin and bone, since he had none, the Fire burned his very essence. Incorporeal meant unkillable, so there was no end to the pain. An eternity of fire. Of agony and betrayal and hatred.

He traveled even further back.

The full moon cast a glow over a sleepy encampment surrounded by tall evergreens. Several small caravans were positioned around a fire, horses grazing nearby. Women gathered around the fire. One cast a small bag of stones upon the ground, studying the contents. The others shared food and drink. A small child sat beside a doting mother.

A shadow descended upon them from the darkness.

They stood no chance against him. His very existence was death, his only purpose to destroy. He simply touched them and unleashed the fire that was within him, and they burned from the inside out. Their screams echoed into the night. The horses whinnied in terror. Blood pooled on the pine needles. The caravans toppled in the chaos of unleashed powers. Defenses that did nothing to save them.

Only the small child remained.

She thought she was hiding, but he knew exactly where she was. He smelled her skin, could have heard her heartbeat from a mile away. He was death, and there was no escape from him.

He descended as a smoky shadow. The child was his final charge for the night. Perhaps then he could finally rest, free from the relentless compulsion to fulfill his vows.

The wraith hesitated outside her shelter, watching her. She didn't cry, didn't scream. He needed only to stretch a claw forward and stroke her tiny face, and she would burn just like the rest of them.

He was bound to do this. Powerless to resist.

He resisted anyway.

The start of fifty years of torture.

He made his own free choice for the first time in his existence, and the agony that consumed him as a result was a thousand times worse than the quick deaths he dealt to the Seers.

His essence dispersed; his power drained utterly. He was whisked away, blown like a feeble wisp of smoke from an extinguished candle, drawn back to the origins of his bondage to face his mistress's wrath.

Raith's spine arched. His claws shot out and dug into the wooden floorboards. His wings burst from his back. He was pure shadow again, but he didn't try to alter his appearance, abandoning all pretense of blending in.

There was no lying to himself anymore, no hiding what he was.

Harrow was gone. He didn't need to wonder what had happened or why she'd left. Everything had been explained in the dream. Darya's intervention, reaching out to her last remaining Seer. Protecting her from the monster that had killed her family and now held her in its clutches.

Harrow had awoken and fled him in horror.

She should have driven a blade through his chest while he slept. He would have helped her sink it deeper.

The door crashed open behind him. Shouts filled the air.

Raith lurched to his feet, spinning around to face the intruders. It was Salizar, accompanied by several others. Raith recognized the blond hair of Loren in the fray. Salizar was armed with his lightning stick and a length of chain that gave off the strong scent of Air magic. They rushed into the room, coming at him. To capture him and deliver him to Darya for extermination. Just like he had exterminated Harrow's family.

But Raith wasn't hiding what he was now, wasn't hopelessly wishing to be something he wasn't. He spread his wings as wide as they would go, and the talons at the tips hit the ceiling. He flexed his fingers and lengthened his claws to their full extent. He may have been broken, but he still had one thing left to live for: vengeance.

He threw his head back and roared.

It was earsplitting, and his enemies stumbled back, hands over their ears. Salizar shouted orders to them over the din. They approached anew. Raith swept out with his claws, too lost in his rage to see who or what he was striking. Blood sprayed, painting his naked chest, painting the walls and the furniture. Screams filled the tiny room.

Salizar swung the enchanted chain, striking Raith in the shoulder. Agony erupted, his body crumpling beneath him—the weapon sapped his strength like a siphon.

He didn't care. He would fight to his own death if he had to.

In this battle, Raith had two major advantages. One, he was a wraith—a living, breathing instrument of death—and he was enraged. And two, Salizar had orders to take him alive, which meant the Enchanter would be measuring his attacks. Raith had no such stipulations.

He swiped his claws again as the chain struck once more. More agony, more weakness. The maddened wraith roared again. The attackers stumbled, hands slamming back over their ears.

Tiny flames erupted around the room from his fury. He no longer possessed the ability to kill with a touch of Fire, but his rage still stoked it into spontaneous existence. He didn't need the Fire to kill anyway. His claws, his teeth, and his body were sufficient. After all, *he* was the weapon.

Salizar struck again. Raith stumbled back, crashing into upturned furniture. Blood poured from his chest, but he was far from done.

The next time Salizar struck, Raith caught the chain in midair. The Enchanter's eyes widened. The chain melted through the skin of his palm almost instantly, draining his consciousness like a sinkhole sucking down water. He ignored it. With a fierce yank, he pulled it from Salizar's grip and tossed it away.

Snarling furiously, Raith advanced on his foe.

Salizar brandished his next weapon—the lightning stick. He swung out, stabbing the staff into one of Raith's wings. Trickles of lightning erupted from the point of contact, spreading through the leathery expanse into his body.

Raith roared in pain, pumping the injured wing furiously to ward off the staff. Still, he advanced, stumbling now.

Salizar swung, striking again. More lightning, until Raith's entire body was coated in it. Still, he advanced. Another swing, another strike. Raith stumbled again, blackness creeping into the edges of his vision. The light of victory shone in Salizar's blue gaze. He swung again, close enough now to stab the sharp tip of the staff into Raith's abdomen. The agony was unbearable, yet Raith had survived worse.

His clawed hand lifted and wrapped around the staff.

Lightning shot down his arm, but he didn't let go. Salizar's eyes widened, but he thrust forward, stabbing the point deeper into Raith's stomach. Still, Raith gripped the staff, fighting to retain consciousness.

It only took one second of distraction for the tide to turn.

Beside them, a man with a bleeding chest wound tried to rise and join the fight but was easily knocked aside by one of Raith's wings. It was Loren, he dimly realized. Salizar's gaze flicked to him for the briefest of seconds. It was all Raith needed.

He jerked on the staff, the tip sinking deeper into his own flesh. It was yanked from Salizar's grip.

Raith caught the other end with his free hand, the one injured by the chain. He didn't even notice because a far worse sensation quickly overrode it.

Lightning shot down both his arms like he'd stuck them into the eye of a furious storm. It traveled over his whole body, frying him from the inside out. But Raith was used to burning.

Roaring with all the fury and agony and hatred of his entire fucking existence, he used all the remaining strength in his wasted body to push the ends of the stick toward each other.

With a booming explosion and a brilliant flash of white, the staff snapped in half.

Instantly, dead silence fell over the room.

He tossed the useless halves of the staff aside. Staggering forward, black spots peppering his vision, he moved toward

Salizar and wrapped a clawed hand around his neck.

A blade sank into Raith's abdomen, just below the ribs.

Raith stumbled, glancing down. Blood flowed out around the wound, down to his hip, soaking into his pants. Magic coated the blade—he could feel whatever enchantment it possessed seeping into his body.

Salizar's palm was wrapped around the hilt. He'd pulled it from beneath his coat.

Raith looked back into the eyes of his enemy. Flexing his arm, he squeezed the hand around Salizar's throat. The Enchanter choked, yet even then, pride and defiance still blazed in those brilliant blue eyes. He jerked on the blade, twisting it in Raith's abdomen, but Raith just squeezed tighter, waiting to see a plea for mercy in that gaze, or even just a hint of fear.

It never came.

Raith tilted his head, studying him. *This is for Harrow*, Salizar had said before he'd blasted him with lightning until he convulsed into unconsciousness.

"You should have killed me when you had the chance," Raith said quietly.

Surprise flickered across Salizar's face.

Strangely, Raith felt a begrudging respect for him. Salizar did what he had to do to protect his people. He had cared for Harrow, kept her safe as long as he could. He obeyed his Queen and fulfilled his duty with honor and pride.

Raith had none of those qualities. Raith had no people to protect. The only person he'd ever wanted to protect was the one he'd hurt worse than any other. Raith's Queen was an unhinged miscreant whom he hated more than he hated his own miserable existence. He had no purpose, no duty, no pride. His life was a curse.

But at least it was *his* life now that he was free of Furie, and it was his choice what he did with it. And who he killed.

Harrow deserved to have vengeance, and he wanted to give it to her. He'd told her he wanted to destroy whoever hurt her, and now, he was actually in a position to do something about it. Delivering himself on a platter to Darya would take care of part of the issue but not all of it.

Killing Salizar seemed unnecessary. After all, he had helped Harrow when she needed it, and he had only tried to do what was right by her.

So Raith shoved the Enchanter away by the hand at his throat, his back hitting the wall, and then he ripped the dagger from his stomach, keeping it in hand. He was going to need it later. Blood pooled around the wound and spilled down his leg. Salizar was already pulling yet another enchanted weapon from beneath his coat, still staring at Raith in shock.

Turning away, Raith folded his wings against his back but didn't disappear them. There was no more hiding what he was. He stumbled across the room to the window, black spots obscuring his vision.

Rather than opening it gently as he had with Harrow, he simply dug the claws of his free hand into the frame and ripped it right out of the wall, tossing it away to smash on the far end of the room. Shards of glass rained down on Salizar's wounded men, who were sprawled about the room in varying states of injury. Everyone was frozen, staring at the wraith as it turned away from the destruction and started to climb through the window.

"Wait," Salizar called out in a hoarse voice.

Raith turned around, seconds before he would have slipped away.

"Why didn't you kill me?"

Raith said nothing. He doubted the Enchanter would believe him anyway. The thought of Salizar's death didn't fill him with satisfaction anymore. He had something else to focus on now.

Vengeance for Harrow.

Turning away, he climbed out the window and scaled the building to the roof. Beneath the moon and stars, he spread his wings wide, shaking off the weakness from the fight. His body was a bloody mess, yet he barely felt it.

He was an abominable instrument of death, after all.

Bending his knees, he pumped his wings and sprang upward, launching into flight. The air rushed by his ears with a roar, the city of Allegra quickly shrinking away as he flew higher and higher, leaving it all behind.

He swooped right, using the constellation Harrow had shown him to navigate the night, though he needn't have bothered. The direction he was heading sang to him, beckoning him to return like a tether on his tainted soul.

He flew directly south.

Raith moved with the deadly speed of his species, a blur streaking through the silent sky, the knife coated with his own blood clutched tightly in his grip. At his rapid pace, it would take him mere hours to reach his destination.

The Queens were immortal, but Raith had been in close contact with two of them, created by their very magic, and he knew their weaknesses.

He knew that not even an Elemental Queen could survive a beheading.

CHAPTER SEVENTEEN

Malaikah was so worried about Harrow she could think of nothing else. After Salizar's pronouncement that night in her caravan, she'd been dying to sneak back into the Underground, but there hadn't been a chance.

Salizar had people watching the perimeters of the fairgrounds relentlessly, and even if she managed to get past them, she wasn't sure she'd get so lucky with Ouro's gang. There'd been a pair of salamander Hybrids hanging around outside the circus grounds all week, making no secret of the fact that they were watching her.

They were Hybrids, and this was their city. Malaikah's sneaking skills were legendary, but she was out of her element here, and they were in theirs.

But what to do? Every night that passed without seeing Harrow tightened the knot of fear for her friend that had taken up residence where her stomach should be. And worse, something big was going down tonight. She could feel it in her bones.

After the circus finished for the night, things seemed business as usual. Mal went to the meal tent and tried to force some food down before returning to her caravan to wash and change into her all-black nightly escape-attempt outfit.

Muffled sounds outside snagged her attention. Creeping to the window, she pushed open the glass and listened with her superior cat senses. Murmured voices floated into her caravan from a distance away. She angled her ears, trying to get a sense of their location.

Salizar's tent, she realized. Some kind of hush-hush meeting was taking place. Once she made the connection, she could hear the unmistakable tone of Salizar's voice whispering commands to whoever was with him.

She was just about to creep over there and eavesdrop when she heard the tent flap open and bodies shuffle out. They headed toward the fairgrounds exit and slunk away into the night.

Where were they going? Had they found a new lead on Harrow and Raith's location?

Questions aside, Malaikah realized that now was the perfect time for her to sneak out. With her speed and agility, she could beat Salizar to the tavern (if that was indeed where he was heading) and warn Harrow and Raith. Or, if it came to it, stall them until Salizar showed up with whatever he needed to recapture Raith.

As for Ouro and his little gang, she'd just have to deal with them if she saw them and hope they didn't—

A knock sounded at her caravan door.

Malaikah spun around, scenting the air. She smelled nothing. Which didn't make sense because everyone smelled like *something*. Well, everyone, of course, except…

Snakes.

The Goddess-damned reptiles were the only ones with the ability to disguise their scent like that. She cursed. Ouro had been content to let her keep her secrets in their last interaction. Now he was knocking on her door.

"I know you're in there, Malaikah. I can smell you."

Oh, great. He smelled her. Good thing she'd showered earlier, and he was smelling her clean scent and not her post-performance sweat. She looked down at herself and cursed again. She was wearing a skintight, sleeveless black bodysuit and men's baggy trousers, which was hardly—

Why in the Goddess's name was she worried about what she was wearing? Shaking her head, she went to the door and threw it open.

Ouro was standing outside, leaning casually against the side of the caravan. "Good evening." One corner of his mouth curved up. "Let me in. We need to talk."

He was bigger than she remembered, and the combination of his patterned skin and jewel-green vertical-slitted eyes was striking. His long leather jacket hung open, the hilt of a dagger poking out from a sheath on one hip, but his hands hung loosely at his sides.

He was trying not to look threatening, she realized, and almost laughed. She ought to tell him not to bother. He couldn't pull off nonthreatening to save his life.

Ouro stepped into the confines of her tiny caravan and closed the door behind him. Turning back, he blatantly bolted it shut, giving her a look that dared her to challenge him.

That's not creepy at all. With a resigned sigh, Malaikah gestured to the table, indicating for him to sit. No point fighting this.

Just like Salizar had the other night, the oversized

Elemental male took a seat at her tiny table, practically filling her entire caravan. Long legs stretching to the side, he crossed his booted feet at the ankles, making himself right at home.

Strangely, the animosity she'd felt toward him the last time they'd met wasn't present. Maybe his attempts at being nonthreatening were working after all. "You want something to drink?" she heard herself ask. Inwardly, she rolled her eyes. Was she trying to pick up a lay or protect Harrow?

"Whisky?"

"Sure." She grabbed the bottle and two glasses from the shelf above the stove and then slid them across the table. He caught them and poured two, handing one to Malaikah as she sat across from him. Her caravan was way too small, and he was way too big. She downed her drink in one gulp.

He lifted a brow but topped her up without comment.

"So why are you here?" she said around the whisky's burn.

"You know why." He sipped his drink, eyes never leaving hers.

"Generally, I make it a rule not to ask questions I already know the answer to."

"It's important your Seer friend speaks to the Oracle. I'm here to make that happen."

Mal frowned. "In case you haven't noticed, Harrow's not here." There was no point hiding Harrow's identity—it was obvious the snake already knew everything. "What did you plan to achieve by coming here?"

He just sipped his whisky, face remaining carefully blank. "You'll see. Won't be long now."

"What is that supposed to mean?"

He sipped again.

"Fine. Say nothing." She refused to play his little game.

"But you do realize that with Salizar gone, tonight's the perfect night for me to sneak out and visit her. Who knows, maybe you could have managed to follow me. But you won't get to her if I'm waylaid here."

"I don't need to go after her."

"Why not?"

He sipped again.

Malaikah actually growled at him. "Why don't you just tell me what the fuck you're doing in my caravan so we can get on with it."

He smiled. "I do appreciate a direct woman."

Was he...flirting with her? She didn't know whether to be flattered or disturbed.

"I'm not buying it."

His smile widened, and there were those lethal fang tips again. She wondered if he was venomous. Not all snake Hybrids were, but this guy? It would surprise her if he wasn't.

"I mean you and the Seer no harm. As for the rest, just wait and see, like I said." He downed the rest of his whisky in one gulp and then stood suddenly.

Malaikah jumped up beside him. "You're leaving?"

"Not yet. But soon. Any minute now, actually. And you're coming with me."

She cocked a brow. "Yeah, that's not looking very likely. Unfortunately—"

And then she scented it.

Her words dried up, and she stared at him. "How did you...?"

All playfulness was gone from his expression. "Here's what's going to happen. When she knocks—"

"You bastard!" Forget his sexy fangs; Mal was going to kill him! "You knew she was coming here."

"Aye." He didn't even try to deny it. "And when she gets here, you're both coming with me."

"Over my dead body," Malaikah hissed, flexing her claws.

He eyed them with a raised brow but had the good grace to look a little wary. "I thought we were past this, Malaikah."

"You set me up to trap my best friend! I'd rather die than give her up. Or better yet, I'll just kill you instead."

"No one's dying. I told you I mean you no harm."

"And I'm supposed to just believe you."

"Doesn't matter to me if you do. Now listen. The Seer's going to knock on the door in under a minute." Mal scented the air and came to the same conclusion. The snake's nose was good, but then, that was no surprise. "When she does, you're going to let her in."

"Not happening."

He sighed. "Look, I really want to keep this civil, but I have a lot to do tonight, and I don't have time for this. Tell me you'll behave, or we'll have to do things the hard way."

Behave? *Yeah, right.* "Hard way it is, then." Malaikah launched at him, claws out and ready to tear some reptile flesh.

When they collided, he crashed backward into the bed but didn't go down. Instead, he caught her wrists again, using his strength to force her back. But the close confines worked to Malaikah's advantage this time.

Twisting and yanking, she clawed up the sleeves of his leather coat, drawing blood at his wrists. As he tugged her arms apart again, she lunged forward, teeth bared, and managed to get a grip on the soft skin between his shoulder and neck. She didn't hesitate to tear a chunk out of him.

He hissed like an angry reptile. Rather than throwing him off his game, however, the wound gave him an extra edge of viciousness. With his next shove, they stumbled backward, Malaikah's spine digging into the sharp angles of the stove, and then he did that same cursed move he'd done in the alley.

Yanking hard on one arm, he tugged her forward and she spun, her back slamming hard into his front. He caught her other arm and held her there, immobilized, lest the hold break her arms.

She cursed herself across the Territory and back for letting that work on her twice.

She tried to headbutt him like she had before, but he, at least, learned from his mistakes. This time, his skull was out of her reach. Still, she thrashed viciously. As a rule, holding a cat that did not want to be held was an impossible task. They were slippery, vicious creatures.

But then again, so were snakes.

The cold prick of fangs against her neck had her freezing instantly in place.

"You wouldn't," she hissed, not daring to move a muscle.

He said nothing, considering his teeth were at her neck and all.

She'd never been bitten by a snake before—or by anyone, for that matter. He had to be venomous, right? Either way, the risk was far too great for her to try calling his bluff.

If she was wrong... Some Hybrid venom was deadly enough to kill in minutes.

"You Goddess-forsaken fucking snake!" Her rage was immense, but her survival instinct was greater. She didn't move.

A knock sounded at the door. They both tensed.

"Malaikah!" It was Harrow's voice.

The fangs lifted from her neck. "Answer the door, Malaikah." His mouth was right beside her ear.

"I told you—I'd rather die. So why don't you go ahead and bite me?" She considered screaming out a warning to Harrow but knew that wouldn't help the situation any. Harrow would just come crashing into the caravan to save her.

"I have men waiting outside. Harrow's not getting away. Don't you want to greet your friend and make this easier for all of us?"

"Mal, it's me! Open the door."

"I'll kill you for this," Mal swore.

"No, you won't. Are you ready to cooperate?"

She growled. "Let me up. I'll do it. But if you hurt her…"

"No one's getting hurt, Malaikah."

"Says the guy with his fangs at my neck a second ago."

"I always carry the antivenom. I wouldn't have killed you. But I need you to cooperate with me tonight, and I will take whatever steps are necessary to ensure that. Now are you ready to answer the door?"

With a final growl, she nodded, and he released her. Spinning around, she stared into his creepy snake eyes. "If you're lying to me, I swear to the Goddess—"

"Answer the door, Malaikah."

With a curse, she shoved him out of the way and stormed to the door.

"Mal? Are you here?"

She quickly unbolted the latch, wondering what in the Shades was going on this Goddess-damned night. Harrow sounded fearful. Distraught, even.

If Raith had hurt her…walking nightmare or not, the bastard would pay.

• • •

Harrow had run out of the Underground as though she ran for her life. In her haste to escape the tavern, she'd left everything, even her cards and her mother's locket. The loss, on top of everything else, made her want to weep, but there was no way she was going back.

Though Malaikah's many turns had disoriented her on their way to the tavern, Harrow's inner senses had shown her the way back. The Water had risen cautiously, as if expecting her to slam it furiously back in its cage, but this time its advice was in accordance with what she wanted, so she allowed it to guide her. She took each turn with confidence as she came to it, knowing exactly which way to go.

At one point, she'd felt a sudden certainty that someone was coming in her direction that she didn't want to cross. Without questioning it, she chose a random detour to bypass the next few blocks. When she was certain the danger had passed, she headed back to the main road once more.

She didn't stop running until she'd crossed the fairgrounds and made it all the way to Mal's caravan. She leaped up the steps in one bound and pounded on the door. "Malaikah!"

Silence.

Or were those murmured voices coming from within? She pressed her ear to the door, but her heart was pounding so hard she couldn't hear anything else.

"Mal, it's me! Open the door."

Still nothing. No, she was certain there were voices inside. Who was in there? Darya had said to go straight back to the fairgrounds, where she'd be safe from the others hunting her. Who exactly was hunting her again? She couldn't remember. Or maybe she'd forgotten to ask.

But Darya had said the grounds were safe, and Harrow was well within them now. Maybe she was overreacting?

She couldn't gauge her actions normally—she was too overwhelmed by everything she'd learned tonight.

She just wanted to see her best friend, the only person in the world she really trusted. With tears in her eyes, she gave one last effort. "Mal? Are you here?"

The sound of the lock unbolting came instantly, and then Mal threw open the door.

They collided in a hug. "I was worried about you." Malaikah squeezed her so tightly she couldn't find the breath to respond. Harrow wished she'd squeeze tighter.

She pulled back. "Where's Raith?"

Suddenly, Harrow was back to choking on her breath. "Mal, he—he—" She was gasping, unable to get the air out.

"Oh, honey." Malaikah's eyes were full of sympathy. She already knew; Harrow could tell. But how?

She was about to ask when she saw a dark shadow moving inside the caravan behind Mal. "Good evening, Harrow," a male voice said, and then he stepped into the lantern light.

It was a reptile Hybrid, immediately obvious from his vertical-slitted eyes and the scale pattern on his skin. A snake, to be precise, judging by the lack of tail. He was so tall he nearly hit the roof, and the hilt of a blade jutting out from beneath his coat didn't exactly make her feel relaxed in his company.

All of Darya's warnings about the people hunting her came back in a rush, and her heart started to pound anew. She waited for her power to rise in defense.

Instead, she felt...encouragement. Expectancy. She frowned. "Who are you?"

"Name's Ouro. I'll explain more on the way."

"The way to where?"

"We've got a bit of a walk ahead of us. Best get going now."

"Where are we going?" Malaikah snapped, proving she wasn't any more excited about the strange visitor than Harrow was.

"I explained this already, Malaikah." They knew each other? This was getting weirder and weirder. "The Oracle wants to meet the Seer and the wraith."

Harrow stared at him. "How do you know...?"

"All will be explained shortly. I mean you no harm. I'm simply the messenger tonight." Ouro flashed a fanged grin.

Darya had told her to remain at the fairgrounds and wait for Salizar. She'd said nothing about going with a strange snake Hybrid to meet a mysterious Oracle. But if Harrow was in danger, then why wasn't her power rising? Goddess damn it, she was getting sick of the Water's conflicting reactions to everything.

She opened her mouth to refuse him but stopped. She'd been blatantly ignoring her power since the moment it had flared up in the dream with Darya. Sure, she had good reason, but of all the things Mellora had taught her, attunement with the Water was number one.

Always trust the Water, her mother had said. *It will show you where you need to go, even if you don't yet understand where that is. Never assume you know better than the primordial force. Instead, feel blessed you were chosen to have a connection with it. If you do, it will guide you rightly in all things.*

Yet how could she follow that advice when her power was still pushing at her to go to Raith and protect him? How could the Water want her to betray her family that way? It hurt, knowing the source of wisdom she was raised to trust infallibly was somehow no longer on her side, yet even then, she hesitated to ignore it.

"Look," Malaikah hissed, going into full defensive mode, "if Harrow doesn't want to visit your creepy Oracle, then nothing you do is going to make—"

"I'll go," Harrow announced.

Mal spun around. "What?"

"I'll go to meet the Oracle."

"Harrow, are you sure? I don't trust this snake."

Ouro chuckled.

"Neither do I. But I'm sure."

Mal searched Harrow's gaze carefully. There wasn't time to explain, but Harrow did her best to let her conviction show on her face. Malaikah knew her well enough to read the expression and nodded. "All right. If you're sure."

They left the circus grounds in silence, meeting up with a group of Ouro's men at the gate. No one tried to stop them. No one was even guarding the entrance. Harrow supposed Salizar had already gone off to recapture Raith.

Had they found him already? Was he hurt? Angry? Scared?

She pushed it from her mind. Whatever Raith felt was no longer her concern. Salizar would recapture him this night, and he'd be transported across the border into Darya's Territory. Justice for her mother's death would finally be served. Harrow could rest easy knowing one less of Furie's killing abominations roamed free.

So why did the thought make her want to throw up again?

"Any chance we can move faster than a snail's pace?" Ouro asked, interrupting her thoughts. "It's a bit of a walk to the portal." Harrow realized she'd been holding up the group and hurried onward.

"The what?" Malaikah asked, keeping close to her side.

The Hybrid just smiled. "You'll see."

CHAPTER EIGHTEEN

H arrow and Malaikah followed Ouro and his men through the belly of the Underground. After dozens of disorienting turns, they headed down a narrow alley, crooked stone walls on either side. The cobblestones were so uneven, the entire lane slanted to the left.

At the end, Ouro stopped outside a tiny, unassuming door.

They entered a large sitting room of faded glory. A single lantern provided the only light, but Harrow's eyes had adjusted, and she could see well enough. Velvet sofas were positioned around an empty stone fireplace. A crystal decanter of liquor sat on another table along the far wall, a group of glasses around it.

At the far end, an open doorway was covered by a beaded curtain. "Follow me," Ouro said, stooping to pass through. Harrow and Malaikah followed, and the rest of the men remained behind. As soon as they went through the curtain, the men seemed to relax, and Harrow heard the murmurs of casual speech and the clinking of crystal as they poured drinks from the decanter.

Then she forgot all about that as she became aware of her surroundings.

It made no sense. She'd seen the building from outside, and there was no way what was here could fit within. Not to mention, it was the middle of the night, yet when she looked up, she saw blue sky and clouds.

In the center of the room, a spiral staircase wound upward at least four stories. High enough that it was difficult to discern what was at the top. This was obviously what Ouro had meant by "portal." But surely it wasn't a *real* portal. Perhaps the Oracle was an Enchantress and had just enchanted the stairs to appear as such?

"Shall we?" Ouro gestured to the staircase.

Malaikah eyed it warily. "Uh, after you."

He shrugged and proceeded up the steps.

They climbed around the spirals for several minutes, finally reaching a door in the surrounding stone wall. Ouro raised a fist to knock but hesitated. "The Oracle can be a little…vague, and sometimes it's difficult to understand her. She sees the past, present, and future all at once. Or at least I think she does." He shrugged. "It's confusing."

"Like a Seer?" Harrow asked. Surely there wasn't another…?

"She's not a Seer." There went that sudden hope.

With that, Ouro knocked, and the door swung open.

A male Traveler stood on the other side, one of the rare and mysterious Ether Elementals, giving Harrow her first clue as to what this Oracle might be. Harrow had never met a Traveler before in her life. Not even Salizar's circus employed one.

Travelers generally lived in secret communities deep in

the Ethereal Forest and rarely interacted with the rest of society. Their inherent Ether magic gave them the ability to teleport as easily as another might walk to move around. They were known to flit about from place to place, jumping instantaneously for even short distances, and it could be extremely disconcerting for those unused to it.

This male was willowy and graceful, with long, silver hair and tattooed skin. Bowing, he spoke with an elegant voice. "Welcome. She will see you now."

He disappeared and reappeared instantly several feet away from where he had been, gesturing for them to enter. Mal and Harrow exchanged wide-eyed looks and stepped into another sitting room behind Ouro. It was similar to the room Harrow had visited in Darya's castle, but instead of fountains, it was all towering windows.

Beyond the considerable book collection, a gilded harp with a stool beside it was positioned by one of the windows. Violins and other stringed instruments hung on another wall. Traces of Ether magic lingered so strongly in the air, it made the hairs rise on the back of Harrow's neck.

The Traveler reappeared beside two sofas at the far end of the room, positioned around floor-to-ceiling windows, and motioned for them to sit with another bow. They followed Ouro's confident stride across the room, Harrow trying hard not to stare at the beautiful Traveler.

She peeked out the window instead, and her mouth fell open. Outside was...sky. Nothing but blue sky and clouds.

Either this was home to a very powerful Enchantress indeed, or they had, in fact, passed through a portal. Into the sky.

"Good evening."

Harrow spun around at the sound of another strange voice.

A woman stood there. Like the Traveler, her hair was silvery white, hanging straight to her waist. Her skin was a rich, earthy brown, and her stunning, pale-blue eyes seemed too large for her slender face.

She wore a long, gauzy dress with a scooped neckline. Dozens of silver bangles covered both wrists, and her ears were lined with rings to their pointed tips. Black tattoos of geometric designs covered every inch of her up to her chin.

In her hands, she held a crystal ball. The inside was full of smoke.

Harrow had never seen her before, but, as with Darya, she knew instantly who she was. This was no Traveler, nor even an Elemental.

Ouro's introduction was unnecessary, but he gave one anyway. "Harrow, Malaikah, this is Queen Nashira of the Ether, otherwise known as the Oracle."

The most elusive and mysterious of the five immortal Queens was right in front of them. Harrow could scarcely believe her eyes.

"We met yesterday," Nashira said, which made no sense.

Ouro shrugged as if this was normal behavior for the Ether Queen.

"Or at least I thought we did." Nashira cocked her head to the side. "Yesterday you were supposed to visit in the day, but you aren't here until tomorrow night, and I've gotten it all mixed up now."

"I found the Seer where you thought she'd be," Ouro said, "but I don't know where the wraith is. I thought we could ask her once we got her here. I didn't want her to sneak away again."

"Yesterday, we had more company. Tomorrow, he won't be able to make it. It's too late now." Nashira looked at

Harrow and Malaikah again as if just noticing them. Her eyes lit up. "Welcome, daughters of the Elements. Please, sit." She looked at the Traveler male who had greeted them at the door. "You may be excused, Remiel. Thank you."

"Your Majesty." Remiel bowed low and then disappeared into thin air.

Utterly overwhelmed by everything, Harrow and Mal obediently sat on one of the sofas, and Nashira and Ouro took the one across from them.

Nashira carefully set the smoky crystal ball in her lap and studied Harrow with a sorrowful gaze. "Where is the other half of your soul, child?"

Harrow suddenly couldn't speak around the lump in her throat.

"You had it, but you let it slip away, and it's too late to get it back. A shame. You can't enjoy the light without first embracing the darkness."

"I d-don't understand."

"Didn't you feel the balance? You must have felt the balance."

Harrow was about to say she didn't understand again, but the words got stuck because she feared she did. "I thought the darkness was evil," she tried weakly.

"Dark is not evil. It is deep. The Deep, you call it, yes? Depth is wisdom. Depth is quietude and acceptance." Nashira shook her head, silvery hair shimmering in the sunlight. "Where is your Deep, shallow one? Did you break the surface and get stuck in the light show? So pretty but so fleeting. And now it's too late."

"I'm sorry, I don't understand."

Ignoring her confusion, Nashira turned to Ouro. "We must retrieve him."

Ouro looked at Harrow. "Where is the wraith?"

"I— He—"

"What's going on here?" Malaikah interrupted. "You're all talking gibberish, and somebody needs to start explaining or Harrow and I are leaving."

"Where's the wraith?" Ouro asked again.

"I left him behind." Harrow's voice was hollow. "Salizar's got him."

"What?" Ouro stood suddenly, causing them all to jump. Well, all except Nashira, who was gazing blankly out the window.

"I— He's a wraith. He k-killed—"

"I know what he did." Ouro waved an impatient hand like it meant nothing. "Where is he?"

"I left him." Harrow wrung her hands together. Why did she suddenly feel so guilty? Raith was a killer. Her mother's killer. "Darya told me what he is. What he did."

Nashira swung her gaze around, suddenly lucid again. "I warned Darya that if she put too much water on the flames, she would extinguish the fire. Did she listen? Nooo." Clearly, lucid still meant cryptic.

"Where's the wraith, Harrow?" Ouro looked angry now.

"Darya told me Salizar was to bring him to her to be..." She swallowed. She couldn't say it. Bile rose in her throat. "I told her where to find him."

Malaikah jerked around on the sofa to stare at her. "You— What?"

"He's the one, Mal." Harrow was suddenly in a rush to justify her actions. "Darya told me. He killed them, Mal." The tears threatened to spill again.

"Salizar told me." Mal reached forward to clasp Harrow's hand. "I didn't want to believe him until I talked to you."

"Who's the one?" Nashira asked. "Who!"

"Raith is," Mal said impatiently.

"No, not him. Raith is brand new. Like a child in many ways." She winked mischievously at Harrow. "And yet decidedly not in others."

"But he's a *wraith*." Did Nashira not understand that?

"Irrelevant! Tell Ouro where to find Dark Half, and I'll explain, though it's too late now."

Confusion made Harrow's head pound, but she was equally curious to hear what Nashira had to say. What could it hurt to direct Ouro there? "I left him behind in our room at the tavern. But Salizar was already on his way there when I left. They're likely gone already."

"Which tavern?" Ouro asked.

"Your tavern," Malaikah said smugly.

Ouro scowled. "You were in my fucking tavern this whole time? And you led Salizar there? Bloody Shades."

Nashira chuckled. "Salizar was surprised at what he will find."

"I'll be back," Ouro said to her. "You'd best explain to them what's going on."

"Already done. We met yesterday, remember?"

"If you say so." He gave them a nod and then swept from the room.

"Why is Ouro helping you?" Mal asked Nashira.

"Ask him." She smiled brightly. "But he won't tell you."

"Why don't you tell me, then?"

"It's not my story to tell. But I suppose you should know. Long ago, an infant child was abandoned on—" She shook her head suddenly. "No, I changed my mind. I won't tell you."

Harrow wasn't interested in Ouro's life story or anything else except understanding what was going on. "What do you want with Raith?"

Nashira's vivid blue eyes snapped to her. "The question is, dear, what do *you* want with Raith? You've only half a soul, after all. Don't you feel incomplete? Haven't you always felt incomplete?"

Yes. Goddess, yes, she had. Except for five short days in a room at a tavern that she'd been telling herself over and over were a lie.

"Who wouldn't feel incomplete without half their soul?"

"What do you mean, half my soul?"

"You're only one half. The light half. It's all very nice, but it isn't much without the dark to balance it out."

"You're talking about Raith."

"Yes." Nashira clapped her hands. "Now you're getting it. You got it much faster yesterday. A shame it's too late. Now you have to wait for him to come to you."

"It doesn't matter," Harrow insisted. "If the other half of my soul is a killer, I don't want anything to do with him."

"We've been over this, Seer." Her voice was chastising yet patient, like she was speaking to a child. "Dark Half is precious and new. I do hope you've been protecting him. Such a vulnerable heart."

Harrow swallowed hard. More guilt surfaced, but she stuffed it down. "If he's 'new,' as you say, then what was he before, when he was killing innocent Seers?"

Suddenly, Nashira's entire demeanor changed. Her eyes became hard, her full mouth pressed into a flat line.

"Enslaved."

"W-what do you mean?"

Nashira's blue eyes grew distant once more. "He was held in forced servitude under the threat of unrelenting agony. Do you understand what that means?"

"Of course," Harrow said, but her voice wavered slightly.

"Really? Because it doesn't seem to me that you do."

"I know the wraiths are bound to Furie's will. Is that what you're saying?"

But Nashira was looking far away again, waving her hands. The crystal ball wobbled precariously in her lap. "Did anyone ask how you felt about this, my poor doves? No. They were too quick to judge, weren't they? Precious creatures, unloved and in the dark. I wish to see you freed from bondage."

"This is wild," Malaikah murmured, shaking her head as Nashira rambled on to her unseen audience.

"I think…" Harrow listened closely, comprehension dawning. "I think she's speaking to the wraiths."

Nashira's gaze snapped back. She pointed a finger at Harrow. "Ding-ding!"

"You're saying the wraiths are controlled by Furie. We know this."

"Did they enjoy being so, do you think? Did they want to serve her? No one ever asks what they think, because they're just mindless killers, right?"

"Wraiths are made of Furie's magic," Harrow insisted, "which is perverted because of her madness. They're evil creatures. Abominations. That's what Darya said."

But Nashira shook her head. "Fire magic is pure. As pure as Ether, Air, Water, and Earth. Fire is Fire, and naught can render it otherwise."

"But the wraiths…"

"Are no more evil than you are. Such silly ignorance from a child gifted with the Water. I had hoped for better. Yesterday you were far more understanding. Then again, yesterday, your soul was still complete. Today, it's too late."

"But they killed an entire group of Elementals," Harrow argued, refusing to accept this so readily.

"Enchained! Enfettered!" Nashira shouted, waving her hands again. The crystal ball wobbled. "Bound by evil!"

"They're cold. Unfeeling. They kill with deadly precision. That's not the work of an unwilling, innocent being."

The Ether Queen jabbed that finger in Harrow's direction again. "Where would your mind go if you were sealed in an inescapable prison and then forced to commit unspeakable acts? Protect yourself first, everyone says. What else to do but turn off the feelings? Otherwise, the pain is too great."

Harrow stared at her. "You're saying they're not evil. That they were just forced to act like it."

"Make no mistake," Nashira said, sounding the most lucid she had since the start of the conversation, "wraiths can be deadly, fearsome creatures. They will always be capable of violence. They will be quick to anger. They will be fierce fighters. But that is the Fire. The nature of that Element is lethal power. And, twisted by their brutal pasts, in this life and the one before, they have become even more deadly, though who could blame them after what they've suffered? We're all just trying to survive. Have mercy, child. Have great mercy."

Harrow went over her memories of Raith, remembering how he'd been confused when she'd told him he couldn't kill Salizar. The idea was incomprehensible to him at first.

But he'd listened, in the end.

He hadn't killed Salizar because he was willing to listen to Harrow, to learn new behaviors. He was open to change, capable of evolving, growing, understanding.

And she had turned around and betrayed him.

Her hand covered her mouth. "He killed my mother," she

said against her palm, desperate to rediscover the conviction that filled her before. "He was the one who killed my entire clan."

"And spared your life," Nashira added.

Harrow swallowed hard.

"A being with no free will, who'd never experienced the concept, who wasn't even aware of its existence, discovered it the very night he chose to spare the life of an innocent child. At great cost to himself. Do you know what Furie did to him when she discovered his defiance?"

Harrow shook her head, not certain she wanted to hear.

Nashira told her anyway. "She trapped him with his own vow so he was unable to escape. Then she made him burn over and over again. It was the same death he gave the Seers, only he could never die from it. You want him to pay for the deaths of your family? Well, he has. A thousand times over."

Harrow had started to shake. She wrapped her arms around herself.

"After several months of this, his essence was so weakened, he had become little more than a wisp of smoke. Darya struck at the perfect time. Capturing him was so easy—she all but trapped him beneath a glass as one might a spider on the wall. And what did Darya do?"

"No…" She couldn't hear this.

"Darya, too, tortured him again and again, trying to force him to embody so she could slay him. She forced him by dousing his Fire essence in Water, extinguishing his inner flame over and over."

"Dear Goddess," Malaikah said.

"But the poor creature was too weak to embody, and his fiery will was unbreakable anyway. He endured the torture for nine years."

Darya had told Harrow this same story from a very different perspective, glossing over the fact that the wraiths hadn't acted of their own volition and convincing Harrow their Fire magic was warped. She'd been more worried about Furie consolidating power, hadn't she? And she'd used Harrow's emotions to manipulate her.

Nashira went on in that cold, detached voice. "After a decade, Darya decided she needed a new tactic. Then came another forty years of trial and error. Endless experimentation until she finally devised a way to merge Fire and Water in perfect harmony, creating a corporeal form for a previously incorporeal creature."

How had Raith endured such torment without losing his mind completely? Perhaps he had, and his rebirth without memories had been his chance at a new life. Until Darya had forced him to relive his previous existence. Harrow swallowed hard against the bile rising in her throat.

Suddenly, it all became clear. Deep within her, the turbulent Water that had assailed her for hours suddenly calmed to glassy stillness in accordance with her new conviction.

Go to him, it said again. *Protect him.*

This time, she didn't fight it. It didn't matter what Raith had done in the past. He'd been tortured, coerced, and tortured again... She couldn't abandon him. How could she have betrayed him like that? He never would have done such a thing to her, no matter what crimes she'd committed.

By the Goddess, she was worse than Furie. At least Furie had avenged her lover with undying ferocity.

Harrow had stabbed hers in the back.

"What have I done?" she whispered in quiet horror.

But Nashira wasn't finished yet. "Of all the Elements, Fire and Water are the most conflicting. Merging them in perfect balance as Darya did? An impossible feat. Yet not so, for it occurred. Even more spectacular, created in part by Water magic, he came into existence with a powerful tie to the only other Water Elemental being in this world—you."

"H-half my soul." That was why her power rose when she was near him. Not because she was in danger. Because the Water in her was responding to the Water in Raith, reaching out to him, strengthening them both. Together, they were stronger.

"But it goes deeper than that. The Fire and Water Elements are restless from centuries of strife. The great Goddess responded to the imbalance. Two beings of opposing natures were brought into existence in the most conflicting scenarios. Is unconditional love and acceptance not the perfect way to heal the rift?"

"We're supposed to heal the rift? How? What do we do?"

"Oh, it's simple. You were already doing it, in fact, until you buggered it up so royally." Nashira shot her a glare. "Betrayal. Abandonment. Why, you're as bad as my sisters."

Harrow couldn't deny it.

"I have to find him." She suddenly didn't care about Furie or Darya's revenge or anything at all except Raith. In fact, she was disgusted she'd ever allowed herself to be caught up in it in the first place. She jumped to her feet, beseeching Nashira. "Please help me find him. I can't believe— I never should have—" She swallowed hard. "Please help me."

Nashira studied her carefully. "You have much to amend, child."

"I know."

"You were given a great gift, and you squandered it."

Tears obscured her sight. "I know. I just want to make it right."

Finally, Nashira nodded, her face softening. "If only you'd been here yesterday. This could have all been avoided. Now, it's too late."

"It can't be too late. I refuse to believe that."

Nashira stood suddenly, setting her crystal ball on the sofa and holding out a hand to Harrow. "Come. We'll visit the tavern."

Harrow took her hand while Nashira held out her other to Malaikah, who grasped it and stood. The Ether Queen's blue eyes started to glow, and the air crackled until it was hard to breathe. Suddenly, they were sucked away into oblivion.

Only to reappear in Harrow and Raith's room at the tavern.

"What was that?" Malaikah shrieked.

Harrow swayed on her feet, feeling a bit green. She knew Travelers could teleport, but only themselves, not others. But it made sense that Nashira, as Queen of the Ether, could—

Everything in the world ceased to matter when Harrow noticed the state of the bedroom.

The bedsheets were torn to shreds, the furniture upended or smashed completely. One window had been ripped from its frame and smashed into a thousand shards. Blood painted the walls.

Raith was gone.

Harrow swallowed her scream as the rest of the room came into focus. There were others there. Ouro was facing off with an imposingly tall male, the two staring each other down.

Salizar.

"Where is he?" Harrow shouted when she saw him, running over to grab Salizar's arm. Ouro's men were backing their boss, facing off with Salizar's people—circus workers Harrow knew, though most of them were bloodied and injured.

Loren appeared at her side, a rag held against a wound on his chest. "Harrow—"

She ignored him utterly and spoke again to Salizar, finally pulling his attention from Ouro. "Where is he?"

Salizar's eyes widened when he noticed her. He was likely wondering how she'd suddenly materialized in the middle of the room, and under normal circumstances, she would have understood his confusion. At the moment, however, it was the furthest thing from her mind.

"How did you—"

"Where is he?" Harrow repeated desperately.

But his eyes had traveled past Harrow to the woman behind her, and, if possible, they widened farther. "Who— Is that who I think it is?"

"Good afternoon, Salizar," Nashira said, though the sky in the window behind her was pitch-black. "You're late. Or you will be."

"Late for what?"

The Ether Queen nodded contemplatively. "For you, yesterday was too early to understand. Today will work perfectly."

Ouro was grinning, obviously enjoying Salizar's bafflement. "Salizar, meet the Oracle, otherwise known as Queen Nashira."

"Where did Dark Half get to?" Nashira asked.

Salizar looked utterly lost.

"She wants to know where the wraith is," Ouro explained.

"He escaped."

"He escaped?" the snake Hybrid hissed.

"Escaped to where?" Harrow asked.

"I've no idea," Salizar replied. "When we arrived, he wasn't under the influence of the dream spell as Darya assured me he would be. He attacked and then fled through the window, but not before I stabbed him with an enchanted blade. The wound won't stop bleeding until it is cauterized with similarly enchanted steel. He'll have no choice but to return when he realizes it."

Harrow stifled a cry by covering her mouth.

"He's a wraith," Ouro said. "I doubt that'll slow him down much."

"He has a body that can bleed, and it will continue to do so until the enchantment is broken."

Desperate now, she searched the room for clues. The blood everywhere horrified her. How injured had Raith been? Judging by the state of Salizar's men, he'd given as good as he got. Her eyes caught on the little table that had somehow remained upright amid the chaos.

Her Seer cards sat atop it in a neat pile, save for one card lying faceup in front.

The Deep.

Her eyes filled with tears for the hundredth time that night. Raith had drawn it, she somehow knew. What had he felt when he pulled that card? Had he wished for Harrow's help in deciphering it? Why had she denied him when he asked her to do a reading for him? Now, she'd give anything for that privilege. Now, she'd give anything for the chance to beg for his forgiveness. If she even deserved to have it.

A warm palm landed on her shoulder, and she turned

to look into the Ether Queen's eerie blue eyes. "It's too late tomorrow," she said sweetly, as if her gibberish was comforting. "Now he has to come to you."

Oddly, it was. "How did you get us here?" Harrow asked, an idea forming.

"Ether transcends time and space. Or is it made of time and space?" She frowned. "Or was that only yesterday?"

"Do you know where Raith's gone? Can you take me to him?"

But Nashira shook her head. "It was too late. It will be too late. Now he has to come to you."

Will you stop saying that! Harrow inwardly screamed at her. "I refuse to believe that."

"Dark Half has spread his wings and flown from my sight. But not yours."

Harrow stared hard at her beautiful, strange face, desperate to understand. "How? How do I find him?"

"I'm not a Seer. No chance of that yesterday or tomorrow, or even one month ago. But you are."

Harrow became aware that the arguing in the background had ceased. Looking behind her, she found Ouro, Malaikah, Salizar, and everyone else watching. With some difficulty, she forced herself to ignore them, turning back to Nashira. "I don't even know where to begin searching for him."

"Where does one go when one has nothing left to live for?"

No! she wanted to shout. Raith had so much to live for. Goddess, this was all her fault. Hers and the infernal Queens'. Darya had played the wounded victim, trying to justify the awful things she'd done, and Harrow had fallen for it hook, line, and sinker.

Well, no more. From now on, she would listen to no one

but herself and her own Goddess-given instincts.

Shaking her head to clear the anger, she swore she would make this right. She would start by finding Raith.

"He went after Furie," Malaikah said.

They all looked at her. "How do you know?"

"Think about it. He loves Harrow. Then he finds out he's the one who killed her family and she's left him. If he's like Nashira described, he's going to feel awful. He'll want to avenge Harrow, but he's also not the type to lie down and surrender. He'll want to go out with a bang. I bet he figures if he can take Furie with him, then it's a job well done."

"Yesterday you were wrong!" Nashira exclaimed. "Today, you make sense. Tomorrow remains to be seen."

"She'll kill him," Harrow whispered in horror.

"Yes," Nashira agreed, though it hadn't been a statement of which she particularly wanted confirmation. "Today, tomorrow, or a hundred years ago, Furie will defeat him if he confronts her. It's definitely too late now."

CHAPTER NINETEEN

Raith had finally figured out what the enchantment was on the blade he'd stolen from Salizar. The wound in his side still hadn't stopped bleeding, though the rest of his injuries had faded in the long hours he'd been flying. The loss of blood was slowly sapping his strength, but it didn't matter.

He just had to make it long enough to fulfill his four-part checklist, and then it was inconsequential what happened to him.

He flew the rest of the night and half the following day before he finally found Castle Fera—Queen Furie's domain. The South was a desolate land. Mostly flat, covered with red sand dunes and the odd towering cliff face, there was little vegetation to be found and almost no water. Here and there, oases sprang up to nourish thirsty travelers, but beyond that, there was nothing but cracked, dry earth. Raith remembered waking up on that very earth with no idea who he was.

Now, he knew all too well.

When he looked at his hands, all he saw was the blood

that stained them. Corporeal or incorporeal, it didn't matter. What he had done... There was no coming back from it, no way to right his many wrongs, especially knowing what he'd done to the one person he valued above all others.

Before tonight, he would have said the one person he loved. Now, he didn't believe a being like him was capable of love. Those blissful days in the tavern with Harrow were a blessing he didn't deserve, and he would greedily cherish the memories until the moment he drew his last breath.

Which likely wouldn't be too long from now.

The wound in his side continued to bleed steadily, and he wasn't deluding himself into thinking he had a great chance of success in killing Furie. Yes, beheading would end her, but she knew this and would have protections in place. In the end, it didn't really matter.

Part of avenging Harrow meant meeting his own end. Possibly taking out Furie was just a bonus.

Within sight of Castle Fera, Raith found a small patch of dying shrubs at the top of a hill to hide behind and rest while he waited for nightfall. He wasn't a full wraith anymore— he was something else entirely, some new abomination that warranted no title—but he was still much stronger in the darkness and could cloak himself in shadows for camouflage.

He studied the castle from his vantage point. He remembered it all clearly now. Too clearly. The hill he was atop sloped steeply down to a moat that surrounded the outer curtain wall around the fortress. The moat had never held water, so perhaps it was best labeled as a pit. The bridge was down. It was never lifted. None would dare attack here.

Fire burned in countless torches atop the stone walls. At the center, the keep rose ominously, its turrets stained pink in the fading sunlight. A row of tiny windows glowed with firelight from the tallest tower—Furie's chambers. At the base of the keep were the dungeons Raith had spent months in, and halfway to the top was the Room of Jars—the place where the wraiths were kept.

Furie had created a hundred of them. One by one, she'd formed them from her magic and bound them with her hatred. It had taken centuries before she'd been ready to strike against Darya.

Years were spent perfecting the process of wording her orders, exacting precise vows, and experimenting to find the limits of a wraith's power. By the time Raith was made, she had finally struck the balance, and he'd been forced into playing Furie's pet assassin for decades until he'd finally been sent to kill Harrow's clan and everything had changed.

Every wraith hated Furie as much as they hated their cursed existence, but it was a futile emotion. Why waste energy on the absolute? They were powerless against her.

When the sky finally darkened to indigo, Raith spread his wings once more and launched into flight, still holding tight to Salizar's blade. He flew high into the cover of the clouds, circling the castle until he was positioned above where he wished to land. From there, he tucked his wings against his body and executed a sharp dive toward the earth.

As if shot like an arrow, he plummeted, wind whistling in his ears, freezing temperatures nipping at his bare skin. He remained clad in only a pair of loose trousers—the ones he'd worn to sleep beside Harrow the last time before everything had fallen apart. He'd taken such a simple act for granted, he realized now.

He had never been worthy of her, had been a fool to believe he could try to be. He was worse than unworthy.

He was her worst nightmare.

Raith shot straight down toward the bottom of the west wall, aiming at a row of windows so low, they were nearly underground. Seconds before he would have crashed into the stone, his wings flared, pumping hard, and he pulled up sharp. It was a flawless landing.

He might have been proud of his aerial abilities had he not been using skills he acquired as an incorporeal assassin. The last time he had swooped down like that, he had solidified a claw to tear open a Seer's throat as he shot past.

He landed in a crouch outside the specific window he'd been aiming for. There were others on the same level, but they were all lined with thick steel bars. Dungeon cells. The window he'd chosen was the only one without bars—they'd been destroyed by Darya on the night she captured him. She'd liberated him from Furie's wrath only to unleash her own special brand.

Stomach churning at the memories, Raith forced himself to climb through the narrow gap. He leaped down lightly into the cell, ignoring the slight trembling of his hands, and surveyed his surroundings.

Steel beams usually barred the outside hallway, but the door was open, still bent out of shape from Darya's damage. The ground was lined with old straw. Manacles hung from the stone beneath the window.

Raith had spent months chained to them.

How had Furie shackled an incorporeal creature? By forcing his vow. He gave it, and that easily, the chains had held him—he hadn't possessed the strength or motivation to fight his vow a second time.

What glaring need had he to save himself from pain? An innocent child had been worth the agony that ensued. He was not.

Again, the memories threatened to overwhelm him, but he forced himself to focus. He had not come to this dungeon to contemplate. He had a purpose—his four-part checklist.

Holding his dagger at the ready, he stepped out of the cell into the narrow passage and crept to the far end, searching in every cell for signs of life. He saw none. At least a dozen more identical prisons lined the hall, but they were all empty. Relief filled him.

Striking step one off the list, Raith focused on his next objective.

Heading back down the passage, he followed his memory and climbed the narrow stone staircase crawling around the inside of the tower. He didn't hesitate as he passed countless hallways and doors. He knew exactly where he was going.

Exiting the winding stairs, he found the hidden tunnel and followed the worn red carpet to the end. A small door waited, bolted shut. Beside it, a lit torch rested in a holder on the wall.

There, he hesitated. Fire in the torch did not necessarily mean someone was inside. Furie was the Queen of Fire, after all. It burned everywhere here. But it did make him pause, scenting the air and listening very carefully for signs of disturbance.

He heard and smelled nothing, so he unbolted the handle and pushed the door ajar. There was no lock. Furie needed none. The tunnel was hidden to all who didn't already know it was there, and no one would dare intrude and risk her fearsome retribution anyway.

No one but Raith.

Inside, more chills raced over his body than even in the dungeon cell. It was pitch-black, but he knew where the torches were, and now that he understood his origins, he understood his strange ability to light fires. He used it now, and the two beside the door flared to life, illuminating the room in a dim glow.

Heart hammering in his chest, he took in his familiar surroundings. The front of the room was empty, the floor singed black by countless Fire traps burned upon it. Behind it, long shelves lined the back wall.

Upon them...were jars.

One hundred jars, to be precise.

Within each jar was a black, smoky shadow, a lid securely fastened to the top. Feeling sick to his stomach, Raith crossed the open part of the room, heading toward a particular shelf and a particular jar.

The top shelf, far left, thirteenth from the end...and there it was.

An empty jar. *His* empty jar.

He had been trapped there. When he wasn't forced into service by his hateful mistress, he had sat in that Goddess-damned jar, confined and isolated. Even if he had found a way to escape, Furie would have simply summoned him back. The very nature of his existence made him powerless against her.

Most of his life had been spent in that tiny glass enclosure, and for what?

Whenever the Fire Queen was ready to release him, she opened his jar and trapped him within a cage of impenetrable magic. She used her magic to force him to vow to commit whatever unspeakable act she wanted done before unleashing him upon the world to obey. When he returned, she forced him back into the jar, securing the lid tightly and placing it back on the shelf.

That was it. That was all he had ever done, all he had

ever achieved.

Imprisonment, mindless obedience, violence. Repeat.

He hated his life. He hated Furie for forcing him to exist and then making that existence worse than whatever oblivion he'd come from. He hated that ninety-nine other beings had lived lives as miserable as his. He hated that they were stuck here even now, at the mercy of one cruel woman with too much power. He hated the injustice of it all, hated his powerlessness, his utter futility. He hated the pain and agony he had caused untold innocents.

With a roar, he struck with the dagger, swiping several jars off the wall. They fell and smashed upon the floor in a great explosion, glass shards flying everywhere as the shadowy beings within braced themselves for whatever fresh horror was surely upon them.

They hung in the air like deathly clouds, and Raith saw their fiery eyes gazing at him in bewilderment. They were like ghosts, but their forms were distinguishable. Shadowy bodies, with pupils of fire and white fangs. Sharp claws and talon-tipped wings. Just like him.

"Go," he told them, using his voice of his own free will. "You're free to go."

Comprehension dawned. They didn't hesitate—within seconds, the wraiths were gone, dissolving into thin air.

Was it smart to release the deadliest creatures in creation? Probably not, but Raith had once been one of those creatures, and he understood their nature. When not forcibly bound to the physical plane, the incorporeal entities generally wanted nothing more than to disappear, dwelling in an unseen realm they called the Void. They were not of this world, and it held little interest to them.

Raith systematically smashed every jar in the room, one

after the next, knocking them from the shelves until there were no more. When he was done, he sank to the floor amid the destruction and buried his face in his hands.

There was no hiding the trembling now, and he didn't try to.

Two of his four objectives had been achieved — check the dungeons, free the wraiths. The third he would likely not succeed in, but it wasn't going to stop him from trying.

The end was finally near.

He thought of those five short days of happiness he'd found with Harrow. He remembered lying in bed with her, stroking her hair. Hearing her laugh. Making love to her. The softness that filled her silver eyes when she looked at him.

His chest ached like he was burning alive, but he took solace in the fact that he was doing this for her. This was the only way he could help her heal the wounds he'd given her.

Raith picked up his blade and his still-bleeding body from the floor and went to hunt down the Fire Queen.

"You have to take me to him," Harrow begged Nashira, all but shaking her by the slender shoulders. "Please."

But the Ether Queen remained impassive. "It's already too late. It will be too late. It was too late. Now he has to come to you."

"I'll die before I sit back and wait for that. Furie could kill him!"

"Yes, she could. She might. She may!"

"Then help me. You brought us here from wherever we were — I know you could find him, and I know you could take me there."

"That's plausible."

"Then please, help me!" Harrow was bordering on frenzied now. Still in her and Raith's bedroom, she and Nashira were surrounded by Salizar and half the circus laborers, Ouro and his gang, and Malaikah, all witnessing her undignified collapse.

She didn't care in the least. She only cared about finding Raith.

"You got us this far. You told me how wrong I was about Raith. Now I want to stop him from getting killed, and you won't help. Why?"

"It's too late," Nashira said yet again. "Will be too late. Was too late. Now he has to come to you!"

"He can't come to me if he's dead!"

"It's too late! Will be too late! Was too l—"

"For the love of the Goddess, *will you stop saying that*!"

"Harrow, honey, maybe we'd better go." Malaikah's hand landed gently on her shoulder.

"No." She was sobbing now. "No, I have to find him. I have to find him!"

"I'm not saying give up. I'm saying that maybe there's another way."

"What other way? She can take me directly to him. What better way is there than that?"

"But she's not going to, Harrow. Take a second and think about it. She's not budging."

Harrow did, gulping air into her aching chest, forcing her head to work through the panic. She met Nashira's blue gaze again. The Ether Queen appeared calm, almost peaceful, as if she had some secret assurance about the future that she wasn't willing to share. Or maybe she didn't care either way.

Beside her, Ouro was running a hand over his skull,

looking uncomfortable. At the far side of the room, Salizar paced while the circus workers rested on the floor. A few of the more seriously wounded had left already, including Loren, escorted by one of Ouro's men to the nearest healing facility.

"How are you so calm?" Harrow snapped at Nashira, not caring in the least that she was being rude to one of the oldest, most powerful beings in the world. "Doesn't it bother you at all that an innocent man is about to be killed?"

Nashira nodded excitedly. "Yes, yes, I'm being terribly coldhearted about all this, don't you think? Best forget about me and take matters into your own hands. It's the only way to get results these days. Folks are becoming so unreliable in modern times."

"Fine. If you refuse to help me, then I will." Harrow spun around and grabbed Malaikah's hand. "Come on, Mal. We're leaving."

She stormed to the door with Malaikah in tow but stopped suddenly. Dropping Mal's hand, she went back to the table and scooped up her Seer cards. Then she grabbed the bag with her scrying bowl, Seer herbs, and jewelry box containing her mother's necklace, and snatched her cloak off the back of the chair.

A week ago, she'd been in a panic over what to pack. Now she knew she'd taken everything of value she owned. Leaving the rest meant nothing.

She went back to Malaikah and threw open the door. Before leaving, she said to the room, "I'll be back at my caravan if any of you decide to help me. But not for long. As soon as I figure out the fastest way to get to Raith, I'm leaving."

Without another word, she strode from the room, Malaikah at her side.

CHAPTER TWENTY

Back on the circus grounds once more, Harrow threw open the door to her caravan—a home she thought she'd said goodbye to forever. Less than a week later, she was back. How had things gone so impossibly wrong?

Because you threw it all away, a hateful inner voice whispered. *Because you couldn't believe in the happiness you'd been given and had to destroy it as quickly as possible.*

"Shut up," Harrow hissed. "I will make this right."

"I didn't say anything," Malaikah said warily, closing the door behind her.

"Not you. Me."

"Right." Poor Malaikah looked slightly afraid of her, but Harrow didn't have time to care. "What's your plan, Seer?"

"I'm going to use my power for its actual purpose for once and figure out where Raith is and how best to get to him."

"Well, he's probably at Castle Fera, no?"

"Yes, I know," Harrow snapped, inwardly wincing at her

rudeness. "But it will take ages to get there. We need to make sure there isn't a better plan."

"Well, look at you." Malaikah perched on the edge of the bed, tail flicking behind her. "I thought you'd lost your marbles back there, but that actually makes sense."

Harrow sat at her tiny writing desk, placing her cards in a neat pile and setting the heavy bag down at her feet. "Nashira may be eccentric, but I think there's truth to what she was saying. And she kept telling me it was too late to go after Raith and that I had to wait for him to come to me."

"So you're actually going to just sit here and wait? That did not seem like what you were planning when we stormed out of that tavern."

"No, I'm not going to just sit here and wait. But I am going to try to understand what Nashira was saying and where Raith is likely to end up. If I can predict his movements, we can be sure to be there to intercept him."

"What if Furie kills him as soon as he arrives?"

Harrow twisted in her chair to glare at Malaikah. "That's not going to happen."

"How do you know?"

"Because it's not!"

"Okay, okay, you're right. I'm sorry."

Harrow sighed suddenly, leaning forward to bury her face in her hands. "No, I'm sorry. I'm being horrible to you, and all you're doing is trying to help me."

"No harm done. You lost the love of your life, and you need to get him back. It's a lot of pressure for anyone. But hey." Malaikah stood and leaned over the desk, pulling Harrow's hands from her face and taking them into her own. Their eyes met. "If anyone can save him, it's you. I know you can do this. Okay?"

Harrow swallowed hard. Nodded. "Okay. Thanks, Mal."

"You got it. Now let's get this reading started. What do you need me to do?"

She snapped into focus. Though she had kept up her daily scrying ritual her entire life, it had been many years since she'd been anything more than a fortune teller, and she had to dig deep into the well of memory to remember what to do.

Scrying for specific knowledge was different than just reaching out to the Water to strengthen the connection as she usually did, and it took a lot more focus. Releasing Mal's hands, she gripped her mother's necklace, silently begging Mellora to help her. Inside the locket, the shard of crystal seemed to throb with reassurance.

"I need my scrying bowl filled with fresh water," Harrow announced with newfound confidence. "I need my bag of vision herbs, a charcoal tablet, and some matches."

"Where is that stuff?"

"It's here." She lifted the heavy bag onto the desk and started pulling out the required supplies. "I can honestly say I didn't expect to be doing this type of magic again."

"Why not?" Malaikah gave her a pointed look. "It's who you are."

"It could also get me killed."

"Not if you've got your wraith watching your back." When Harrow's eyes filled with tears yet again, Malaikah grabbed her hand and pulled her to her feet. "So let's get him back, yeah?"

A few minutes later, the supplies were gathered and positioned on the desk. The caravan was dark save for a few candles, and the heavy scent of smoking herbs filled the room with a haze. In a small silver dish, a charcoal tablet burned steadily, the vision herbs smoking atop it.

Malaikah sat cross-legged on the bed, tail curled around her. At the desk, Harrow wrapped her hands around the scrying bowl. In the still water, her reflection stared back at her. Her eyes were haunted, full of regret and pain.

She exhaled and took a deep breath of the smoking herbs, allowing their effects to take hold and draw her deeper into the trance. The Water stirred in the depths of her soul in a way she hadn't felt since she was a child, since her beautiful mother had sat her down and shown her what it meant to be a Seer. Staring into the scrying bowl, she let her vision unfocus, her mind quiet, and her thoughts drift.

The Water rose within and took her down like a great tidal wave crashing overhead.

Instead of being transported into a vision as she expected, however, she found herself standing in Darya's library. She looked around in confusion. How had she ended up here?

Darya emerged from a door in the wall and rushed toward Harrow, silky black curls streaming behind her. "There you are. I thought you'd never come." Her arms were out like she meant to embrace her—

Harrow stepped back. "Why am I here?"

"Because I brought you here." She was still reaching out. "I just needed you to stretch your magic a little to complete the connection, and you did. I'm so happy you came to me—"

"I didn't come to you," Harrow said coldly. "I was trying to find Raith."

Her arms dropped to her sides. "What?"

"I was trying to find Raith." Harrow's voice went flat. "After I betrayed him, he escaped. I realized my horrible, unforgivable mistake, and I'm trying to get him back."

When Harrow expected Darya's argument, she was surprised to see her sigh tiredly instead. "Nashira just paid me a visit."

"She did?"

"Yes, she did. She explained everything. Specifically, about your wraith and who he is to you."

Harrow narrowed her eyes.

Darya turned to stare out the window into the darkness. "You need to understand. I was once rich beyond measure in the blessings of those I considered my own. Now I am alone. I've outlived every one of my children—a mother's worst nightmare. All except you. The idea of something happening to you haunts me."

"So you wanted to kill the man I love," Harrow said dully.

"No, I— Yes, I did. But only because I didn't understand." Her silver eyes were beseeching. "Harrow, I swear to you, I didn't know. How was I to know his true nature and what he had become? I was so consumed by my grief and fear for your future, I didn't consider that this could be something greater than a simple vendetta between sisters. And, though I wish I'd broken the news to you differently, you needed to know the truth. Even if you chose to love him still, you needed to understand the connection between you and why it is there. I'm sorry if it seems like I intentionally manipulated you."

"A simple vendetta between sisters?" Harrow couldn't believe her ears. "Do you know what this *simple* vendetta has cost? The Territories have been at war for centuries, and my people are dead! If you really saw yourself as our mother, you would have found a way to stop this long ago, before I became the only survivor. My family and my real mother are gone because of you. Because of what *you* did. You started this."

Darya had the grace to look ashamed.

"And it didn't *seem* like you manipulated me," Harrow

continued, her anger pouring out freely now, "you did manipulate me. You knew exactly what to say to make me doubt myself, and you used me as a tool to achieve your own selfish aims. Which is all you've ever done, I see now."

Darya's mouth opened as if to retort, and Harrow readied herself for an argument. She almost wanted it to happen; she needed to vent some of the helpless rage that filled her whenever she thought of her clan's deaths and the pointless, never-ending war—and now, Raith's tragic history.

But the Water Queen closed her mouth again and then took a deep breath for composure. "You are right, Harrow," she finally said. "I have been selfish, and I did use you, which I regret immensely. My feud with Furie has hurt those I loved and those I was supposed to protect more than anyone else. It is time to make things right, beginning with an apology." Darya looked her in the eye. "I am sorry I manipulated you."

"And I'm sorry I was weak-willed enough to believe you," Harrow said quietly. "I'm sorry I didn't trust in myself and my connection to the Water enough to realize I'd been manipulated. I'm sorry I didn't choose to trust the man who'd done nothing but protect me over the word of someone who would torture an innocent being for fifty years. I'll have to live with that shame for the rest of my life, but let it never be said that I don't learn from my mistakes."

Darya smiled ingratiatingly, the relief plain on her face. "Of course you do, child, and I'm so proud of who you've become. If your mother was alive, she would be too. And I encourage you to deepen that connection with the Water. I should've been there to teach you, but I thought you were better off without me in your life. I realize now that was a mistake. I should have been there to guide you. Maybe if I'd gotten to know you better, I would've been able to see past my grief and spare you this pain. It's too late to change the past now, but I can still try to influence the future."

"If you want to influence my future, let me go back to scrying for Raith," Harrow said impatiently. "I think he's gone to Furie's castle to try to kill her, and I need to figure out what's going to happen so I can stop him. Every second I spend here is a second wasted."

Darya blanched. "He's going to try to kill her?"

"That's what Malaikah thinks, and I believe she's right."

"But he won't be able to."

"How do you know? Raith is strong. If anyone can do it, it's him."

But Darya shook her head. "Furie is the most paranoid woman this world has ever known. She lives in constant expectancy of attack, though not a soul has dared set foot in her castle in centuries. She uses her wraiths as servants, since her human staff long ago fled her domain, and she's constantly surrounded by powerful magic. Even alone in her chambers, she keeps a shield of Fire around her, so thick it would burn alive any who touched her. Besides, our powers are very great. The chances of an Elemental being able to hurt us are low."

But the opposite certainly isn't true, Harrow thought bitterly.

She stared at Darya, dread consuming her. "So what do I do? How can I stop him from going after her?"

"Nashira won't take you there?"

"No." Harrow gripped her hair in frustration. "I begged her over and over, and she refused. I don't understand why, since she was the one who explained everything to me in the first place."

Darya didn't look surprised, however. "Nashira sees

things differently than you or I. What seems logical now may not be so in the future, and her magic goes against the natural order in many ways. Her direct intervention often has adverse effects. Perhaps she's seen things play out a certain way and knows that without her interference, it will turn out for the better."

A tiny ray of hope sparked within. "So that means Raith won't be killed, then, right?"

"Unfortunately, we can't make that assumption." To her credit, Darya looked innocently sympathetic. Harrow wasn't that trusting anymore, though. She needed Darya's help now, but she wasn't naive enough to believe the Water Queen wouldn't turn around and try to kill Raith as soon as she got her hands on him again.

But right now, Harrow didn't care about Nashira's choices or Darya's supposed turnaround. She just cared about Raith. "So what do I do? I have to go after him."

"Return to your scrying. I'll join you as well, and we can merge our magics for a clearer result. Your line of thinking was good—perhaps in the present we can't be of much use, but we can influence the future by gaining knowledge of it now."

She wanted to scream in frustration. "But there *is* no future for Raith if Furie kills him."

"The drop of a stone in the ocean can create a ripple that washes the shores of another land. You can't know that we can't influence the future from here if we don't try."

Raith flew to the top of the tallest tower and landed noiselessly on the windowsill. Peering through the glass to the room within, he was afforded a perfect view of his target. It was all so simple.

There was Furie, kneeling before a roaring fire in the hearth. The rest of the room was dark, but the fire was so great, flames licked up the outside of the stone chimney and around the sides.

Red hair tumbling down her back, a blood-red gown pooling at her feet, Furie stared into the flames, muttering to herself.

With careful claws, Raith eased the glass open and climbed quietly inside the room, freezing in place, certain she would sense him. Black spots peppered his sight—the wound in his side continued to bleed steadily, and the blood loss was taking its toll.

Barely daring to breathe, he raised his blade and approached. He was a physical entity now, but he embodied the wraith he'd been in every other way. His every footstep was silence itself, his skin the shade of the blackest shadows, the talons at the tips of his wings poised and ready to strike.

He crept across the room, choosing each step with precision so no floorboard creaked. Passing the sitting area, he stepped onto a large rug. There, he hesitated.

Two more steps and he would be within striking distance.

Raith was an assassin, not a storybook villain. He was not going to approach Furie, put his blade at her throat, and then stop to speak a lengthy discourse. When he took those final steps, he would swing the dagger instantly, giving her no chance to engage her defenses.

So why was he hesitating now?

Curiosity ate at him. Furie's nonsensical whispering was audible from where he stood, and he tried to make sense of it.

"My love..." Her voice shook as she rocked gently back and forth. "You're so beautiful, so strong and fierce. My everything."

Peering around her shoulder at the fire, Raith saw the object of her attention.

Images flashed in the flames, created by Fire magic. Images of a man. A warrior, with leather armor and a heavy broadsword, swinging it mercilessly in the throes of battle, roaring cries of victory. His skin was desert bronze. A thick black braid fell down his broad back. A jagged scar cut across his face, over one dark eye and down to his lip. He wore no helmet, and his arms were bare, powerful ridges of muscle rippling with strength as he wielded the sword like an extension of his arm.

The scene changed.

The same man was standing in a tent, unbuckling his armor, staring into the eyes of the viewer. He tossed the breastplate aside and tackled the viewer onto the bed with laughter in his eyes...

The image changed again.

He was in a bed. The viewer's arms were out, tracing the defined ridges of his pectoral muscles while he looked on with a ravenous gaze. Feminine hands smoothed over his strong body with obvious adoration. They were Furie's hands, Raith realized, recognizing the rings upon her fingers, and suddenly, it became clear.

These were Furie's memories of her human lover, Ferron the Conqueror, the great warrior — the one Darya had killed long ago. The one whose death Furie had created the wraiths to avenge.

The reason the Seer line had been obliterated.

"You're so beautiful, my love," Furie cooed at the fire. In

the memory, she was kissing her lover's chest, working her way slowly down his body.

It was...pathetic.

The entire scene was so pathetic, Raith nearly turned and fled out the window the way he'd come. The powerful, immortal Queen sat alone and unloved in her tower, reliving ancient memories of her lost mate.

Worse, Raith knew exactly how she felt. It was how he felt.

If he had the power to conjure images of Harrow in the flames, he might have flown to a high tower somewhere and done exactly that. And he doubted his ability to ever recover from losing her, either. If Harrow was killed, the vengeance he would unleash upon the world would make Furie's brutality look tame.

He...understood her. He related to her. He even sympathized with her.

But he was still going to kill her.

She'd wrought far too much damage for him not to take this chance. Maybe her death would take her to wherever her lover was now, maybe not. It didn't matter, in the end, because he wasn't going to pass up this opportunity. Furie, alone, undefended, oblivious to her surroundings—there might never be a chance like this again.

He would do it for Harrow.

Fingers tightening around the dagger's hilt, he lifted it high and took one step forward. Furie rocked back and forth, mumbling at the flames. He took another step. Still, she rocked.

He swung the blade.

His aim was true, his strength immense. The blade whistled through the air to connect directly with the soft skin of her neck. It was a clean, powerful strike. It would have beheaded any other foe in an instant.

Instead, the steel melted.

The instant it touched her skin, the metal turned red-hot, softened, and then melted into a molten goo. He dropped it instinctively when the hilt started to melt his hands with it.

Furie didn't move immediately. For a second longer, she stared into the fire as if loath to leave the memories within. But the images faded as she withdrew her magic and seemed to shake herself back to the present. Drawing her skirts about her feet, she rose gracefully and turned around. For the first time in half a century, their eyes met.

She was, like all the Queens, impossibly beautiful. Her skin was a perfect alabaster, as flawless as porcelain. Her hair was deepest red, falling in glossy curls over full breasts. Her eyes were the blue of the center of a flame, her lips luscious red.

All that beauty disguised a volatile beast.

Raith could do nothing but stand there, awaiting his fate. He knew well what her magic could do and didn't delude himself into thinking he could escape her now. No, he'd had his chance already.

The assassin had taken his strike and failed. Now, he faced retribution.

Furie's blue eyes widened with recognition. "You."

Raith just stared at her. He wasn't fool enough not to be afraid. His heart thundered in his chest, and he flexed his claws to keep his hands from shaking.

He was afraid, but he wasn't a coward. He stared his death in the face, looking right into her eyes. Whatever happened, he would keep his eyes forward and his chin lifted. He would meet his death knowing it was the only noble path for a creature like him.

"You came back to kill me," Furie said.

Raith nodded. He would never speak in her presence unless she forced the words from his throat. And she couldn't now, he realized. The Water magic that helped create his physical form negated her absolute control.

"When I heard what Darya had managed to do, I could scarcely believe it. Yet here you stand. A brand-new Elemental. A perfect fusion of Fire and Water."

She stared at him like she was looking at a finely crafted object she desired to possess, the glint of covetousness in her eyes.

"You're so beautiful," she whispered.

Hearing those words on her lips moments after she'd said them to the dead man in the flames sickened him, but he allowed no outward reaction.

Then she sighed. "What a shame I have to destroy you."

CHAPTER TWENTY-ONE

Almost instantly, Raith started to burn.

It was all so familiar. He'd been stolen and transformed into another being, had his mind erased and his existence reborn…only to end up exactly where he'd started.

Burning alive at the Fire Queen's mercy.

But the pain's familiarity didn't make it any less intense. A cry was torn from his lips, and his knees buckled beneath him. The wound in his side became the equivalent of a tiny sliver as searing agony incinerated every inch of his being. It felt as though his skin was being flayed from his body while his internal organs were stabbed repeatedly with hot pokers. It felt as though his very soul was being boiled alive.

Through the haze, he saw Furie's beautiful, blank face staring down at him. Her head cocked slightly, and her bright blue gaze was inquisitive, like she was wondering with scientific curiosity what his suffering felt like.

"You were always one of my favorites, Thirteen."

Thirteen. That was his real name, his real legacy.

She laughed distantly. "My lucky number Thirteen."

That was all he'd ever been. The thirteenth wraith. The favored assassin.

His hopes of having a new life and identity were nothing but a cosmic joke. The truth had been there all along, plain as day—even in the name he'd chosen. *Raith*. From the beginning, he'd simply labeled himself as what he was, and he hadn't even known it.

"Your body isn't nearly as impervious to harm in your new condition." Furie's voice seemed to come from farther and farther away. Or maybe he was the one drifting? "A weakness rather easily exploited, don't you think? Ghostly wraiths are much stronger than flesh-embodied ones."

Raith had tuned her out after the first sentence, for it was then he realized…that feeling of being boiled alive while his skin was flayed off? It wasn't just a feeling any longer.

It was really happening.

His body was being incinerated. It said a lot for Darya's Water-enhanced embodiment that Furie hadn't just blown him to smithereens—he had seen it happen before. One touch, or even just an enraged shriek, and the enemy's body simply…exploded.

Raith, on the other hand, was lasting. He wasn't sure that was a good thing. A quick death was a mercy he didn't deserve but one he wished for anyway, though he'd never lower himself to beg for it.

"So you thought you could be free, did you, Thirteen? You poor, wretched thing. Oh, I saw it all in the flames. How you found the Seer you failed to kill and fell in love with her. How you were foolish enough to believe she could love you back."

Not Harrow, Raith wanted to beg. *Do anything to me, but*

don't torture me with thoughts of her. But he wouldn't beg for mercy he knew he wouldn't receive.

"Such a silly, naive creature. How could anyone love a monster like you? When she found out what you were, how you had slain her beloved mother and family, how you were my obedient assassin for centuries, she fled from you in terror, didn't she? She was horrified she had welcomed such a beast into her body. She fled back to her real protector, Salizar, and begged him to kill you."

It was all true. Raith wanted to howl with misery, but he kept his resolute silence. To not scream was the only dignity he had remaining, and he clung to it.

"Rejected by your beloved, you came back here to have your vengeance, is that it? To strike back at me for all the pain I've caused you? Or was it more selfless than that? Perhaps you came back to kill me to avenge your Seer. Perhaps you hoped she might forgive your crimes if you were successful. How romantic."

She paused for effect and whispered, "A pity you failed and will die here instead."

If she meant to frighten him, she failed in that. Raith could have cried with relief. She was finally going to end him. The agony would be over.

He could tell by the pain in his body, or lack thereof, that he hadn't much time left. Or much body left, for that matter. Most of him was numb now, probably melted or burned away. His vision was black around the edges. Soon it would be over. He allowed his consciousness to fade to a gentle wisp until he felt nothing but a soothing caress against the edges of his soul...

And he suddenly knew.

When he died, he wouldn't go to a shadowy void of

isolation in the blackest pits of the dark Shades. He would go somewhere peaceful beyond the Veil. He felt it there, just outside his reach, though he was now grasping at it with both hands. It was welcoming him. Reaching out for him as he reached out for it.

Tears of gratitude would have streamed from his eyes if he'd had eyes left to cry with. Surely a purely evil being couldn't find such peace? Surely this meant he wasn't evil after all?

With a final, grateful exhale of his shredded lungs, Raith relaxed into death.

"Or maybe," Furie said from a thousand miles away, "you're even nobler than I thought. Maybe you came here knowing full well you wouldn't succeed in killing me. Maybe you came because you knew that when you failed, I would kill you. Oh yes, you wanted to die, didn't you? This was all an epic gesture for your true love — sacrificing yourself to restore the balance. What better way to avenge your Seer than by killing the one responsible for her mother's death? Yourself."

She laughed, and it reverberated around his blissful haze like a wildfire sparking in a peaceful forest.

"You clever beast! You manipulated me! And by the Goddess, I nearly fell for it. I nearly gave you exactly what you wanted. Oh, this is too much."

No! Raith screamed mentally. *Finish me!* He was so close to the edge. Seconds from falling over it.

"Let me tell you something, Thirteen. Something you should already know from your years of service to me. I don't like being manipulated. And I punish those who try in the worst ways imaginable. So now, I've changed my mind. You will not be dying today. I have something much greater in store for you."

In an instant, the pain vanished, and with that, he finally broke.

If he could have, he would have begged for mercy. He would have pleaded for his own death. But he had no more strength left for begging, and no tongue left to speak with.

He had failed both his final tasks—Furie lived, and apparently, now so would he.

He could already imagine what she had in mind for him. Before, going to his death had seemed a dark sacrifice but a necessary one. Now, death would be a merciful gift—one he wouldn't be receiving.

Had he the strength, he might have laughed at the cruelty of the Goddess for saddling him with such a miserable existence. It seemed even his desire to die honorably would be denied him. For he knew with certainty:

What awaited him now was a fate worse than death.

R aith must have lost consciousness, because the next time he was aware, he opened his eyes—he could see again?— and recognized the inside of the Room of Jars. Whatever was left of his body lay paralyzed upon the floor in the center of the scorch marks, right where Furie used to trap him with Fire magic when he'd been a full wraith.

"You're awake," she said from somewhere, though he couldn't see her.

He saw above him and to the sides, as far as his eyes could travel, but he couldn't turn his head or move his body in any way.

"I thought you might die on me on our way down here, so

I had to heal you a little bit. Then I almost killed you again when I saw what you did to my wraiths." She chuckled. "Very bad, Thirteen. But it's no matter—I made them, and I can summon them back to me again. And perhaps one of your first tasks when I'm finished with you will be cleaning up all the glass in here. That'll take ages."

Finished with him? Raith didn't like the sound of that at all.

Why can't I just die? Never had a being wanted it more, he was certain.

"Darya did amazing work on you. I would never have thought it possible to do what she did." Furie strolled into his line of sight then, looking down at whatever mess was left of his body. "I've gone and ruined all that hard work, now, haven't I? A shame. But I have no use for you in a form I can't control. And, since Darya isn't here to claim you, I think I'll make you back into something that is useful to me."

Horror suffused him. Surely she wasn't saying what he thought she was? Surely that wasn't possible? Darya had made him a physical body and tied his spirit to it, effectively rebirthing him. Surely the process was irreversible? *Please let it be irreversible.*

If he'd even considered that the remotest possibility, he never would've flown within a hundred miles of the castle. But he'd dismissed it, thinking it impossible.

What a sad, sorry fool he'd been. In so many ways.

"I hope you enjoyed your little stint with a body, Thirteen, because it's time to go back to how I created you. 'That's impossible!' I can almost hear you thinking. I'm here to assure you, it is not. Darya overrode my magic with her own to create you, and I can do the same in reverse. It's just going to be a little uncomfortable."

A pause, and then...

Agony. Indescribable torture. Pain beyond measure, belief, or comprehension. Fire consumed every inch of him, down to his very soul.

Mercifully, he passed out.

While unconscious, he had a dream of sorts. He was swimming underwater in the quiet dark where no sunlight could penetrate. He felt peaceful, whole again. After the torture he'd endured, the feeling was such a relief that grateful tears poured freely down his face to merge with the oceanic depths.

He felt rather than heard a disturbance in the water above. Twisting around, he looked up, searching for the cause, and saw something moving toward him. A dark shape. It drew closer.

Hands. There were hands reaching out. Instinctively, he reached back. They were almost touching. So close...

Then he saw her. Harrow.

She was swimming toward him. Indescribable joy suffused him. He hadn't known it was possible to feel such happiness.

She reached for him, straining to grab his hand. He strained back, stretching his fingers, desperate for even just a single brush of skin. A certainty filled him that if he could touch her, he could go to her, and he needed to go to her. So badly, in fact, that his very life might depend upon it—

He never got the chance. The next instant, he regained consciousness in his new reality.

The ocean vanished, replaced by that familiar stone room.

Instantly, he recognized what he'd become. It was familiar, as familiar as slipping into a worn jacket or pair of shoes. It was more familiar than his old life had ever been, for he'd lived in this condition far longer.

His body was weightless. He could dissolve it into the ether or gather it into a dark shape at will. Neither state was more comfortable than the other. He could become any color he wished, camouflaging to any surrounding, turning invisible. He could also solidify himself completely for a short time, but the state of being solid brought with it glaring weaknesses.

How could he have ever wanted to remain permanently so?

In this spectral form, he was untouchable.

His emotions were dampened, a memory attached to the physical world he was no longer part of. As he floated, he felt a sense of lightness, of disconnect from everything, as though he was watching the world through a veil. Nothing seemed to matter, and why should it? Why bother caring about anything?

He was nearly invincible, free from bodily troubles, gifted with unimaginable power. He moved unseen in the night, cloaked in shadows, as silent as a whisper, as deadly as death itself.

"There you are," Furie cooed, and the wraith spun around to face her.

Hatred filled him at the sight of the sorceress who bound him, the only blight on his powerful existence. He was free in every way except for her.

If only he could kill her... But she'd prepared for this. He was surrounded by magical bars of flame on six sides—she was careful to cage him at his feet, too. If not, he would have sunk through the floor and come up behind her to slit her throat before she could blink. As it was, he was well and truly trapped.

A beatific smile adorned her flawless face. "Yes, you're much better like this, I think."

The wraith stared blankly, his hatred of her the only emotion to penetrate his smoky existence. And even that felt numb and far away.

"Now that I've restored you to your former glory, we have work to do. Since you freed all my other wraiths and I don't have time to fetch them back just yet, you'll have to do all their work combined. A suitable punishment for your insubordination, I think."

He pumped his wings lazily, awaiting instruction or a chance to escape.

"But before we begin, we need to take care of your earlier indiscretions. You made quite the mess, Thirteen. I've got not one but two of my sisters breathing down my neck, and a piteous group of Elementals coming to stir up trouble on your behalf, including one short-sighted Seer." She chuckled at her own cleverness.

Her humor abruptly died as she began to pace back and forth in front of him. He watched disinterestedly, his attention rapt on the cage he was trapped in. If her concentration lapsed for even the briefest instant, he would slip free and strike.

"That Seer has proven to be trouble. Oh, I've known about her all along, though the poor child probably thought she was hidden from me. I chose to let her live, thinking, 'What could it hurt to let Darya have one last daughter to dote upon?' But now she's gotten on my nerves, planning to come here and take my wraith for herself."

A flicker of recognition passed through the wraith. The Seer wanted him? Why? In his old life, she hated and feared him. What interest would she have in him?

He inwardly shrugged. It didn't matter. Life was fleeting. Death could strike at any moment.

"And Darya helping her?" Furie continued her tirade, waving her arms about for emphasis. "My sister has gone too far. I must retaliate before she believes I've gone soft. Before she forgets what it means to incur my wrath." She spun suddenly around to face him, a smile spreading across her face. Her eyes glinted with crazed anticipation. "You, my wraith, will remind her. Vow it."

The wraith narrowed his eyes in loathing. She would force his vow now. The humiliation of the act never ceased to incur his own wrath, but again—against her, he was powerless.

"Vow you will remind the world what it means to challenge me." The power stirred beneath her words, her blue eyes glowing from it. The Fire tugged at his essence, forcing him to obey.

"I vow I will remind the world what it means to challenge you." His disembodied voice echoed around the chamber. He loathed the sound of it nearly as much as he loathed her.

Furie's gaze lit with triumph. "You're truly back, my treasured one. I shall be very careful with your vows this time, putting extra power into them. There won't be any disobeying me again. Are you ready to hear your first task?"

His glare promised an excruciating death. His hatred of her burned deep.

"Vow to me you will find the Seer, wherever she lurks. You will not stop searching until you have found her. You will do nothing else but search for her."

The Fire scalded him until he was forced to say, "I vow I will find the Seer. I will not stop searching until I do. I will do nothing else but search for her."

"Vow to me that when you find the Seer, you will kill her."

Deep within, a part of him cried out in horror. He knew that but a few hours ago, he would have given anything in the world to avoid such a compulsion. Yet he could do nothing about it, so why waste energy fighting it? Still, he hesitated, though it cost him dearly. The agony was quick to strike, and he knew it would only worsen until he said it.

So he did.

"I vow to kill the Seer."

Furie's eyes glowed with power and the light of victory. "Vow to me that you will never stop trying to kill the Seer until you are successful."

The power behind the command hit him so hard, his essence briefly dissipated into smoke before reforming again. Again, the pain was excruciating. Quickly, he said, "I vow I will never stop trying to kill the Seer until I am successful."

"Vow you will never disobey your vows again."

Such a permanent promise was highly inadvisable, but again, there was nothing he could do about it. "I vow I will never disobey my vows again."

"Vow you will kill the Seer!" It sounded more like a battle cry than a queenly injunction.

"I vow to kill the Seer," the wraith repeated, feeling the binds tightening around him.

"Again."

"I vow to kill the Seer."

"Again!"

"I vow to kill the Seer."

Finally, it was done. His words were given, and his bondage was complete. Unnecessary now, the fiery cage dissipated, and he was free to go—unable to strike at the Queen now that he was committed to another objective.

Without hesitation—as per his vow not to rest or do

anything else—he shot instantly out of the room, through the walls, and into the night to find his prey.

His vow had been given. The Seer's fate was sealed.

CHAPTER TWENTY-TWO

Harrow tugged on Fiona's reins to slow her down—not that she needed to. Fiona's default pace was stationary. Getting her moving in the first place was by far the more difficult task.

As predicted, with the slightest tug, Fiona came to a grateful halt, and Harrow hopped down from the caravan's seat to pat her horse on the neck. As she went about taking off Fiona's harness and tethering her to a tree by the stream, she watched the moon rise.

Full tonight.

She'd traveled an entire day out of Allegra yet was still in the depths of the Ethereal Forest—the vast old-growth woods covering most of the Central Territory. It was later than advisable for setting up camp, but they had a lot of ground to cover, and Fiona wasn't exactly the world's fastest driving horse. Nor was Harrow the world's most skilled driver.

All her life, she'd had Salizar's laborers helping her out

with the horse-care aspect of caravan living. Now, she was all by her lonesome and figuring it out herself. She gave thanks hourly that Fiona was so easygoing—a feistier horse would have long since kicked her in the head for her clumsiness.

She was alone by choice, however, so she refused to utter a word of complaint. After Darya had released her from their conversation, she'd dived right back into the scrying bowl, coming back to the world an hour later with a burning need to take her horse and caravan and head south immediately.

So she had.

The Water had been very clear, and though she didn't understand it in the least, she'd learned her lesson well. From now on, no matter how confusing or nonsensical it seemed, she listened to the Water.

So Harrow had made a quick trip to the tavern for her bags, fetched Fiona from the stables, and rolled out of town amid hearty protests from both Salizar and Malaikah. So hearty, in fact, that she still didn't understand how she'd managed to shake Malaikah. She'd been certain Mal wouldn't give up and was still expecting to find her hiding beneath the bed or in the wardrobe.

With Fiona settled for the night, Harrow built a fire and sat close to it for warmth. The tall trunks of ancient cedars towered above her, creating a thick canopy that bordered the clearing's view of magnificent stars. The forest floor was covered with mossy logs and lush ferns. Nocturnal creatures chirped their lonely calls, but beyond that, the night was quiet. Still. Utterly peaceful.

Lying back on the soft ground, Harrow stared up at the sky. As an old habit, she used what she could see of the constellations through the trees to orient herself. With another pang in her heart—a sensation that was becoming too familiar of late—she remembered showing Raith how to find the Tidal Wave and navigate by it. Was he out there somewhere looking at the same stars, thinking of her as she was of him?

A shadow streaked briefly across the full moon's face.

Harrow tensed but quickly dismissed it, certain she was imagining things. But her heart rate had sped up, and her sudden nervousness had shattered the peace of the night. Though she told herself she was being silly, she held her breath and listened intently for sounds of disturbance.

She heard nothing but jolted upright a moment later regardless. The hairs on the back of her neck rose as her gaze darted around the clearing, searching for something. There was nothing to see, nothing to hear. Everything was still.

Too still, in fact.

The chirping insects had fallen silent. Not a single sound disturbed the quiet.

Her heart started to pound. From her seat on the moss, she twisted this way and that, searching the surrounding forest. Something was out there. Something ominous.

Fiona gave an anxious whinny from the darkness. Harrow's power stirred within, and she let it rise, gathering her defenses.

A sudden suspicion hit, and she gasped, jumping to her feet. Holding her breath, she peered harder into the dark, still seeing nothing. Now her pulse raced for a different reason.

"Raith?" she whispered into the silence.

A cold wind gusted past, lifting her hair.

"Raith, is that you?"

The ferns across the clearing ruffled suddenly, and Harrow jumped. Tamping down her fear, she forced herself to sound calm.

"Are you there? It's me, Harrow. I—" She swallowed hard. "I missed you." It felt wrong, exposing her vulnerabilities to the seemingly empty forest, but if he was truly there... "I'm so sorry, Raith. I should never have left you that night. I can't believe I hurt you that way. I should have trusted you, and I'm sorry."

Was he even there? Was she just imagining this entire scenario? Perhaps it was for that reason that she finally found the courage to say what she wished she'd said days ago.

"Raith, if you're even there, you should know... I love you. It sounds absurd, but I think I loved you from the moment we met, and I never stopped. Even when I left, I still loved you. I loved you then, and I love you now, no matter what happened in the past."

Silence. A breeze ruffled her hair again. Nothing moved; nothing changed. And yet she found herself holding her breath in expectation...

And then, there he was.

He seemed to materialize out of thin air, standing before her in all his wraithlike glory. His skin was deeper than shadows, his irises burning brighter than the fire beside them. Long claws curved from his fingertips, and his enormous wings rose high above him, half spread as if ready to launch into flight.

"Raith," Harrow breathed. He had never looked more terrifying than he did right then.

He had never looked more beautiful.

She ached to run to him, to throw herself into his arms and embrace him with all the longing that had been tearing her to pieces since she left him.

"You came back to me." She thought of Nashira's words

suddenly. *It's too late. Will be too late. Was too late. Now he has to come to you!* Was this what she meant? Could it really be that simple?

But Raith didn't move. His face was blank, devoid of emotion. He was so wrapped in shadows, his body almost didn't look solid. Goddess, he was terrifying.

But terrifying or not, this was the man Harrow loved, and she forced herself to take a step closer, though every instinct in her body screamed at her to run. Raith did nothing, didn't move, didn't even twitch. A trickle of unease ran down her spine.

"Raith?"

Nothing.

She took another step closer and lifted a hand. Reaching, reaching, she could almost touch him—

He jerked away.

Her hand dropped instantly. Of course he was distrustful of her. She had betrayed him. Was it even possible to make it right? Did she even deserve his forgiveness? "I'm so sorry for what I did, Raith. Betraying you was the worst decision I ever made. I should have believed you were different. I should have—"

"Don't come closer." His voice seemed deeper, strange. His eyes were wild.

"Okay." She swallowed back the tears. "I won't." But she wasn't giving up that easily. She tried a new approach instead. "I left Allegra to search for you. I thought I'd have to travel for days. How did you find me?"

A flicker passed over his features. Why did she suddenly have the impression he was in pain? Though it was impossible to see him clearly, he seemed rigid with tension, as if he was barely holding back from doing…something.

"For me?" he whispered.

"Yes, for you." She spoke quickly, encouraged by his reaction. "I was searching for you to tell you I was sorry, that I don't care what happened in the past, and that I love you."

His brow furrowed. "Love?"

"Yes, I love you, and I'm sorry I left. I was wrong. So, so wrong."

He said nothing.

"I know what happened to you—that you were forced to do those things against your will. I could never hate you for that. It's the opposite. I love y—"

"No!" he suddenly shouted, and she lurched back involuntarily. It was the first time she'd ever heard him raise his voice. It sounded strangely disembodied as it echoed around the clearing. "No!"

She raised both hands in a placating gesture. "I'm sorry I upset you. I just need you to know that I love y—"

"Stop!" he cried as if her words scalded him.

He dropped to his knees suddenly, gripping his head in his hands.

"Raith!" Unease forgotten, she rushed to his side, hovering over him. She was desperate to touch him but didn't dare ignore his vehement warning. "Raith, tell me what's wrong, please."

"Harrow…"

"What is it? Please tell me so I can help you."

"She…changed me."

"Who did? What did she do? Tell me what happened, Raith. We can get through this together. I'm not going anywhere this time, I swear it."

"Furie…"

A feeling of certain doom cascaded down her spine like

a frigid waterfall. "What happened?"

Crouching beside him, she reached out slowly. He didn't flinch this time, just remained hunched over with his head in his hands, gripping his hair with lethal claws. She was inches away from tracing her fingers along his shoulder, and when she finally made contact—

Her hand passed right through him.

With a gasp, she jerked back.

"No..."

This wasn't happening. She had imagined it. She reached out again. Again, her hand went right through his dark shape. She could see the ghostly outline of her own hand inside his smoky form. "No!"

Raith was a wraith once more.

"Did she do this to you? Did Furie do this?"

"Harrow..." He gripped his hair tighter, moaning as if in great agony.

"It's okay." The words for her benefit as much as his. "We'll figure this out together. Darya made you a body once, right? She can do it again. We'll be fine."

"Can't...fight it."

"Can't fight what? Are you in pain? What's wrong?"

"Vowed...not to fight it."

"You vowed?" She swallowed a lump of dread and tears and panic. "Did Furie force you?"

Through the tight grip on his head, he nodded.

Oh sweet Goddess, this was bad. This was the worst-case scenario, in fact. Raith had evidently gone back to Furie, and she had made him a wraith again and made him vow to...

To what?

"What did she make you vow to do?" Harrow whispered.

But suddenly, she was pretty sure she knew.

Raith moaned again. "Vowed not to fight my vows. Already broke one. Can't do it again."

"What do you have to do, Raith? Tell me."

Suddenly, his head snapped up. He went rigid with tension as his fire-ringed black eyes met hers. His fingers curled, claws sharpening to razor-sharp points before her very eyes.

"Kill you."

"Oh, Raith…" Right now, he almost seemed to be in some kind of trance—likely a result of the compulsion of his vow— but after the deed was done and Harrow was dead, he would snap back to reality. He would realize what he had done.

Her sweet, gentle Raith would never recover.

But what could she do? The Water had told her to come here. She'd been so sure of everything, so sure it would all work out. How could she have been so misguided? Or maybe the Water wanted her to die at Raith's hands? But what purpose would that serve?

She'd sworn to never doubt her instincts again, but this? It seemed she'd made a catastrophic error—one she had no clue how to extricate herself from.

Raith was going to try to kill her; she could see it in his eyes. He wasn't going to be able to fight it as he'd done when she was a child.

This time, Furie would force him to finish what he'd started.

"Oh, Raith," the Seer said, her silver eyes brimming with tears, the tiny crystalline droplets containing oceans of sadness and…compassion? But why would she feel compassion for the monster about to take her life?

He couldn't think through the haze. All he knew was the compulsion to fulfill his given word. He had already reneged on two vows—not to hesitate before killing her, and not to fight his vows—and was already battling the insanity-inducing agony as a result.

Why was he delaying? Even now, through the fiery torture, he still couldn't bring himself to act. Though his mind was numb, consumed with his objective, he still had the vague thought somewhere that killing her would be a terrible mistake.

It didn't matter. He couldn't fight it any longer. His broken vows were clawing into him, pushing him to act, blurring all coherent thought into one straight track—get the job done and be free from the compulsion.

He looked into those luminous silver eyes and studied those delicate features as if some part of him was memorizing them for the last time. Tears poured freely down her face, and she made no effort to stem them. The sadness and compassion were still there, but there was something else now...

Acceptance.

She had accepted her fate, yet she still felt compassion? He couldn't comprehend it—couldn't fight the pain long enough to try. He would think about it later when he was free again.

The wraith spread his wings wide and climbed to his feet.

One touch. One touch was all it would take to end her as he'd ended countless others before her.

"Whatever happens," the Seer whispered, looking up at him with those fathomless eyes as she climbed proudly to her feet, "I'll always love you."

The wraith tilted his head, certain this was important. But

he couldn't think, couldn't decipher why. Later, he would reflect. Now, he had to act.

Without a whisper of sound, he struck.

R aith lunged. Harrow screamed. She couldn't help it—whether she loved him or not, he was here to kill her, and she was scared.

She didn't want to die. She wanted to help Raith find his freedom. She wanted to go with Malaikah back to Kambu one day and help her retake her homeland. She wanted to learn more about her Seer roots and practice her craft. She wanted to *live*.

They collided, falling to the ground, Harrow landing hard on her back. Raith's enormous wings curved forward around his body, just the taloned tips solidifying. With lightning speed, he stabbed them deep into her shoulders to pin her to the ground. Another scream was torn from her lips as her blood began to flow.

She felt the razor-sharp tips of his claws at her throat. A flex of his fingers, and she would be dead.

But the wraith froze suddenly, head cocked in that feral way again.

He's hesitating! Harrow tried to think through the haze of pain. Maybe she could reach him. Deep down, he didn't want to hurt her. He was compelled by his vows, but her Raith was still in there somewhere.

"R-Raith." Her shoulders were soaked with the hot stickiness of her spilling blood. Where his talons pierced her skin, a pain like fire scalded her. "Fight it. I know you c-can."

Her teeth were chattering. From shock? Blood loss? Did it matter?

Still, he hesitated, and feeble hope began to rise in her chest. He was so shadowy, it was impossible to read his expression, but she swore she saw a tortured look in those fiery irises.

"Raith, fight this!"

His eyes narrowed. He was fighting. He was—

He shook his head roughly, face clearing. Blank again.

His claws flexed, but instead of tearing out her throat, he wrapped his hand around it. Squeezing tightly, though not enough to asphyxiate her. What—?

She started to burn.

This was the wraith's killing touch she'd heard about. The agony was unbearable. Through his grip on her throat, somehow, she found air enough to throw her head back and scream to the sky. Was this what her mother had felt before she died? Was this what all the Seers had suffered?

In a way, it was strangely comforting that Harrow would die in the same manner as her family. Perhaps she was never meant to have survived that tragic day at all. Perhaps this was why the Water had led her here—she'd dodged her fate then, and now it was just correcting the oversight. And now, she would die with only love in her heart for the creature delivering her death.

Did Raith know that? Had she made that clear? Years from now, if he was still trapped and forced to do Furie's bidding, would he be able to think back on this moment and know she didn't blame him for what he'd done? She had to be sure.

Through the agony, through her screams, she managed to say, "L-love you… Know you have to…don't have a choice…

Already forgive you...just l-love—"

The burning stopped suddenly.

Was she dead already? Was it over? But no, the pain from her injuries lingered, and she was vaguely aware of Raith's shadowy shape above her.

Had he stopped himself again?

"Harrow..."

Even through the haze, she stilled. He sounded like himself. Could he actually fight this?

But she never got the chance to find out.

A powerful explosion of magic split the night. Instantly, the darkness became blazing white light, the pressure so immense, it was nearly as agonizing as burning alive. Tornado-like winds whipped the air into a frenzy, and heavy rain pelted the ground. Harrow screamed again.

Raith did too.

And then he was torn away from her, talons ripping out of her shoulders, causing fresh waves of blood to spill. She didn't even notice. The power... She recognized its signature.

Water magic.

But Harrow hadn't done this. So who...?

Raith roared from somewhere, swallowed by the all-consuming light.

She sat up with a jolt, invigorated by adrenaline-fueled panic. "Raith!" Where had he gone? What was happening?

Scrambling to her feet despite her injuries, she stumbled through the torrential downpour, screaming his name. Tears streaked down her face, mingling with rainwater and her blood. She'd been seconds from death at his hands, but it didn't matter. She didn't want him hurt, and his tortured howl was an obvious indication that he was.

"Harrow!" Malaikah came out of the whiteness, fighting

through the storm to reach her.

What in the world was Malaikah doing here? Harrow's addled brain struggled to make sense of it and failed. Weakness overwhelmed her, and at the sight of her friend, she started to fall. Malaikah caught her as she went down, and they ended up on their knees, water drenching them and wind whipping around them with an earsplitting roar.

"Where's Raith?" Harrow cried, clutching Mal's shoulders.

But Mal wasn't listening. She was saying, "Oh Goddess, oh Goddess, oh Goddess," again and again, her hands fluttering over Harrow's bloody body. Still, Raith's howls of agony rent the air, audible even amid the roaring wind.

"Raith…" Harrow was losing consciousness at last. "Malaikah, help…Raith."

"It's over now," Malaikah was saying. "You're safe from him."

No, no, she didn't understand. Harrow needed her to understand. But her tongue felt like a rock in her mouth, and she couldn't see straight. "Raith…"

Suddenly, the downpour stopped. The light dissipated. The magic was withdrawn, and the air became breathable again. The forest clearing with the starry sky returned. Silence reigned. Malaikah still clutched Harrow, holding her upright, both of them soaked to their skin.

But where was Raith?

Harrow's question was answered the next instant as Queen Darya stepped into view. Her hair was windswept yet somehow dry, her face pale from exertion. She crouched beside Harrow and stroked her bloody face with a trembling hand. "There, there, child. It's all right. He can't hurt you anymore."

"No…"

"He'll never be able to hurt you again."

Harrow wanted to scream, but she didn't have the strength. Her vision was going black, head swimming, thoughts muddled. But she was clear-thinking enough to realize before she finally slipped into unconsciousness...

Darya had betrayed her again.

CHAPTER TWENTY-THREE

Harrow jerked upright the moment awareness returned. Or tried to. What she actually did was flop like a fish out of water, a low moan rasping from her bruised throat as she rediscovered the pain of her injuries.

"Whoa, easy there." Gentle hands pressed her back into the soft mattress. "Just relax for now, yeah?"

Eyes racing beneath her lids, Harrow fought as never before to regain consciousness. "Raith…"

"He's not here. He can't hurt you—"

"No."

"Calm down—"

"No!" Invigorated by her fear for Raith and her frustration at being helpless, Harrow fought off the hands holding her down and the remnants of unconsciousness.

With a jolt, she sat upright, fully awake.

She was in her caravan. Why this surprised her, she didn't know. Malaikah was beside her, eyes wide, reaching out as if to force her back down. Her hair was dry, her clothes fresh.

Sunlight streamed in through the windows, and the door was open, a gentle breeze teasing the edge of the sarong hanging over it.

"Where's Raith?" Harrow demanded, the betrayal of what Darya had done eating at her heart.

"Harrow," Mal said softly, "he was one second away from killing you."

"No, he wasn't! He was fighting it. He was going to fight it and then— What happened? How did Darya get here? What did she do, Mal?"

"What she did was for the best—"

"How can you say that? She'll kill him! I have to go after her. She manipulated me. She lied to me about what he was and convinced me to run from him. It's my fault this happened. I have to—"

"Harrow, calm down! No one is killing Raith. He's okay, I promise you."

"You can't know that. You can't trust Darya. You can't—"

"If you'll shut up for a second and listen, I think you'll find that I can know that, and I can trust Darya. For this, at least."

"But—"

"Just let me explain, okay?"

Harrow took a deep breath and willed herself to calm. She trusted Malaikah, and after everything Mal had done for her, she owed it to her to listen. "Okay. Just make it quick."

"Your shoulders have gigantic holes in them, and your throat is purpler than my stage makeup. You're not going anywhere."

"Please, Malaikah. I have to."

"Fine, fine. Just listen first. After you came out of the vision and told me you were heading South to find Raith alone, I... Well, understandably, I wasn't too keen on the idea. So I went back to the Underground to find Nashira, and I told her what had happened. She was her usual weird, vague self, but she seemed almost excited, which struck me as odd, considering the circumstances."

"I don't see what that has to do with Raith."

"Harrow." Malaikah gritted her teeth, and silence fell between them. They rarely argued, but Harrow had promised to listen.

"You're right. I'm sorry. I won't interrupt."

Malaikah smiled wanly. "Thanks. So after I told Nashira, she sprang into action. She grabbed me and portaled me all the way to Darya's bloody castle in the Western Territory. The jump we did before was a short distance and disorienting enough, but this one? I passed out, and then when I came to, threw up. It was gross, and Nashira was all surprised, like she hadn't known it would affect me that way." Mal scoffed. "Anyway, so Darya was there, of course, and she told us that she talked with you and was helping you scry for Raith or something. She was half crying the entire time because, apparently, she had this vision of Raith killing you, and she didn't know what to do and couldn't reach you with her magic anymore."

"I felt her trying to tug me into a vision," Harrow grumbled, "but I ignored her. I don't trust her."

"Yeah, she figured as much. So she was devastated about Raith killing you, but Nashira insisted it would be all good if we just sat and had tea for eight hours."

"Eight hours?" Harrow snorted a laugh despite herself. "Nashira is something else."

"I know. Darya was as incredulous as me. But she refused to take us anywhere or do anything before then, so we didn't have much choice. Darya left and did some more scrying before she finally agreed. So yeah, basically we had tea for eight hours until suddenly, Nashira jumps up and says, 'Time to go!' But I wouldn't let her take us anywhere without first figuring out exactly what Darya was planning. I swear, Harrow, I didn't want Raith hurt any more than you did. I told Darya over and over you'd never forgive her if something happened to him, even if he tried to kill you. I told her that to protect you, she had to find a way to save Raith."

Harrow should've known better than to doubt her best friend for even a second. Mal always had her back in all things, no matter what.

"So finally, we made a plan that we all agreed on, though Nashira acted like that had been her idea all along, of course. We would jump to wherever you were—Darya figured that out by scrying—and Darya would use her magic to capture Raith as she'd done before. This time it would be a lot harder, since he wasn't weakened, but she also had years of experience and knew what worked and what didn't."

"Years of experience torturing him," Harrow murmured.

Mal's mouth twisted. "So that's what we did. We jumped. I passed out again, of course, but only for a moment, since Raith was literally seconds from ripping out your throat and I had good motivation to stay awake. Harrow—" Her voice hitched, her eyes filling with tears, though, in typical Malaikah fashion, she didn't allow any to spill. "I was so scared for you. I thought we were too late. I thought he was going to kill you."

"He wasn't," Harrow insisted. "He was fighting the compulsion."

"Whatever the case, Darya freaked and just kind of...

exploded. I've never seen magic like that before. The clearing just lit up, and that rain and wind..." She shook her head. "It was like we were in the middle of a cyclone made of Water magic."

"I'd never seen anything like it, either." Just remembering the stark terror Harrow had felt for Raith made her shiver.

"And you know the rest. Darya caught Raith in her magic trap, and when the storm died, both of them were gone, along with Nashira. I reckon Nashira jumped them back to Castle Vari."

"To do what? Figure out a way to kill Raith?"

"No! Haven't you been listening to anything I'm saying? She's going to figure out a way to embody him again."

"She...what?" Harrow blinked, certain she had heard incorrectly.

"She's going to repeat what she did last time and create a new body for him. That way he'll be free of the vows he made to Furie."

Harrow's heart started to pound. "How do I know she'll actually do it? How can I trust she won't just try to kill him like last time?"

"She told me you'd ask that. And she told me to tell you that when she completes the embodiment, there will be another magical explosion, and, like last time, Raith will be transported to the land of his origins. She told me to tell you that, just like before, she won't be able to kill him before the embodiment, and she won't have a chance to kill him afterward before he ends up in the South."

Harrow considered this. It was true—while Raith was incorporeal, Darya had been unable to kill him, even with all her considerable power. And once she had finally made him corporeal, he'd been transported to the South, out of

Darya's reach. It was the only reason he was still alive, in fact.

She didn't have to put any faith in Darya. She just had to make sure she beat her to finding Raith wherever he ended up.

There was just one problem. "How do I know she won't keep Raith imprisoned in Castle Vari forever instead of embodying him?"

Malaikah chuckled. "She told me you'd ask that too. Amazing."

Harrow scowled. "It's hardly a great stretch of the imagination to guess I wouldn't trust her."

"She told me to tell you it takes considerable power to keep Raith imprisoned, and she can't afford to waste any on keeping him any longer than she absolutely has to with Furie breathing down her neck. She said it was 'time to do what she should've done fifty years ago.' Whatever that means."

"She's planning to go against Furie?" Harrow shook her head. "Look where that got her last time."

"Yeah. But I think she's planning something different this time. She and Nashira were whispering for hours while we were waiting to go after you. I think they're planning something together."

"Hm." Harrow found she didn't particularly care what happened to Furie. She'd lost too much, suffered too much, to want anything except a little slice of happiness for herself and Raith. "I still don't trust Da—"

"She told me to tell you, if you had any further doubts after I explained all that, to turn to the Water. She said, 'the Water will guide you rightly,' or some Seer mumbo jumbo."

"It's not mumbo jumbo."

"Whatever. But you know what to do. You can rest here and trust that everything will be taken care—"

"I need to gather my scrying materials immediately."

Malaikah sighed. "There's no rush—"

"I need to speak with Darya."

"I really wouldn't recommend—"

"I won't be taking her at her word. I need to see Raith myself and make sure he's okay."

"You shouldn't—"

"I also need to know how long the process will take—"

"Harrow!" Malaikah suddenly shouted.

"What?"

Her friend opened her mouth. Closed it again. Sighed heavily. "Look, there's one more thing you need to know. I was hoping you could rest a bit before I told you, because you're not going to like it, but I can see that's not going to happen."

"What?"

"Silly of me to even try, honestly. You're the most stubborn person I've ever met—after myself, of course, but that's a given—"

"What is it, Mal?"

"All of what I said before is true. You can trust Darya, and she is working hard to help Raith. But...there's a catch."

"What catch?"

"Well, the first time, it took Darya forty years to make Raith's body."

"Because she didn't know how, right?"

"Right, so it won't be that long now. But...she said it could still take time."

Harrow forced herself to speak slowly. "How much time?"

"Lots of time. As in...years."

"Years?" Harrow stared at her. "But that's— I can't— The process is torture for Raith. And he's going to be in a lot of pain already from breaking his vows."

"I know," Malaikah said softly.

"You heard him b-before—" Harrow's voice hitched. "He was in agony. Years of that?"

"I know. But it's the only way."

"It can't be. There has to be a way to make it faster."

"There isn't. Look, Harrow, Darya promised to work as hard as she possibly can, but there's no way to speed it up. And at least this time, Darya won't be trying to hurt him. She'll be kinder."

"I can't trust her with that. I'll go there myself. I'll lend her my magic, and we can work together."

"No, Harrow. In fact…" Malaikah dragged a hand down her face. "She told me to tell you that you're forbidden from entering Castle Vari until the process is complete."

"Why?"

"Because of what Raith has to go through. It's the only way, Harrow, and Darya knows you won't be able to stand it if you're there."

"No way. No way!" Harrow threw back the blankets covering her with a jerk that sent pain shooting up to her injured shoulders. She gasped reflexively, head spinning.

"Get back in bed," Mal protested.

Harrow ignored her, lowering her feet to the floor and gently easing up to standing.

"You lost half the blood in your body. You can't be up and about yet!"

Harrow took a step, but black spots winked in her vision and she stumbled into the wall. Malaikah was there to catch her before she went down. "Please get back in bed?"

"Need my scrying supplies. And a healing brew."

"You have healing herbs? Thank Goddess. Where?"

"They're in the bag with the rest of my Seer supplies." Harrow gritted her teeth and took another step toward her desk. "Pull everything out for me, would you?"

"I still think you should be lying down," Mal tried weakly.

"Not lying down, Mal. Help me or go outside with Fiona. Your choice."

"Hey now, Fiona's all right. You make it sound like she's bad company."

Harrow snorted a laugh despite herself. "You're right. That wasn't fair. Sorry, Fiona." Leaning hard on Malaikah, she painstakingly turned to look at her best friend. "Please help me? I know you've already done so much, but I just... need to do this."

"What exactly are you going to do?"

"I want to talk to Darya. I want her to look me in the eye and promise Raith will be okay. And I don't care what anyone says, I want to see him."

Malaikah sighed. "If I help you, will you promise to go back to bed afterward?"

Harrow frowned but realized that even if she did decide to travel to Darya's territory to break Raith out of there, she still needed to heal from her injuries first. A Seer's healing brew wasn't an instant cure. It certainly sped up the process, but it would still take a couple of days for Harrow to feel like herself again. "Fine. You win. I promise I'll go back to bed afterward."

"Excellent. So what do you need first?"

"I knew you'd come," Darya said from the far end of the room.

Harrow spun around. It was a sunny day in the Water Territory, but the air was cold. Though the temperature didn't affect her in a vision, she could still feel it. Still, no fire burned in the hearth. Harrow had a feeling Darya never lit any no matter how cold it was because it reminded her of Furie.

"Everything Malaikah told you is the truth," Darya said before Harrow could speak.

"I want to see him."

The Water Queen looked exhausted. Dark shadows lurked beneath her arresting silver gaze, and her normally silky black curls were frizzy and wild—looking more like Harrow's did on a regular basis. Even more surprisingly, Darya wore a plain, undyed dress with tears in the worn fabric. None of her regular fineries were present. If not for the aura of power and charisma that surrounded her, she would have appeared no more royal than a scullery maid.

"You can't, child," she said softly. "I'm sorry."

"Why not? Why should I trust you mean him no harm?"

"Because I gave you my word. And because a Seer knows when another has told her a bald-faced lie, especially one of as great importance as this."

Damn her, but she was right. The Water gave Harrow no inner indication of falsehood, but again, Harrow had been ignoring it because she wished for a different reality. When would she learn? Perhaps this was to be a lifelong lesson, then?

"I will embody him again," Darya said, "but as I told Malaikah, it may take time. I intend to do nothing else until I achieve my desired result, but I don't know when that will be."

Harrow listened to her every word through the filter of

her inner guiding voice and heard nothing but truth. "Can I see him?"

Darya shook her head.

"Why? If we're to be separated for an indefinite amount of time, you should let me see him before I go."

"I cannot."

"Why?"

"Because..." The Water Queen sighed. "Because I made him a promise."

"Raith?"

She nodded. "After I captured him, it broke the trance of the compulsion. He was aware of everything he had done. Child, he feels great shame. He made me swear not to let you near him."

"Why would he do that?" Harrow's throat constricted painfully.

"I see now how wrong I was about him." Darya's gaze softened. "He is noble, and he loves you."

"Then why doesn't he want to see me?" To her dismay, a tear trickled from the corner of her eye. She was sick to death of crying. Sick of it. But circumstances kept coming, one after the next, that forced those tears to flow.

"He's ashamed of what he did. He carries a great weight of regret."

"I don't care. I know it wasn't his fault. I know he didn't want to hurt me. I need to tell him this."

"I know, daughter, but I must respect his wishes. He asked for my given word, and I gave it. Knowing how much weight a being like him puts behind a vow, I have no intention of breaking mine to him."

"He has to know I don't blame him for anything. He has to know that I love him."

"And I give my vow to you, too, that I'll tell him. Oh, and before you go," Darya added, though Harrow had no intention of leaving so easily, "there's one more thing you must know. I'm telling you this now so you can prepare yourself."

"What? What are you talking about?"

"When I eventually succeed in embodying your wraith and when you finally reunite with him, it will be exactly as before in more ways than one. He'll be transported to the South, and, as before, he'll come into his new body with no memory of who or what he is."

A pit opened in her stomach that seemed to suck everything left of her into it. "No…"

"Unfortunately, yes. There's nothing I can do to prevent that. I will have to restore his memories for him to remember you. Unfortunately, it won't be pleasant."

"Why not?"

Darya's mouth twisted. "His past is dark, Harrow. When I returned his memories the first time, it was a form of torture. I'm not proud of it now, but that's the truth of it. He was forced to relive every pain he'd endured and caused others as if it happened anew, all compressed into the length of a single dream. And that's exactly what he'll have to endure again to regain his memories a second time."

Harrow covered her mouth with a hand. That hand dropped back into her lap and twisted with the other. "Do you have to restore them at all? Wouldn't he be happier not knowing what happened to him?"

"No. Just as before, he'll retain his subconscious memories and will still feel great shame and guilt, only he'll have no understanding of why. He needs to remember everything in order to heal. Even the worst parts."

She was right, of course, though Harrow didn't like the thought of Raith being tortured with this. He'd been tortured enough. "Can you give us a few days first? A week?"

"I don't know, Harrow..."

"Just give us one week to be together without the memories haunting him. That way, I can show him how much I love him, and it'll make it easier for him to accept the rest."

The Water Queen's expression softened. "I'll give you one week, but I warn you, Harrow, even without his memory, he will need an explanation for what happened, or his feelings will haunt him." Harrow nodded eagerly, and Darya's gaze sharpened. "You have to tell him everything, no matter how unpleasant. Do you understand?"

She swallowed hard. "Okay."

"In the meantime, remember the Water will guide you in all things. And don't try to come here before I've finished. I'll bar the gates with impenetrable magic, so don't waste your time journeying here. When the time is right, the Water will tell you. Use your Goddess-given gifts as you were born to use them."

"But—"

"Goodbye for now, daughter of the Water. May you live your life with all the glory you were destined for until fortune smiles upon me and grants me the gift of our next visit. Knowing you has been my greatest joy in many long years."

"But—"

Darya threw Harrow out of the vision. With a gasp, she jerked back from the scrying bowl, back in her caravan, thousands of miles away from the Water Queen and the male she loved.

And apparently, she was banned indefinitely from seeing either of them again.

• • •

Of course, Harrow was far too stubborn to accept her fate and Darya's dismissal that readily. As soon as she regained her strength and fulfilled her promise to Malaikah to rest—briefly—she went right back to the scrying bowl and dove into another vision.

This time, she was after a different Queen.

With the combined power of Nashira's Ether magic, Harrow found herself back in the sorceress's airy chambers in the sky. Nashira sat beside the towering windows, playing the harp and singing softly. The ethereal music blended with Nashira's hauntingly beautiful voice to create a magic of its own. Her strange crystal ball sat on a cushion on the table beside her.

The Ether Queen stopped playing abruptly. "You're here. Later than I expected. You rested first? That's good. No, I can't help you today, tomorrow, or yesterday. My sincerest apologies." She turned back to her harp.

"You didn't even let me explain."

Nashira looked back again. "No need. I know everything, remember?" She chuckled to herself, but Harrow couldn't tell if she was joking or not.

"Why doesn't he want to see me?" Harrow found herself asking, though she didn't understand why she sought answers from this bizarre, infuriating woman. She supposed it was because a part of her recognized there was wisdom in the Ether Queen, even if it was buried beneath so much outward strangeness.

"Oh, he does. He longs for it as much as you do."

Harrow gaped at her. "But Darya said—"

"A promise given is a promise kept."

"But why—"

"Guilt is a weight to be carried by the bearer alone. The forgiveness must first start within before it can be accepted from without. But how to share a burden we can't release?"

"But if—"

"And what a burden to carry alone, only to discover it was weightless all along. When the fingers are pried loose, it drifts up to the clouds like a wayward feather. Free at last!"

"Why can't you say anything plainly!" Harrow cried, patience finally at its end.

Nashira just smiled. "Don't worry. You'll understand soon enough."

"When?"

But the Ether Queen had turned back to her harp, strumming it lovingly and humming softly. Harrow ground her teeth, swearing she wasn't leaving until she heard something remotely useful, which didn't include more wistful philosophical ramblings or—

"So lovely to see you again, dear. Do pay us a visit when you pass through. Oh, and congratulations!"

"On what?"

But she never got a chance to find out. The next instant, Harrow was jerking back from her scrying bowl, back in her caravan, yet again ejected from her own vision by another bloody Queen and her bloody magic. And this time, she was finally starting to realize there might truly be nothing she could do but wait.

But she'd be damned if she wasn't going to keep trying anyway.

CHAPTER TWENTY-FOUR

Six months later...

Harrow adjusted the covering over her mouth and nose and wiped the sandy grit from her eyes, the only part of her exposed to the merciless sun. Ahead of her, Fiona trudged wearily forward at a snail's pace, not that Harrow blamed her. Her gentle horse had once been unaccustomed to such harsh weather conditions.

Needless to say, after six months, she was now.

Still, no matter how acclimated one became to the Southern climate, it never ceased being a formidable foe. Only the foolhardiest of travelers dared journey through the heat of the day — those unfamiliar with the severe conditions, and those in a great hurry to reach some destination.

Harrow fell into the latter category.

After six months of constant wandering, the time had finally come. As she'd done daily since the beginning of her travels into the barren South, that morning, she'd set up her scrying bowl and dived deep into the Water for signs of the one she waited for.

Finally, she had found results.

For months, she'd traveled with little knowledge of where to go or where he might end up. All she had was a strong conviction that she needed to continue roaming through the desert. She was certain that if she were ever to retreat to fairer lands, she would be in the wrong place when the time came.

After her vision-conversations with the Queens months ago—the last contact she'd had with either of them, though not for lack of trying—she'd turned to the Water as Darya instructed, searching for her next course of action, only to discover she was already on the right path. Her decision to leave Allegra by herself and head South still held up.

So she'd rested a few days in that forest clearing with Malaikah by her side, and then, when she was well enough to travel, said goodbye to her dearest friend and recommenced her journey alone.

Predictably, Malaikah hadn't left without a fuss. But Harrow had stressed the importance of her travels being completed solo and the fact that Mal was safest at the circus under Salizar's protection, and in the end, Malaikah relented, returning on foot back to Allegra. Harrow had thanked her profusely for her help, knowing it couldn't have been easy for her to leave the circus behind. Even going back wouldn't be easy. There was no way Salizar would take kindly to all the chaos the two of them had managed to wreak.

And so, alone again, Harrow, Fiona, and her caravan traveled south.

It took the better part of a month to cross into Furie's

territory, and another two months to finally penetrate the region known as the Far South. From there, Harrow had traveled through Kambu, saddened to see the deteriorated state of Malaikah's homeland under the corrupt leadership of the traitor who'd taken it from her family years ago. She'd taken care to hide her identity to protect herself from both Furie and her supporters.

Another month later, the Water had urged her to roam deeper into the desert, where few travelers dared venture and where she was safer. She had loaded her caravan with supplies and obeyed her instincts without question—something she was finally becoming accustomed to doing. Months spent alone had increased the volume of her inner voice and her trust in its wisdom.

For two months she traversed the desolate wilderness of cracked earth and rolling dunes. Her days were spent seeking shelter, traveling from water source to water source. Her nights were spent bundled in her caravan or seeking warmth by a fire.

Every morning, without fail, she filled a bowl with precious water to scry. Always, the sun shone mercilessly down from clear blue skies. The days were sweltering, the nights freezing. It never rained. Bush fires frequently raged across any landscape brave enough to grow vegetation.

Her thoughts were consumed constantly by survival—water, shelter, food, rest, repeat—and yet, in a way, it was a peaceful existence. Just a woman and her horse, braving the desert, searching for her lost love.

And today, she would finally find him.

The vision hit her unexpectedly. One moment she was wiping sand from her eyes, squinting into the desert sun, and the next...

She came back to reality with a gasp, jerking Fiona to a halt. Throwing herself off the side of the caravan, she began to sprint, though exerting oneself to such a degree was never advisable in this climate.

It didn't matter. Nothing but this moment mattered.

She ran faster, hope filling her heart. Hope that after all these months, her search had finally come to an end.

The sun crept under his eyelids as he gradually pulled himself from unconsciousness. Instinct told him to sharpen his awareness, survey his surroundings, scan for threats. He only managed to shift his eyes beneath their too-heavy lids.

Pain assailed him as he slowly became aware of his body. Everything hurt.

He finally peeled his eyes open, only to close them immediately as the glaring sun scalded them. He tried again, squinting into the intense light, and saw blue. Clear sky, not a cloud in sight.

Battling intense weakness, he turned his head to one side. Beside him, the ground was cracked and dusty, an impenetrable hardened crust. In the distance, a lone shrub struggled for life.

A ghost of familiarity assailed him—a certainty he'd been here before, lived this before—but that didn't make sense. He had no memory of ever—

His thoughts ground to a sudden halt as realization suffused him.

He had no memory of anything.

He had no idea who he was or how he'd come to be

stranded naked in the desert. He didn't even know his own name.

He did, however, feel a strange gratitude for the sensation of flesh bound to his spirit. As if he'd experienced the reverse and much preferred his present condition, weak and pain-riddled though he was.

Unpreferable, however, was the haunting feeling of grief that weighed upon his soul. He felt as though he'd lost something treasured, only he couldn't for the life of him remember what it was.

Was life worth living in such a state? He was too weak to move with his body's debility and the burden of grief weighing him down. Perhaps without that disembodied longing, he might have summoned the will to save himself, but with it? Death would be a welcome relief.

Funny. He was suddenly certain he'd had that thought before.

With an exhalation through that haunting pain in his chest, he relented. He let life beat him. He gave up. Finally. He relaxed his will, released his instinctive urge to survive, and waited for darkness to claim him—

A voice cried out from a vast distance, pulling him back from the edge.

No, he thought, *let me go. Let me slip away.* Would death forever be denied him?

"Raith!" This time, the cry seemed louder.

Something about that voice struck him right in the center of that ocean of inexplicable grief. The pain was so intense, he gasped, lifting a heavy arm to clutch at his chest. Suddenly, he couldn't seem to get enough air.

"Raith!"

It was beautiful, he realized. Though he hadn't a clue what

it was saying, the sound of that voice was so inexplicably glorious, it brought tears to his eyes. To hear such a voice again...

Perhaps there was something worth living for after all.

A s Harrow ran, finally, she saw it—a dark shape upon the earth a distance away.

Immediately, she cried, "Raith!"

The shape didn't move. She ran faster.

"Raith!"

Nothing. Still, she ran.

And then she could see him. He lay on his back, head turned to one side, the inky shade of his naked skin seeming to swallow the midday sun. She ran faster, calling his name repeatedly to no effect.

Finally, she reached him, dropping to her knees at his side. He didn't move. Tears of gratitude filled her eyes, blurring her sight, but she blinked them away, determined not to miss a single detail of his beautiful face.

After six months of searching, here he was.

But he was weakened, unconscious. She had to get him back to the shelter of her caravan. He needed to be out of the direct sun, and he needed water.

Wrapping her arms around him, she dragged his massive form into her lap. His massive, *solid* form. Even unconscious as he was, his strength astounded her. His body was so huge, so lethal.

Tearing off her headscarf, she draped the fabric over him to cover him from the sun and then unhooked the water flask from her waist belt.

She stroked his cheek gently, fighting back the sobs in her throat. "Raith, my love, wake up so I can give you some water."

He groaned softly, eyes shifting beneath closed lids, and she was so happy she could cry. She did cry.

"My love, you need to drink." Gently, she tipped the water to his lips.

They parted, and she poured a little of the life-giving liquid. He swallowed. "That's it. Take more." She poured a little more, and he swallowed again, this time with more vigor.

After draining her entire flask sip by sip, he began to regain awareness. She stroked his silken hair, murmuring words of encouragement, telling him how much he meant to her, how desperately she'd missed him, and how long she'd searched for him.

Finally, he blinked his lids open. Through her tears, she beheld those all-black eyes with their fire-wreathed centers. "You're safe now. I promise I'll take care of you."

When he spoke, his voice was hoarse. "Who...are you?"

Eventually, Harrow got Raith back to her caravan. First, she tried getting him to stand up and walk. He made it three steps before his legs crumpled beneath him, and he passed out again.

Rather than repeating that agonizing endeavor, Harrow had been forced to leave his side and run back to the caravan. She then made poor Fiona trot back beneath the merciless sun to where he lay.

Raith drained two more flasks of water before he was

strong enough to stand again. From there, Harrow helped him into her caravan. He fell straight into her bed, asleep before his head hit the pillow.

She directed her exhausted horse to the nearest oasis—a Seer who drew her magic from the Water could always sense a nearby source. She tied Fiona to a tree beside the spring so she could drink at leisure and keep cool in the shade, and then she went back into her caravan.

Raith was awake, sitting up in bed, already looking stronger than before. Feeling somewhat awkward, especially knowing how much explaining she had to do, Harrow busied herself opening the windows and door to let fresh air in. The inside of the caravan was stuffy, and though it was hot outside, too, a gentle breeze blew through and brought relief.

All the while, Raith watched her closely.

When she could find nothing else to do, she took a seat on the chair by the bed. "Would you like some more water?"

He shook his head. His skin was still midnight shadows, and she realized that he'd changed its color before only because of others' negative reactions to it. Something Harrow would never do. Black, brown, that brilliant orange he'd once turned… She didn't care what he looked like.

He was here, alive and well, in her caravan. Finally.

And now it was time to tell him who he was.

"You don't know me anymore," she began, "but I know you. I'll start at the beginning, I guess. Your name is Raith. Well, that's the name you chose. When we first met, you didn't have a name. You see, Salizar had asked Loren to paint a sign—" She shook her head quickly. "Never mind. That's not important right now. Just know that your name is Raith. With an R, not a W."

"Raith," he repeated, exactly how he'd said it the day they met.

"Yes." She smiled. "And my name is Harrow."

"Harrow." His face softened slightly. "Harrow." He appeared to enjoy saying her name.

Her heart felt like it would burst. "And we are... Well, we— I—" How could she say this? Her cheeks were already flaming, and she hadn't even managed a complete sentence. Finally, she gritted her teeth and just spat it out.

"We're in love."

His eyes widened. He looked so utterly shocked, she might have laughed had she not been busy trying to hide her embarrassment.

"Or at least we were in love. Before."

Now, he looked stricken.

"No, I didn't mean we don't— I just meant— We still love each other. Or rather I still love you, and I think you would've felt the same before you forgot me."

Now he just looked confused. Great. She was doing an excellent job bungling this up. "Let me just start at the beginning, okay? I'll tell you everything, and then you can ask me any questions at the end."

So Harrow started at the beginning. She told him about how they'd met at Salizar's circus and how they had escaped. And when she told him about their nights in the room above the tavern, her cheeks burned so badly she was forced to skip the details. By the look on Raith's face, however, he knew what she was talking about. And finally, she told him about coming after him in the desert.

And...glazed over the rest.

She lied.

Well, it wasn't actually lying. She just...dodged the truth

a bit. But his eyes were as wide as saucers, and she'd just dragged the poor man inside, and surely, she could give him a little respite before burdening him with the dark details of their twisted pasts?

"So what do you think?" she asked when she finally finished sharing their incomplete story. Guilt niggled at her, but she pushed it aside for now.

He cocked his head in that feral way of his. "The most beautiful female in the world just told me she loves me. I think I'm not so foolish as to question my good fortune."

Happiness burned so fiercely in her chest it was nearly unbearable. Her smile was so huge, her face ached. She scoffed to hide the depth of her pleasure. "You don't remember anyone else. How can you know I'm the most beautiful?"

"I know."

Their eyes met. Stayed locked.

"Will you come closer?" he asked quietly. "So I can see you better?"

She practically ran to his side, all but throwing herself at him. *Easy, Harrow. He doesn't remember you.* She forced herself to sit beside him on the bed rather than climbing into his lap. Their gazes met again. Connection sparked between them, as powerful as magic.

"Definitely the most beautiful," he murmured, leaning closer.

She leaned closer too. "I missed you so much."

He studied her face intently. "When I awoke, I felt I was missing something important. I think it was you." His hand lifted to rub his bare chest absently.

"I don't care what happened in the past." Harrow knew he didn't remember, didn't understand what she was talking about. But maybe, somewhere deep inside, he did. "I don't care what you did or who you were. None of it matters."

He frowned like he was struggling to make sense of things. All the while, he rubbed at his chest like it was paining him.

"The past is in the past. As long as we're together."

Somehow, the space between them had shrunk down to mere inches. Still, his eyes searched hers so intently. She stared back into those fiery irises with equal intent, daring him to see into her soul, to see what she truly felt for him.

"Is this real?" he murmured.

She nodded, lifting a hand. She stroked the edge of his jaw, tracing that flawless bone structure, nearly impossible to see for its incredible darkness. She remembered wanting to scream in horror at her first sight of his true appearance. The memory filled her with shame. Looking at him now, she saw nothing but the man she loved. Thinking him anything else was a mistake she would never make again.

Lost in thoughts of his own, Raith reached up to stroke the frizzy mess of her hair, reminding her she hadn't brushed it in days or taken the time to put on a nicer dress. Her face was likely caked in sand.

"So beautiful," he murmured, and she flushed with pleasure.

And then he leaned down to kiss her, and she melted against him without a thought.

CHAPTER TWENTY-FIVE

Some force had taken over Raith, and he was powerless to resist the exquisite creature sitting beside him on the bed. She had run to him across the sandy desert—how had he gotten there in the first place?—and then taken him back to her little home on wheels and told him she loved him. This woman, this indescribable, glorious woman, had crossed the desert to find him because she loved him.

It seemed impossible. He was likely dreaming.

If so, he was determined to enjoy every second of it before he awoke to whatever dismal reality awaited him. The woman called Harrow melted in his embrace, moaning softly like his touch was her greatest pleasure. It floored him.

It encouraged him. He deepened the kiss, pushing her lips apart with his own to dive into her mouth with his tongue.

He had done this before, he realized. Somehow, he knew what she liked. He knew how to cradle her head in his hand in the way she craved, trapping her against him. He knew what the curve of her waist would feel like as he ran his other hand down her back. He knew how firmly she liked to be gripped on her voluptuous hips, and when he did so, he was instantly rewarded with another soft moan.

Excitement coursed through his blood. Confidence filled him.

Maybe he could actually give her what she sought from him. Maybe he could be good enough for her.

He gripped her waist and hauled her into his lap, her shapely legs straddling his hips. Forgetting he was naked beneath the blankets until they slipped down, he was about to cover himself again when she rocked against his hard shaft with another moan of pleasure, nothing but her thin dress between their bodies.

His eyes fell shut. This pleasure, this familiarity… It felt like coming home. It felt like the only place he ever wanted to be, the only place he was meant to be.

So why did he still feel such debilitating grief?

It didn't matter now. He couldn't let anything distract him from this precious moment. Harrow rocked against him again, clutching his shoulders with soft hands, and he forgot everything else. He slid her dress up to grip her bare thighs, moaning at the feel of her supple flesh beneath his fingers.

She pulled back, looking at him with so much desire, he affirmed again he must be dreaming.

Then she tugged the whole dress off and threw it over her shoulder.

He sucked in a breath, his hungry gaze devouring her. The fullness of her breasts, the softness of her belly, the thick curves of her backside and thighs…

Goddess, he wanted to grab all that flesh at once and feel it spilling over his hands. He wanted to feast on every inch of her until she was crying out his name—

What was his name again?

"Raith," she said, squirming beneath his hungry gaze. "You're teasing me." Her eyes were playful as she stretched her arms up to gather her hair in a wild bundle atop her head.

He nearly died at the sight.

Fisting a hand in those lively curls, he pulled her in to kiss him again, pressing her lips apart with his own to conquer her mouth with his tongue. The way she moaned and writhed against him set his lust ablaze.

Releasing her hair, he bent his head to suck her perfect nipples. She threw her head back, her spine a sensuous arch, her fingers clutching the muscles of his shoulders. He palmed the breast not in his mouth but froze suddenly, lifting his head to study the contrast between their bodies.

Her skin was tanned, like the color of sand. His was… shadow itself, absent of all color. The sun's glow shining through the windows didn't reflect but seemed to be absorbed into it. Nothing else in their surroundings reacted similarly to light, and it struck him as strange. He straightened abruptly, holding his arm out and staring at it.

"Raith?"

"What am I? Why do I look like this?"

Harrow's grip tightened on his shoulders. "You look perfect to me. The most beautiful man I've ever seen. And I, for one, have my memories."

He tilted his head, meeting her gaze. "Does anyone else look like me?"

"You can change your appearance if it bothers you. But don't do it on my account."

He noticed she'd avoided answering the question, but he was too intrigued by what she'd said to care. He stared at her earthy, tanned skin and then willed his own to match it.

And...it did. Amazing.

Harrow gasped and then laughed. "That's a neat trick, but I think you should change back."

"Why?"

"Because I want you to always remember that I love every part of you, exactly as you are. And I don't want you to feel you ever have to change yourself for me."

He leaned in to kiss her again in response and then quickly forgot what he'd been so worried about in the first place. Being with her made him feel like he belonged. Who cared about anything else?

He promptly engaged in his prior task—sucking on her nipples. They hardened to peaks amid her soft moans as he held her at the curve of her waist, his hands nearly meeting in the middle. Encouraged by his ministrations, she began rocking her hips again, and a growl rumbled from his throat when her soft core, already wet from arousal, stroked against his shaft.

"Raith—"

He lifted his eyes to hers in question.

"Change back." Her words were breathy.

"Why?"

"Want you...as you are."

He shrugged, not understanding why this was important, but obliged her. His skin reverted to shadow, and then he pulled her in again for a kiss.

She wrapped her arms around his neck, holding him close, and continued rocking herself against him, the movement of her hips driving him mad. Her arousal coated his shaft where they pressed together, and the sound of her soft moans flooded him with a sense of desperation. He needed this. He needed to see her come undone.

Tightening his fingers around her waist, he pulled her even closer. His erection, aching and hard, stood up between their bodies, as Harrow worked herself faster and faster against him, riding along his length without taking it inside her.

If he only tilted his hips, he would penetrate her, but he didn't. He wanted to see her climax like this, to watch her pleasure herself with his body. She was as desperate as he was, and he loved it.

He loved her.

Was that ridiculous for a man whose entire memory spanned the length of several hours? Maybe. Did he care? At that moment, not in the least.

Faster, she moved against him, bracing her arms against his shoulders for leverage, her thighs trembling from the force she exerted. The way she reveled in her sensuality, unashamed to take what she needed to achieve her pleasure, was beyond the most intoxicating thing he could have dreamed of. She was a goddess, and he worshipped her.

Again, that feeling of familiarity seized him. He knew she was nearing orgasm by the way her breath raced and her moans escalated in volume. He knew how she would respond if he grasped her hair and demonstrated his strength. Full of anticipation, he did just that, pulling her head back so he could feast on the column of her throat.

She cried out and writhed faster, grinding furiously against him. When her cry turned to one of frustration, as though she hovered on the brink but couldn't quite reach the peak by herself, he knew just what to do to push her over the edge. He met her thrusts with his own, syncing the pace of their movements, tightening the hand in her hair to show his dominance.

Her ecstatic cry filled the cabin. Her head dropped back and her whole body shook with tremors. His own climax came suddenly, his control shattered at the sight of her ecstasy, and he erupted in the space between their bodies, slicking their skin with his release.

Harrow went limp and sagged against him, so he gathered her in his arms and held her close. His own body trembled, every nerve tingling with life. His lust may have been sated, but his passion burned on. He didn't think it would ever cease with her.

The way she laid her head on his shoulder with a soft hum of contentment made him feel like the most powerful being in the world.

For a man with no memories, it should have been impossible to feel such belonging so soon after experiencing isolation, but he couldn't deny it. It was not a fleeting sensation, brought on by the frenzy of their ardor. It was deeper than skin and bone, deeper even than thought.

Whatever it was, whatever strange twist of fate had landed him here, he would not squander his blessings. He would cherish and protect his Harrow, shower her with love and affection.

Yet it was she who lifted her head and stroked his hair back, telling him how wonderful he was, how strong and capable. And in the end, all he could say of his feelings was, "You are mine."

"Yes," she agreed. "I'm yours, and you're mine, and I'm never letting you go."

Eventually, they rose from the bed to wash. Harrow cooked them a small dinner with what little remained of her food supplies. He tried to help, but she insisted he rest, though he no longer felt weak.

While they ate, she told him how she'd spent months in the desert searching for him. He couldn't believe the loyalty this woman demonstrated, couldn't fathom what he'd done to deserve it, but he swore he would do everything in his power to be worthy of it.

If only he could figure out why his chest still ached. If only he could understand why he still felt he was missing some crucial detail.

Tomorrow, they would travel north, Harrow said, out of the desolate South into fairer lands. From there, they would decide together where to go, but Harrow said she wanted to intercept the circus she'd once worked for to visit her friend Malaikah. Raith would go wherever she wanted to go. He didn't yet know where he fit in the world and looked forward to discovering it by her side.

He just wished he could understand the aching hole in his chest.

He knew he had done something wrong. Something terrible. Something that might be unforgivable.

But he couldn't remember what it was.

How could he move on with his life with Harrow if he couldn't find forgiveness for his terrible deed? How could he ever let this go if he didn't know what haunted him in the first place? Despite her constant assurances, he couldn't shake the feeling that he didn't belong in Harrow's bed—that she deserved so much more. He couldn't shake the feeling that he'd hurt her in some horrible way.

Looking at her sleeping beside him later that night, a gentle smile touching her lips, he couldn't imagine how he could ever do such a thing. He loved her. He wanted her safe and happy.

So why would he hurt her?

But he had. He was certain of it, and it tore him up inside like a knife stirring his guts. If he'd hurt her before and couldn't remember it, what was to stop him from doing it again? How could he ever trust himself in her presence? He should leave her now and spare her from the harm he might inadvertently do her.

No. His arms tightened around her, a growl rumbling in his chest. He was never leaving her. Never. His cold, dead arms would have to be pried from around her to separate them.

Still, the thought haunted him. How could he trust she would be safe with him if he didn't remember what he'd done?

Finally, he drifted into an uneasy sleep, praying to the Goddess he wouldn't accidentally hurt his love while he rested. As he slept, nightmares plagued him.

He woke with her lifeless form in his arms, blood dripping from her mouth. He had crushed her in his sleep. He screamed.

No! It was just a dream. He was still asleep.

He awoke again. Wet blood soaked everything. He had stabbed her with his claws in his sleep. His cries of horror filled the air.

No! Still a dream. He awoke.

Her neck was torn open—he had ripped it open with his teeth in his sleep. *Dream.* Her throat was slit. *Dream.* Her body was burned to a crisp. *Dream.*

Her blood was on his hands. Always, her blood coated his hands.

• • •

"Harrow!"

Harrow drifted on a cloud of bliss, annoyed at the panicked voice trying to drag her from the realm of pleasant dreams.

"Harrow!"

It was Darya's voice. Go figure.

"Harrow, hear me now!"

She snapped to awareness, but not awakeness—she was in a dream vision. Back in the room of fountains, she was seated across from the Water Queen, who looked even more haggard than she had during their visit six months ago. Her skin was paler than before, the shadows beneath her eyes darker, her hair messier, and her dress seemed to hang limply off her.

"What happened to you?" Harrow asked before she could stop herself.

"Good to see you too." Darya lifted a brow. "I see you've reunited with your wraith and things have gone well."

"Yes, they have." Harrow flushed. How much had Darya seen?

"You didn't tell him everything."

She sighed. "I know, but I wanted to give it a day or two. If I can show him how much I love him before he remembers, then maybe—"

"Right now, he dreams over and over of waking to find he's accidentally killed you in his sleep. He realizes he's dreaming, falls asleep, and awakens again in the same scenario."

Harrow covered her mouth with a hand.

"He knows he's hurt you in some way he deems unforgivable, but he can't remember how or why. He can't imagine why he would ever hurt you and is afraid of himself and what he might do. You're torturing him by withholding critical information."

"I didn't— I had no idea. I just thought he was confused."

"I warned you he would have subconscious memories. I warned you he needed to know."

"I know." Shame filled her. How could she have ignored something this crucial?

Because of her own selfish fears, she realized. She didn't want Raith to remember her leaving him. She didn't want him to experience the hurt of remembering how she'd betrayed him. She was afraid he wouldn't forgive her.

"You're right," Harrow said. "He has to know everything. And not through me telling him. You have to restore his memories now."

"I agree." Darya smiled sympathetically. "I know it's hard, child, but you're making the right choice for your mate, and that's what's important. Now, I'm going to dissolve our dream spell so I can focus on weaving the memory spell for Raith, which—"

"Wait." She stared at the Water Queen. "You really did it. You made him a new body, and you're really going to let him go."

Darya frowned. "Of course."

"You don't hate him anymore."

"On the contrary, we bonded during our six months together."

"You did?"

"Oh yes. My child, if I'd wanted to kill him, I could have done it on the first day."

"How?"

"As soon as Raith realized where he was and what he'd done, he solidified himself, as wraiths can do for short periods. As you know, I once tortured him for years, trying to force him to do that very thing so I could kill him, and he never broke. But this time, as soon as he was strong enough, he did so."

"Why?"

"Harrow… He begged me to kill him for what he'd done."

Harrow's eyes filled with tears.

"I didn't, of course, for I had made a promise to my daughter of the Water. Instead, I told him how furious she would be if she heard him talking such nonsense."

"You did?" Harrow wiped her eyes roughly.

"I did. And I told him my daughter was not only beautiful but stubborn. And she had her heart set on him and would not take kindly to anything happening to him, especially while he was in my care. Your Raith and I shared much over the last six months and grew to know each other. Already I miss his company. You have chosen your mate well. He will be a perfect companion for a Seer."

"I thought the embodiment process would be torture for him."

"It wasn't pleasant, certainly, but I couldn't always be blasting him with magic. And this time, he was working with me, so it wasn't as difficult. While I rested, we passed the time together."

Several things finally sank in fully. Darya had truly kept her word. She had embodied Raith solely to give Harrow and him a future together. She had not only relinquished her desire for revenge, but she had also found friendship with the man she'd once wanted to kill.

"Thank you," Harrow whispered.

"There's nothing to thank me for, child. I can't undo my mistakes, but I can try to make amends." Darya rose from her perch on the sofa and smoothed her skirts. Her dress was elegant, but the way it hung from her gaunt figure detracted from its loveliness. "Since I've done it before, this spell will take less effort, and I can do it tonight. Go back to your sleep, and when you awaken in the morning, Raith will remember. Be prepared."

"Okay." Harrow was still studying the Water Queen. "Are you...okay?"

"Of course."

"Are you sure you can do this tonight? Last time you said it took days."

"As I said, the second time is always easier."

"You should get some rest after. You look exhausted."

Darya smiled tiredly. "We go up against my sister soon. With any luck, we'll be successful. I will rest then."

"When was the last time you slept?"

"Several decades ago."

Harrow stared at her. "Are you serious?"

Darya flicked a wrist. "Don't concern yourself with me. I've been around for countless centuries and will remain for countless more." The way she said this made it seem like a wearisome burden. Harrow supposed that if she was immortal and alone as Darya was, she might feel the same.

She decided that, since Darya had made an effort to heal the rift between them, she would do her best to stay in contact with her. "Thank you. For everything."

"Providing for you is something I should have been doing from the beginning. I'm only sorry it took me this long to discover how to do it properly."

"Well, for what it's worth, I'm glad you're in my life now. And even if you had the wrong motives in the beginning, it was because of you that I met Raith in the first place."

Darya smiled. "Such wisdom for one so young. Go now,

child. Go and find your happiness."

With that, Harrow slipped away, back to the cradle of darkness in the realm of dreams.

She would need her rest. When she awoke, she and Raith would be facing a very different battle.

CHAPTER TWENTY-SIX

The next morning, Harrow woke to feel the weight of another's gaze upon her. Everything came back in a rush, and she jolted upright.

Raith was sitting in the chair at the end of the bed, clad in a pair of pants she'd given him the night before. He stared at her with haunted eyes. His skin was deep bronze again, the shade it had been when they first met.

"Raith." She clutched the sheet over her bare breasts. "I'm sorry I didn't tell you the truth sooner. I was afraid, and it was selfish."

It was like he hadn't heard her. "You came back for me."

"Yes."

"You left. But you came back."

"Yes." She swallowed hard. "And I'm never leaving again."

"I hurt you. I—" It was his turn to swallow. "I tried to kill you." He looked sick at the thought.

"No, Furie tried to kill me. You fought with everything

you had not to."

"I hurt you. I made you bleed. I — "

"No, Raith. Furie did those things. You fought her. Even after I betrayed you, you still fought to protect me."

"You were right to leave me."

"No." Her fingers clenched around the bedsheet. "No, I was wrong. I can't believe I doubted you for a second."

"Harrow, I killed your family. Your mother. How can you even stand to look at me?"

"I can look at you because I know it wasn't you who did those things. Furie bound you and the other wraiths — your actions weren't your own. I saw how you were under the compulsion of your vow. You weren't yourself; you weren't thinking clearly. You couldn't fight what you were doing. Anything you've done with your own free choice has been the opposite of how you were under Furie's control. All you've ever done is protect me and love me and make me happier than I've ever been in my life."

Raith's eyes were haunted as he stared at the floor. "I killed so many. Not just Seers. For years, she sent me after anyone who angered or threatened her. After enough time, I obeyed without a second thought."

"I want to kill her for what she did to you."

"I went back to her the night you left. I tried to cut off her head."

So Malaikah had been right. "What happened?"

"The blade melted when it touched her skin." He shrugged. "I knew I would likely fail. I hoped that when I did, she would kill me."

"Raith." Harrow's vision swam with tears.

"She almost did. But she realized it was what I wanted, so she stopped and sent me after you instead." He shook his head. "I was a fool."

"*I* was a fool. If I hadn't left that night, you never would've gone back to her."

But he shook his head again. "Darya gave me my memories back that night. It changed me. Whether or not you left, I doubt I'd have been able to stay, knowing what I'd done."

"You're still not getting it, Raith." He had so much to live for, and it was time he started fighting for it. "You were just doing what it took to survive. Your whole life, you've been forced to do that horrible woman's bidding, and then I came along and judged you for that. I've never felt more ashamed. That I could doubt you for even a second—"

"How could you not?"

"Darya planned to kill you, and I knew it, and I still told her where to find you. How is that any better than what you did to me?"

"Your entire life has been shaped around the horrors I did to you. You have no family, and you're the last one left of your kind. How can you say that doesn't matter?"

"I'm not saying it doesn't matter. I'm saying you aren't to blame for it because you didn't have a choice."

"There is blood on my hands that can never be washed clean!" She flinched at his raised voice, though a part of her was satisfied to see him pushing back. A will to fight was a will to live. "You told me you could never care for the monster who killed your family. Harrow, I am that monster!"

"And I also told you I was wrong to say that. I didn't understand at the time what you were or how Furie had controlled you, and—"

Her words suddenly dried up as she stared at the man

sitting before her. His fiery eyes were blazing, his strong body dwarfing the delicate chair, his golden-brown skin contrasting against the plain undyed pants she'd given him.

All of a sudden, tenderness filled her. The fight drained out of her, and she could only look at him and give thanks to the Goddess he was here in her caravan, alive and well. They were two lost souls who'd been collateral damage in a senseless war that wasn't even their own. Why should that divide them when they were finally together now?

"Raith, I'm so sorry I doubted you. I'm sorry I told Darya where you were hiding. I'm sorry I left you, and I'm sorry to myself for ignoring what my own instincts were telling me from the start. And I'm sorry I let you believe I didn't love you, because I never stopped for a second. Will you forgive me?"

He stared at her. "There's nothing to forgive."

She smiled softly. "Thank you." She let the relief wash over her for a moment, not realizing how much she'd needed to hear him say that. "Now, it's your turn. You ask me for forgiveness, and I'll grant it, and then we can finally move on with our lives."

He looked uncertain. "You could actually forgive me for what I've done?"

"I already do. I just want to leave the Queens' war where it belongs—in the past—and start fresh together. Darya gave us both a second chance to get things right, and we'd be fools not to take it."

Still, he hesitated, searching her face. There was so much longing in his expression. He wanted to believe her, she knew, but couldn't quite take that step yet.

"I can't tell you what to do, Raith, but the way I see it, Furie wins if we let her actions divide us. All I want is the chance to make a future with you that doesn't involve anyone else's conflicts."

"How can I know I won't be forced to hurt you again?"

"Furie can't control you with a body."

"She took my body away last time."

"And Darya gave you a new one. And maybe she'll find a way to stop her, and things will change, but if not, we'll get through it like we're going to get through this. I'll always come for you, no matter what. And I trust you. I know you wouldn't have killed me that day in the forest, just like you didn't kill me all those years ago."

His expression was tortured. "I didn't want to hurt you. Inside, I was screaming at myself to stop, but I couldn't."

"You did stop, remember? Plus, remember Darya's powerful magic storm? If she stopped you like that once, she could stop you again. But she won't have to. Once we leave, we never have to set foot in the Southern Territory again in our lives if you don't want to."

She waited for him to respond, wanting so badly for him to agree with her, to say he was ready to move forward, but he didn't speak. His gaze transferred to the floor, and he seemed to go somewhere far away in his mind, his eyes growing distant.

"She called me Thirteen," he finally said, and Harrow knew he was talking about Furie again. "That's my real name. The name I had forgotten."

She opened her mouth to refute him, to tell him his name wasn't some hateful number and could be whatever he wanted, but he kept speaking.

"When we met, I didn't remember. And when you asked me what my name was, I just picked the first thing I read off that sign."

"I guessed that," she said softly.

"I should have known right then." His mouth twisted with a bitter smile. "I went around with the name 'Raith,' wondering who I was, when I'd labeled myself correctly from the beginning."

"But you know now, and you also know it doesn't matter."

"It does matter."

"Okay, so it matters. You're right. But it's part of who you are, and that's something to be proud of." Harrow leaned forward to emphasize her point. "Look at what you've been through. Look at the person you are—this amazing, strong, caring man. What you are—a wraith—isn't despite that, it's *because* of it. I love that about you. I love who you are, and I hope you can love yourself too."

His gaze lifted back to hers, and he went silent again, but his eyes narrowed slightly as if he was considering her words. She hoped he was. She meant them down to her bones.

"I know my feelings for you don't change anything," she said, "but I—"

"They change everything."

She nodded mutely.

"And knowing you love me...if you really do love me..." He glanced away. "Maybe I can forgive myself. Accept myself." He shrugged lightly. "If you can accept me."

"I do love you. And I do accept you. That's what I've been saying all along. How many times do I need to tell you that before you believe it?"

The edge of his mouth curved. "Maybe a few more."

She smiled back, though her sight blurred slightly with tears. "I'll tell you as many times as it takes for it to sink in."

They smiled at each other in silence for a moment, and

Harrow could sense the darkness of the past finally starting to lift, the heavy storm clouds lightening to clear skies.

"Harrow." Raith's gaze shifted away again. "I'm sorry for what I did to you and your family and for the crimes I committed in the past. Will you forgive me?"

He was actually doing it—asking for her forgiveness like she'd suggested so they could move on together. Her heart swelled with happiness.

"Of course I forgive you," she said fervently. "I love you."

Studying his hands with intense focus, he murmured, "From what I understand about love, I think I love you too."

Her eyes filled with tears. Again. But this time, these were the kind of tears she wanted to spill.

"You really want this. With me." His head lifted, and he searched her face carefully as if looking for signs of doubt. She let him stare all he wanted—he wouldn't find a single one.

"Yes, you silly man. I already told you that."

He smiled slightly, though it was still hesitant. "Darya said you were stubborn."

She chuckled. "The most stubborn. And I always get what I want."

"I've never had what I wanted before," he said, breaking her heart into a hundred pieces. "I never even knew how to want something. Until you."

"I want you to have what you want."

"You're what I want."

"And you have me."

He was still smiling softly at her, but he looked so uncomfortable, his big body squished into her tiny chair, that she felt compelled to say, "Will you come closer so I can see you better?"

His smile widened. "When I said that to you yesterday, you ran at me so fast, you blurred."

She grinned. "I bet you can go faster."

She was right. She didn't even see him move. One moment, he was in the chair, and the next, she was flat on her back with him above her. Their eyes met. He was still smiling, and it was so pure her chest ached.

But then, he brushed her hair aside and saw the scars on her shoulders where his taloned wingtips had pinned her to the ground. His face fell.

"Don't go there," she said. "Stay with me."

Their eyes met again. "Always."

"Always."

He lifted a finger to trail down her cheek. "You let me touch you with my wraith skin."

"Mm-hmm." She squirmed at the memory.

"You liked it." His gaze heated.

"Oh yes." She shivered in appreciation. "And I want to do it again."

Fiery eyes burning, he dropped his head and kissed her, needing no further prompting. Immediately, she wound her arms around his neck, pulling him closer, as close as she could get him. Their bodies pressed together, the heat of his skin like a brand against her, even through the barrier of the bedsheet.

"I want everything," she murmured, his taste and scent swamping her senses. "Don't hold back."

Despite her urgings, however, he continued to kiss her leisurely. Forearms braced on either side of her head, he simply covered her with his heated body and explored her mouth with lazy flicks of his tongue.

With her arms still wrapped around his neck, she tried

to pull him even closer, lifting her pelvis to seek the friction she craved. He let her play, but he was in no hurry to give her what she wanted.

The sheet tangled around her suddenly felt obtrusive, and she unwound her arms, struggled to yank it off, and then kicked it away, leaving her naked beneath him. Still, he never moved to assist her, content to watch hungrily as she wriggled beneath him.

Sliding her hands up his strong back, she buried her fingers in his silky hair and clenched them slightly, enough to convey her impatience. "Raith."

It was all she needed to say. His lips curved into a devastating smile, and she just knew he'd been waiting for her to beg a little.

"Are you going to let me take you, sweet one?"

"Yes," she breathed, her body aching at the mere thought. "Please, Raith."

One palm landed on the side of her ribs, sliding down to the curve of her waist, his big hand spanning half her body. "Or shall I torment you until you're crying for mercy?"

"*Raith.*"

Down his hand traveled, over the curve of her hip, his fingers clenching her soft flesh as if he could possess her with only a touch. The breath gusted out of her as his hand slid back up her inner thigh, and that breathlessness turned to a gasp as he finally touched her where she craved him the most.

Her legs widened and her hips tilted of their own accord. Every part of her body wanted to open for him—to spread wide and be taken. Consumed.

Dexterous fingers slid through her arousal, dipping inside and spreading the wetness around. As he grazed lightly over her clit, her whole lower body lifted off the mattress, and she had no hope of stifling her moan. She didn't try to. This pleasure was shared between them—she wanted him to know how he affected her. She wanted him to feel what she felt.

His eyes positively ablaze, he did it again, this time circling around. As she squirmed and moaned her pleasure, he kissed her again, trapping the sound in his own mouth. She lifted her chest, pressing her naked breasts to his heated skin, her nerves alive and singing as he continued to tease her with his fingers.

Her toes curled as she envisioned taking his hard shaft in her hands and stroking it, making him moan as she did, and then guiding him into her body. Eagerly, she reached down, fumbling with the fastening of his pants, barely able to concentrate on her endeavors when the movement of his fingers continued to consume her attention.

But that empty ache inside her demanded fulfillment, and as soon as his pants were open, she shoved them down his narrow hips as far as she could reach, taking a moment to appreciate the strength in his muscled backside. Then she bent her knees, catching her toes on the waistband and wiggling expertly to aid her efforts to slide them down.

He pulled back with a breathy laugh, watching her struggles, once again making no effort to aid her. She scowled at him with mock frustration, though secretly, she reveled in his teasing. This playful side of him was new, and she wanted to nurture it and see it grow.

Finally, he rolled off her, tugged the pants down, and tossed them away.

He was back over her in a second, his heat like a blanket, his hard shaft a heavy weight against her thigh. Without further torment, he scooped up one of her legs behind the knee and hitched it high, spreading her wide. The head of his erection aligned with her entrance, and she squirmed in anticipation.

"Is this what you want, my Harrow?"

"Oh yes." She arched into him, trying to take him inside, but he held himself away. "I need it. I need you, and if you make me wait any longer, I don't know if I'll— *Yes!*"

His hips surged forward, penetrating her aching core in one deep thrust. Her inner muscles rippled around him, the edge of pain from the tightness quickly dissolving under waves of pleasure.

He didn't move, giving her time to adjust to his size. "So tight."

It had been six months since they were together, after all. "So big." She stroked her palms down his chest. "You feel so good inside me."

He bent down and kissed her, and she wound her arms back around his neck. His movements were slow, leisurely, as he eased out of her and then sank back in.

"Change your skin again," she whispered. "I want to see your true form."

He stilled, lifting his head to meet her gaze. Yesterday, when she'd told him to change, he'd frowned, not understanding why she would care what he looked like while they were intimate. But today, she saw in his eyes that he understood well what it meant.

Instead of any shame or hesitation, his gaze heated as if her request pleased him. And then, he granted her wish.

The color faded from his skin like the moon eclipsing the sun and shadowing the day. She held a palm against his chest, marveling at the difference between them, and he watched her with a fervent gaze. His eyes blazed from amid the darkness, the fire in them brighter than ever.

Looking into the flames, she smiled. He was so beautiful, and he was hers.

And then, suddenly, they couldn't get close enough. Their lips crashed back together, tongues dueling. He crushed her into the mattress and thrust deep, his pelvis grinding against hers, the friction making her see stars. She angled her hips to fit him even deeper, grinding against him in turn.

Clutching his powerful back, she wrapped her arms around him, her nails sinking into his skin. Her legs encircled his hips, heels digging in, encouraging his relentless movements.

They made love with ferocity. With passionate desperation.

He thrust so hard into her, she slid across the bed until her head was crushed against the wall, so he scooped her up and sat her in his lap. From there, he lay back to watch her ride him, but neither of them lasted long like that. Always hungry to control her movements, he sat up again to meet her kiss, holding her still above him while he drove his hips into her from beneath.

Still, they needed more.

He picked her up and stood, tossing her on her back on the bed. He entered her again, and she cried out, wrapping her legs around him to take him deeper. She threw her arms overhead, savoring his low moan as he watched her breasts bouncing, his shadowy body moving in and out of her while his dark hands clenched around her thighs.

Lifting her again, he crossed the caravan to her desk and set her upon it. He took her desperately, his fingers caressing her clit while she cried out against his lips. Next, he dropped her on her hands and knees back on the bed. He entered her again, reaching around her hip to keep stroking her in time with his frenzied thrusts.

The orgasm climbed up from the base of her spine and crested overhead like a tidal wave. Her ecstatic cries filled the caravan as he bent and fixed his teeth around her shoulder. The prick of his fangs against her skin was sharp but careful so as not to hurt her. She didn't care about pain. She reached back to grip his head, willing him to bite harder as she rode out the final waves of her peak.

When she could take no more, she pushed his hand away from her sensitized clit, head spinning from the pleasure. He released his bite, pulled out, and flipped her over once more onto her back. Her body flopped limply, weak from her climax, and she could do nothing but cry out as he thrust back into her, reveling in the hoarse shout that burst from his lips as he finally gave in to his release.

Hips still rocking, he collapsed atop her, and she wrapped her arms and legs around him as far as she could go, wanting to hold him in the cradle of her body forever. He dropped his head to her neck, breathing hard against her skin, and she thought her heart would burst from fullness.

Eventually, he rolled them to their sides, and she cuddled into his chest, feeling tiny and vulnerable and yet safer than she'd ever felt. Together, they were stronger. Together, their vulnerability *was* strength.

She pulled back enough that she could look into his eyes. He smiled at her, the subtle crinkling of his cheeks nearly hidden by his shadowy skin.

"What are you thinking?" she asked, remembering how

they'd often asked each other that in their room at the tavern.

"That...I love you," he murmured, those fire-wreathed irises glancing away.

Her heart swelled until it nearly hurt. "And I love you. So much."

He looked back at her, and this time, he didn't look away.

This was really happening, she realized, a sudden exhilaration seizing her until it felt like she was flying. They were really going to make it. They were here together, starting over, their future wide open before them. They could end up anywhere in the world, and she wouldn't care. Just as long as they were together.

"You know," she mused, "if you wanted, you could choose a new name." This was their new beginning, and she wanted him to feel as ready for it as she did.

"No," he replied immediately. "You were right before. This...us...is because of what I am, not in spite of it. If I'm truly going to move forward, I need to accept my past. The name I chose is part of it, and I'm not going to pretend to be something I'm not." He glanced down at himself and smiled, the tips of his white fangs a stark contrast against his skin. "I mean, look at me."

She breathed a laugh, lifting a hand to trace his jawline. "I think you're perfect. And I like that. I love your name. It suits you."

Still smiling, his brow lifted. "Because I'm a wraith?"

"No—well, maybe a little. But mostly because it reminds me of how we met. How sure I was from the beginning that you were meant to be in my life."

"I like that memory."

"Me too." She placed her palm on his cheek and leaned in to kiss him. "And now let's make some new ones."

One week later, Harrow awoke to uncomfortable heat in the caravan. She must have slept in again—something she never did when she'd been on her own. Traveling in the desert meant leaving before the sun rose, resting in the heat of the day, and traveling until it was too dark to see. But since reuniting with Raith, she'd relaxed her schedule considerably. They had nowhere to be, nothing to do except be together and enjoy each other's company.

It went without saying they'd been doing that a lot.

Throwing back the thin sheet, she padded naked to the wardrobe and donned a light robe. The windows were open, and a gentle breeze ruffled the sarong over the open door. Harrow went there and peeked around it.

Yesterday, they'd found a little spring surrounded by scruffy trees. Clean water and shade—out here, this place was paradise. Outside, Raith was keeping Fiona company by the water's edge.

Harrow had taught him everything she knew about caring for her horse (which wasn't much), and he'd proved to be a fast learner. In fact, he seemed to enjoy the tasks and was already much better with Fiona than Harrow was. And of course, the horse loved him, nuzzling him at every opportunity, far more enthusiastic about putting on her harness if Raith was the one doing it.

Smiling, Harrow ducked back inside and went to the desk to commence her morning ritual. She filled her scrying bowl with water, lit a stick of incense and a charcoal tablet, and then placed a pinch of her dwindling supply of vision herbs atop it. At some point, they would have to journey to the Western Territory to gather more from the lakes and marshes where the plants grew.

Exhaling deeply, releasing all distracting thoughts, Harrow gazed into the bowl and let the Water rise...

Moments later, she jumped upright with a gasp, stumbling backward into the stove and nearly knocking over the chair.

"Raith!"

She sprinted outside, practically ripping the sarong off the doorway and taking the steps in one leap. Raith looked up in alarm, dropping everything to run toward her.

"Raith!"

They reached each other. She clutched his arms, staring into his eyes.

"What is it?" Poor Raith didn't know what was going on.

She was so excited she could barely speak. "Raith, I was just scrying! Sweet Goddess—"

"What, Harrow?"

"We're— I'm— We're having a baby! She's so beautiful, Raith. She's the most perfect—"

"A what?"

"A girl! A baby girl!" She had to laugh at the look on his face. "I'm pregnant."

"P-pregnant..." He was swaying on his feet. Was he going to faint? "A girl...?"

"Yes, a baby girl. You're going to be a father."

"A fath—"

He dropped right to the ground as if his legs couldn't support him any longer. Laughing in sheer happiness and exhilaration, Harrow dropped beside him, and they clutched each other on the sandy desert floor while Fiona stared at them as if they'd both lost their minds.

"You're pregnant?" he asked when he'd recovered enough to speak again. "How do you know?"

"The Water showed it to me just now."

"How long?"

"We conceived the first night we reunited," she said with a grin. "My mate was in a hurry." Elemental children were incredibly rare, and the offspring of two different Elementals even rarer—so rare, many believed it impossible. For her to get pregnant so quickly... It was a miracle. A blessing from the Goddess.

Harrow had never seen Raith's eyes so wide. "A girl?"

"Yes. I saw her, Raith. She's so beautiful." Her eyes filled with tears.

But he looked suddenly stricken. "Harrow, does she... look like a wraith?"

She knew he was afraid their daughter would face the same cruelty he had, and she shook her head. "But even if she did, she would still be the most beautiful—and only— Seer-wraith in existence, and we'd love her just as much."

Raith nodded fiercely. "And we'll kill anyone who even thinks to harm her."

They were in perfect agreement on that one. "She has your eyes."

He frowned. "My eyes?"

"And they're beautiful," Harrow said firmly, daring him to disagree. "Just like her father's."

His face softened again. He lifted a hand to stroke Harrow's hair from her face. "I already know she's perfect. She's our daughter."

"Exactly. That's exactly right."

They stared at each other, hearts overflowing.

"Let's go home," Harrow declared.

Raith frowned. "Where's home?"

They had Fiona and the sturdy caravan. And, more importantly, they had each other.

Harrow smiled up at him. "Wherever we want it to be."

EPILOGUE

One year later…

"Oh good, you're up." Malaikah ducked under the awning and took a seat in the customer's chair, looking as though she was about to receive a reading from the great "Seer Who Survived," as Salizar had dubbed Harrow. Not that the Seer was even doing readings today—the circus was en route at present, stopped for a rest day outside a small village.

"Barely." Harrow yawned from the lounge. She was "up," but her hair was an unbrushed tangle of frizz, and she still wore her nightgown. Other than her mother's locket, she hadn't opened her jewelry box in months, and any dresses that didn't have easy breastfeeding access were collecting dust in the wardrobe. "I don't know how human women can handle having more than one child."

Malaikah chuckled. "You told me you guys conceived

on your first night back together. Human or not, you're definitely having more than one."

Harrow winced. "Let's not think about that just yet." Baby Mellora's birth had been about as easy as giving birth could be on a woman, but that wasn't saying much. Three months later, Harrow's poor body was still recovering.

Excruciating agony aside, it had been by far the most wonderful, beautiful experience of her life. Her loving mate had held her hand throughout the hours of labor, despite his nearly fainting a dozen times, and he had endured without complaint all the threats she hurled at him amid contractions. The result had been a gorgeous baby daughter passed into their arms, her cries filling the air while their tears of happiness fell onto her perfect, tiny body.

They'd named her Mellora, after Harrow's mother. Her skin was light brown, her hair dark, her tiny ears pointed, and her eyes like Raith's—the outer edges as black as her pupils. Instead of fire-wreathed irises, however, hers were a luminescent silver that identified her as a Seer.

The moment she saw her, Harrow knew she would be just like her father. A father who was going to spoil her rotten, if his behavior thus far was anything to go by. Harrow expected nothing less, for they were both heartily in agreement:

Mellora was obviously the most perfect child ever born.

"Where is the miracle baby, anyway?" Mal asked.

"She's inside with Raith. She just woke up and will want to nurse soon, but Raith's taking care of her until then so I could nap."

"Good man."

"I know." Harrow sighed.

Before meeting up with Salizar's circus in the Western Territory, Raith and Harrow had traveled together for five months, Harrow offering readings as they went to keep them afloat. It had been Raith's suggestion to rejoin the circus. Though Harrow had protested for his sake—she never wanted him to feel obligated to return to the place he'd been treated so horribly—Raith had argued that Harrow would want Malaikah close when Mellora was born, and that having Salizar taking care of the business aspect of her Seer duties would give her more time to focus on being a mother. He was right, and his selflessness meant everything to her.

Contrary to what Harrow had once feared, Salizar had not been the least bit hesitant to have the last surviving Seer under his protection. On the contrary, he saw her presence as an investment in his enterprise and a way to draw even more clientele to the circus.

In order to secure her reemployment, however, Harrow had demanded Salizar offer Raith a sincere apology and a promise to behave respectfully in the future. She needn't have bothered. Raith seemed to have gotten over his hatred of Salizar after learning he'd been protecting Harrow since her childhood. And Salizar had begun to respect Raith after their fight at the tavern. The two might never be friends, but they tolerated each other, and it was enough.

Though Salizar charged customers an arm and a leg for a reading with Harrow, her popularity had only continued to grow. The "Seer Who Survived" drew crowds of humans and Elementals alike wherever they traveled. Salizar had even commissioned a new advertisement banner for the circus with both Malaikah's and Harrow's faces on it.

Raith took care of Mellora while Harrow did readings, lingering nearby in case of trouble. Sometimes he helped the laborers with odd jobs around the circus, but mostly, he was content to be a father to Mellora.

Harrow thought that was perfect. After everything he'd been through, he deserved a little peace and quiet, and who wouldn't want to spend every available moment looking into the tiny, angelic face of their daughter?

And Raith truly could have peace now. Several months ago, Darya had sent word that for the first time in centuries, she, Audra, and Nashira had gotten together and merged their magics to bind Furie's powers. They had also surrounded her castle with an impenetrable barrier to imprison her within. No one could come or go.

The Fire Queen had fallen but was still protected from any who might wish to take advantage of her defenseless state. Despite everything she'd done, her sisters didn't want her dead. As long as Furie remained trapped and powerless, Harrow supposed she could accept this.

She hoped them banding together meant the Queens were working toward solving their differences. While there was a part of her that would never forgive them for what they'd done, she could only hope all that was behind them now.

As for the ninety-nine other wraiths that Raith had liberated, they had vanished completely, likely from the physical world altogether. Considering what they were capable of, however, Darya hadn't been thrilled to learn they were loose and had been searching for them. So far, she'd found nothing. Harrow figured that since no rumors were abounding of powerful, shadowy creatures wreaking untold havoc, there was no harm leaving them be.

A baby cried from inside the caravan. Though she quieted again instantly — Raith was truly a miracle — Harrow's breasts had begun to ache. "I should go feed Melly. Do you want to hold her first?"

"Nah, I'll come back this afternoon. Let you guys have your family time."

"You're family too, Mal."

Malaikah smiled. "Oh, I know. I plan to take full advantage of my role as the eccentric aunt."

"Goddess forbid."

She chuckled. "You have any new advice for me?"

"Nothing yet." A few days ago, Harrow had received a vision telling her the time was coming for Malaikah to return to Kambu. Unfortunately, it hadn't been forthcoming with details, and she was still waiting for more information to come. "I've been scrying constantly, but I'm only getting this vague image of a crossroads. I have this sense that you're approaching something big, and you'll be forced to make a difficult choice, but I don't know more than that. It's frustrating, to say the least."

"The Water knows best," Mal replied easily, though Harrow knew her well enough to tell she was nervous. "It'll show you more when it's time, I guess."

Harrow nodded, wishing things were different. The thought of her best friend leaving the circus forever was heartbreaking. But she knew how deep Malaikah's need to return home ran. If she gave up on it, who would she be?

"Don't worry about it. It'll happen when it's meant to, right?" Mal stood. "For now, you have a hungry baby to feed, and I need to find Salizar. I want to get his opinion on the new routine I'm working out."

"He'll obviously love it. You're the 'Amazing Malaikah,' after all."

Mal grinned. "Obviously. I'll see you at dinner, yeah?"

"Definitely." Harrow embraced Mal before she whirled away like a mini cyclone. Harrow smiled to herself. Malaikah was truly a force to be reckoned with.

Mellora gave another squabble from inside, reminding Harrow she still hadn't eaten. Not to mention, her leaky breasts were seconds away from soaking through her nightgown. Again. She climbed the stairs and went into the caravan.

Inside, Raith was cradling Mellora against his bare chest with one strong arm. His free hand was held above her tiny face, and she sucked on his finger while he whispered soft endearments.

Harrow's heart nearly burst. Was there anything more perfect in the world?

Their gazes met.

"She wants her mother." He smiled with such easy contentment now. The change was night and day from the tortured man he'd been only a year ago. A loving mate and child would do that, she supposed.

She took Mellora, tugging her gown down to free one breast. Immediately, her daughter started to nurse, making happy slurping sounds. Harrow looked back at Raith. "Thank you for looking after her so I could rest."

He bent down to kiss her. "Helping you with Melly is a gift."

She sighed. Did he have any idea how amazing he was?

"You look beautiful this morning." He stroked a hand over her tangled mop of frizz.

She snorted. "I look like I haven't slept in three months, which is actually pretty accurate."

"You look like the mother of my child. There is nothing more beautiful."

She sighed again. *Definitely amazing.*

"You didn't manage to sleep outside?"

She shook her head. "I was worrying about Malaikah. I still don't understand that crossroads I keep seeing. It feels like something big is coming into her life—a new person, maybe. Except I have this feeling that person has been there all along, right under her nose. Which doesn't even make sense. And if the choice is about whether to choose the circus or her homeland, why would another person factor into it at all?"

"You're worrying too much."

"I can't help it."

"She's your sister, not your second child," Raith teased. Yep, he teased her now. And not just in bed.

"Yes, but—"

"No more buts." And interrupted her too. She scowled. "You said it yourself. This is who she is."

"I know, I know." She shot him a mock glare. "You look so smug when you're right."

With a completely straight face, he replied, "Then I must look smug all the time."

"You're terrible." But she chuckled despite herself.

"Yes, and you're mine." He kissed the end of her nose and the top of his nursing daughter's head and then snatched a shirt from the pile on the bed. Oh, and he was messy now, too, not that Harrow cared. She was probably messier than he was.

He threw the shirt over his head and slipped past her to the door, giving her ass a pat as he walked by. Another new habit. "I have to go get some supplies from the meal tent, but I'll be back."

"Supplies? For what?"

"For our picnic."

"What picnic?"

"Since we're not traveling today, I thought we could take Fiona and go somewhere quiet to have lunch."

She smiled. "That sounds lovely."

"Then wait here, and I'll be back in a bit with food and our horse."

"But I'm not dressed, and Mellora's still nursing."

He gave her a blank look. "You're wearing a dress."

Typical man. He didn't even notice the difference between her nightgown and her regular clothes. *Then again*, she thought, glancing down at herself with a shrug, *maybe he's on to something*. If anyone could justify spending the whole day in a nightgown, it was a new mother.

"I guess I'm ready, then," she said with a grin.

He flashed a dazzling smile in return and then ducked out of the caravan.

A couple of hours later, they were on Fiona's back, riding through the silent forest. Raith sat behind Harrow, his strong arms wrapped around her, steering the horse. Mellora was swaddled carefully against Harrow's breast. She wasn't worried about falling—Raith's reflexes were lightning fast, and her motherly instincts were amplified by her Seer abilities. There had never been a more protected child, she was sure of it.

They stopped at the top of a rise, finding a clearing on the cliff's edge with a breathtaking view of the valley below. They ate a simple meal and then lay down on the blanket, watching the clouds move, their little daughter asleep between them.

Later, Harrow pulled her Seer cards from the bag and shuffled the deck. Since Darya's magic had been the catalyst for Raith's corporeal body, he had a bit of Water magic in him, and Harrow had learned he felt a connection to her cards. She'd begun teaching him what they meant.

They did a reading together, taking turns drawing until there were six faceup.

First, Harrow drew the Waterfall—a symbol of change and new beginnings. Raith drew the Mist, symbolizing the intangible and mysterious. Next, the Spring—life-giving rejuvenation. Then, the River—water seeking its origin, a journey of perseverance. The fifth card was the Ocean, the source of all life.

The sixth and final card was Raith's, and it was no surprise which one he drew.

He laid it down beside the others. "I always get this one."

To Harrow, Raith's card had taken on a newer, more personal meaning. "It represents the choice to dive headfirst into the unknown. To confront grief and conquer fear."

"To embrace the darkness and find peace."

"Exactly." They exchanged smiles.

Between them, Mellora made a tiny sound in her sleep, her little hands twitching. They both looked at her with soft expressions.

"I think she's dreaming," Raith said.

Harrow thought of her own dream. The nightmare that had become a blessing. The choice she'd made to dive. The wisdom she'd gained from the darkness.

"I hope she chooses the deep," Harrow said, smiling up at her mate.

ACKNOWLEDGMENTS

Thank you, dear reader, for coming along on Raith and Harrow's journey with me. This story means so much to me, and I'm so grateful to be able to share it with you.

The first inspiration for this book came when I was driving across Canada. Somewhere along the Trans-Canada highway in Ontario, there is a very small community called Raith with a single road sign that somehow caught my eye as I drove past. My immediate thought was, *That's my next hero's name!*

The next book will be about Malaikah and her destiny to return to her homeland. I loved her character from the moment she sauntered onto the page, so I can't wait to dive into her head and bring you along with me!

A lot of people were involved in making this story into what it is today, but first and foremost, I have to thank my editor, Molly Majumder. When we first started working on this together, I can honestly say I had no idea we would end up where we did! It's been a wild ride, and I'm so grateful and excited for what's to come. Thank you for helping me build my vision for this world.

I also want to express my gratitude to the entire Entangled/Red Tower team, including Liz, Bree, Curtis, Meredith, Stacy, Jessica, Toni, and everyone else who worked on Sanctuary. Also Rae, for your assistance with inclusive language and the sensitive and authentic portrayal of all my characters. Thank you all so much, it's been an absolute joy working with you. The cover and map and all the little details that went into this book are beyond beautiful, and I can and will stare at them for hours.

As always, thanks to my husband Orion for supporting my creative endeavors, listening to me rant about my characters (and life in general), and helping me brainstorm my way out of any plot hole. I feel like I can do anything when you believe in me!

And last but certainly not least, I want to give a huge shout-out to every one of my Patrons, readers, mailing-list subscribers, social-media followers, and fellow romance lovers. Your support, passion, and general awesomeness is what makes this community such a special one to be part of. I hope one day we take over the world, because I know we'll make it a better place!

xx Aurora

P.S. If you want to keep in touch, come find me on social media (@aurora.ascher.author), join my mailing list, or even better, become a Patron and get access to exclusive short stories and monthly character art. You can find links to everything on my website: www.auroraascher.com

Firefly meets The Breakfast Club *in this snarky new-adult romance from #1 NYT bestselling author Tracy Wolff and Nina Croft*

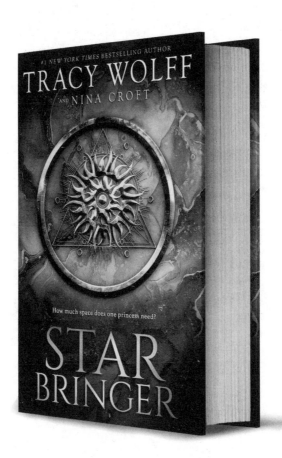

The only thing standing between a dying sun and ultimate salvation is seven unlikely misfits... ahem, heroes.

Turn the page for a sneak peek...

CHAPTER 1

Kalinda, Crown Princess of the Nine Planets

"That's it. Your privileges as companion-in-waiting have been officially revoked."

Lara lays out the giant purple monstrosity she's selected for me to wear, undeterred. But I see the tiniest hint of a grin start to slip onto her lips. "And what privileges would those be, Your Highness?"

"You don't think you've got privileges?" I send her an arch look from where I'm sitting on the bed, but she's already returned to smoothing out my dress. "So ungrateful."

One of the best parts of having your best friend also be your companion-in-waiting is that you can give her shit. Sure, Lara tends to stick to propriety even when it's just the two of us, but our best moments are when I can get her veneer of decorum to crack. And the full-on grin she's giving me now warms me up from the inside out.

Of course, when your best friend is also your companion-in-waiting, she can talk you into *doing* shit you don't want to do—like wearing giant purple dresses that make you look like a Kridacan desert slogg with a nasty case of space pox.

"If by privileges, you mean the honor of waking up

before five every morning, then may the Ancients bless you for the honor." Lara continues unbuttoning the ugliest dress in existence before retrieving a matching pair of high-heeled shoes.

I bat my eyes. "Admit it. You love our early-morning swims."

"Oh, absolutely, Your Highness." She shoves her long brown hair out of her face, then picks up one of the heels and undoes its delicate jeweled clasp. "Almost as much as you love dates with ambassadors' sons. Maybe I should mention to the Empress how much you miss Jorathon."

I narrow my eyes at her. "You wouldn't dare."

Before she can answer, the pod we are traveling in comes to a stop. We have officially docked on the Imperial Space Station *Caelestis*.

My stomach twists with a combination of nerves and excitement. I've been dying to get a look at the crown jewel of the Empire's science program since the spacebreaking ceremony several years ago. But this is the first time I've actually gotten near her, and I'm practically coming undone with excitement.

The fact that it's also my first official duty away from the palace negates some of that excitement—as does the fact that I have to tour it in full Imperial Regalia while doing my level best not to screw anything up. If I make one mistake, the Council's doubts will be confirmed, and I'll be stuck in the palace for the next fifty years.

Which is why I have no intention of messing up. The consequences don't bear thinking about.

"Give me your leg." When I continue to scowl at her, Lara grabs my leg herself and starts shoving my foot into the shoe. She snaps the clasp shut hard enough to have me yelping, then reaches for the second one.

"I keep telling you—I can do that myself." I try to take the purple heel away and get a hand slapped for the effort.

"Companion. In. Waiting," is all she says as she starts slipping on the second shoe, albeit much more gently than the first.

"Exactly. Waiting, not dressing."

"It's the same thing, and it's my job." She snaps the second heel into place, and her expression softens. "You're going to look gorgeous in this dress, Your Highness."

I sigh. "So gorgeous I might even find some hot Corporation guard or science nerd to show me a *good* time?" I waggle my eyebrows, just in case she didn't get my emphasis on the word "good."

Her firm mask of propriety is back in place, her russet skin smooth and unmarred by so much as the tiniest grin. "Absolutely not. For so many reasons."

Lara holds the dress out for me to slip on feet first—less chance of me messing up the elaborate hairstyle she spent the last hour twisting my long hair into.

"Kidding. I haven't forgotten we're here to talk about saving the entire system from total annihilation. I feel like that's more important than me getting laid."

Lara mutters something that sounds a lot like, "Debatable," but it's so fast that I can't call her on it.

"Plus," I add, "my mother went against the Council to send me on this trip. She's trusting me to do a good job and not screw anything up. Sleeping with some random in a space lab seems like the definition of screwing things up."

I try to take a deep breath, the weight of everything I'm about to do suddenly way more substantial than it was a second before, but Lara is already buttoning me into a dress so heavy and jewel-encrusted, it might as well be body armor. There's no longer room for movement of my diaphragm, which means joking around is definitely out. Unfortunately, so is breathing.

"You look so beautiful, Your Highness." Lara steps back as she finishes with the last of the tiny jeweled buttons. "What do you think?"

"Are there any sloggs bigger than the ones from Kridacus? Because if there are, I definitely look like one of those."

"Nope," she replies as she turns me to face the full-length mirror that runs along the wall. "Kridacans are definitely the largest."

I sigh glumly as I survey my reflection. "Then I'm definitely a new species. Hopefully of the nonpoisonous variety."

She takes the dress's cape out of the closet and wraps it around my shoulders. Because, obviously, a giant purple cape is what it was missing.

I glare at her, which she completely ignores as she fastens it with a brooch in the shape of a starburst just beneath my neck.

Before I can try to talk her into leaving the cape off — overkill is an actual thing — the comms beep. Lara and I exchange a look, and I sigh heavily. Only one person would be calling the comms link right now, and her title begins with E and ends with double S. Lucky me.

"What does she want now?" I mutter as I slide into the seat in front of the screen. Or, more accurately, try to slide. The dress makes it impossible, so I end up moving the chair aside and just standing.

"To wish you luck, I'm sure." Lara's answer is circumspect — exactly how a companion-in-waiting should answer.

Her expression, however, falls for a second into total annoyance.

I snicker as I answer the call.

The Empress narrows her eyes on me from the viewscreen. "I hope you don't plan on laughing like that when you get off the ship, Kalinda. What is it I always tell you?"

"A royal's mask never falters," I recite for the millionth time.

"That's right. I know you have this, Kalinda." She sends me a smile that, for just a second, actually appears indulgent. But then naturally, she follows it up with, "Don't make me regret sending you off-planet. Do I need to go over how important this is?"

I mentally roll my eyes. "I know how important it is, Mother. And I've wanted to come aboard the *Caelestis* since before she became operational. I promise I won't embarrass you or the Empire."

"See that you don't. Also, make sure Ambassador Holdren doesn't get you alone. He has an agenda that doesn't coincide with ours, and I don't want you making any promises to him. And avoid the delegate from Glacea. From what I understand, he tends toward inappropriate conversation, and I would prefer to avoid any more *unfortunate incidents*."

She gives me a look that I know is supposed to shame me. But I stand behind my decision to push Councilor Samalani into my mother's Verbosnia bushes. Well, except for the fact that my hands had to actually come in contact with him to do it.

On the plus side, he hasn't said a single thing about my breasts since.

A knock sounds on the door. "Sorry, Mother, but Arik is here. I have to go."

"He'll wait until our conversation is through, I assure you." But she relents. "Don't overpromise. Don't ask too many questions. Don't forget the Imperial face, and you'll do great."

As if I could ever forget the Imperial face. Don't smile. Don't frown. Look interested but bored at the same time—all without actually moving a facial muscle. She's had me practicing since I was five.

"I won't. Thank you for this opportunity, Mother." I sign off before she can say anything else. I'm nervous enough already without any more of her awesome pep talk.

"We're so lucky to have her," Lara says. Again, totally circumspect. But also totally not.

There's another knock.

"Coming, Arik," I call.

Lara opens the door for me, then steps back to let me precede her into the main section of the pod—which is about half the size of the royal quarters I was just in.

"I'm sorry to rush you, Your Highness," Arik says with a respectful bow of his head. His green eyes glow with amusement.

"Not at all," I tell him. "I was just speaking with the Empress."

He gives me a sympathetic wink. Like Lara, he's been with me all my life and was a friend of my father's. I trust him implicitly.

My other bodyguard, Vance, is a new member of my entourage, and I'm pretty sure he's reporting to my mother. I'd trust him with my life but not my secrets—if I had any.

A sudden, sharp beeping splits the air. I jump, and both Arik and Vance look concerned. I mentally roll my eyes again—like they're the only ones who are allowed to be a little on edge? This is my first time representing the Empire. Surely I'm allowed a few nerves.

I'll be fine once I'm out there.

The pilot must have noticed my reaction, because he smiles at me before continuing to press a bunch of buttons that all look exactly the same to me. "It's just the final system-check indicator, Your Highness," he says. "We're cleared to disembark."

"Thank you."

Lara reaches a comforting hand toward me, then stops at the last second. From now on, we're on strict royal protocols, and a person doesn't just reach out in public and touch a Princess of the Senestris System—even if that person happens to *dress that same princess every day*. Just another of my mom's bizarre rules, and I add it to my mental list of things to change when I'm Empress.

I take another deep breath and give Lara my cockiest I've-got-this smile. She returns it with a little head tilt that tells me to get moving.

But as the shuttle's disembarkment ramp extends, my stomach flips with nerves. I ignore it and focus on my job instead. Toe the line. Deliver the message. Don't shame the Empire.

I straighten my spine and settle my best regal, I'm-so-bored look on my face. Then turn to Lara for an inspection.

She looks concerned.

Less grimace, more grin, then. Got it.

"Ready?" she asks.

"More than," I answer.

I'm ready to step onto the ramp, but Vance and Arik beat me to it. One quiet look from Vance's steel-gray eyes has me standing down despite the impatience gurgling inside of me. It's his job to make sure no one gets a clear shot at me. Except, of course, the Empress...

While I wait, I study the docking bay further—a huge, cavernous room with silver walls and a curved ceiling high above us. It's crowded with sleek and shiny shuttles of various designs. They all look new and impressive—even the patched ones—like every delegate is determined to put their best foot forward.

Then my gaze snags on something that doesn't quite fit in. It's dry docked in the far corner of the bay. I presume it's a ship, much bigger than the shuttles, but it's hard to tell anything else as it's covered by some sort of dark cloth.

To protect it or to hide it?

I love a mystery, and I itch to head over there and take a peek. But at that moment, Arik gives the all-clear from below and we're ready for business. My heart rate jumps. I'm trying to be cool, but this is a huge deal. And not just for me.

Because the reason we're here is to find out exactly where the oh-so-brilliant Dr. Veragelen is with her very important and very expensive research.

Is the massive amount of money poured into this research station going to save us all from a fiery and very imminent death?

Or to put it frankly—are we all going to die?

CHAPTER 2

Rain, High Priestess of the Sisterhood of the Light

"Oh, Merrick, look. There she is. She's so perfect. She looks just like a…" My mind goes blank, the way it does when I'm excited. Thankfully, that doesn't happen very often: the blankness *or* the excitement.

Maybe it's due to the drugs they gave me to help my body adjust to the much higher gravity here on the *Caelestis*. The space station is set to Askkandian gravity, which is more than twice that of my home planet, Serati. All I know is I've never felt this heavy before, like I'm fighting through mud with every step I take.

Then again, that could just be my nerves. Of all the places I'd ever imagined standing, here on this space station isn't one of them. Not just because its mission—stopping the sun from exploding—goes against everything it's pretty much my job to help bring about, but because high priestesses don't usually do this sort of thing.

"I think the word you're looking for is 'princess,' High Priestess." Merrick's tone is dry, but then, it's always dry. I think sarcasm is his second calling, right behind being my bodyguard.

"Maybe so, but how am I supposed to know that? It's not like I've ever seen a real live princess before." It's not like I've seen much of anything before. But that's not Merrick's fault.

It's no one's fault, really. It just is.

The princess glides to the top of the ramp, and I push up on my tiptoes to get a better look at her. She's tall, really tall, and though I tell myself that it doesn't matter, I can't help being a little jealous.

Not of her tiara or her amazing dress but of her long, willowy height.

I know high priestesses aren't supposed to care about their looks, and most of the time I don't. But every once in a while, being the shortest person in any room I'm in really stinks.

Today it stinks more than usual. Partly because I'm lost in the crowd and partly because in every glimpse I manage to get of her, the princess looks perfect. Regal. Serene. Confident.

I'd really like some of that serenity—and that confidence. Both are hallmarks of every high priestess the Sisterhood has ever had. Until me.

The princess floats toward the dais, her feet barely touching the ground. As people lean forward, eager to get a glimpse of her, I realize Merrick and I will soon be face-to-face with her. "Merrick?"

"Yes, High Priestess?"

"What do I call her again?"

He sighs, and in it I hear all the disappointment he doesn't voice. But he doesn't have to. I get that I'm a trial and a tribulation to him most days, but I also suspect that deep down, he cares about me. "If she addresses you directly—and let's all send up a special prayer that *doesn't* happen—then you must call her Your Highness."

His words momentarily quash my excitement at being here. In the same room as the princess, yes, but also here on the space station, so far from the only place I've ever lived. Home.

But then the energy of this place—of these people—has my blood fizzing in my veins. "Got it. And, Merrick—?"

Another sigh. "We went through all of this on the flight. You should have been paying attention."

"I know. But I was in space, Merrick. In *actual* space." And I wanted to know how everything worked. I think I annoyed the poor pilot with my incessant questions.

But what does Merrick expect? I've spent my entire nineteen years of existence in the monastery on Serati. And except for this one trip, it's likely where I'll spend the rest of my life—as all the high priestesses do. So I intend to make the most of it.

"Don't curtsy," he tells me, and I glance over at him as he smooths a large hand down the front of his white robes. "It's not required of an ambassador, and for the love of the Dying Sun, do not touch her. That's punishable by death. Just remember you're representing not only the Sisterhood but the planet of Serati."

How could I possibly forget? My own importance has been drilled into me every day of my life.

Though I'm honestly still scrambling to believe that I'm here. I shouldn't be. But at dinner four nights ago, the ambassador who was supposed to go— I cut off the thought before the picture of her choking and foaming at the mouth forms in my brain yet again.

She was poisoned, Merrick says. By someone who hates

the Sisterhood, obviously. And someone who wanted her to suffer.

Even after what happened to that poor woman, I didn't think I'd be selected for this trip. As high priestess and the second-ranking person in the Sisterhood's hierarchy, I know I'm important—to the Sisterhood and my planet. But I don't normally play an active role in anything. I just...wait. And have faith. And when the time is right, I'll... Well, no one actually knows that bit. Or if they do, they haven't shared it with me yet.

Still, all will eventually be revealed.

Or not.

Like each of the high priestesses before me, I'll likely die not knowing, then be reborn to live this life again.

Except, for the first time, that might not be true.

Merrick says we're in unprecedented times. My spiritual advisors tell me everything is different now.

Because the time of the Dying Sun is upon us. It began nearly twenty years ago. At first there were only a few signs of instability, mainly solar flares, but as the years passed, our sun began changing color—first orange, now tinged with red. Plus, it's expanding, causing system warming that is—at the moment, anyway—mainly affecting the inner planets. Serati was always hot, but now it's *seriously* hot.

Despite the downsides, it's been an exciting time for the Sisterhood, with a record number of new members. Unfortunately for me, that excitement hasn't managed to extend to the monastery.

But thoughts of rebirth remind me of something. "Did you know we're both from Askkandia?" I ask Merrick.

It's unusual for a high priestess to come from anywhere but Serati. I'm apparently an anomaly, but the portents were all in place. When the old high priestess dies, another is reborn. And there are all sorts of signs and precursors that guide the Sisterhood to the new priestess. In this case, those signs guided the Sisterhood to me.

"Me and the princess," I clarify.

"Yes," Merrick replies shortly. But then, Merrick knows everything.

"And we're both nineteen?"

"I'm aware of that as well." He jerks his chin toward the princess. "Now pay attention."

Merrick's watching everyone carefully. He's a warrior priest and has been my bodyguard for the last four years. Though honestly, it's a pretty cushy job. He's trained to fight, but it's not like there are a lot of threats in a monastery. Except poison, but that's a very new development. A four-day-old development, to be exact.

Ever since that night, he's been eating a bite of my food and drinking a sip of my drink before I ever get to touch it. Bodyguard *and* poison tester now.

No wonder he's in a bad mood.

Plus, this gathering is a whole different situation, and he's been distracted since we got the news. I can't decide if it's because he's worried about protecting me or if he's just wondering why I, of all people, was chosen to be the ambassador from Serati.

Of all the people on our planet, how could the Sisterhood really think I should be the one to replace Ambassador Frellen when she died? Surely there was someone more suitable for the job. Someone who was actually trained in the protocols of the Ruling Families.

I don't even look Seratian.

The people from Serati, where Merrick was born, are

unique—they've adapted over the generations to cope with the planet's less-than-ideal conditions of high heat and low gravity, not to mention off-the-charts levels of radiation. While I'm short, with pasty white skin, Merrick is tall and quite thin. His skin is tanner than mine because he's outside more, but it also has faint silver lines in a beautiful swirling pattern that is common to all people of Serati, as it helps keep them cool in the brutal temperatures. He has narrow, slightly tilted eyes with dark black irises to cope with the radiation, and his hair is platinum blond.

He's very striking, and I always feel insipid standing next to him.

At least our trip has taken his mind off his other issues. Merrick's father died recently, and it hit him very hard. I sense they were close, though he's never spoken to me about his family.

I turn my attention back to the side of the dais just as the princess is ascending. She doesn't even climb stairs like a normal person—she seems to float majestically up them.

I think I have a crush.

As she moves closer to us, I glance around at the other delegates. They're so colorful, like the exotic flying creatures from the rain forests of Ellindan. I sigh and peer down at my ugly white robes. I know it's beneath me—my mind is obviously meant for higher things—but the fact is, I long for color.

Plus, it's just one more thing that separates me from them, as if our belief systems weren't enough.

I know from my reading—I read a lot; there's not much else to do in the monastery—that each delegation is decked out in a different color, as dictated by tradition. Blue, green, purple, red, yellow, orange, and white. Of course, only members of the Ruling Families are allowed to wear these colors. The workers' guild wears browns and grays. The technicians who work for the Corporation wear black.

Mingled with all the color are the black-and-gray uniforms of what I presume are the station's security officers. There are a lot of them about. Are they expecting trouble? Maybe that's why Merrick is so tense.

We've all been standing on this dais in the center of the docking bay for an hour now, lined up in order of the farthest to the nearest planet from Serai, our sun. First, the outer planets of Glacea, the farthest, then Vistenia, Askkandia, Ellindan. Then the inner planets: Permuna, Kridacus, and finally, Serati—where I live. Serati is the only planet not governed by one of the Ruling Families. It's run by the Sisterhood. Obviously there's no one here from the outermost "dead" planets of Tybris and Nabroch—they're too cold and inhospitable to support human life.

At the very end of the line, dressed in a long blue coat trimmed with fur, is the delegate from Glacea. He's short, even shorter than me, like most Glaceans, and has a lot of hair to protect him from the cold. He smiles, showing really sharp teeth, and his taupe skin is chapped and peeling from the wind and freezing weather. The princess nods back and speaks briefly, then moves on.

See, Rain, not so scary. You can do this.

For a second, I imagine how our exchange will go. She'll smile at me, her eyes a kindly silver—I love silver—warming as they meet my plain brown ones. She'll ask me a question about Serati, and I'll dazzle her with an answer that makes those same eyes widen in surprise. Her smile, already more than polite, will grow more interested and—

"Pay attention," Merrick hisses again.

I sigh, but to show that I heard him, I stand up so straight that my back muscles hurt a little bit in all this dense gravity. It's not nearly as much fun as my imaginary life, but I'll admit, finally getting to see people from all across the seven inhabited planets is pretty fascinating.

The next in line is the delegate from Vistenia, Glacea's nearest neighbor and the main grain producer in the system. The ambassador is a tall, blond woman with pearlescent skin and the large eyes with big pupils so common on her often dark planet. She's dressed all in green and reminds me of the graceful gala lilies that bloom on Vistenia only one month of the year.

"Your Highness," she murmurs.

The princess nods more warmly this time. "Ambassador Terra, I hope you had a pleasant journey."

Then Askkandia, in purple like the princess.

And so it goes.

She greets the ambassador from Ellindan, who's dressed in a tight-fitting red jump suit only a few shades darker than her copper skin. The ambassador flashes a showy smile — I've heard that everyone from Ellindan has red teeth, stained from drinking too much akara juice, and it's fascinating to see that's true. To me, it's not exactly a good look, but apparently everyone on Ellindan is super proud of it. Plus, the juice is addictive enough that they'd probably deal with it regardless.

The princess is getting closer, and I can feel my muscles tensing up. It will be my turn soon.

Don't touch her. No matter how kind her silver eyes look smiling into yours, don't so much as skim a finger along her cape. Princesses aren't to be touched.

Although the closer she gets to me, the more I wonder if she really will be kind. Or if she'll be upset that I'm here because of who I am and what my religion believes.

The fifth delegate is from Permuna, the first of the inner planets. He has a barrel chest and large ears like most Permunians and is dressed in long robes the yellow of the desert sands of his planet. The skin around his eyes is darker than the rest of his face. I glance down and see his hands are the same color.

Apparently, from an early age, they dye those exposed areas to avoid sunburn, until the dye becomes a permanent mark. It looks like he's wearing a mask, and it makes his yellow eyes stand out even more. They seem like the eyes of a predator, but I read that the color is a side effect of a diet rich in starburst cactus, one of the only plants that grow prolifically on Permuna.

The ambassador doesn't look happy. His eyes are narrowed, his lips pinched, and his hands clench into fists as he steps forward to meet the princess. In a blink, a huge man with sepia skin and close-cropped gray hair in purple-and-black body armor moves between them—the princess's bodyguard, presumably—and I feel Merrick tense beside me.

"Stand down!" The princess's command is nearly inaudible, but it freezes her bodyguard in his tracks. It's a neat trick—one I wish I had in my repertoire. Then again, bodyguard or not, Merrick doesn't listen to anyone but himself.

"Speak, Ambassador Holdren," the princess says.

"Your Highness, I wish to ask, on behalf of the people of Permuna, why the last two grain deliveries have been rescheduled. My planet is running short; people are going hungry. I—"

The ambassador from Vistenia steps forward. "I hardly think this is the time or the place, Holdren."

"I think it's exactly the time and the place. We were promised the deliveries would not be interrupted. And now—"

I watch, fascinated, but the princess holds up her hand and the ambassador stops speaking immediately. "I'm sorry for your hardship, Ambassador. I will bring this matter to the Empress's attention when I return."

"You think she doesn't know?" His voice is bitter, irreverent, and an answering murmur runs through the increasingly tense crowd. It also causes the princess to raise her brows, but in surprise or arrogance, I can't quite tell.

Merrick moves in front of me, and though I want to push him out of the way, I understand why he's nervous. While Serati is tightly controlled by the Sisterhood and we hold ourselves separate from the other planets, even in the monastery, I've heard rumors of unrest among our neighbors. For decades now, the temperatures in the system have been rising and the agricultural productivity declining. Frequent solar flares are wreaking havoc with communications, and the exponential warming is making parts of the inner planets completely unlivable.

Our scriptures tell us that it will be okay, that a period of great joy will follow the upheaval. I know I just need to have faith. But it's hard when so many people are suffering.

As the sounds of dissent grow louder, the princess's eyes sweep the crowd. "Silence, please," she starts. "Let's not forget why we are here today. I'm sure Dr. Veragelen will have news of a solution to all our problems." She turns back to the ambassador. "I promise I will look into this matter."

He looks doubtful but bends his head nonetheless. "Thank you, Your Highness."

I half expect the same sort of comments from the

ambassador from Kridacus, a shrewd-looking woman in an orange gown, but the expression on her sun-lined, white face seems purposefully blank.

And then it's my turn. Princess Kalinda shifts her stern face and kind—I knew they'd be kind—eyes to me.

"Be calm. You can do this." Merrick's hand touches my shoulder, and immediately my racing heart slows as I feel his strength, both mental and physical. He might find me a trial, but for the last few years, he's been family, teacher, friend, protector, all rolled into one.

If he says it will be okay, then it will be okay.

The princess is even more beautiful close up, with the same light golden-brown skin and dark red hair of the Empress. But her skin has the same swirling silver pattern that Merrick's does, and in this light it's like she almost glows. Standing next to her makes me feel drab and young, despite the fact that we're the same age.

"Ambassador Fr—" A frown flickers across her face. "You're not Ambassador Frellen."

It sounds like an accusation, and I wonder if she recognizes me and if that's why she's frowning. Because she is here for a solution to the Dying Sun and I exist because there is none.

For a second, I can do nothing but blink up at her and wait for her to say something to me about our beliefs. When she doesn't, and instead just continues to frown at me, instinct takes over, and—even as I'm thinking *don't bow*—I do it anyway. I drop into a low, deep curtsy that has Merrick's hand tightening on my shoulder as though he can stop my descent.

Too late, Merrick. Way too late.

I'm nearly to the floor before he pulls me up like a puppet.

But the damage has been done. Everyone saw what I did—most especially the princess.

I'm expecting the worst when I finally work up the nerve to glance at her face. But she's actually smiling, amusement flickering in her eyes.

"I don't think I know your name," she murmurs.

"I'm Rain," I say. "It's an honor to meet you, Princess."

I hear Merrick's indrawn breath behind me, because, of course, I've made another mistake. Flustered, my face burning with mortification, I do the only thing I can think of to make this better. I reach out to touch her…and… Yes, it's official. I am a total and complete disaster.

Thankfully, Merrick yanks me backward before my hand can connect. At the same time, the big man in the body armor pushes himself between the princess and me. As he does, he reaches for the weapon at his side.

"For goodness' sake, Vance," the princess mutters. "Stand down."

Vance looks like he wants to argue, but eventually he steps back. And I don't blame him, which is why I do my best to look harmless. It's not hard, considering I'm 1.6 meters tall with a total baby face. But still, after the mess I just made, I'm not taking anything for granted.

Except the princess's lips are twitching. I'm a source of amusement, which is completely humiliating.

"I think proper introductions might be in order," she says.

Merrick steps forward. "Your Highness. May I introduce Rain, High Priestess of the Sisterhood of the Light and *temporary* ambassador of Serati."

"High Priestess?" Her eyes widen, and I wonder what her feelings are toward the Sisterhood. Our relationship with the Ruling Families has often been a little…fraught. "Well,

I'm glad I didn't allow Vance to shoot you. It would definitely have caused a diplomatic incident."

"Yes, Prin—" I suck in my breath. "Yes, *Your Highness*," I say. "I'm glad as well. Very glad."

She laughs then, holding my gaze as she does. For a second, I think I see wariness, or maybe pity, in her eyes. But then she reaches out and touches a finger to the emblem of the second sun on the upper left lapel of my robe. As she does, a murmur goes up around us and Merrick stiffens beside me.

But before anyone else can throw a fit, a loud buzzer goes off. The blaring shifts the tension as across the docking bay, a light flashes above a set of double doors.

The princess drops her hand and steps back. "It looks like something is finally happening." Then, just like that, she turns and walks away as the sound continues.

Something *is* finally happening. Seems it's time to shift focus from the disaster that I am to the disaster that I'm supposed to save us all from.

RED TOWER
BOOKS™